The KINDER GARDEN

BY THE SAME AUTHOR

Walking Shadows

FREDERICK TAYLOR
The KINDER GARDEN

Carroll & Graf Publishers, Inc.
New York

Copyright © 1990 by Frederick Taylor
Published by arrangement with the Random Century Group.
All rights reserved

First Carroll & Graf edition 1991

Carroll & Graf Publishers, Inc.
260 Fifth Avenue
New York, NY 10001

Library of Congress Cataloging-in-Publication Data

Taylor, Fred.
    The kinder garden / by Frederick Taylor. — 1st Carroll &
    Graf ed.
        p.   cm.
    ISBN 0-88184-697-X
    1. Berlin (Germany)—History—Allied occupation, 1945–
    —Fiction.
    I. Title.
    PR9619.3.T318K56   1991
    823—dc20   91-12568
                                                    CIP

Manufactured in the United States of America

For Alice

ACKNOWLEDGMENTS

Almost twenty years ago in Berlin, a German friend introduced me to Arno and Yogi. They had been 'cellar children' there after the war, without family or protection and living on their wits. Some of the stories they told me about that time have been incorporated, in various forms, into *The Kinder Garden*. I wish them well, wherever they are now, and offer my thanks.

Mr Norman Kitson, who taught me German at Aylesbury Grammar School, was kind enough to share with me his recollections of his experiences as a Public Safety Officer in the British Zone of Germany during the period depicted in this novel.

I wish to thank Mr John Maclaren for his information, his introductions, and—last but by no means least—the pleasure of his conversation. My gratitude is also due to the staff of the Corps of Military Police Museum and the instructors of the Special Investigation Branch's training wing at Chichester Barracks, who gave generously of their time and expertise.

If I have succeeded in introducing some leavening of authenticity into this fictional entertainment, the credit is largely theirs.

PART 1

BLESSED

Who could be strong and refrain from murder? Who in that age did not know that the worst was inevitable?

Rainer Maria Rilke,
'The Notebooks of Malte Laurids Brigge'

ONE

IT WAS SHORTLY AFTER SEVEN O'CLOCK on the morning of June 26, 1948. The risen sun shone kindly on the fallen city, gilding its charred buildings and ravaged parklands, filtering down to warm even the most desperate of cellar-refuges, and promising at last a respite from Berlin's wettest summer in thirty years. Hard by the skeleton of a bombed-out secondary school, within traffic-sound of the Potsdamer Strasse and a lazy lovers' stroll from the Tiergarten, those same healing rays cast light on the bodies of a murdered British soldier and a murdered woman, sprawled awkwardly among rubble that was overgrown with weeds and stained with freshly-spilt blood.

The stillness of the dead contrasted weirdly with the relentless activity animating the ruins. Everywhere the machinery of post-mortem emergency was in full operation. A military police photographer had just finished taking pictures with a flash-camera. Careful men trained in forensic procedures picked their way; their scholarly, almost priestlike, reverence marred only by the routine obscenities that spiced their muttered consultations.

Out on the Potsdamer Strasse, a khaki-painted Horch sedan approached the site at speed, swinging across the tramlines, mounting the kerb, and bumping over cleared waste ground towards several parked vehicles. Here a small posse of military policemen stood vigil. A stockily built sergeant abruptly detached himself from this group and hurried over to greet the new arrival.

For some time after the car had halted and cut its motor, no one emerged. Then a driver got out and opened the rear door. The man in the back seat wore a British army officer's uniform under his vintage

11

trench coat. He eyed the flattened debris beyond the running-board with the wan disgust of one who has been keeping early hours for years and still hates it. Finally he eased his lean frame out into the day.

The stocky sergeant saluted, wished him good morning.

'OK, Kelly,' the officer began, with a gesture of gentle impatience. 'You know I can't stand suspense. Before I go and get my feet dirty, just give me a simple answer: Is this our elusive Corporal Price or is it not?'

'Well, I reckon so, sir. They found his paybook on the body.'

'Forget the bloody paybook. You spent an entire night questioning the fellow last winter. *Is that his corpse over there?* Yes or no.'

'Yes. Yes, sir. He's been hacked about a bit, and it's a few months since that raid in the Kantstrasse, but I remember Price's fat face well enough.'

'Right. Thanks.'

It was hard to tell whether the officer was pleased or disturbed by his companion's admission. Captain James Blessed of the Special Investigation Branch practised an economy with words that emphasised his powerful air of detachment. Perhaps every policeman shares this quality: the nature of his job places limits on how close he can get to his fellow men. In Blessed's case, his appearance also set him apart. Though he stood a little under six feet, something rigorous—his enemies would say arrogant—in his presence made him seem taller. High cheekbones and arctic-blue eyes gave him an altogether un-British look. To be more precise, despite the uniform he wore, he seemed classically, strikingly Prussian.

Blessed's next move was to produce a packet of cheroots from his coat pocket. In a way that held a strong sense of ritual, he lit one and enjoyed a first, solemn intake of smoke.

'So Price came back,' he said quietly. 'He came back to Berlin, despite being warned off. And this is what he got.'

Sergeant Kelly let out a short, honking laugh. 'When we picked him up last February it broke my heart to let him go. I thought the bugger had got off scot-free. Funny, eh? Because if we'd managed to put him behind bars—'

'He wouldn't have ended up here,' Blessed finished for him. 'Life, Kelly, is full of might-have-beens. Now be quiet for a bit, will you?' Just take me, in silence, to where we need to go . . .'

Their arrival at the scene of the crime was signalled by the distinctive butcher-shop smell of bodies left in the open. Blessed paused at the edge of the clearing, delivered a general, matter-of-fact greeting to the forensic team. Then he stepped forward to see what had to be seen. As Blessed knew from long experience, neither the murdered man nor the murdered woman would ever look like this again, and never again would his own impressions have such awful, perfect freshness.

The male victim was about thirty years old and distinctly overweight. Kelly's reference to his 'fat face' was graceless but accurate. The man was wearing fawn civilian slacks and a white open-necked shirt. The shirt was torn and stained with blood, which had already soaked into its fabric and dried dark and hard. His throat had been cut. Around the wound, the skin, which was elsewhere a wan shade of grey, had turned purple with congealed blood, as if a livid and heavy cravat had been knotted round his neck. It gave the dead man a macabre, raffish look that belied the terror still captured vividly in his lifeless, popped eyes. No wonder there was so much blood on the grass. When the carotid artery is severed, the lifeblood gushes out with great force, sometimes jetting up to ten feet. A victim can lose consciousness within seconds, bleed to death in a few more.

The sight of the woman was much harder to take. She lay four feet or so away, on her back. Her dress, a flower-patterned cotton frock with buttons at the front, had been ripped apart. It was impossible to be sure of her age, though her face was one of the few unmarked parts of her body. She had been blonde, probably with the aid of a bottle, and quite pretty. On the rest of her body a furious assault had been carried out: a deep incision from pubic bone to navel; criss-cross slashes on her breasts, stomach and legs—some deep and others hardly breaking the skin, but raising welts much like African tribal markings; and a big, decisive stab-wound under the heart. Blessed made a mental note to confirm with the pathologist whether this coup-de-grace had been delivered before or after the mutilation.

The flies were gathering. The captain turned away, nodded to the man who was waiting to replace the protective tarpaulins.

'That's all for now. Thank you.'

He shielded his eyes for a moment with one hand. A spurt of nausea came and went. He had never become altogether inured to the sight of violent death, of a mutilated human body. In his early days, this queasiness had seemed an embarrassment; he had since come to regard it as comforting evidence that his finer instincts were still in working order.

'We've got a ripper on our hands here, sir,' Kelly said, grinning with grim relish. 'Nasty. *Very* nasty.'

'Yes, yes. Now, where's the boy?' Blessed asked.

'What boy, sir?' Kelly's smile faded. He became wary, defensive.

'The one who found the bodies. When you phoned me first thing, you said a German kid stumbled across this mess. So, who's got him?'

'Um, with respect, sir, I didn't say anyone actually *had* him . . .'

'Christ. Are you telling me he's gone missing? I hope you—or someone around here—has a very good explanation for that.'

'I think it's the Germans as has to come up with the excuses on this occasion, sir,' said Kelly huffily.

The sergeant had been Blessed's assistant for eighteen months now. He was thickset, of about average height, with a permanent five o'clock shadow, and jug-handle ears. He was not someone the captain would have chosen as a social companion, but then that was not his role. He was superhumanly hardworking, with a ravenous appetite for detail. The ideal subordinate. Blessed had come to rely on him and to ignore his less attractive features.

Kelly relaxed as he warmed to his story, which absolved himself and as a bonus shifted the blame firmly onto the despised local police—the 'poe-litz-eye' as he always called them in his atrocious German.

'The story I heard was, this ragged-arsed urchin flags down a cop on night patrol over there on the Potsdamer Strasse,' he explained. 'The kid's all het-up, gabbling on about how he's found these dead people. Anyway, chummy from the poe-litz-eye duly launches himself off into the undergrowth, following the little blighter's directions. He gets here, shines his torch on the dirty doings, turns round, and . . . well, our rascal's cleared off, hasn't he? You've got to remember, it was half-three and still pitch dark.'

'Just a moment. How old was this kid?'

'Nine. Ten. No home to go to. You know how things are here in Berlin.'

'I do.' Blessed nodded in acknowledgment that the boy-witness was lost to them, apparently through no fault of Kelly's. 'I'll interrogate that German police officer later. I suppose this must have given the kid a hell of a shock. Maybe that's why he ran away.'

'Oh, I don't know about that, sir. The nippers here have pretty strong stomachs. They've seen more than their fair share of beastliness, after all.'

'I suppose you're right.' Blessed glanced at his watch. It was twenty past seven. His own, British-born daughter would be waking up about now, in her cosy bed in their comfortable requisitioned house on the outskirts of the city. Thank God for that. 'Where's the pathologist?' he said. 'He should have got here just after the forensic boys.'

'Our man's been caught out by the Russian blockade, apparently. Still stuck in Hamburg, waiting for a seat on a plane. The Kripo are supposed to be sending along one of their police surgeons. He should be here soon.'

'Fair enough. We seem to be organised, then—apart from the fiasco with the mysterious disappearing witness.'

Kelly looked relieved, as he always did when the captain expressed satisfaction with his work. He didn't drink or smoke, and his one obvious vice was a passion—almost literally, a lust—for promotion. Kelly dreamed of the dizzy heights of Warrant Officer and higher, the way other men fantasised about winning the pools or having sex with Rita Hayworth. Since advancement would depend largely on Blessed's recommendation, the sergeant was obsessed with keeping in the captain's best books.

Grisewood, the senior forensic officer, stout and fiftyish, had been writing in his official notebook. He suddenly snapped it shut and walked over to where the two SIB men were standing. 'So you've decided you're interested in this poor bugger Price, are you, Captain Blessed?' he said. His flat Black-Country accent made every aspect of life or death, no matter how terrible, sound like a question of weights and measures, but until his team had finished its work he had tyrannical powers at the scene of a crime. No one made a move around here—not even the Military Governor himself—without Grisewood's say-so. An investigating officer annoyed him at his peril.

'Good morning, Mr Grisewood,' Blessed said. 'Yes. If this is the right man, that is.'

Grisewood's curiosity about Blessed's presence here was natural. As the Corps of Military Police's equivalent to the civilian force's CID, the Special Investigation Branch was still struggling to control the epidemic of crime and corruption that had swept starving, desperate occupied Germany in the aftermath of defeat. Murders, even murders involving Allied soldiers, were commonplace. Grisewood knew that an experienced SIB sergeant would normally be considered competent to handle an investigation such as this one. For an officer of Blessed's rank—a section commander, no less—to put in an appearance must mean there was more to these killings than met the eye.

'Anyway, how are things going?' Blessed said.

Grisewood smiled sourly. 'Pretty slim bloody pickings so far.'

'Prints? Weapon?'

'No luck yet, I'm afraid. Our villain used a five, six-inch blade, I'd guess, but I can't be dead sure.'

'You say "villain", singular. You're sure of that?'

'That's what the tracks say, Captain. Footprints of the two victims. Plus one other set of bootmarks and one only. As for the weapon, I was hoping he might have ditched the knife somewhere in the vicinity, but so far we've found nothing. He probably tied it to a brick and chucked it in the Landwehr Canal.'

'Pity. What about access? Which direction did the attacker come from?'

'From the park, it looks like. Only a couple of hundred yards away.' Grisewood jerked a thumb to indicate the area behind where he was standing. There were clear signs of disturbance to the grass and vegetation.

'From the Tiergarten side. All right. What about the victims?'

'Likewise. Perhaps they knew the murderer. Perhaps they were threatened, forced to accompany him to this spot.' Grisewood tapped his teeth thoughtfully with his pencil. 'I suppose it's also possible he followed them, surprised them when they were settling down to have a cuddle . . . Anyway, we can't find any other tracks—except those of the policeman and the boy who found the bodies. Of course, like you they came from the direction of the Potsdamer Strasse.'

Grisewood's team had already marked out the permitted entrance route to the scene. The path, indicated by twine stretched between wooden stakes, was as close as they could get to the route taken by the people who had found the bodies, because along this route the terrain and the evidence it might hold had already been disturbed. To step outside these limits was forbidden until the forensic team and the pathologist had finished their work.

'Fine. Well, personally I'd be prepared to give even money that these people knew the man who killed them,' Blessed said firmly.

'Oh yes, Captain? And what brings you to that conclusion, pray?' There was such a ponderous deliberation in everything Grisewood did and said that Blessed often wondered if there was in it a hint of some private, deadpan campaign of mockery. Perhaps that was what kept him sane; everyone here had their methods.

'Their fingers,' Blessed pressed on, using the opportunity to think aloud. 'In the case of a knife-murderer's victim we invariably find marks or cuts on the fingers, where the hands have been raised in a desperate attempt to deflect the blade. This defensive reaction is instinctive, no matter how hopeless the situation. In fact, if you ever doubt the word of a man who claims to have been attacked by someone with a knife, just check for scars on the pads of his fingers. There were none on the dead man's . . .'

'How true. But scars all over the lady's, eh?'

'You're with me, of course, Mr Grisewood. I think he went for the man first, taking him by surprise, slashing deep into his throat, leaving him no chance to raise his hands in self-defence. By the time he turned to the fellow's lady-friend, she was able to put up some resistance. Hence the cuts on her hands.' Blessed shrugged. 'They must have known the murderer and come here with him willingly. That would explain why they were totally unprepared for what happened.'

'He must have been bloody quick off the mark, that's all I can say,' Grisewood said sceptically. 'And that must've been quite some blade he used.'

'There are plenty of weapons in this city, Mr Grisewood. And plenty of characters who know how to use them.'

'Watch out, sir,' said Kelly, his eyes on the Potsdamer Strasse end of the site.

Blessed and Grisewood followed the sergeant's stare. A thin, sharp-faced German in a raincoat and a dark-grey trilby was trudging towards them. With him were a couple of younger men, also in civilian clothes.

'How did those Germans get in here? Did you invite them?' Grisewood demanded irritably.

Blessed shook his head. 'No, but they're known to me. They're from the Kripo, central district.'

'Jesus, the way things are going here, we should start charging admission. Which of those types is boss-man?'

Blessed indicated the man in the raincoat and hat. 'He's the senior one. I'd like to talk to him.'

'Just him, then. Those two spear-carriers of his can bugger off.'

'All right. I'll take responsibility.'

'Darned right you will, Captain,' Grisewood snapped. 'And keep him from under our feet, will you?'

When he reached the edge of the clearing, the man in the trilby signalled with casual authority for his companions to hold back while he came on alone.

'Good morning, Manfred,' Blessed said in perfect colloquial German that held a strong hint of the rapid-fire, guttural Berlin dialect. 'Always the early bird. How're things?'

They shook hands. Kriminalinspektor Manfred Weiss's gaze flicked around appraisingly. His grey-blue eyes were bright, almost feverish in their intensity, a contrast with the ease of his manner, the wry smile he habitually wore to face the world. Blessed could feel the bones of his hand and wrist. As a middle-ranking Kripo official, the inspector got a more generous ration than most Berliners, but he had a large family to feed. Blessed knew only too well the problems Weiss faced. The captain himself owed his looks, and his command of this language, to the fact that he was half German. His father had supplied him with a British name and nationality, but Blessed's mother had been a Berliner. This city had been familiar to him since childhood; he kept in contact with members of his mother's family who were struggling to survive here.

Blessed explained that Weiss's two men would have to wait back on the street. He told Kelly to escort them back along the path. While he was at it, he could radio into the office and put out a description of the missing boy-witness. The captain had worked together with the inspector often enough—in raids on black-market restaurants, on warehouses full of contraband, on basements where illicit printing-presses and stills were making fortunes for a few—to be relaxed in his company, respectful of his experience.

Meanwhile, Grisewood had turned away and gone back to his work, without directly acknowledging Weiss's presence. Like many colonial-minded British officials—he had spent fifteen years with the Indian police—he was constitutionally incapable of dealing with subject foreigners on equal, familiar terms. To him the Berliners were 'natives', just like Sikhs or Bengalis, and that was that.

'I was told of this affair as soon as I got into the office,' the inspector said when Kelly and the others had gone. 'A patrolman from our district found these bodies, as I'm sure you know. But then your people sealed off the area and would allow no one near. "No one", of course, meaning no Germans. Nevertheless, since the female victim seemed to be one of our citizens, I decided to try my luck at the scene of the crime. I would say I intended to "show the flag", except that since forty-five we Germans don't actually have one.'

In Weiss's words Blessed sensed yet again the dumb weeping of the national wound. 'Well, you seem to have elbowed your way through to the members' enclosure without too much trouble,' he said briskly, refusing to take the bait. 'Tell me, Manfred, how did you manage it?'

Weiss dropped the resentment and grinned. 'Simple,' he said. 'I lied. I recognised your car parked out there, and so I told the MPs on guard that you had sent for me. I assumed that you, of all people, would forgive such a minor untruth—in the interests of justice and Anglo-German cooperation.'

Blessed laughed. 'You took quite a chance. If Mr Grisewood knew what you'd done, you'd be out on the Potsdamer Strasse so fast you'd wonder what hit you.'

'Maybe,' Weiss said with a fatalistic shrug. 'But in Berlin these days we have four occupying powers constantly contradicting each other and several different political factions fighting for power in the police department. No one even knows which currency we're going to be paid in at the end of the month! To do this job at all efficiently, one must always be taking chances.'

'I'm glad you're here. Have a smoke.'

Weiss gazed hungrily at the cheroot Blessed had offered. Then he shook his head. 'Thank you. Later. Definitely later. But first . . . The victims are one off-duty British soldier and his Fräulein? This has been established, yes?'

'There were identity documents on the man's body, but nothing on the woman's,' Blessed said. 'It seems probable she was a German civilian, though we won't know for certain until we manage to identify her. As for her relationship with the soldier, who can tell whether it was a long-term affair or a hurried fumble in the bushes. This is Berlin . . .'

'Yes. It certainly is.' Weiss rubbed his hands together as if it were winter. 'I should like to see the bodies. Will this be possible?'

After negotiations with Grisewood, the tarpaulins were raised again. Weiss stood for a long time, just looking. Then he turned back to meet Blessed's gaze. 'I'd appreciate that cigar now, please.'

Blessed nodded to Grisewood's man. 'OK,' he said in English. 'I think we've all had enough for now.'

They moved a few feet away and settled by a half-demolished wall. Blessed handed Weiss a cheroot, lit it for him. 'Everything indicates that the victims made their own way here, probably in the company of the man who killed them,' he said. 'So two human beings were brutally murdered within a stone's throw of the Potsdamer Strasse on the one side and the Tiergarten on the other. How many worthy citizens within earshot, do you think?'

'Come, James, you are half a Berliner yourself! You know this city well enough to realise that a scream, especially a woman's scream, coming from a place such as this at night would be unlikely to bring anyone running to the rescue!' Weiss shook his head, drew deeply on his cheroot. 'At night only a fool would venture in here under such circumstances.'

Blessed nodded. 'The obvious supposition is that she was a prostitute, he was her client, and they were surprised when they came here to have intercourse. A classic sex-murder. Committed by someone with a grudge so terrible that only carnage on this scale would satisfy it.'

'The work of a madman. I too would believe this. If only the great Captain Blessed, scourge of the black-market gangs, had not seen fit to hurry to the scene.'

Like Grisewood, Weiss was of course curious to know why Blessed had got up so early. The captain, for his part, was not yet prepared to discuss his reasons, even with Weiss. Grisewood solved his problem by materialising at his elbow.

'Seen enough, gents?' he demanded. 'Wouldn't like to take a stroll, would you? The photographer's got to take some more snaps, and my boys will soon be wanting to do where you are. So if you'd like to continue your chat elsewhere while we all wait for the man with the little black bag to put in an appearance . . .'

Blessed and Weiss set off back towards the Potsdamer Strasse together, following the stakes-and-twine path. Since the end of the war, nature had reclaimed this deserted couple of acres of Berlin, and the prescribed route took them along a path newly trodden through long grass and flowering weeds as tall as fruit trees. So far, the sun from the east was on their backs. Then, suddenly, they came to a high, buttressed wall that cut off their previous direction of advance and cast them into an almost wintry gloom. In this part of the ruins, sunlight hardly penetrated, and earth and air alike were damp and sour. All they heard was the scolding *chook-chook* of a song thrush protecting its nest nearby, and the distant rattle of a tram on the street ahead. There were bullet holes in the masonry that must date from the battle for Berlin at the end of the war. Finally they stepped through a gap in the wall and found themselves on the cleared area of flattened rubble bordering the Potsdamer Strasse.

Kelly and Blessed's driver were standing by the remains of the main school building, where the vehicles were parked, chatting to the military policemen on guard duty there. The cluster of caps, each with the distinctive scarlet cover of the military police on its crown, gave the group the look of a gathering of colourful, busy birds. Weiss's men, who were some distance off, made to approach, but the inspector waved them away.

For some time the German and the Englishman smoked in companionable silence, waiting for the Kripo's surgeon to arrive. Blessed found himself unable to forget the frenzied damage that had been done to the female victim's body. It was unlikely that a professional killer would take the time to commit such a time-consuming extra atrocity. Unlikely, but not impossible. It all depended . . .

'You know something, Manfred?' he said, tossing away the end of his cheroot. 'I'd give a great deal to know whether the woman was killed before or after her mutilation. I mean, a professional killer would go for a clean, quick death, first of all.'

Weiss looked at Blessed sharply. 'You're suggesting this may have been the work of a paid assassin?'

'Every possibility is worth considering. The only question is, why mutilate the woman's body? Why complicate matters?'

Weiss laughed in the grim, pleased way of a Berliner who is proud of his capacity for self-mockery. 'You could say,' he suggested, 'that as a nation we are fond of complicating things. See how under Hitler we insisted on declaring war on almost the entire world, so that we were bound to lose! See how we, maybe the most hardworking, ingenious people on earth, have managed to lose our independence and our dignity—so that we now have the Russians squatting on the Hanover autobahn, stopping the trucks of turnips from reaching our beloved Berlin! You think we Germans don't like our lives to be complicated?'

'I wondered when you were going to bring up the subject of the blockade.'

'Did you? But this is my city. It is effectively under siege. Did you expect me not to talk about the fact?'

Blessed shrugged. 'The crisis is a problem for the politicians, and perhaps for the fighting soldiers—but certainly not for policemen like us.'

Weiss had made his smoke last a surprisingly long time. He seemed to be savouring the cheroot as if, like the rest of the population of beleaguered Berlin, he was determined to live as well as he could, while he could.

'It is all connected,' the inspector said after a while. 'Don't forget, the blockade has only just begun. The West is still making brave, defiant noises. But for how long? Maybe in a week, a month, your government will decide that the two million people of this city, who were your enemies not so long ago, are not worth defending after all. They and the other western powers will tell their armies to pack up

21

and go, and when you have left, the Russians will take over the whole of Berlin. Now tell me, who will bother with this murder then?'

'Come on, Manfred. We can't let that affect us. I know there's a crisis, but I can't believe the Soviets will refuse to help us with a straightforward murder case. What's political about a pair of mutilated corpses, a squaddie and his Fräulein, found on a bomb site by a ten-year-old boy?'

Weiss thought about that, clearly considering his reply with great care. Then he said gently, 'Please don't misunderstand me, James. You may be right in this particular case, that there will be no problems. But there's one important truth, and it is perhaps the only truth any of us can rely on.' He looked intently at Blessed. 'My friend, in this city at this time, especially so far as the Russians are concerned, everything is political. Everything.'

The Berlin crisis had been brewing for months, because the great powers could not agree on the future of Germany. In May 1945 the last government of the Reich had been deposed. By agreement among the victorious Allies, the defeated, starving country was placed under military government and divided into four Zones of Occupation. The Russians got everything east of the Elbe, the Americans the rich southern provinces, including the Alpine regions, while the British acquired the northern plains and the smoky industrial powerhouse of the Ruhr, leaving the French to lord it over the western marches and the coal-rich Saar. Berlin, in the middle of the Russian Zone, was also divided into four separately-governed parts, or 'sectors'. The inter-allied Control Commission—set up to coordinate policy towards Germany as a whole—was also based in the former Reich capital. Under an informal 'gentlemen's agreement', the Soviets allowed the Western Allies to transport supplies and personnel to and from Berlin by specific road and rail routes. That agreement had held until two days ago. At midnight on June 24, 1948, Moscow closed the transit-autobahns and stopped all rail and water traffic, thus cutting off all movement between the three western-ruled sectors of Berlin and the outside world, except by air. In their bare-faced peasant way, the Russians blamed 'technical difficulties', but they fooled no one. Would the democracies let themselves be starved out of Berlin? Was the Russian blockade the spark that would ignite a new war, this time between the West and the Soviet Union?

So peace was once more in the balance. There were many different opinions as to what should happen next, but few doubted that the city and its inhabitants were in for a thin, nerve-racking time. And everyone, foreigners and Germans alike, agreed on one thing: three years, one month and eighteen days after the end of the Second World War, if the victorious alliance between America, Britain and Russia could ever have been described as a party, then the Berlin Blockade showed plainly that the party was over and the hangover—which would later be called the Cold War—had begun.

Whatever Weiss said, therefore, it wasn't only Germans who liked to complicate things. Even Corporal Ronald 'Taffy' Price of the Royal Medical Corps had managed to pick a very inconvenient time to be murdered; and his violent demise among the rubble between the Tiergarten and the Potsdamer Strasse had already set in train complications and dangers beyond anyone's imagining.

In fact, it was from these routine beginnings—if murder can ever be called routine—that James Blessed was about to embark on a descent into hell. Perhaps, as some would later say, it was a destination partly of his own devising, but then, what personal hell is not?

TWO

'HELLO!' BLESSED called out, laying aside his briefcase on the table by the front door.

He heard the chink of cups in the kitchen, and frowned as he began to unbutton his coat. His pleasure at arriving home had been diminished as the Horch rounded the bend in the tree-lined drive and revealed a black Military Government Bentley in front of the house, complete with a chauffeur dozing in the driver's seat. These limousines were reserved for the most privileged members of Mil. Gov.'s elite, and Blessed had harboured a strong suspicion as to who this particular nabob might be.

A cupboard door closed, another chink signalled continuing activity in the kitchen. Now he could hear the sound of over-animated laughter from the far end of the house, possibly the music room, probably the conservatory. Those two rooms took up a considerable proportion of the ground floor. The previous occupant of the house—a Nazi Kreisleiter—had apparently adored the piano and the sub-tropical lily in just about equal measure. Or perhaps his wife had. It was impossible to say, because the entire family had decamped during the last night of April 1945 and had never been seen again since.

'Good morning, Gisela.'

'Captain. A very good morning,' said the young woman who had just come out into the hall from the kitchen, still wearing her apron.

The English she spoke had a distinctly German rhythm, but it was beautified by the kind of perfect Victorian diction that no one except foreigners could be bothered with any more. For a year now, Gisela Bach had been employed as nanny to Daphne, the Blesseds' daughter,

24

and the captain still found her both impressive and mysterious. He knew, for instance, that she had learned her English from a tutor who had been at Oxford in the '80s of the previous century and claimed to have swapped *mots* with Oscar Wilde. She had been brought up by academic parents in Königsberg who saw it as absolutely normal for their child to master three languages with fluency, to play the piano and cello and to sing, to paint and draw, and to have read most of the major writers of the last century. There was the German glory—and the German tragedy. Stripped of their teaching posts and expelled from their home when the Russians occupied East Prussia at the end of the war, Gisela's parents died somewhere on the frozen road out of Königsberg and were buried in the snow where they had fallen. Now in her early twenties, without money or family, Gisela looked after Daphne, made tea for the household, did the shopping.

In their requisitioned houses, with servants readily available from among a destitute German population, British officials and their families lived in some style. The captain's driver, Thwaite, occupied the chauffeur's flat above the garage. Gisela completed the immediate household. A cook and gardener—*de rigeur* in self-respecting Occupation circles—came in as required. British-occupied Germany was being ridiculed as 'the new Raj'.

'You left the house very early,' Gisela continued. 'Daphne missed you.'

'Something important came up. It couldn't wait.'

'Anyway, welcome home. We expected you to go straight into the office afterwards.'

'I . . . I've got a report to write, and I decided to work on it at home. Once I get to the office, I won't get any peace . . . Where's Mrs Blessed?'

'She is in the conservatory, Captain. Would you like some breakfast?'

'Mr Redman, is it? The visitor, I mean.'

'Yes.' Gisela paused. 'Breakfast?' she repeated patiently. 'To keep your strength up? I must say, you look tired. And also, perhaps, irritable?'

'You're right about that. I'm sorry. It's been a nasty sort of morning so far. Look, you mustn't take any extra trouble.'

'You haven't eaten yet today, I am certain of it,' Gisela told him firmly. 'I am already preparing morning tea for Mrs Blessed and your visitor. It is no trouble to find an extra cup and saucer, and to make some toast.'

'You're very kind.'

Blessed still wasn't sure of the feelings behind the smile that greeted his weary gesture towards good manners. Gisela's pointed, pretty face was dominated by a luxuriously wide mouth that commanded a huge but obscure vocabulary of smiles for every occasion and every feeling. He sometimes felt himself wondering if, when she was alone in her room, she ever smiled a funeral smile for her parents.

Gisela took herself back into the kitchen. Blessed hung up his coat and cap, straightened his tie, and set off along the high-ceilinged central hallway. The laughter in the conservatory was louder now. He distinctly heard Harriet saying, 'Larry, you're outrageous! You can't—' Then he opened the cloakroom door under the stairs and went in, losing the rest of her sentence.

Going into the tiny room was like entering a sound-proof booth. With the staircase directly above, Blessed had to duck slightly to get to the handbasin. He turned on the tap, splashed his face, bathed his eyes, swilled out his mouth, meticulously spat the bile of the morning into the Italian marble bowl. Finally, he rubbed his face all over with the hand towel. When all these processes were done, the features that looked back at Blessed from the mirror were pale and gaunt, the lines around his mouth well-scored. Overwork and irregular hours had given him a puffy look around the eyes, but unless he was deceiving himself the whites were still youthfully clear, the irises a healthy blue. He still had all his hair, and he hadn't started to sag in the face or waist. The only part of himself that he really disliked were his lips, which he thought were a little bit too full for a man's. Women didn't seem to mind, though.

Blessed quietly closed the cloakroom door behind him, walked down the remainder of the hallway to the conservatory.

His wife, Harriet, and her guest were standing with their backs to him on the far side of the room, viewing the garden through the high windows and laughing loudly. One of her beautifully-manicured hands was resting on the sleeve of Laurence Redman's well-tailored jacket, perhaps for support because his story was so hilarious.

'Hello, darling,' Blessed announced himself. 'Hello, Larry.'

Harriet Blessed, née Fiske, turned on her high heels like a mannequin. 'I thought you were gone for the day, Jim,' she said. 'Well, well, well . . .'

'Larry,' Blessed acknowledged the visitor again. 'I didn't know you were back in town.'

'Yet more ruddy fact-finding, Jim,' Redman said. 'The usual ghastly saga . . . the PM's office phones up, tells me I'm booked onto a draughty old Berlin-bound Dakota, and that's that. Less than two hours' notice. No time to ring before I left London.' He made a waggling motion with his hands to indicate his helplessness in the face of such uncaring masters. 'So how are you? Madly busy since this Soviet blockade I daresay, like the rest of the military.'

Blessed nodded. 'We've always had our hands full in Berlin. Now we've got them even fuller.'

Redman was a Labour Member of Parliament, recently appointed as a junior minister at the Foreign Office with special responsibilities for occupied Germany. He had been a close school-friend of Harriet's brother, who had been killed in the war. This had given him an excuse to look them up during his first official mission to Berlin the previous autumn. Redman's visits had become frequent since then, because of the deteriorating political situation, and he always dropped by when he was in town. Blessed supposed that for Harriet he represented a link with her dead brother. For his part he disliked Redman, but since he disliked every politician he had ever come across, there didn't seem much point in making an issue of it.

Harriet grabbed the opportunity provided by the men's stilted attempts at conversation and made purposefully for the door. She brushed past Blessed, caressing his cheek with her lips so quickly and lightly that it was like a bat flitting past in a dark attic. She said from the threshold: 'I'll leave you boys to chat. I'm going to see what Miss Germany is up to in the kitchen. She went out to make tea about a year ago and hasn't been seen since.'

Blessed heard Harriet's heels clacking along the parquet floor in the hall. As she neared the kitchen, her voice pealed out in a mocking yodel: 'Geeee-sss-ell-ay-ay-aaa . . .'

Almost all of the ex-Kreisleiter's moveable possessions had disappeared in the wave of looting that accompanied the Russian conquest. His lovingly-tended collection of exotic flora had survived, however. At this season, the conservatory was filled with eccentric flesh-coloured lilies, *Amaryllis Belladonna*, which bloomed on bare stalks.

'The place is looking thoroughly impressive,' Redman said, staring round rather wildly. 'You could mount an opera in that music room of yours.'

'Everyone's done their best to make us comfortable. With a requisitioned house, of course, you've basically got to like it or lump it.'

Silence fell. In fact, this was a pretty ridiculous building, as both men knew. Named the Villa Hellman after the wealthy tea importer for whom it had been built in the early 1900s, the house's design was based on that of a Tyrolean hunting-lodge. Harriet had come to refer to it in her best American accent as the 'Villa Hell, man' ('Hello there. So you're Lieutenant Smith, and you work with James keeping the streets of Berlin safe. Welcome to the Villa Hell, man. Have a drink or three. It's the only way to get through the day.'). The Kreisleiter had taken the kitsch content to the limit (a huge swastika mosaic had to be removed from the main bathroom). Now the place resembled an empty film set, with just a scattering of Blessed furniture, shipped out from England, to absorb the echoes.

Nevertheless, the Villa Hellman was roomy, and anyway, the captain and his family had lived here together for longer than anywhere else. While he had done his war service in the Middle East, Harriet and baby Daphne had lived with his wife's father, dividing their time between London, where Sir Hugh Fiske had a flat, and the old man's country house in Cornwall. After Blessed's return to Europe, around the time of VE-Day, they had spent a delightful summer together in England. But thereafter, during his first German posting, they had been crammed into a depressing flat in Cologne. His promotion to head this section in Berlin had brought with it the bonus of the Villa Hellman. He and his family had been here for almost two years.

Although he would never have confessed it to his family, one reason for Blessed's attachment to this place was its removal from the raw realities of postwar Berlin life. The street was part of a leafy garden development, planned in those far-off prosperous days before the First World War for individuals of middling to high income and middling to low taste. The area had escaped serious war damage, apart from a few pot-holes in the cobbled road, and now most of the German inhabitants had been evicted to make way for soldiers and officials of the British occupation. The Americans had created a similar enclave for themselves in Dahlem, in their own sector, a Little Connecticut where the British had made a Little Surrey. Of course it was an artificial existence. But it was safe. To Blessed that was everything. He could come back here after a morning, a day, a night, on duty in the wild, unprotectable centre of Berlin, and know that Daphne was all right, that Harriet—if she was in the mood—would have been able to relax.

For want of something better to do, Redman had sat himself down in a wicker chair, and was fumbling for his pipe and tobacco. He wore an expensive, well-pressed linen suit and an old Reptonian tie, but the collar of his white shirt was slightly frayed. Blessed suspected this was a deliberate affectation, an attempt to convince his political friends that at heart he was actually an untidy socialist idealist. Redman was slender and wore spectacles, which gave him a misleadingly donnish look. His legs were as long as a high-jumper's and his movements extravagant.

'I had a murder this morning,' Blessed found himself saying. He stayed on his feet because he didn't want to settle into a cosy social occasion. 'Two murders, to be precise.'

Redman got his pipe going, then took it out of his mouth and waved it about. 'I didn't realise you were involved in that sort of thing. You told me your section is chiefly concerned with vice, the black market, corruption, all that. Is there some connection?'

'I don't know yet. The victims were one of our servicemen and an unknown woman. I've taken personal charge of the investigation because the man may have been involved in black-market dealings. In fact, he had already been interviewed by people from my section, some months ago.'

'I see. A gang killing? A shoot-out in a bar? Isn't that usually the form?'

'Not in this case,' Blessed said coldly, irritated by Redman's flippancy. 'The bodies were found on a bomb-site. The woman had been badly mutilated.'

Redman nodded uncomfortably. He was obviously learning more about Blessed's morning than he cared to know.

Silence returned. Blessed felt like a swimmer who has reached the end of the baths and is enjoying a brief respite while he turns, breathes in, and prepares to strike out on the return lap.

'I . . . I was telling Harriet about Ernie Bevin, among other things,' said Redman, apparently deciding to get himself away from talk about cadavers. 'Ernie's furious with the Russians, of course. He rang the State Department in Washington, bellowed down the phone that there was to be no surrender. "You never retreats in the face of a commie, George," he told Secretary Marshall,' Redman continued in a fair rendering of the British Foreign Secretary. ' "It was true in the Bristol docks, and by God, it's true in Central Europe. Listen to a man what knows!" '

Blessed grunted. 'Are we prepared for war, then?' he asked. He hadn't laughed at Redman's story about Bevin. Its real purpose had been to remind James Blessed that he was talking to a dynamic young member of the government who was privy to all sorts of off-the-record information.

'Oh, I don't know about that,' Redman said quickly. 'Diplomatic channels haven't yet been exhausted. Nowhere near it. That's why I'm here.'

'Well, it sounds like Mr Bevin's prepared to take us all to the brink. If he's really intending to steamroller the Soviets, he'll have to be prepared to do something dramatic if need be. Rattle your sabre at the Red Army and you have to mean it. The Russians can see through an empty threat quicker than any people on earth.' Blessed shrugged. 'For what it's worth, I think it's also important that the Berliners realise we're determined to stay put here. If they were sure of that, it would encourage them enormously. God knows, they need it. Things had been improving for the past few months as regards food and fuel. Now they're frightened it will be back to starvation rations and freezing bedrooms. The authorities reintroduced electricity rationing this morning, I heard.'

Redman puffed sagely on his pipe. 'I think they'll get the message pretty quickly, actually.' He leaned forward confidingly. 'To tell the truth, Jim—this is between you and me and Harriet—I'm here to help show Stalin we really mean business. We're not going to take his damned blockade lying down!'

'Do you mean the government will be reinforcing the Berlin garrison?'

'Ah . . . not exactly. As you know, we've already stepped up the quantities of provisions we're flying in for the military and their families. But—and this will be officially announced today—we're willing to take on far more. We intend, Jim, to outdo what the Yanks achieved in China, when they flew over the Hump to supply Chiang Kai-Shek's armies who were fighting the Japanese, and our own efforts, when we kept occupied Holland from starving during the last winter of the war.' Redman paused dramatically. 'We're going to supply the population of the western sectors of Berlin by air.'

'Christ. Military and civilians alike? Two million people?'

'That's the idea.'

'Food, fuel, clothing . . . everything?'

Redman nodded.

'Good luck,' Blessed said. 'I hope it works. For all our sakes.'

'It has to, Jim. We've got to show we have the political will, or the Russians will just walk all over us, and probably keep walking until they get to the English Channel.'

Just then, Harriet came back in. For the first time, Blessed noticed that she was wearing a new blue blouse, made of what looked like silk.

With her fair skin and hair, and a pair of turquoise ear-rings, it looked very good indeed. Eleven years ago he had married a beautiful woman, and she was still beautiful. He felt a twinge of sexual pride in the fact that she was his. It occurred to him, not for the first time, that he loved his wife for most, if not all, of the wrong reasons.

'I know what you're doing,' Harriet announced brightly. 'You're talking politics. Will the Russians invade? Will they manage to starve us out?' She followed up with a husky laugh. There was a dangerous twinkle in her eye. 'Well, you've heard the official version from Larry,' she said to Blessed. 'Now what do you think's going to happen? Shall we be calling in the movers? Shall we pack up our troubles and head back to dear old Blighty, leaving the Russians and their local commie chums in sole command of these ruins? Do we actually give a damn? When you think about it, all these freedom-loving Berliners were Nazis not so long ago, weren't they?'

Blessed was used to this. 'Berlin never voted for Hitler. Most Berliners always voted for the left, for democracy, as you know full well,' he said calmly. 'Anyway, I'm on the government's side in this case. I don't want war either, but I believe we've got to dig our heels in, say "thus far and no further". We can't let the Russians take Berlin the way they've already helped themselves to the rest of Eastern Europe. The communists grabbed Czechoslovakia just this last February. Surely you're not saying the Czechs were Nazis too?'

'Of course not, darling. But as *you* know full well, half your relations here were. I can see why you wouldn't want the army to leave Berlin. You'd have to leave them—which means the German bits of you as well—behind, and you'd hate that.'

'That's all got nothing to do with the crisis, Harriet,' Blessed insisted with quiet emphasis. 'My job is here. I do the job well because I know Berlin. And I enjoy the job because I do it well.'

Redman was looking very ill at ease. Harriet seemed to find this amusing. 'See, Larry?' she said. 'What did I tell you? Jim's just an old Prussian at heart. He believes in working hard and playing as little as possible.'

'You're embarrassing our guest, Harriet,' Blessed said. 'Undermining his morale when he's come here to lie for his country, like a good diplomat. That's not considerate.'

Redman coughed. 'Jim has other things on his mind, anyway. He was telling me just a few minutes ago that he had to go and investigate a murder. Two murders, in point of fact.'

31

Harriet had snapped open the velvet box on the table in the corner, taken out a cigarette. 'Sounds about right,' she said. 'There's a lot of that sort of thing about in dear old Berlin. Brits were they, Jimmy, these corpses of yours, or more wretched Germans?'

Before he could answer, Gisela arrived, carrying a well-loaded tray. There was a fine porcelain teapot, with matching cups, saucers and plates. A selection of butter-biscuits was provided for Harriet and Redman, toast and marmalade for Blessed.

'Anything else?' Gisela asked, turning to face Blessed. 'If it is all right, I will go and tidy Daphne's room. It is a mess.'

Blessed frowned. 'You spoil her, Gisela. She should learn to look after her own things.'

'We had to hurry to catch the school bus. She—'

'Oh, for God's sake, let the girl go and clear up Daff's room, will you?' Harriet said. 'Once we get back to England, we won't be able to afford servants, so our darling daughter might as well enjoy having someone to tidy up after her while she's got the chance.'

Gisela's face, usually pale, had turned distinctly pink. Blessed realised that the flush came from suppressed anger. The daughter of Professor and Frau Bach of the University of Königsberg did not relish being referred to as a 'servant'.

'Oh, Harriet. Shut up,' he said. Then to Gisela: 'All right. But I intend to have a word with Daff about her untidiness. There's no reason why you should have to take care of her room for her. You have enough to do already.'

After Gisela had left the room, Harriet poured the tea. 'Sit down then, James,' she said, without looking at him.

'Thanks, but I won't. Perhaps I'll take my tea and toast into the study. I've got a report to write.'

'Get it down on paper while the gruesome memories are still fresh, eh, husband?'

'Something like that. I'll have to go into the office later this morning. I'm afraid this case will mean a lot of extra work. I have a feeling there may be more to it than meets the eye. There are connections. You know.'

'Jimmy is convinced he can clean up wicked old Berlin single-handed,' Harriet explained to Redman in a stagey aside. 'A task which makes Hercules's assault on the Augean Stables look like a breeze. He tried to do the same thing when he was stationed in the Lebanon, and nearly got himself killed.'

Blessed frowned. 'You weren't there, Harriet.'

32

'Damned right! Your daughter and I were at home in England. Daff wasn't even four years old, and she came within a hair's breadth of growing up fatherless! All because you were out to get some Arab thug.'

She was surprisingly calm. There was something cold-blooded about this goading, as if she were rehearsing something rather than airing a real grievance.

'He wasn't an Arab,' Blessed said. 'He was a Druze. As for what happened, I'm afraid it could happen to any soldier. Or to any policeman. It comes with the job. And besides, you heard a distorted version. A dramatised one. You got the story secondhand.'

'I had to.' Harriet turned back to Redman. 'Jim never told me about it, you see. *Didn't want me to worry.* I'd never have known if it hadn't been for a friend of his who told me about it when they all got home.'

'This has got nothing to do with anything,' Blessed said.

'Hasn't it? You've got a strange gleam in your eye, and I suspect it's the same one you had then. You're out to get someone!'

Blessed shrugged, picked up his plate of toast and marmalade and his tea. This was another old argument. 'I have to go. Sorry.'

'So you should be,' his wife murmured. She squashed her cigarette in the ashtray in a way that showed she considered the skirmish over but the war undecided. 'Anyway, I hope you're going to be able to honour our next social commitment.'

Blessed smiled. His daughter would be eight years old tomorrow. 'Daff's birthday tea? I'll try . . .'

'No, *no*, my Prussian. Of course, we all hope you can attend your own daughter's birthday. But first, tonight, there's the dinner party at the Donaldsons. We've already postponed twice. You swore you'd manage it this time.'

'I may be rather late, but I'll show my face.' Blessed had forgotten the Donaldsons' dinner completely, as Harriet knew. 'Who else did you say was coming?'

'Who's going to be there? Oh, the de Ventoux couple, and that funny American air force colonel and the Italian wife he picked up in Naples . . . and . . .' She made an open-handed gesture towards their guest. '. . . Mr Laurence Redman, MP, Parliamentary Under-Secretary at the Foreign Office! Gillie Donaldson phoned earlier to make sure we were coming, found out Larry had landed at Gatow, and promptly insisted on feeding him too.'

'What, Larry, isn't the city throwing a state banquet in your honour?' Blessed asked.

33

Redman managed a grimace that passed for a smile. 'This is a working visit, of course,' he muttered. 'I may be held up, too.'

'In which case, you can both bloody well take a taxi home,' Harriet said. 'Sometimes I think you men deserve each other.'

Blessed repeated that he had better be off to his study. He would see Harriet before he went into the office, he said, and he would see Redman again at the Donaldsons if all went well. As he climbed the stairs, still feeling irritated by the contest of wills with his wife, he gave some thought to the coming evening and decided that Redman would probably turn up, despite his protestations. Harry Donaldson was the doyen of the press corps in Germany; he headed Central European operations for an international press agency. More to the point, his wife, Gillie, was a cousin of Clement Attlee, the British Prime Minister, and she and Harry were often invited to dinner with him when they were in London.

In other words, for Laurence Redman, being nice to Harry and Gillie Donaldson would not come at all amiss. For James Blessed, on the other hand, though he liked the couple, all that made not a ha'pennyworth of difference. The only thing that mattered was finding out how those bodies had ended up on that wasteland behind the Potsdamer Strasse. Oh, and his daughter's birthday. He had to find time for Daphne tomorrow, no matter what.

THREE

'YOU SHOULDA BEEN THERE for that blood-spilling, Benno!' said Gurkel. 'Wow!'

Benno answered with a non-committal shrug. But there was no stopping his friend now. An eager smile played on Gurkel's eleven-year-old face. He put two homemade cigarettes in his mouth, lit them skilfully, handed one to Benno.

'That Hershey, that Gee-Eye-Joe,' he continued. '*Ach scheiss* you know, we beat him up good! Banana, he stood on his belly while Granit lifted his boot and kicked Joe's face to *sweet pink pulp*. Then they took his wallet, his everything . . . Wow, you shoulda been there—you and the Wonder . . .'

Sitting waiting at the disused slaughterhouse for their black market contact, Gurkel was bragging about how he and two of the older orphans had robbed an unwary American serviceman in broad daylight by the Landwehr Canal. Gurkel had lured him into the trap.

'Easy, you beddabelieve, Benno! I give him my cutekid grin. I say, hello Joe, I got a sister, you come with me for best frat, she is mad for fucking. And that Hershey he laughs, with his crazy red drunk-eyes looking at me, so I tell him my sister got tits like melons, beautiful ass, blonde hair . . . Marlene Dietrich! Eva Braun! And this dumb Gee-Eye, he follows me into that cellar like a dancing bear!' Gurkel exploded into a high-pitched, machine-gun laugh. 'And then those big Kinder get him, and they punch him and kick him and take everything. He moans. He looks at me. And even though he is choking on his teeth he is mumbling, "Nice boy. Oh I thought you wuz a nice boy . . ."!'

35

Naturally, Benno chuckled at the GI story, if only out of tribal loyalty. Gurkel was rangy, eleven years old but looked thirteen. Benno was square, shorter, and though they were the same age he looked appreciably younger. His features were saturnine, dark and thoughtful. Not for him the freckled, deceptively open kid-brother look that made Gurkel so popular with the soldiers, especially the 'Hersheys', as they called the Americans. But Gurkel was one of Benno's two special friends among the gang of homeless children who called themselves the Kinder—the other was the Wonder.

'The big Kinder don't like the Allied Occupation,' Benno said. 'Sometimes I think maybe they don't really care about the thieving, they just wanna *hurt* those soldiers. This I think they get from Boss-Kind. He's been talking a lot of hate about those Allied soldiers lately—Tommies especially. Why don't he hate the Soviets too?'

'This is a mystery, Benno,' Gurkel said with a loose little shrug. 'But he's the Boss, and he always has good reasons. Maybe . . .' His brows knitted as he rehearsed in his mind what those reasons could be. '. . . Maybe because those Russkies don't have so much you can steal.'

They were perched on upturned petrol drums in the slaughterhouse, waiting for a man they knew only as 'the Slovak' to arrive and take delivery of a package. Both wore old, patched shirts and shorts. Gurkel's bare feet were protected by a pair of battered sandals, Benno's by heavy army boots, several sizes too big for him and stuffed with newspaper to help them fit.

Until the end of the war, the slaughterhouse had been just that: a busy municipal abattoir. Since then the high, vaulted roof had been partly destroyed, wooden frames and beams scavenged for firewood, opening it up to the elements. All the butchering equipment and holding-pens had gone too, looted by Russian reparation squads. There were great double doors at one end—once the place's steel-hinged mouth—while at the other was a maze of smaller rooms—processing-chambers, the various stations of its great intestine. In there the carcasses would be broken down into digestible hunks, stored, prepared for distribution.

The room where the boys were sitting had been a cold store. Boss-Kind had chosen it for their official pick-up point inside the Soviet sector. And although the entire building had a feeling of cavernous gloom, an after-reek of death, to Benno and Gurkel this did not seem a sad or frightening place. Since they were small, the boys had lived among death and destruction, had accepted these scourges as normal.

If they felt fear, it was of a manageable, necessary kind, like the sailor's fear of the sea.

'I tell you the time,' Gurkel said. 'Then we know if the Slovak is late.' He pulled up his long, baggy shirtsleeve, and proudly revealed a watch strapped to his skinny forearm, several inches above the wrist. It was a cheap American timepiece with a worn brown leather strap, but it had a second hand, which was ticking round, evidence that the mechanism worked. 'Ah . . . you know that it is twenty minutes past ten. The Slovak is late!' he said in triumph.

'Good watch. American,' Benno said with mild envy. 'You got that from the Hershey?'

Gurkel nodded. 'Banana, Granit, all the big Kinder got plenty watches. So Banana said to me, you take it! We won' tell the Boss, no.'

'I still don' understand why you can't just *have* that watch,' Benno said. 'You rolled that Hershey, you made that *Spritze*, that piece of thieving, happen, just as much as the others.' He frowned. 'I mean, you know Gurkel, we work so hard. What do *we* get?'

'We are free, we are safe,' Gurkel said solemnly. 'Remember how that was in '45 at Point Null and how it is now, Benno.' He began to chant the child-gang's anthem:

'Altogether Kinder swing,
Unity is Kinder thing
Every little Kinderwaif
In Kinder Garden he lives safe . . .'

Just as he finished there was a sound at the far end of the room. Benno quickly pinched off the end of the skinny hand-rolled cigarette he and Gurkel had been sharing, put the remainder into the pocket of his shirt. He and Gurkel both slid off the petrol-drums, ready to flee if necessary.

The ill-fitting steel door scraped open, and there, huffing and puffing, stood the Slovak, in his habitual dark glasses, with his white stick and the old Panama hat he wore all the time, even in deepest winter. The Russians laughed at him but in their superstitious way left him alone—thirty years of communism had not cured them of the belief that cripples were holy, chosen.

'*Na, Kinder,*' the Slovak said in his slow, slavic-accented German. 'You are here and now so am I.'

All anyone knew about this man's background was that he was down on his luck and that he came from Bratislava, which was why they called him 'the Slovak'. Also that he was not really blind; he didn't

37

see well, but he saw as much as he needed to. The blindness was just a device, one that earned him a little living if there was no better way available, and that made him seem harmless, less-than-human. He was about sixty, thick-set, with a pepper-and-salt beard and an incongruous, sensual little bud of a mouth set among otherwise coarse features. The small, round dark glasses that he wore gave him the look of an extremely poisonous deep-sea fish.

'*Na, Kinder.*' He made slow progress towards them, his difficulty the result of a war-wound from 1916. Or so he had told them. But, like much of what the Slovak said, this claim was to be treated with caution. He could move very quickly if he so desired, as the boys had long since found out. '*Na, Kinder,*' he wheezed yet again when he was within two or three feet of them, 'what do you have for this old man today?' He held out his right hand like a supplicant.

Benno reached under his shirt, took out a small package about the size of a packet of cigarettes, wrapped in newspaper. He did not hand it over immediately, instead waited.

The Slovak laughed. 'All this time, we do business, and still you do not trust me. Are you frightened that I will betray you to the Russians because of the blockade? Boys . . . rest assured. I don't like the Russians, and I don't like the atheistic Reds who run my beloved country now. So you are safe. And here . . .' He reached into his coat, pulled out a small bag. 'Tell your Boss these are best quality diamonds, worth a great deal in Antwerp or New York. They once belonged to a Russian grand-duchess, I know that for a fact.'

Benno silently held out his package in one hand, prepared to take the bag with the other.

The Slovak made to hand over the bag, then held back, keeping it just out of Benno's reach. 'You boys, you think I was always like this,' he murmured. 'Ah, but I was not. I was an officer in the Imperial and Royal Army of Austria-Hungary. I owned land, big estates. I *danced* with grand-duchesses in those days.'

'We are in a *hurry*, Slovak,' Benno interrupted him. 'We got many things to do.'

Gurkel grinned. 'And Boss-Kind don' care if these diamonds come from a duchess or from a pig's arse, so long as they earn *valuta* for the Kinder.'

Benno lunged forward, snatched the bag from the surprised Slovak, pressed the package at him. The Slovak took it eventually.

'If it were not for my beloved apartment, so close to the most beautiful parts of Berlin, I would move to the west, away from the filthy Russians,' the Slovak said, still trying to delay the end of the transaction. He wet his lips. 'I have candy at my apartment. I have nice clothes. If you boys—'

He had produced from the depths of his coat a chocolate bar. It had a Red Cross on the wrapper, so had probably come from a United Nations supply. He was holding it up, ogling each of the boys in turn. 'See? See?' he repeated.

Benno's attitude changed. He came closer, smiling bashfully. 'You bring for us . . .?'

The Slovak nodded, trying in his greasy way to twinkle. 'Just a short visit to my place. I have so many other beautiful things . . .'

'We will go.' Benno reached out, looking his dubious benefactor in the eye with a hint of coy promise.

'Yes, yes. We will go,' the Slovak agreed, captivated by Benno's pliant attitude, and so moved that he let the chocolate go without protest.

Immediately Benno sprang back, clutching his prize. 'We will go *home*! Home to the Kinder Garden!' he crowed. 'You can stay here and find a grand-duchess to talk to, you old Slov-oh hom-o!'

When the boys ran past the Slovak to get to the open door, he made a determined grab at them, but they were too quick for him. In fact, Benno even had time to drag the door shut behind them on the way out. As they ran laughing down the alley towards the street, they heard the Slovak's stick banging on the door. The old *Drecksack* would get the door open eventually, but it would take a few minutes, or he could get out of one of the windows. Two minutes later they were out on the street, where they slowed down to a normal walking pace. Benno had the chocolate in his pocket, the bag of diamonds concealed under his shirt.

The disused slaughterhouse was near the Weissenssee marshalling yards, close to the old working-class suburb of Prenzlauer Berg. The two boys attracted no notice, from soldiers or civilians, as they walked westward through the drab, grey streets. Only once did they worry, when a Russian captain got off a tram and shouted at them—although western officers were driven around in staff cars, Red Army officers, even quite high-ranking ones, used public transport. The boys relaxed when they realised that he was merely drunk, and shouting at everyone he saw. They passed gangs of labourers at work on bomb-sites, busy erecting huge billboards of Lenin and Stalin, and of the geriatric German communist leader, Wilhelm Pieck. They passed bands of communist 'Free German Youth' in their uniforms of red bandanas and khaki shirts and shorts. They carried flags and placards; probably they were heading for some 'spontaneous' anti-western demonstration at the Brandenburg Gate. Benno and Gurkel didn't care either way, though they registered everything carefully, as creatures trained to survive must do. Mostly, though, they were as happy as they reasonably could be. After all, they were young, they had food in their bellies, nothing bad had happened to them today, and the sun was shining. So on they sauntered, vaguely aiming for the sector border. Then suddenly Gurkel stopped and pointed upward. To the south, over the American sector, a big cargo plane was circling. The Kinder had heard vague, distorted rumours of the blockade and the airlift.

'Maybe other Kinder are on that plane already,' Gurkel said. 'Boss-Kind told Granit that many Kinder will go. Maybe the Wonder tomorrow.' He glanced furtively at the precious bag concealed under Benno's shirt. 'And maybe the Wonder will take those duchess's diamonds to Rhein-Main, to the Hershey-Zone.'

Benno shrugged indifferently. 'You know I don't understand this flying to the West. I just do my job for the Kinder. Sometimes, though, I wonder what Boss-Kind is really doing.'

'Doing? Boss-Kind is doing the best for us Kinder!'

'I still don' understand this flying to the West, this *Fliegerei*. And Boss-Kind, he's not telling. These days, with the Boss everything is so secret . . .'

'Maybe *you* could lead the Kinder instead of Boss-Kind, Benno,' Gurkel hissed, his mood suddenly less amicable. 'Maybe you'd just like to call a Kinder-meeting, and ask them whether they want *you* to be responsible for keeping the Kinder Garden safe!'

Chastened, or at least cautioned, Benno shrugged. 'Nix leader,' he said, reverting to comic Russkie-German. 'Me nix leader, me *watcher*. I make joke, yes, Jurrman comrade?'

'You beddabelieve!'

FOUR

STRANGE, EVEN DISTURBING, how vividly Harriet's jibe had brought back that terrible incident in Lebanon. While he had been roughing out an account of the Price murder, the dark images and emotions of three years ago, of events in a different country, had threatened to overwhelm him. Now Blessed sat smoking a cheroot in his study, the draft report completed. He knew he should already be on his way back into the centre of the city to take charge of his section, but the memories of that nightmare in the hills outside Beirut would not recede . . .

As Blessed's wife had said, he had been absolutely determined to catch Jamail. The bandit leader, chieftain of a Druze village high in the hills twenty miles or so from Beirut, had been running Berka Valley opium down to the docks in a big way for years, using his own secretive, clannish people as couriers, and crossing a few important French and Lebanese government palms with silver. Blessed, then leading a small unit with special responsibilities for British interests on the waterfront, had managed to intercept some embarrassingly large shipments, and the Lebanese chieftain had been furious. His and his people's livelihood put at risk! All those expensive bribes gone to waste!

That was when the word had come through the usual channels: Jamail had decided to run his latest supply of opium down to Tyre, far to the south, out of Blessed's jurisdiction altogether. The stuff would be stored for one day only in a cellar beneath the house of X, in the village of Y—close to Jamail's fiefdom—and Jamail himself would be there, with a few supporters, to supervise the opening of the new export route.

How could the opportunity be missed? After a pleasant al fresco breakfast in the garden of the Grand Hotel Ain Sofar, Blessed had set off for the cool of the hills, taking two open jeeps, plus a light Dodge truck for transporting prisoners. The party was made up of three English military policemen, a Lebanese interpreter/guide, and seven Jewish-Palestinian auxiliaries.

Everyone felt grateful to be free of the city's stifling heat. Blessed was in the front passenger seat of the leading jeep. Beside him sat his driver, a stocky, fierce Polish Jew named David Lemberger with wire-grey hair, five children, and an Eastern-European penchant for strongly-scented eau-de-cologne. They had passed a solitary, whitewashed house draped in flowering hibiscus, and were toiling up the steep, twisting road with woods to their left, and high, rocky slopes to their right, when suddenly the world seemed to fall in on them all.

One rifle-shot was followed almost simultaneously by another. The jeep shuddered and swerved, and Lemberger slumped hard over, almost pitching his passenger onto the road. Somehow, Blessed managed to stay in the jeep, and heave his dying driver back far enough to enable him to seize the wheel, as the jeep rumbled off the road and was brought to an abrupt halt by a clump of young trees.

The firing continued. It was coming from rocks a couple of hundred feet up, and it was unpleasantly accurate. Blessed and the two survivors rolled out of the jeep and took cover among the trees. Meanwhile, the following jeep had reversed into the Dodge, and both vehicles had slid back down the road for a hundred yards or so before being brought to a halt by a rocky outcrop.

One man in the jeep had been badly wounded by a bullet, another thrown onto the road by the sudden tumble into reverse. The rest survived and were soon keeping up a steady fire in the direction of the invisible assailants among the rocks. Blessed took the decision that they must cut down the hill through the trees, one at a time, to join the others. First a man called Heller set off, stumbling, slithering through the pine-needles, on a rough zig-zag course. He reached the Dodge, disappeared behind its bonnet to cover and relative safety. The second man went immediately after and was running like a hare until suddenly, about twenty yards from home, he was hit. He stumbled, then continued a little more slowly, clutching his left arm. Then it was Blessed's turn.

Of course, the dash towards safety seemed to last forever. As Blessed ran, his eyes filmed over with salty sweat, so that all he could make out between the tree-trunks was the blurred outline of the covered truck.

At last he swung himself behind the sturdy bonnet of the Dodge, as the previous fugitives had done. A bullet hit the headlight, exactly where the small of his back had been a second previously. After that, strangely, the fire stopped almost immediately, as if the reuniting of the raiding-party and its commander's survival destroyed the whole point of the exercise. Someone yelled something incomprehensible but obviously insulting from the enemy-occupied heights. Then there was silence.

Jamail was hauled in a couple of weeks later. Even the French-Lebanese authorities couldn't ignore the deaths of two military policemen. They never found out how he had managed to feed Blessed's unit with the misleading information that had led them to the ambush in the hills. They never managed, either, to pin the murders on him. But some opium was found at his village, an old kidnapping charge was dusted down, and he spent some time in prison. Meanwhile, Blessed's superiors had decided that his German-speaking abilities required his return to Europe for occupation duties . . .

He was brought back to his study in Spandau by the sound of Gisela singing. She had, he realised, just thrown open a window in order to air Daphne's room, and the sound of her well-trained, pleasant soprano was suddenly amplified sufficiently to wrench him out of his reverie. Donizetti, he thought a little hazily; that catchy, sad aria from *Lucia di Lammermoor*. Sometimes it was a mystery to him why Gisela stayed here. Certainly she seemed to have developed a quite touching rapport with Daff, but considering that she could make twenty times what she did here by working the GIs on the Augsburger Strasse, Gisela was proof that some Germans, at least, wouldn't do just anything for dollars.

His study was a tiny attic tucked under the carved eaves of the villa. On a clear day Blessed could see the church spire in Falkenhagen, a mile or so away inside the Russian Zone, and the azure meniscus of the nearby Falkensee lake. He had rejected the Kreisleiter's mahogany-panelled retreat on the floor below: he preferred a cosy little room with a view. And the house-martins had arrived for their summer stay, busy in the roof above his head. He had learned to distinguish between the even chirrup of the parents and the raucous pleas of the hungry young.

On the simple pine desk facing the window were his notepads, his legal reference books, the paper he used for writing letters and for drafting reports. And perched on the corner of the desk, a crystal

43

paperweight—a beautiful turquoise blue, shot through with purple and black and silver veins, that his German Aunt Lotte had given him on his tenth birthday. He had always treasured it above his train sets, his lead soldiers, his toy cars. It still went with him everywhere, perhaps because it connected him to those days of childhood visits to Berlin. And he still had a very special affection for Aunt Lotte. His mother's sister had sacrificed much in Germany's last two wars. Her newly-wed husband had been killed in 1915, leaving Lotte, by then pregnant, alone to bring up the child. Thirty years later almost to the day, she was bombed out of her precious Berlin apartment. She now lived in the American sector with Gerhard, Blessed's cousin, a young man who had never known his father.

But at least Lotte had survived. Blessed's mother, widowed under very different circumstances and trapped in her London exile by the war, had not been so lucky. Hardly more than a girl when courted by his father—then a handsome English medical student attending lectures at the University of Berlin—in her nineteenth summer she had abandoned her homeland and family for love. Her reward had been early widowhood, the remains of her youth spent raising Blessed alone in what always seemed to her a strange and unforgiving country. She had been only fifty-four when one fine afternoon late in 1944 her mansion-block flat in Highgate was annihilated by a German flying-bomb. And only her son had ever understood how desperately homesick she had always been for the Kurfürstendamm and KaDeWe, for Lotte and for *Erdbeertorte* with real coffee at the Cafe Kranzler.

There was Blessed's mother now, in one of several photographs arranged on the small shelf above his desk. The snap had been taken soon after Daphne was born. His mother was smiling stiffly, as she always did when confronted by a camera, but there was no mistaking the joy and pride with which she cradled her granddaughter.

Blessed picked up the next photograph. This one showed himself and his family, snapped by a German photographer the previous summer while on holiday at the Steinhuder Meer, a lake resort near Hanover. In those days the Zone borders had been easy to cross. He remembered how smiling Russians had waved their car through the checkpoints. So, there was Blessed and, to his right, Harriet. Daphne, then just turned seven—it had been almost exactly a year ago—was wearing a cotton pinafore dress and smiled at the camera with a kind of generalised, happy trust. She had a tooth missing, as children of that age often do. She was a pretty child, though in a round-faced way that came from her stolid German grandmother rather than from

44

Harriet, the highly-strung English thoroughbred who had carried her and brought her into the world.

At that point his wife walked into the room. Inexplicably, Blessed panicked. He hastily returned the family photograph to the desk, turned wildly to face her.

'Christ, Harriet. What do you want?'

She glanced at the photograph, then back at him in a peculiarly blank way. 'I surprised you,' she said at last.

'Yes. I'm tired, and I'm under a lot of pressure.'

'You always are tired and under pressure.'

Blessed shrugged. Harriet was still wearing the blue blouse, and over it a cream-coloured suit adapted from a prewar ensemble. Her shoulders were heavily padded. She looked tall and slightly masculine and terrifically sexy.

'You look ready for the social fray,' Blessed commented. 'I'll be off into the city myself in a few minutes. Can I offer you a lift anywhere?'

'Larry's waiting for me, actually. I'm going swimming at the Blue-White Club. He has a big meeting with General Herbert at the Villa Lemm in half an hour. The Club's on his way.'

Somehow, though he hadn't heard the car, Blessed had fancied that Redman must have gone by now. How wrong he had been. 'Fine,' he said.

'I'll be meeting some of the girls afterwards in the bar,' Harriet continued, as if anticipating the question in his mind. 'We're having lunch at someone's house . . . Anne Garfitt's, I think. Though I'm not absolutely certain.'

'I see. That explains the outfit, then. Very nice too.'

'Thank you. Mustn't let standards drop just because the Cossacks could come thundering up the drive at any moment.'

Blessed laughed. It did nothing to relieve the tension between them. Then the telephone rang. Harriet's gaze was curious, challenging. He picked up the receiver: 'Yes. Blessed speaking.'

It was Sergeant Kelly, ringing from the office.

'More about Corporal Price, sir,' Kelly said, going straight to the point. 'Looks like a certainty, the identification. I phoned his unit in Wolfenbüttel and found out he's been listed AWOL. Didn't return from home leave. Told everyone he was going back to Wales to see his wife and family. Even had a travel warrant issued, right through to Caerphilly.'

'We need to know if he actually went home.'

'We're trying to contact Mrs Price to clear that up. The poor woman's in for a shock. I'll lay odds he told Wolfenbüttel he was off home to Wales, then grabbed his chance to sneak off to Berlin. Crafty little git. Once his missus confirms he's not in Wales, I suggest we fly her over here for a formal identification of the body.'

'Just find out if he went home first,' Blessed said. 'We'll think about the rest later. The family will need to be handled carefully. The implications of Price's death could be very far-reaching, and we don't want the wrong kind of publicity.'

'Very well, sir. Anything else?'

'No. We'll be pulling in his associates later according to plan.' Blessed was making hurried notes. 'Well, it looks like I'd better come in immediately. We have to talk about this afternoon's business, and I'd like to speak to Price's unit myself . . . Could you hold on a minute, Kelly—'

Blessed glanced up, only to realise that Harriet had slipped quietly from the room. He had missed his chance to ask her to wait.

'No Price in Wales,' Kelly announced the moment Blessed came through the door. 'Nor was there at any time during the past few weeks.'

Pursued by the sergeant, Blessed walked on into his office. 'That was quick work, Kelly.'

'Sheer luck. Mrs Price has a job as a filing clerk at the local colliery, so it was easy to contact her by telephone.'

'And she didn't know anything about Price's supposed home leave?'

'No, no. She hasn't clapped eyes on hubby for almost a year, apparently. Not exactly your ideal of wedded bliss, in other words.'

Blessed hung up his coat and cap. 'I was wondering why she hadn't moved into married quarters over here. Most army wives are very keen on staying close to their husbands, if only to keep an eye on them. They've heard all the stories about those wicked German Jezebels.'

Kelly leered mechanically. Despite his extreme shyness with women —it was generally agreed that he could well be the only virgin of either sex left in Berlin—he knew the correct army response to any sexual allusion.

'Perhaps she'd already given up on the philandering sod,' he suggested. 'Anyway, her story was that she earns good money at the pit office. And, of course, "our mam looks after little Caradoc, see".' Kelly gleefully mimicked Mrs Price's South Wales bleating. 'Blowed if she was going to sit in some freezing, horrible Nissen hut, surrounded by lousy, dirty Germans, and have her Caradoc catching all kinds of awful diseases. I quote.'

Blessed sighed. 'So, there's a son. How old is he?'

'Coming up to five, the wife said. Due to start at the local school in September.'

'Well, she'll miss Corporal Price's pay, office job or no office job,' Blessed said. 'How did you get her talking, by the way?'

'I told her I was from army welfare.' Kelly was delighted with this new opportunity to prove his cunning. 'I said we were doing a survey, trying to find out why some army wives accompany their husbands on overseas postings and some don't. I didn't see much point in getting her upset at this stage.'

'No. She'll have enough grief coming later.' Blessed looked at the pile of mail on his desk but made no move towards it. 'Any other urgent business?'

Kelly handed him an itemised list of the morning's phone calls. Blessed sat down, pushed the mail to one side to make room, and started studying the sergeant's notes. There were a couple of fairly straightforward enquiries which Kelly seemed to have answered quite adequately. Also, Colonel Harrison, the Acting Provost of Military Police, wanted him to stroll over during the course of the morning for a chat. Blessed frowned. Harrison, based a short distance away in the Knesebeckstrasse, was his immediate superior. His invitations often signified bad news, administrative problems, or complaints from officers who'd had their nose put out of joint by some SIB investigation. It was also possible that Harrison had heard about the Potsdamer Strasse murders and had some inkling of their potential significance. Something told Blessed that it might be a good idea to get the case really moving before Harrison had a chance to interfere. A few quick *faits accomplis* would do no harm, he told himself before his attention moved to the last message.

'Ah. I see Inspector Weiss rang,' he said to Kelly, who was still hovering at his elbow. 'Has he got the policeman who found the bodies?'

'He has. He wanted instructions on what to do with him.'

'We'd better get the chap over here as soon as possible. Send a car. Weiss is to escort him and assist with the interrogation.' Blessed tapped on the desk with his pencil. *Fait accompli* number one coming up, he decided. 'You can also draft me a formal letter to the German President of Police at the Alexanderplatz, requesting—no, *informing* him that Weiss and three of his men will be working with us on the Potsdamer

Strasse murders. Prepare copies to be sent to Colonel Harrison, to the Public Safety Officer, and . . . most important . . . to the Soviet Liaison Officer at police headquarters.'

Kelly gave him a sideways look. 'Perhaps a letter to *The Times* as well, eh, sir?'

Blessed grinned. 'Not yet,' he said. Kelly knew as well as he did that once those demands had been made in writing, there was nothing Harrison would be able to do to stop him co-opting Weiss and his men. In fact, after the Russians had been informed, the colonel would be duty-bound to support Blessed to the hilt. He wouldn't like it, but that was just too bad.

'Oh, we've put out a description of the dead woman, by the way,' Kelly said. 'I've told the boys in Vice to check all their records against our details, but so far they haven't turned anything up. Early days yet, though.'

'It's also possible that she has no form. Make sure they keep looking, though, just in case. Anything else I need to know?'

'We're still waiting for the German pathologist's written report. Funny how those blokes really like to take their time over these autopsies,' Kelly remarked. 'Anyone'd think they enjoyed themselves in there in those brightly-lit rooms, with their saws and their scissors and their sewing kits.'

Blessed nodded absently. He was already making equations with the details he had culled so far. If the corpse was Corporal Price—and there now seemed no doubt about it—then they might have to extend the enquiry westward into the British Zone itself. This would not be easy, especially with the land routes from Berlin to the Zone blocked by the Soviets. He decided that when he went to see the colonel later that morning he would box clever, for the moment only supply information when he was asked direct questions, and even then stick to Berlin, the murder details, the known facts—some of which would first have to be clarified by a telephone call to Corporal Price's unit.

Blessed knew the town of Wolfenbüttel quite well. It was quaint and small and also very close to the border with the Russian Zone, which was why it had a sizeable British garrison. Before the Soviets closed the land corridors, it would have been easy enough for Price to hop on a train, or hitch a lift, and be in Berlin in as little as three or four hours. So, say Price had sneaked off to Berlin a couple of weeks ago, having told everyone that he was making a sentimental pilgrimage back to his native Wales. (How much home leave had he been granted? A note to ask his CO.) Then, of course, he would have been marooned by the sudden, unexpected imposition of the Soviet blockade. The only way for Price to return to his unit would have been by applying to the military authorities in Berlin for a seat on a transport plane. And odds-on, once he did that, that someone would check his papers, establish that he was supposed to be on leave in Wales, and want to know what he was doing in Berlin instead. A routine enquiry to the Military Police here would then, of course, reveal that Price was known to them, having been interrogated by Blessed's unit the previous winter and released for lack of evidence, with a warning to stay away from Berlin in future . . . Given those options, Blessed thought, it was altogether plausible that Price preferred to go AWOL, or even to desert outright. Particularly if he had a bolt-hole at his girlfriend's place—if the dead woman was his girlfriend, of course, and not just a casual pick-up. These equations still didn't solve the mystery of what she and the corporal had been doing, dead, on wasteground between the Potsdamer Strasse and the Tiergarten, but first things first.

After Kelly had left the room, Blessed tackled the task of phoning the RAMC in Wolfenbüttel. The telephone connections between Berlin and the outside world were under enormous strain, as the frantic operators kept telling him, but after half an hour he got through, by dint of ruthless rank-pulling. Once an RAMC clerk from Wolfenbüttel came on the line, however, Blessed transformed himself from a bullying SIB captain into 'Sergeant Grimes' of the Military Police in Brunswick, investigating the 'disappearance' of Corporal Ronald Price. The CO and his deputy were both unavailable, but in the event, as often happened, the clerk proved franker and more knowledgeable than any officer would have been.

'Oh yes,' the man told Blessed. 'I heard this morning—someone said he never went to Wales to see his missus and the kid. Never went near the place. What a laugh! I mean, for weeks he'd been shooting us all this line about how he was lookin' forward to being with his family and breathing the clean air of the valleys. Old Taffy Price could tell a tale and no mistake. He brought tears to the eyes of grown men the night before he left.'

'Had he been home—to Wales, that is—before in your experience?'

'Let me see. It would have been last July. And I think he definitely went there, because he brought back some peppermint rock from Barry Island.'

'What about other time off? How did he spend that? Where did he usually go?'

'I dunno really,' the clerk said cheerfully. 'I hardly ever saw him in the gasthofs or the usual places the rest of the lads go. I reckon he had some bird tucked away, and he used to stay with her.'

'Would he go away when he had, say, a forty-eight hour pass?'

'I suppose so. All I know is, we never used to see the blighter around the camp, or around town. He'd just disappear. So what do *you* think?'

Blessed thought for a moment. 'I don't think anything in particular at this stage,' he said. 'My job is to establish some basic facts, you see. Now just tell me, if you don't mind, who was Price's best friend, his closest mate.'

'A *mate*? He didn't really have any. He was a solitary bloke, for all his mouth, and . . . well, to tell the truth, no one liked him much. He was clever. Too bloody clever by half.'

'Let's put it another way. Who knew him best?'

'Oh, I suppose that'd be Whizzer Whalley. He'd served with Price in the war. They were both clerks in medical stores. You couldn't exactly call them bosom pals, but you'd see them having a jar together once in a while.'

'I'd like Whalley's full name and rank, please.'

'Just a sec.' The man went to consult his records. 'That'd be Whalley, with a "h". Anthony Leonard. Lance-Corporal. A good bloke, Whizzer. Probably used to buy Taffy a drink because he felt sorry for him.'

'Probably. Thank you very much.'

Blessed put the phone down, summoned Kelly.

'Any luck with Weiss?' he said when the sergeant came back into the office.

'He'll be here in just a few minutes, sir, along with our jolly wachtmann. Want me to keep 'em amused while you're seeing the colonel?'

Blessed cast a baleful look at the still-unopened mail. He shook his head. 'Phone 248 Provost and tell Colonel Harrison's office I'll be with him as soon as I can,' he said. 'I want to get this interrogation over with first.'

Kelly smiled indulgently. 'Sticking to your priorities, sir?'

'We have to keep our end up as best we can,' Blessed said. 'While Inspector Weiss and I are busy with our man in here, you can be making sure you've got that letter, and the copies, ready for me to sign as soon as I've finished. In other words, they're to be sent off *before* I go over to the Knesebeckstrasse to see the colonel. Once you've got the letters prepared, you can double-check our plans for this afternoon's surprise party for those black marketeers in the Tiergarten.'

'Yes, sir. Of course, sir. Will you be taking part personally now?'

'Not directly. You'll still be in charge of the actual arrests, Kelly. And don't forget that we're clearly playing a much harder game since those bodies were discovered than we thought. Until this morning, we were aiming to crack a fairly routine black-market ring. Now that's all changed. A member of His Majesty's Forces has been killed. If, as we must suspect, there's a connection between this murder and the drug racket, then our suspects will be prepared to use extreme force to avoid arrest.'

'I'm aware of that, sir,' Kelly said stiffly, barely concealing his offended pride. 'We'll still be following the original party-plan. But everyone will be issued with extra rounds, and they'll be warned to anticipate serious armed resistance. They're experienced lads, though, sir; they've all been in shoot-outs in their time.'

'Good. And now, show in Inspector Weiss and friend just as soon as they arrive, will you?'

As it turned out, Wachtmann Hermann Gottlob Pilzinger was not a born Berliner. He lived in the Russian sector but his name, and when he opened his mouth, his accent, marked him out as a Swabian from southwest Germany. The wachtmann, an overweight, florid man of about forty, used a Berlin vocabulary, but he still spoke in the lazy, singsong rhythms of his home province, which most other Germans found irresistibly comical.

'I've got three kids of my own,' he told Blessed. 'They have a place to live, they get just about enough to eat, thank God. These street-children, though, they tear at my heart.'

'How did you encounter this particular one last night, Wachtmann?'

'Ah. It was some time still before daybreak. The chilliest part of the night. I saw him emerge onto the Potsdamer Strasse. You see, my beat always leads me there at that time. I take my meal-break—'

'Come to the point, please, Pilzinger. We haven't got all afternoon,' Weiss interrupted him. The inspector was sitting on a chair against the wall to Pilzinger's right. The professional persona he had chosen, by agreement with Blessed, was that of the 'hard' interrogator.

'Yes, Inspector. Well, this kid was wild-eyed, waving frantically.' The policeman mimed his own surprise at seeing such an apparition at three in the morning on the Potsdamer Strasse. 'I thought, it's not often that such children come *looking* for a cop. Usually they are trying to keep out of your way.'

'Describe the child, please, Wachtmann,' Blessed asked politely.

'Let me see. Nine, ten years old—hard to tell when these kids are so undernourished. He was very small for his age, I think. He had dark hair but pale skin. What in the Hitler time they used to call "alpine" facial features. A couple of front teeth missing.'

'Eyes?'

'Hazel.' Hesitation. 'Perhaps even darker. Big, dark eyes. But it was not yet light, you know, and such details didn't seem so important at that point.'

Blessed grunted sceptically. 'Clothes?'

'Baggy, threadbare shorts. An old sweater.'

'Colour?'

'The night was very dark. I don't know—' Pilzinger had begun to sweat. He ran one porky hand through his thinning yellow hair.

'I want to know, what did the boy *say*?' Weiss barked.

Pilzinger whirled around to face him. 'He . . . he said, "Herr Wachtmeister, excuse me, but I have found a man and a woman and I think they are dead. Please come and look." '

'And what did you say?' Blessed took over again. It was astonishing how engrained were German habits of flattery. Even a street urchin would instinctively bump up a policeman's rank, automatically address him not as a simple wachtmann or constable, but as 'Wachtmeister' or Sergeant. In the same way, in a restaurant it was polite when trying to attract the very humblest waiter's attention to refer to him respectfully as 'Herr Ober' or Headwaiter.

'I asked him what he was doing here at this hour—it was three twenty-seven precisely.' The fact that he could name the exact time did something to restore Pilzinger's dignity. He looked at Weiss with mild defiance: 'I see you have my written report on your desk, Herr Inspector, but just in case you have not read it, my words were: "Where I come from, you would be in bed with angels watching over you. What are you doing in this godforsaken spot?" '

Blessed couldn't suppress a grin. Even Weiss, still playing the hard man, had to struggle to keep a straight face.

'Then you followed him?'

'I drew my service pistol first. And I said, "Do you know these people? Are you related to them?" '

'A wise question.'

'He said "no" and made off into the ruins. Naturally, I went after him and followed until we arrived at the place where the poor man and his girl lay.'

As a matter of routine, Blessed asked Pilzinger to describe the positions of the bodies, and their condition. It was clear from what he said that they had not been moved afterwards.

'So why do you think the boy ran away?'

'I don't know, Herr Captain. I had no reason to believe that he would do such a thing. Of course, with hindsight . . .'

'You said yourself, just a few minutes ago, that street children don't usually welcome encounters with the police,' Weiss corrected him. 'That implies you were aware there might be a problem.'

Wachtmann Pilzinger, who had not slept since the previous day and would dearly have loved to be in bed at home, with angels watching over him as well, hung his head and said nothing.

Eventually Blessed leaned forward. 'Look, Wachtmann. I understand how it was. You were tired. You thought that since this child had sought you out, informed you of the location of the bodies, he was prepared to cooperate fully. Why should he suddenly disappear?'

Pilzinger nodded gloomily. 'Why?' he echoed.

'If we knew that, we would know a lot, eh? It's a pity you let him go, but the damage is done. Perhaps we can find him again. We're not trying to trap you, Wachtmann, but it is our duty to enquire into every detail.'

'Did the kid say anything else, before he ran off into the ruins?' Weiss took over the questioning again.

'He did not, Inspector.'

'But he gave no indication that he intended to flee?'

'None, Inspector. He seemed frightened, grateful that I had come along. Again, that was why—'

'Just answer the questions, all right?' Weiss snapped. 'Are you sure you didn't see anyone else around?'

'No, Inspector. Not a soul.'

Blessed glanced at Weiss, as if warning him to ease off.

'All right. Now, you're a Swabian by birth, Wachtmann. Tell me, how long have you lived in Berlin?' he asked then.

'Since 1937, Herr Captain,' Pilzinger said. 'After leaving the *Realschule*, I was apprenticed to Mercedes in Stuttgart as a mechanic. I worked there, among my own people, for years. Then the company transferred me here to work in a service depot in Pankow. Soon after, I married a Berlin girl—my family never forgave me, they couldn't believe I hadn't chosen a good, hardworking Swabian maiden. Well, I intended to save up, maybe open my own garage, but then the kids started coming, and the war, and—'

'Slow down, Wachtmann. What did you do in the war?'

'I was in the Motorised Corps, naturally enough. First in North Africa, which was fine, then in Russia, which was not so fine, in fact it was terrible . . . In Russia I was wounded and invalided home. I still walk with a slight limp, and my stomach . . .'

'Was that when you joined the police?'

'Yes. The authorities drafted me into the Protection Police as an auxiliary constable, because all the fit cops had been sent to war. This was in the summer of forty-four.'

'The SMA left you where you were, I see.'

'Pardon, Herr Captain?'

'The Soviet Military Administration didn't purge you from the police when they took over the government of Berlin.'

Pilzinger shook his head emphatically. 'Why should they? I was never a member of the Nazi Party. I never fired a shot in anger. Most of the time I just fixed officers' staff cars, or I fixed armoured cars, trucks. I tried to fix tanks but I could never get on with them. I got my wounds from Russian bullets, when the Red Air Force strafed division headquarters. I was working in the motor pool. This was a hundred kilometres behind the front. I can't claim to be a hero, Herr Captain, but at least I was no Hitlerite . . .'

'Are you still interested in cars? Do you still fix them?' said Inspector Weiss. In this mood, he could make an interest in automobile repair sound as if it was on a par with child-molesting.

'Maybe in my spare time. A little . . .' Pilzinger mumbled, caught off balance. He smiled, shrugged, as if to say, you know how it is. Weiss stared at him stonily, making it clear that, no, he didn't know.

'So, whose cars do you fix?' he snapped.

'I . . . I do it for Soviet officials. And for the few Germans, mainly communists, who are allowed private cars by the Russians. Herr Inspector, I know such unauthorised work is frowned upon, but even in these terrible times the man still calls for the rent every month. And living in Pankow has never come cheap. They toss me a few lousy cigarettes. Every little bit helps . . .'

Blessed suddenly changed tack. 'I don't understand,' he said. 'You're attached to the Brandenburger Tor station, which is in our sector. Yet you prefer to live in the Soviet sector. Why is this, eh?'

'Pankow is adjacent to the British sector. The border is less than a kilometre from where I live.'

'But nevertheless, you are in the Soviet sector.'

'The Herr Captain will permit me to remind him that when I first rented the apartment, it was two years before the war,' Pilzinger explained with dignity. 'There were no such things as sectors. And the only Russians in Berlin in those days were the exiles who played the balalaika in borscht restaurants.'

'So you have no problems with the Soviet Military Authorities in commuting to the British sector?'

'None whatsoever. I tell you here, with God listening to my every word, that I cross the sector border every day on my bicycle, in full uniform. Then I report for duty on the western side. The Russians never bother me. Never.'

'Maybe they are being nice to you because they want their cars fixed,' Weiss said sardonically. 'Maybe to them you are a VIP. A Very Important Pilzinger.'

After the unlucky constable had been ushered from the room, Blessed shook his head in amused exasperation.

Weiss yawned, lit an acrid German cigarette. 'It was difficult playing tough with that poor fellow. I liked him too much.'

'That's hardly the point.'

'One cannot expect an amateur to do a professional's job. Pilzinger was only kept in the force because he was politically clean—no Nazi background. Of course, these days that isn't good enough. The way our communist Police President Markgraf is purging us, before long we'll all be faced with the sack—except for the hundred-and-ten-per cent reds, that is. How will Pilzinger pay his Pankow rent then, eh?'

'Mercedes will soon be allowed to start making cars again. Then he'll be able to discard his nightstick and pick up his wrench once more.'

'That will make him very happy. Pilzinger's a good-hearted man. Germany depends on millions of ordinary, decent people like him for its future.'

'I'm sure you're right. The trouble is, he lost an important witness. Perhaps a crucial one.'

'Perhaps, and only perhaps. A child . . .'

'OK. You win,' Blessed conceded with a shrug. 'Now, would you like a sandwich? Made with English Spam and English bread, and washed down with English tea, including the traditional milk and six spoonfuls of sugar? While you get some nourishment, I can explain my real reason for bringing you here.'

'I was hoping you had an ulterior motive for asking me along to help with the interrogation. I would certainly be delighted with the sandwich.'

The captain pushed a bell on his desk. Kelly was still busy with the paperwork. It was Sergeant Brownlow who took the order for sandwiches and tea.

Blessed eased himself back in his chair. 'I need reliable German help on this case, Manfred,' he said. 'How would you like to work with me?'

'You want me to be seconded to work with BlessForce?'

'Yes.'

'Well . . . in principle I am only too willing.' Weiss hesitated. 'As long as you can sort matters out with my immediate superiors. Kommissar Escher is the real man to ask.'

'I've drafted a formal notification to the Alexanderplatz. I want you to start immediately. This morning. I've also asked for three reliable footsloggers to be seconded along with you. Just in case. OK?'

'I certainly hope so,' Weiss said. He sucked in his cheeks thoughtfully. 'A word of warning: Escher's job depends on keeping Police President Markgraf sweet. Since Markgraf is the Soviets' man, this means making the right Marxist-Leninist noises. Markgraf gave Escher his promotion, he can take it away. For this reason, the Kommissar will not be eager to be seen doing the Western Allies any favours. Especially during the present political crisis.'

'I'll make sure my own chief, Colonel Harrison, gives us all the support we need,' Blessed reassured him. 'Just don't worry about the formalities. If I really want something, I usually get it.'

'So I am told, James. So I am told. Well, with the two big guns, you and Harrison, on my side, we may be all right. I'll have Schmidtke, Auer and Katzenbach report to me here. They're excellent plain-clothes operatives.'

'Good. We've put an office aside for you. You can move in this morning.'

Sergeant Brownlow brought in two mugs of tea, and a generous-sized Spam sandwich for Weiss. The inspector attacked the food with such urgency that there was an enforced lull in the conversation.

'To work, then, eh?' Weiss said when he had consumed half of the sandwich. 'I must earn my bread, as they say.' He took a gulp of the hot, sweet tea. 'I recall that when we met this morning we discussed sex-killings. Do you think we are faced with another Haarman or another Grossman?'

The notorious murderers named by the inspector had flourished in Germany in the 1920s. Both had been solid citizens who led lives of unimpeachable outward respectability. Both had slaughtered upwards of twenty human beings during their careers. Haarman would lure unemployed youths to his rooms with promises of lodging and work. Once behind closed doors, he would tear out his victims' throats with his teeth before sexually abusing the bodies. Grossman, by contrast, specialised in young women—especially farm girls who had run away to Berlin—whom he engaged as 'housekeepers'. After torturing and killing them, he dumped their corpses in the River Spree that flowed through the heart of the city.

'I'm not at all certain we dare ignore the pathological element.' Blessed paused. 'Equally, I'm forced to look very hard at other motives.'

'Any valuables taken from the victims? Money, jewellery, ration coupons?'

'In the man's pockets we found about five pounds in English currency. Plus forty new Deutschmarks in nice, crisp notes. And a gold-plated watch.'

'Then we can rule out robbery.' Weiss looked at Blessed shrewdly. 'So, are we faced with the policeman's worst nightmare, the motiveless crime?'

'Personally, Manfred, I doubt there is such a thing as the truly motiveless murder,' Blessed said. 'But the point here is, the male victim had close business connections with a local black-market ring, a gang I've been investigating for some time.'

'Ah. Now you tell me! I suspected something of this kind when I saw that you had taken personal charge of the case,' Weiss noted with dry satisfaction. 'So references to perverts and sex-killers were, in effect, a smoke screen?'

'You saw the bodies. Do you think whoever inflicted those wounds could reasonably be described as normal?' Blessed asked. 'It's the aspect of the case which puzzles me most.' He shrugged. 'But I'll admit I didn't want everyone to know exactly why I'd come rushing to the scene of the crime. Gossip spreads quickly . . .'

'I thought the British Military Administration was just one happy family. Surely you and your colleagues have no secrets from each other?'

Blessed made no comment. Weiss's little barb, though delivered with a smile, cut dangerously close to the bone.

'The thing is, I happen to know quite a lot about the man who was murdered,' he said instead. 'Actually, he was stationed in the British Zone and had no earthly right to be hanging around Berlin with a mysterious bottle-blonde.'

'No right, perhaps. But he must have had a reason. Why don't you unravel the mystery at your own pace while I finish this?' Weiss said, and started on the second half of his snack.

'OK. Well, his name was Ronald Price, known to his associates as "Taffy",' Blessed began. 'He was a corporal in the RAMC, and he worked as a storeman at a medical supplies depot near Braunschweig. We suspect that he was heavily involved in the theft of prescription drugs from those same stores, and in the illegal selling of the drugs on the Berlin black market—some morphine and cocaine, but more especially penicillin, which as you know is still not generally available to civilians.'

Weiss nodded. 'You certainly identified him very quickly.'

'His paybook was still in the hip-pocket of his slacks. Anyway we'd first come across Price five or six months ago. He was pulled in after a routine raid on a dive in the Kantstrasse frequented by black-marketeers and drug-dealers. The men he was talking to there were known to us. ' He took a sip of tea before pressing on. 'Price was questioned for some time—by my Sergeant Kelly, as it happens—but we couldn't prove anything. So, we shunted the chap off back to the Zone with a stern warning not to show his face in Berlin again.'

'A lucky escape for him.'

'In a way. He must have thought he'd got off clear, but actually he was a marked man. I opened a file on him, and he also went onto the military police Register. I'd told the people at 248 Provost that if his name came up again in connection with any kind of trouble, I was to be called in immediately.' Blessed shrugged. 'Well, of course, Price got into terrible, fatal trouble. The moment they matched the paybook with the name in their records, they rang my office. Kelly phoned me at home not long after six o'clock this morning.'

'Fascinating. And now you are getting to the conclusion of your story, I am allowed to make a contribution, I think.' Weiss smiled. 'I believe you have a suspect. Isn't that true?'

'Perhaps . . .' Blessed expressed himself with caution. 'A good working hypothesis, at least. Tell me, does the name Floh mean anything to you?'

'Not off-hand, no.'

'A veteran pimp, lately turned drug-dealer. He relies for muscle on a man named Panewski.'

'Now, that name does ring a bell.'

'He's done time for manslaughter. I have his file.'

'Fine. These were the men Price was with in that bar when you raided it?'

'Quite right.'

'I assume your people are already busy rounding up these villains?'

Blessed shook his head. 'Actually, Manfred, it's not quite that simple. You see, we've been planning these arrests for weeks now. Precise arrangements had already been made before Price and the woman were killed, and I'm reluctant to change them now. I think we can wait a little longer.'

'How much longer?'

Blessed checked his watch. 'About six hours. If all goes well.'

'I see. And what do you plan for us to do in the meantime?'

'Brownlow will show you to your office. He'll bring you the relevant files. Meanwhile, I have some documents to sign. Then I'm booked in to see Colonel Harrison over at the Knesebeckstrasse. When I get back, we'll talk.' Blessed smiled enigmatically. 'And afterwards we'll go for a nice walk together in the Tiergarten.'

'People think that the famous Captain Blessed is so ruthless, so dynamic!' Weiss exclaimed with a laugh. 'If only they could hear you now, talking of leisure and strolls in the park! It would ruin your reputation!'

'Oh, you just wait until *after* that walk, Manfred. From then on, I assure you, your feet won't touch the ground.'

FIVE

SIB 'BLESSFORCE' (officially but hardly ever known as 89 SIB (B) [Centre]) was crammed into a huddle of cell-like rooms above a barber's shop a heartbeat from the bustle of the Kurfürstendamm, in an anonymous grey-stone block that before the war had been a place letting rooms by the hour to prostitutes and their clients. Blessed remembered that time, and in his mind's eye he could still see the garish sign of the *Stundenhotel*, the crowds of eager pleasure-seekers, the whores under the street lamps outside with their fox furs and their umbrellas, each woman's personal erotic speciality indicated by the precise height of the boots she wore. All twenty years ago, before Hitler, before the slaughter and bombing, before Berlin had been turned into a city of troglodytes, of cowed beggars, of refugees.

Blessed emerged from his headquarters, followed the path between banks of uncleared rubble. He walked quickly down to where the sidestreet met the broad boulevard of the Ku-Damm, where the clearing work had made real progress and a once-famous restaurant on the corner had recently re-opened for business, its tables out on the street almost like in the old days. As was Blessed's habit lately, he paused at that junction by the tables, to light a cheroot, check his bearings, and consult his instincts about the condition of Berlin.

Of course, the Ku-Damm was not Berlin, any more than Oxford Street is London, but as the most conspicuous urban artery it was the best place to go if you needed to feel the city's pulse. Though the morning's sunshine had dried out the pavements, there was no breeze and the air was heavy, laced with the invisible dust that the ruins still gave off. It would be a long time yet—some said a hundred years at present rates of progress—before the bomb-sites would be cleared, but nevertheless, as he had told Redman earlier that morning, things had started to improve. The old shops and restaurants were returning; in some cases the owners had conjured up the means to rebuild at least a storey of their old premises, while in others kiosks had been knocked together so that they could recommence trading, even though the sites were still mounds of debris. The usual energy, the cheerful cynicism of the Berliner were there as Blessed stood and watched the people of the Ku-Damm go about their business. But he could also sense a tension, a hollowness in the greetings, a special stillness in the way the early customers sat under café awnings, cups of ersatz coffee untouched as they scanned their newspapers for the latest news of the Russian blockade of their city. Food and fuel shortages were already apparent, and electricity rationing, which had been abolished in the spring, had been re-imposed earlier that morning. Many Berliners expected the western Allies to abandon them to the communists; some were already saying that it was better to give in now than to starve, and few were optimistic about the city's chances of surviving as an enclave in the middle of the Russian Zone.

'*Der Herr?*'

Blessed turned and saw an elderly waiter smiling his professional smile from the edge of the tables, indicating a clean tablecloth and a breakfast setting ready for occupation.

'*Der Herr Hauptmann möchte frühstücken?*' The man had now seen the insignia of rank on Blessed's coat and seemed to think his invitation might be more successful if he addressed him by rank.

'*Nein. Danke. Schon gefrühstückt, Herr Ober.*'

The waiter was surprised by the fluency of Blessed's response. '*Der Herr Hauptmann ist Deutscher?*'

Blessed shook his head. '*Ich bin Engländer,*' he said, then explained about his German mother. '*Aber meine Mutter stammte aus Berlin.*'

'*Dann werden wenigstens Sie uns nicht verlassen, Herr Hauptmann,*' the waiter said with a strange kind of sad satisfaction. So you, at least, won't desert us, Captain.

'*Machen Sie sich keine Sorgen, Herr Ober. Berlin hält aus.*' Berlin will hold out. These days it was best to keep one's expressions of hope for the future suitably general, Blessed thought.

With an expression of polite regret, Blessed made to continue his walk. A short distance away along the Ku-Damm stood the blackened tower which was all that remained of the Kaiser Wilhelm Memorial

Church. The hands of the clock set into its mock-gothic tower still stood at seven-thirty, as they had since the night in '43 when British bombs had destroyed the rest of the structure. But Blessed's watch told him that the real time was at half past noon, and that he was running late for his meeting with Colonel Harrison. He tossed his half-smoked cheroot away, stepped off the kerb and crossed the Ku-Damm, stopping briefly to buy a newspaper at the entrance to the U-bahn station that stood on a concrete island in the middle of the street. When Blessed reached the opposite pavement, he looked back to where he had been standing a couple of minutes earlier and saw the elderly waiter arguing with a young, one-legged war cripple. A small but growing crowd of onlookers were taking sides. He realised that they were fighting over what remained of the cheroot he had discarded so casually.

A further five minutes' walk took Blessed to his destination, the headquarters of Military Police Provost 248 Company in the Knesbeckstrasse, between the Ku-Damm and the Savignyplatz. From here, 248 policed the British-controlled parts of the city centre, including the nearby fleshpots, which attracted the soldiers of the four Allied powers, as well as Germans of all possible sexes and a rich mixture of displaced persons of various nationalities. The suburbs were left to 247 Company, based out in Spandau, not so far from the Villa Hellman. Today Blessed noticed several faces from 247 in the entrance hall of the station, an indication that the two units had buried their rivalries and united in the face of the blockade crisis.

The atmosphere in the building was of constant talk, activity, doors slamming and phones ringing, a machine in top gear and quickened by a salutary following wind of fear. The fear was of a shooting war, naturally, but also of the task ahead, even if it never came to that. The challenge of keeping order among two million Berliners, in a half-city that was now under siege, was truly intimidating. Few of the officers he saw bothered to greet him. No one seemed to know, or care, about the Potsdamer Strasse killings. The blockade was beginning to overshadow everything else, even murder.

Blessed walked into the anteroom to Colonel Harrison's office and told the clerk-sergeant, Mulroney, that the APM was expecting him.

'I'm afraid he's on the phone to RAF Wunstorf at the moment, sir,' said Mulroney, a tall Ulsterman with laughing eyes and bad acne. 'They're going to be handling most of this Carter-Paterson business.'

Carter-Paterson was the name of a well-known London firm of

furniture removers. 'Why Carter-Paterson? Is the colonel moving? Going home?'

'Oh no, sir.' Mulroney chuckled. 'Carter-Paterson is the codename for the airlift, sir. Now that Stalin's put the complete, de luxe blockade on us, we'll be supplied completely by air. Or at least, they're going to have a shot at it. You can imagine all the work this will cause for us in the CMP, can't you?'

It was very strange that Whitehall, or some unknown comic talent at RAF High Command, had chosen to name the big airlift for Berlin after a removals firm. If you were a Berliner, or for that matter a Russian, you might reasonably assume that the choice of such a codeword implied that the British were planning to move *out* of Berlin rather than stay where they were.

Blessed thanked Mulroney for the information and agreed that the airlift would make a lot of work for the military police. He then asked if it was worth his waiting until the colonel was free, or should he come back later.

Mulroney leaned over towards the door to Harrison's office, listened intently, then said: 'I think he's signing off now. If I were you, I'd nip in there before his phone rings again. It's been bedlam this morning, I'll tell you.'

Colonel Harrison was a handsome, tousle-haired man in his fifties, Hollywood's ideal of an English country squire. When Blessed entered he was jotting notes down on a desk-pad. Harrison looked up with a frown which quickly slid into a smile, then addressed Blessed as 'Jim' and told him to take a seat. The casual manner, the use of first names, the welcoming smile, were his trademarks. The colonel's charm was his miracle weapon.

'It never rains but it pours,' he said. 'I don't know if you heard, but there was an "incident" during the night. A bunch of Russians sneaked across a railway cutting and camped inside our sector. It took several hours of hard talking before they agreed to withdraw. Hardly an invasion—in fact, it all seemed a bit of a joke—but who knows? Next time they could refuse to pull back, and what do we do then? Start a war?' Harrison didn't wait for Blessed to answer. 'We've been asked to step up our border patrols to ensure the Reds don't catch us napping again.'

'In view of the crisis, perhaps they'll fly out an extra company or two from home, sir,' Blessed suggested.

Harrison shook his head. 'Not much chance of that. Believe me, I've asked. No, we'll be expected to patrol the borders, man the autobahn checkpoints—even though the Russians aren't letting anything through, we've got to keep up appearances—ensure public order is maintained . . . *and* we'll be expected to lend a hand with this ruddy airlift. All without a single extra man! I've just come off the phone to Wunstorf. They're worried some of the stuff they're flying in might get pinched, and how are *we* going to stop that happening? Who'd be a military policeman, eh, Jim?'

There was a silence. Harrison had run out of steam. Blessed said, 'Was that what you wanted to see me about, sir? Do you need the Branch to help out? We'll do what we can, especially in the way of criminal intelligence.'

'Oh, we might indeed at some point, but that wasn't why I wanted this chat,' Harrison said. He took off his half-moon reading spectacles, rubbed his eyes. 'You see, the fact is, the powers-that-be are not just refusing us the extra manpower we need to cope with the present crisis. They're demanding that we actually cut our forces here in Berlin—especially administrative and headquarters staff.'

'*Now?*'

'Yes. Now.'

'Does that mean we're not serious about staying put in Berlin, sir?'

'No, not exactly,' Harrison said. 'The fighting units and the essential administrative structure will remain. But it's obvious that the situation has changed fundamentally. Stalin doesn't want us here now, and he has no intention of allowing Berlin to resume its status as the capital of a united Germany—unless he succeeds in his aim of overrunning the entire country, of course.' The colonel shrugged in a peculiarly comfortable, English way, implying that the prospect of Germany going communist was about as likely as a snowstorm in June, or a bookie going broke. 'On our side, it's taken for granted that, whatever happens to Berlin, a "West German" state will be set up soon, with its capital in one of the western zones. So you can see that it'll be safer and more convenient to transfer most of the admin people over there, perhaps to Cologne or Hamburg, with staff officers based at Mil. Gov. HQ in Bad Oeynhausen.'

Blessed was beginning to sense what was coming. 'Good Lord,' he said. 'Are you saying that the four-power Control Commission for Germany, based here in Berlin, is going to be scrapped?'

'It's already a dead letter. The Russians have effectively pulled out. We don't intend to give up Berlin, because of its symbolic value, but it looks as if what we're going to be left with is just another garrison town.' Harrison chuckled drily, pleased with the image he had hit on. 'A garrison town, admittedly with two and a half million people, and inconveniently stuck slap in the middle of the Soviet Zone of Occupation, but there you are.'

'So is this going to affect my unit, sir?' Blessed asked bluntly.

Harrison got to his feet. He was not very tall, but barrel-chested and powerful in the arms and legs. He clasped his hands behind his broad back, whistled a quick, tuneless theme through his teeth.

'I was getting to that, as I'm sure you realise, Jim,' he said, moving out from behind his desk so that he could pace the room. He took a couple of steps, turned to face Blessed. 'I have to give *them* a list of officers who could conceivably be transferred away from Berlin.' *Them*, as ever, indicated the Office of the Military Governor.

'And would this list include me?'

'It doesn't really include anyone yet, Jim. I'll be discussing the problem with each officer under my command over the next few days, conducting informal soundings, so to say.'

'All right, then *might* it include me, sir?' Blessed persisted.

Harrison hesitated before answering. 'All things being equal, I think it would, yes,' he conceded.

'I object with the utmost force to being transferred from Berlin. I consider my continued presence here to be essential, sir.'

The colonel sighed. 'I'm sorry to hear you say that.'

'Did you really expect anything else?'

'I suppose I didn't.' Harrison sat down again, heavily. 'I know how attached you are to Berlin, Jim. I know about the family connections you have with this place, and like everyone I appreciate your absolute integrity as an officer and as a policeman . . .'

Harrison faltered. 'Look, there's a shake-up on the way whether we like it or not,' he continued. 'Our present political problems apart—and they can't last forever—the Germans are doing most of the routine police work nowadays. Gone is the time when we were the only force that stood between this city and chaos. So it's become impossible to justify having two separate military police commands in Berlin. Soon 248 Company and 247 Company will be combining to form one unit. The same logic applies to the Branch, Jim. BlessForce and SIB 89 Section will be merged into one unit as well.'

Blessed nodded. 'I see. And who'll be in command of the merged SIB?'

'I'll be honest. They won't be looking for a serious crimes specialist to run the show, Jim—not even one as good as you.'

'I'm beginning to get your drift, sir.'

'The belief is that the new situation calls for an administrator,' the colonel ploughed on grimly. 'A chap who's also something of a diplomat.'

'You mean, someone who'll turn a blind eye to what's been going on in the army over here.'

'You're being unfair, Jim. This is precisely the attitude that's made you so many enemies. I know you've got a particular bee in your bonnet—'

'You're quite right I have. Because no one else seems to give a damn. In fact, most officers seem to regard the opportunities for corruption here as a kind of unofficial pension scheme, a short-cut to that nice little bungalow in Littlehampton they've always dreamed of retiring to.'

'Now, we all know there are some bad eggs . . . some chaps who abuse their privileges . . .'

'*Some?*' Blessed snapped. 'Occupied Berlin makes Chicago look law-abiding. At least Al Capone wasn't a government servant. And as far as I know, he didn't divert food from starving families, or steal drugs that could save children's lives. The criminals I'm talking about are British officers, men I rub shoulders with at the club, probably men you play golf with . . .'

'That's enough of that!' The reference to his golfing partners—he played every Sunday without fail—had finally goaded Harrison into returning fire. 'All right,' he said sharply, 'Berlin's a cesspit. Who'd deny that? But we have to be realistic. The mess can't be cleaned up overnight, not even by Jim Blessed. Christ, anyone would think you were the first policeman to have noticed that the world is by and large a wicked place. These things are inevitable when you put a foreign army in control of a country where the local money's worth nothing, the economy's in ruins, and there's a shortage of everything except pretty young women.' He continued in a more level voice, 'We can only prosecute a fraction of the offenders, hope that those few examples will have a deterrent effect. If you want my opinion, these problems will disappear like magic when the German currency reform takes effect, when Germans can buy something with their cash, and the economy gets back on its feet.'

There was an uncomfortable pause. Harrison started fiddling with his fountain-pen, uncapping and capping it repeatedly.

'That may well be,' Blessed said. 'But I intend to continue to make a few examples, as you put it. Until they sack me. I hope I shall have your support for as long as I remain in Berlin, and in charge of BlessForce.'

Harrison nodded, relieved that the confrontation seemed to be over. 'Absolutely.' He put down the pen, smiled. 'Not that I shall be around for all that long myself,' he confessed. 'If it's any consolation, I'll be getting my marching orders in the autumn too. I'm hoping for a home posting that'll take me through to retirement. I shan't be sorry to see England again. Neither will my Margaret.' Mrs Harrison was a good-natured woman, as handsome as her husband, whose main discernible interest in life was the breeding and training of golden retrievers. 'And how's Harriet, by the way?' Harrison added a little too casually to be entirely convincing.

'Very well, sir.'

'Good.' The colonel paused for a moment. 'She's a . . . spirited woman, Harriet. I'm sure she won't mind going home either, eh?'

It was an opening of sorts. Blessed looked at the time, said, 'Army wives often find foreign postings difficult. I know that. Luckily, Daphne is in a good school, and we have excellent help in the house.'

'Ah, yes. Wee Daphne. She's well too?'

'Thriving, thanks.'

Just when it seemed the moment might be past, Harrison suddenly leaned forward in a confiding way and said, 'Bugger it, let's talk man to man, and never mind the army. I'm going to take a risk and offer you some advice, Jim. Not as your superior but as a friend.'

'Yes, sir.' Blessed carefully chilled the words.

'You're probably not going to like what I have to say, but here goes. All right?' Harrison asked rhetorically. 'Well then, if you were to ask me—which I know you haven't, but never mind that—I'd advise you to leave Berlin, and the SIB . . . Go back to legal practice. My Margaret hears things, you know. Just women's talk, nothing specific. But it's clear that Harriet's unhappy. Really unhappy.'

There was a lengthy, painful silence before Blessed answered. 'As I've already said, sir, I recognise how difficult it can be for one's wife. Married couples have to work these things out. Thank you for your advice, anyway.'

'You're being bloody stubborn,' Harrison said with a sigh. 'And more than a bit pompous, damn you. But at least I tried. No one can say I didn't.'

'No, sir.'

Harrison's manner, though still affable, became impersonal again. 'Well, I daresay you're champing at the bit to get back to BlessForce, and I've got half a dozen more phone calls to make before I can start to think about lunch . . .'

'There *is* one thing I'd like to talk to you about, sir. Between ourselves.'

Harrison recoiled in mock surprise. 'Don't say we've suddenly found an area of life where I can be of service!' he exclaimed. 'My, oh my. Well, fire away, old chap.'

'It's the double murder this morning. Have you heard?'

'Kelly mentioned it when I rang your office earlier. You'd already visited the scene of the crime. Sounds grisly. But I'm surprised you've decided to get personally involved. You've got some very capable chaps who usually handle this sort of thing, haven't you?'

'It was a particularly unpleasant piece of butchery, sir. More importantly, though, I have reason to believe that the murders may be connected with drug-smuggling and black-market dealings by British servicemen which were already being investigated under my personal supervision. In fact, we could be dealing with a major black-market ring.'

'I see.' Harrison raised a bushy, knowing eyebrow. 'That makes more sense, then. And no wonder you're so jumpy! Well, if there's anything I can do . . .?'

'Sir, I know that German criminals are also involved,' Blessed said. 'So I want Inspector Manfred Weiss of the Kripo to be formally seconded to the case, along with three of his best footsloggers. I'll need an extra car . . . and the use of your cells here. I may need your backing if the Russians or their protégés in the police department object to Weiss's working with me. I'm not saying they will, but you know how bloody-minded they can be sometimes.'

'Don't I just.' Harrison stroked his chin doubtfully. 'Jim, if only we could work out who's really in charge at the Alexanderplatz these days,' he said. 'The main problem is that dreadful little shit, Markgraf. Stumm, his deputy, seems a sound enough sort of chap—at least he's not an outright commie, anyway—but half the time you don't know who's giving the orders. It's certainly not the Lord Mayor of Berlin, though. Or us.' He looked at Blessed almost pleadingly. 'Are you absolutely sure you need this Weiss fellow seconded to your investigation? Him specifically, I mean?'

'He's a very competent, experienced officer with an unblemished political record. Never liked the Nazis. Doesn't think much of the communists either.'

'Another postwar convert to democracy, eh?' Harrison said with a sly grin. 'Come on, Jim. They all secretly hated the Nazis, if you believe the yarn they spin you now.'

'I've looked at his record very carefully, sir,' Blessed said. 'I like to check on all the Germans I work with on a regular basis. And I can report that he's whiter than white. Weiss never joined the Nazi Party or any of its associated organisations. In fact, he had his promotion barred during the Third Reich because he expressed disapproval of the way the Kripo was being turned into an adjunct of the SS. I've seen the Gestapo documents, and at one time they were even thinking of arresting him. Instead—in forty-two, I think—Weiss resigned and went into the army. A friend warned him of the Gestapo's attentions, he told me. He had a very rough war, mostly on the nastiest parts of the Russian Front. Fortunately he survived and was able to return to his police career.'

'An excellent type, obviously. Marvellous. But nevertheless . . .'

'He's ideal for our purposes,' Blessed said. 'I'll be honest, sir. Weiss is already working with me, as a full member of my team. Because of the urgency of the situation, I've already submitted the necessary written request to the Police President's office, with a copy to the Soviet Liaison Officer there. It's just a formality, after all . . .'

'You should have—' Harrison realised he had been outmanoeuvred, checked himself. 'What I mean to say is, I'd have been grateful for advance notice. Relations with the SMA are difficult at the moment, for obvious reasons.'

'Luckily, Weiss lives in the American sector. There's nothing the Reds can do to prevent his working for me, short of kidnapping him.'

'It wouldn't be the first time they've sent a snatch-squad across the sector border, Jim,' Harrison said. Then he sighed in a resigned sort of way. 'All right, though. If you want him—and you evidently have a soft spot for the chap—then I suppose you must have him.'

'I'm very grateful for your support, sir. I know this is a difficult time, but justice still has to be done—and be seen to be done—even when there's a threat of war.'

Mulroney stuck his head in, interrupted the conversation to say that 'Lancaster House'—the British Control Commission headquarters on the Fehrbelliner Platz—was on the phone asking about border patrols and wouldn't take no for an answer. Could the colonel come to the phone and shut them up? Harrison said he'd be available very soon, if they could hang on.

'Lord, I'd really like to know what drives you, Jim,' he said after Mulroney had gone. 'What makes you run, eh?'

'The usual things, I expect.'

'Whatever *they* are.' The colonel ran a hand through his beautiful head of hair. 'Well, just be careful, won't you?' he said, suddenly serious.

'Careful? I'm only trying to do my job, sir.'

'Come off it! You and I have knocked around a bit. We both know it's not that simple!' Now there was something quietly forceful, even—could those kindly, country-gentleman looks be deceptive? —a little menacing, in Harrison's manner. 'The fact is, you're determined to hang a few more really good scalps on your belt, and to hell with the cost, aren't you, Jim?' he said softly. 'Even if it's the last damned thing you do in Berlin.'

Blessed didn't flinch. 'You may be right, of course.' He got up to leave. 'Especially then, in fact. Most especially then.'

SIX

BENNO AND GURKEL approached the invisible sector border for all the world as if they were returning from running an errand for their non-existent parents, hands in pockets, talking casually. Their hearts always beat a little faster at this moment, but fear never showed. They were proud professionals.

> Us Kinder know what
> Us Kinder know how
> Us Kinder survive
> Us never kowtow . . .

That was what Boss-Kind always said.

The Bernauer Strasse is a long, undistinguished residential street that runs from northeast to southwest close to the centre of Berlin. Its northern edge lies in the borough of Wedding, while the opposite side of the street belongs to the borough of Berlin-Mitte, the old heart of the German capital. Before the war this technicality had mattered little. Since June 1945, however, when Berlin had been divided into sectors of occupation, the significance had been much greater, because under the four-power agreement, Wedding had become part of the French sector, while the Soviets had been assigned Mitte, which included most of the government buildings and cultural foundations, as well as Prenzlauer Berg's forbidding tenements and rundown factories. By 1948, though as yet there were few physical barriers between the Soviet and the western-ruled parts of Berlin, and none at all in the Bernauer Strasse, everyone was aware that the divide between East and West, capitalism and communism, ran right down the middle of this once unremarkable street.

But so far as Benno and Gurkel were concerned, everything was fine. They strolled past the sign that told them they were leaving the Soviet sector. A few more steps and they were inside French-administered territory. A young woman wheeled an infant in a very old baby-carriage that looked like a Victorian hip-bath on wheels. Old people queued patiently at a grocer's shop on the corner. A hundred yards or so away, two men with suitcases were walking in an unhurried way along the French side of the Bernauer Strasse towards the boys.

Benno and Gurkel registered the men with the suitcases—solid, early middle-aged, dressed in old suits and wearing homburgs—because they stood between them and their destination, further on past the Bernauer Strasse U-bahn station. But they didn't look like cops. Cops, at least in their young experience, didn't carry suitcases.

Nevertheless, they were poised to take evasive action as the men approached. A few more paces and they would be level. The men showed no interest in them. In fact, the men's faces were rigid with very much the same kind of intent as the boys'. It occurred to Benno that they might be on a very similar errand, with their suitcases, their nondescript clothes. The boys stepped off the pavement onto the cobbled street to let the adults pass, the men strode on by without a glance. Benno looked at Gurkel, let out a little puff of relief. Gurkel grinned. Just another couple of minutes. Past the next cross-street, and . . .

A jeep swung round the corner with a shriek of tyres, came to a sudden, juddering stop. The submachine gun in the hand of the soldier in the passenger seat was already sweeping the street, covering the boys and the two men with the suitcases. Somewhere a voice was bawling, 'Halt!' in German with a French accent. Benno and Gurkel froze. They heard the sound of another vehicle behind, between them and the street they had just come from. Two jeeps had bottled up the street. There was the sound of running feet. 'Halt! *Arrêtez-vous!*' the voice shouted again, louder. Almost immediately, there was a burst of automatic fire, an instant's silence, then a scream.

The man with the submachine gun, wearing French battledress and a beret, got out of the jeep. Keeping the weapon trained on the boys, he was waving for the two other men from the jeep to go and help where the shooting had occurred. Benno and Gurkel had raised their hands and had backed against the bullet-pocked façade of a tenement wall, turning their heads to see what had happened back towards the Eberswalder Strasse.

One of the men was sprawled in his own blood just a few feet short of the entrance to a block of flats on the Soviet side of the street. His hat and suitcase lay nearby, just where they had landed. He was moaning, clutching his chest with both hands, writhing on the soaked cobbles. Benno had seen a woman give birth in a cellar once, during an air raid. She had looked remarkably like that. Eck, he thought despite his terror, but how strange.

The wounded man's suitcase had broken open—it was only cheap cardboard, with a tin catch—so that pairs of contraband nylon stockings had spilled out and were beginning to blow all over the street. They delicately brushed the road surface, attracting tiny flecks of dust and blood, before being picked up by the wind and borne away. The man's companion was standing in the gutter some distance away, and had placed his own suitcase carefully on the ground beside him, like a traveller waiting for a train. He was quite silent, and his hands were raised above his head also. He was paying no heed to his wounded friend; he was just staring at the French soldiers.

The armed man from the nearest jeep clumped over to the two boys, chose Benno, swung him round. A young conscript, the soldier had dark, curly hair and a thin, fine-boned face. His breath smelled of pungent herbs.

'*Ver—beest—doo? Papee—eere!* Papers!' he demanded in very bad German.

'Name is Benno. This Gurkel. Nix papers.'

'Aha. I arrest you, *hein?*'

Benno stared straight up at him with a terrified, beseeching look that was only partly assumed. Since he had been forced to stretch his arms above his head, the waistband of his shorts had started to slip down ominously. He was painfully aware of the bag of sharp, hard little diamonds against the flesh of his stomach, and of the fact that his cargo was not securely lodged there. What if the diamonds suddenly fell out from the waistband? And surely this soldier would notice the telltale bulge?

'I . . . live . . . in . . . street . . . here . . .' Benno stammered, gesturing to embrace Gurkel as well. 'We . . . ' He indicated the direction they had been walking before the trouble. 'There . . . *waisenhaus* . . . orphanage!'

The French soldier hesitated. He couldn't have been older than nineteen, and beneath his tough manner he was obviously unsure of himself. He kept glancing past Benno to where other French soldiers

73

were surrounding the wounded suspect. The other suspect had been herded over at gun-point and was being questioned, none too gently, by a tall, hawk-faced lieutenant.

'*Mon lieutenant!*' the soldier called out. '*Que faire avec ces enfants?*'

The officer made a gesture of irritation. Then he strode over to them, looked Benno and Gurkel up and down.

'No papers, eh?' he said. He talked down his nose and from a great height. It was disconcerting. Also disconcerting was that he spoke excellent German. The boys couldn't know it, but the lieutenant was from the border-province of Alsace, specially selected for duty here because he had German as his second language. 'Have you anything to do with the men we just arrested?'

They both shook their heads energetically. 'We are orphans,' Benno said.

'And how are you going to prove that? Why shouldn't I take you in?'

'Sir . . . sir, we are from the orphanage in this street. Yes. Right here.'

The lieutenant was frowning. Benno could see he had enough on his plate, with one man wounded, possibly dying, down there on the street, and another he needed to interrogate without delay. Finally he said: 'How far from here is this orphanage of yours?'

Benno felt every nerve in his body flood with relief. Confidently, yet respectfully, he pointed again along the street. 'Two hundred metres, sir.'

The decision was made. The lieutenant shrugged, said something in French to the soldier, motioned with his right hand at them and said, '*Vite, vite!*'

Benno had hoped that they would be set free on the spot, but the lieutenant was too canny for that. The soldier ushered them away from the scene, clutching his submachine-gun. 'You . . . take me . . . *waisenhaus*-orphanage, *hein?*' he said, and they set off down the street.

For propaganda purposes, Benno had halved the distance to their destination when making his suggestion to the lieutenant. It was actually between three and four hundred metres to the pompous, rendered-brick building with its big Imperial eagle sculpted over the door. Benno saw one of the other Kinder look down from a second-floor window, then disappear. The French soldier seemed to notice nothing. They arrived at the door, Benno said, 'Here!' The soldier indicated for him to ring the bell.

They waited for almost a minute. Benno kept smiling encouragingly, for the French soldier's benefit. 'The—director—comes—soon,' he told him.

When he finally opened the door, Doktor Barnhelm was looking more than usually dazed and confused. This was evidently not one of his better days. At least his shirt was clean, but his eyes were so glassy, his bony hands were trembling so much, that Benno was certain the French soldier would become suspicious. Barnhelm stared at them as if he were inspecting a deputation of creatures from outer space. Then he said, 'Yes. What do you want?'

'*Ces enfants . . .*'

'Yes, these children. They live here, yes.'

'*Ah. Alors . . . ce sont des orphelins?*' the soldier pressed on, apparently quite oblivious to the fact that he was conversing with a human wreck.

'*Wie bitte?*'

'Orphans . . . zey are orphans?'

'*Ach,* yes.'

'*Et vous êtes le directeur de cet orphelinat?* You . . . director . . .?'

'Yes. I am Doktor Gustav Adolf Barnhelm, director of this children's home.' Barnhelm drew himself up to his full five feet seven inches.

The French soldier sighed with relief. '*Alors . . . adieu, mes enfants!*' he said, and set off back down the street to rejoin his comrades.

They were left on the threshold. Doktor Barnhelm stood in silence, staring at them both fixedly as if trying to recall exactly who they were. His lower lip was trembling; his eyes were vague. There was a red scab to the right of his nose. It was astonishing to think that this pathetic, lost old man in a threadbare suit had once been capable of terrifying them beyond measure. Although he was still under sixty, since the end of the war Doktor Barnhelm had aged by twenty years.

'Eck, it's time to go in, eh?' Benno coaxed softly.

'I am the director of this children's home, yes,' Barnhelm said. 'What do you want?'

Gurkel stepped forward, looked to the right and the left to ensure no one on the street was watching them, then quickly pushed Barnhelm in the chest. The shove sent the old man staggering back into the hall. Gurkel kept going, pushed him again. Barnhelm ended up sprawled at the bottom of the hall stairs.

'I am the director of this children's home. Yes,' he mumbled. 'I used to speak a little French, you know. I have forgotten so much.'

'That's good,' said Gurkel with a laugh. 'I reckon that morphine Boss-Kind gives you don' improve your memory, eh?'

This seemed to rouse Barnhelm. He suddenly looked up at Gurkel and for a moment the look in his pale eyes was penetrating. 'I know you. Your name is Mielke. You have been here for many years, since you were very small.' He nodded to Benno, who had also come inside, closing the street door behind him. 'You . . . you are Brauer. Yes. You have been here since . . . oh, it was very cold. It must have been the Stalingrad winter when you came to the orphanage . . .'

'Shuddup, old man,' Gurkel sneered. 'No one calls me Mielke. And this isn't no orphanage any more. This is the Kinder Garden, and don't you forget it!'

'Help me up . . .' Barnhelm pleaded feebly. The light, the keenness had gone out of his gaze again now. 'Help me.'

'*Help him!*'

Granit was standing at the far end of the hall, by the door to the cellar, puffing on a hand-rolled cigarette. He was seventeen, six feet two, weighed some twelve-and-a-half stone. Some of it was fat, but not much.

Gurkel looked at the older boy, then at Benno. They went to it immediately, pulling Barnhelm to his feet. He was light as a skeleton.

Granit was generally acknowledged as the second-in-command of the Kinder. He was muscle and organisation where Boss-Kind was the quick blade and the inspiration.

'We need Barnhelm, and don't *you* forget that,' he rasped while Benno and Gurkel were busy with the old man. 'For these times, when Froggie soldiers arrive at the door like just then, or when police come. So we gotta keep the old shit alive. If I see you hurt him again . . .'

'Sorry, Granit. Sorry.'

Barnhelm was shuffling off to his quarters, behind the door to their left, guided by Gurkel. 'So you tell me, what was *that* about? Froggie asking questions at the Kinder Garden, what?' Granit demanded.

'Froggie *Razzia*,' Benno explained hastily. 'Just this side of the sector border. Two jeeps, big patrol. They catch two Hats with suitcases, maybe black-market nylons, I think. They pick us up 'cos we are nearby—'

'OK, OK . . . Why did you bring them *here*?'

'Otherwise they would arrest us, Granit. That's the gadawlmighdy truth. No papers. Maybe they think we're working with those Hats with the suitcases. And if they search me . . .' Benno reached into his shirt, pulled out the bag of diamonds. 'Best quality. They be-long to a grand-duch-ess, I guarantee it . . .' he said, mimicking the Slovak's pitch back at the slaughterhouse. 'This way they bring us home, check our story with Dok-tor Barn-helm, everything is OK. *Ach scheiss*, all they are doing, so far as they know, is returning two poor little orphan boys to the *waisenhaus*.'

Granit looked at them both appraisingly. 'All right,' he conceded. 'You give me the diamonds—those exchanged for morphine?'

Benno nodded, handed over the bag. 'Fifty grams. Big delivery.'

'I won' tell Boss-Kind 'bout Froggies, Hats with suitcases, anything like that,' Granit said. He weighed the diamonds quickly in his hand before pocketing them. 'If you're smart, you say nothing either. Boss-Kind is *hiding* in his lair. He won' come out. Something happened last night. What, I don't know . . . but you beddabelieve he don' wanna hear 'bout Froggie *Razzias*.'

Granit opened the door leading down to the cellar, started off down the stairs. The boys followed suit. Gurkel carefully shut the door behind him. An outsider would have been mystified when he reached the bottom of those stairs. All that greeted the eye was a filthy, empty cellar, with garbage on the floor, holes where the panes of the one, grilled window had been, and graffiti scrawled over the concrete walls. One slogan, written in red paint on the right-hand wall, said: '*HIER IST KEIN KINDERGARDEN*'—this is no Kindergarden. To one side of that, hardly visible until the eyes adjusted to the gloom, was a cupboard. Granit was already opening the door of the cupboard and ducking to pass inside it.

In fact, the cupboard was no cupboard, and the door led to another door, this time a steel air-raid shelter door. Such doors had been fitted in large cellars all over the city during the later part of the war, when the Allied bombing raids became regular affairs, night after night, for months on end.

The door opened into a low-ceilinged antechamber, a kind of guardroom, where two boys in their mid-teens sat at a table. They had been smoking and playing cards by the light of a paraffin lamp. Both wore old sweaters, long trousers that had been adapted from army uniform pants.

'Hey, where you two been?' asked one of Benno and Gurkel.

'Russkie-sector. Slaughterhouse,' said Gurkel. 'Swapping dope with the fat slug called Slovak,' he added, making a wry face.

The older boy laughed. 'He still like little boys, he still run so fast, so *blitz-schnell* when his old blood is up?'

'You bet.'

'You young Kinder are welcome to him. Give me this guardhouse anytime.'

'You get no excitement, you know that's your trouble,' Benno said. He mimicked the Slovak again: 'I got nice clothes, candy . . .'

'You cut the banter and get something to eat, eh?' Granit interrupted sternly. 'Something tells me we still got a busy day ahead.'

He had opened the far door. Benno followed Granit and Gurkel through into the room beyond. The guards returned to their cards.

The place they entered was a huge, concrete bunker lit dimly by oil-lamps, with one thick, gridded skylight at street level to provide some natural light. This must have been the main shelter in wartime. Now it was a living and sleeping area, filled with twenty or so old iron bedsteads and twenty or so German boys. The bunker was gloomy, it didn't smell good, but it seethed with life. Most of the boys saluted Benno and Gurkel in a casual, comradely way. The youngest was about nine, the eldest seventeen, perhaps eighteen. Some of the younger boys wore shorts, but most wore long pants and sweaters, shirts, of varying provenance and in different degrees of repair. There was a lot of smoking going on, by all ages; the dominant sounds were whistling, excited chatter, the rattle of dice. One boy was sitting on his bed with a needle and thread, sewing a short army tunic which had been cut down to his size. There was a silent radio in the corner, but music was in the background somewhere, coming from yet another room, a scratched phonograph record of a recent American hit song:

> 'Roll me over
> In the clover
> Roll me over, lay me down and do it again . . .'

'So Boss-Kind got his old wind-up machine going,' Benno said to no one in particular. 'Cos we got no electricity, so no radio, eh?'

The sewing boy, who was a little younger than Benno, looked up from his work. 'You beddabelieve. I tell you, Benno, the Boss been in there the whole gadawlmighdy morning, just playing that same disc over and over and over. 'Cept when some Hat came by just a little while ago. Then Boss-Kind went upstairs to talk to him.'

'A long talk? Who was this Hat?'

The boy—his name was Flix—shrugged. 'They talked for a couple of minutes, that's all. One of Riese's gang, I think. I don' know. Hats just don' interest me.'

'One day, when you're not paying attention to some Hat, he'll catch you and hurt you, Flix.'

'Maybe. You ask me about the Boss, and I tell you. Apart from that break for business, that is all there is. Boss-Kind, he laughs and he cries in that room of his, so they say, behaving ab-so-lute-ly crazy—I mean *verrückt*!'

Benno grunted. 'He's been like this before. Wild stuff. When he been out hunting with that blade of his.' He looked round. 'And where's the Wonder?'

'The Wonder is in there with Boss-Kind. We are waiting to go to the Tiergarten, you know that, Benno?'

Benno took a moment to absorb this information. 'All of us?'

'Every Kind called to arms, as they say!'

Benno groaned, trying without success to conceal his sudden, unaccountable nervousness. 'Flix, why's the Wonder in there? He was out with Boss-Kind all yesterday, all last night. I just saw him once, first thing. *Ach scheiss*, he looked like he spent the night in the cooler instead of out on the tiles.'

'The Wonder, he is becoming the Boss's Kind. He do anylittlething Boss-Kind says. And I mean *any*littlething,' Flix said with a sly smirk. 'Maybe the Wonder gets special treatment, special cigarettes and food . . .'

Benno scowled at Flix. 'You are jealous. Jealous of the Wonder.' Benno's eyes narrowed further. 'And you tell me, Flix, when did you join the Kinder, eh?'

'It . . .' Flix hesitated, knowing he was on weak ground. 'Well, you know, Benno, it was before Point Null . . .'

'*Just* before. And, Flix, how old were you? Tell me that.'

'Maybe six, ach OK, nearly seven . . . but it was before Point Null, when this place was still a shit-orphanage, so don' you start on 'bout those "special" Kinder, like you and Gurkel and the Wonder . . .'

'Since we was s-o-o-o little, we have been here, me and those two, Flix,' Benno hissed. 'Since we was tiny *Kleinkinder. Ganz klein*, yes. Since the war time, way before Point Null, way before the Kinder Garden . . .'

Benno and Flix stared each other out. The younger boy dropped his eyes back to his unfinished jacket. 'OK, OK. So you and your friends, you are the originals, the Ur-Kinder, the ones who can do no wrong,' Flix mumbled.

Benno was about to get roused when Gurkel ambled back. He had been to the kitchen beyond the dormitory and had two bowls of lung-soup and a hunk of bread for them to share.

'Ach, Benno,' he said. 'You already fighting with ol' Flixie?' He handed Benno his bowl of soup. 'You better eat this, 'cos word is that Boss-Kind will be coming out of his lair at any moment now, and then there will be no more resting for any Kinder. Not even the likes of you.'

'Flix says the Wonder is the Boss's Kind,' Benno grated.

Gurkel smiled. 'He's busy these days, the Wonder is,' he said in a peacemaking voice. 'He is the Boss's special fetcher, just as you are the watcher, Benno . . .'

Benno had already shoved a lump of the spongy grey bread into his mouth. He tried to say something else, but it was lost in the movement of his jaws on the food. Fighting was good, but it was a fundamental truth of the Kinder's life that *nothing* was better than a feed.

The music suddenly got louder. It was coming along the corridor behind the guardroom, from the direction of Boss-Kind's room, his private place where he slept and thought and listened and planned. There he had his wind-up phonograph. There Boss-Kind also had his maps, his steel safe with the things in it that he bought and sold on behalf of the Kinder, and there he met with his allies—who were the Kinder's allies too, of course—and his informants.

'Roll me over . . . In the clover . . . Roll me over, lay me down and do it again. . . .' the record crackled, then there was an abrupt scratching noise, and the music stopped dead.

First the Wonder flitted into the room. He was almost freakishly undersized. With his little pointed face and his bright eyes, there was something of the marmoset about him. Now he looked tired, more than a little frightened, but strangely exhilarated. Then in stalked a boy, almost a young man, with long dark-blond hair that cascaded over his forehead, so that he was constantly shaking or pushing it away from his gaunt, high-cheekboned face. He was nearly six feet tall, somewhere between seventeen and eighteen years old. He wore a long black coat and a bright blue-and-scarlet bandanna around his neck. He was extraordinary-looking on many accounts, but his most striking feature was his eyes, which were fever-bright and yet expressionless, like a caged animal's stare.

All movement, all conversation, ceased. It was as if this being had stolen everyone's energy—almost expropriated their souls—so swiftly and totally did the room and all the Kinder in it become his to command.

Boss-Kind tossed his hair. Then he clapped ostentatiously for silence, though in fact by then you could have heard a rat fart in that cellar.

'We got a real *emergency*, Kinder,' he said in a voice that was never far away from a chant. 'Urgent business in the Tiergarten. All Kinder are called to arms! Are . . . we . . . ready?'

There was a shuffling, a general expression of assent.

Boss-Kind waited until he was satisfied with the response before he continued. 'This business is to help some friends. But it is also important Kinder-business, and this is why I tell you we got an *emergency* . . .' He nodded slowly to emphasise his words. 'You know we must protect the Kinder Garden, and we must protect it now against a Hat who brings deadly danger—so deadly that all means against him are necessary. I am talking about a Tommy Herr Officer, no less, whose name means the Sainted one!'

A few of the Kinder, Benno and Gurkel included, sneaked doubting looks at each other. They knew that Boss-Kind liked theatricality, but this thing today was just a little too alien for comfort. Particularly the meaning of the Hat's name. They were going to the Tiergarten to protect themselves against some Hat graced by *God*? Had Boss-Kind suddenly gone crazy-*Christian*?

But the surprises were not over yet. Benno, who had been furtively guzzling down the last of his lung-soup, almost choked on it when he heard Boss-Kind call out his name.

''Cept for you, Benno,' Boss-Kind said. 'You are the watcher, and you got other things to do, you alone. I tell you later.'

Gurkel dug Benno in the ribs. Benno felt slightly sick. He hadn't wanted to go to the Tiergarten, but neither did he like being singled out and excluded. For some reason, Boss-Kind liked making him feel special and yet also somehow inferior. He would have felt much safer if Boss-Kind had treated him as one of the crowd.

'You see, Kinder,' Boss-Kind continued, returning to his main theme. 'You see the urgent and deadly danger is this person, this Hauptmann of His British Majesty's Army of Occupation in Berlin.' His lip curled in a slow sneer. 'So this is a *Kep-ten* we are talking about, and his name, in English, is *Bless-ed*.'

Some laughed dutifully, others just waited for Boss-Kind to get to what they had to do, how long it would take. They knew the Tiergarten and the area surrounding the park like the backs of their hands. Many a Tommy, a Hershey, a Froggie had they rolled there, or conned into parting with cigarettes or hard currency. Many an illegal errand had they run, dangerous substance ferried there, protected by their supposed youthful innocence.

'Blessed? That's a name so *strange*, even for a Tommy officer!' someone yelled out. 'You sure you're not making that Hat up, eh, Boss-Kind?'

That got a laugh. But Boss-Kind was unfazed.

'This is one Kepten Shems Blessed I am talking about,' he said. 'We will see this Hat in the Tiergarten, Kinder. Yes, while we are there, helping our friends by whatever means are necessary . . .' Boss-Kind made a sudden, violent slicing motion in mid-air '. . . all this time, we will see *him*. But this Kepten Blessed, this dumb Hat, *he will not see us until it is too late!*'

SEVEN

A COUPLE OF HUNDRED YARDS from where Blessed and Weiss stood, a massively overloaded S-bahn train was rattling across a viaduct, heading southwards from Potsdamer Platz towards the Anhalter Station. Desperate commuters with their briefcases and bags, bundles and knapsacks, clung to the open doors of its cars like Indian or African peasants. The city-wide commuter railway, with its administration based in the Russian-controlled part of Berlin, was the only overground rail service still running since the blockade, and even the S-bahn's operations were limited by electricity shortages in the western sectors. The Berliners' frantic determination to get a ride was understandable: even though it was only just past six o'clock in the evening, this train might be the last.

The two men had just spent an hour where Corporal Price and his woman had been murdered. The bodies and the forensic boys had now gone, though the immediate area was still cordoned off. They had ended up on this vantage-point, atop a pile of cleared rubble on the corner of the Kluckstrasse and the Schöneberger Ufer, looking north across the Landwehr Canal towards the Tiergarten and the former government district. They had been propositioned by prostitutes twice in the past half-hour.

Blessed had changed into the nondescript German-made outfit that he always kept at the office for use on plain-clothes operations. He took off his homburg, fanned his face, which was hot from the late-afternoon sun.

'You mentioned that you know the suspect Floh surprisingly well,' Weiss was saying. 'What exactly do you mean by that?'

'Oh, that's a sordid tale, Manfred.'

'We still have some time to spare. And if I didn't like listening to sordid stories, I don't think I would have joined the Kripo.'

'All right,' Blessed said with a laugh. 'Well, I was over here in Berlin for a year when I was a young man, on an allowance from my rich uncle. To spend some time with my mother's family, to polish up my German. Those were the excuses. My real aim was to have a fling before I took articles with Uncle's legal firm.' He let out a snort of pleasure at the memory. 'I stayed with my maiden aunt, Lotte, but at nights I used to go drinking with the English exchange students from the University. We toured all the bars and cabarets—this was just before Hitler came to power, so things were still pretty outrageous. I got to know most of the characters who frequented those places. Floh was one. You'd see him around the dives—the White Mouse especially. Do you remember the White Mouse?'

'Of course. It was notorious in its time. The owner set up in business directly across the Friedrichstrasse from the more famous Black Cat. The name was a cheeky joke. The place aimed to shock, I recall.'

'Oh, yes. We went there because the show featured a marvellous-looking girl who danced with no clothes on, none at all. Anyway, Floh would often be in there, downing cocktails and doing some discreet pimping. He made his living off a stable of five or six girls, but he seemed harmless enough by the standards of the time. God knows, though, he was no spring chicken even then. I assumed he must be dead . . .'

'And when did you realise he was still alive?'

'Last year. He was pulled in by my lads, on suspicion of organising Saturday-night orgies that had become very popular with certain officers and Mil. Gov. officials. Some of the girls Floh supplied were only twelve or thirteen years old.' Blessed snorted with disgust. 'We couldn't get the case to court—partly due to the military government's fear of scandal, though don't for Christ's sake tell anyone I said so.'

'Of course not, James. I wasn't born yesterday, by the way. I know such things happen under all political systems, even democratic ones.'

'Anyway, I don't give up easily,' Blessed said sourly. 'I marked Floh's card, put the word out that I was willing to pay well, in hard currency, for information about his activities.'

'And?'

'Earlier this year, someone told us that he and a partner were running drugs these days. I've been out to nail him ever since. We made one unsuccessful attempt when we raided that bar in the Kantstrasse, which was where we first came across Corporal Price. That's the connection, and that's why we plan to try again in the Tiergarten later this evening.'

'I'm very impressed, James,' Weiss said with a chuckle. 'So the upright Captain Blessed has a murky past, eh? A misspent youth! But this also means you are aware that Floh is almost seventy years old now, and not a violent type. Do you think he can have had anything to do with such a brutal double-murder?'

'Not necessarily. But his partner, Panewski, seems to have a tendency in that direction.'

Weiss shrugged. 'What can I say? He's a typical small-time hoodlum. I've dealt with a hundred characters like him during my career. Violent? Maybe.'

'There was a murder charge twenty years ago, reduced to manslaughter.'

'A fight in a bar that got out of control. The victim was a fellow-criminal. Apart from that, Panewski's done time here and there for assault, burglary, pimping—and for knocking his girls about when he had had too much to drink. The usual Ku-Damm catalogue of misbehaviour. I also saw he volunteered for the army during the war, because otherwise the Nazis might have put him in a concentration camp as a "persistent offender".'

Blessed nodded. 'He was captured in Italy, shipped off to a POW camp in Canada, resurfaced in Berlin about a year ago. Soon afterwards, he teamed up with Floh, and they took up drug-dealing. Just like Price . . .'

'That's all very well, but there's a difference between drunken brawling and the kind of butchery we're faced with here,' Weiss said. 'Apart from anything else, the murder of a British serviceman is a very risky affair. Conviction would mean a British military court and death by hanging.'

'We live in violent times, Manfred,' Blessed said. 'People are hungry, desperate. They've become capable of things they would never have contemplated before.' He gave Weiss a cheroot. The German sniffed its aroma but left it unlit for the moment. 'In any case, there's little doubt Floh was Price's main criminal contact in Berlin. Even if he weren't a suspect, we'd want to talk to him and Panewski, pump them about Price's other associates and how the drugs ring worked.'

'You're right, of course. Murder overwhelms everything. One forgets there are other crimes.' Weiss paused, playing the cheroot between his fingers, then asked: 'How much do you actually know about the connections between these people? I mean, how much solid evidence do you have?'

'I'll be honest with you. The only thing we know for absolute certain is that Floh and Panewski are dealing in illegal drugs. We suspected Price of being one of the suppliers, but the evidence was almost all circumstantial. Since I didn't have enough resources to mount an investigation in the Zone, I decided to concentrate on the Berlin end of the business, which meant keeping tabs on Floh and Panewski.'

'Hence this evening's operation.'

'Yes. We'd heard through our informant that a suspected drugs courier—an RASC driver named Mitchellson—is due to meet Floh in the Tiergarten this evening. The raid we planned was going to be our big breakthrough in the drugs case. But now that Price and his woman have been killed I believe that if we can find out who killed them and why, we may have the key to the whole drug-smuggling and distribution system between the Zone and Berlin. In other words, although I hate to say it, Price's murder could turn out to be a gift from the gods.'

Weiss thought for a while. 'For my part, I will concede one thing,' he said eventually. 'I acknowledge that Panewski could have committed these murders. But if he did, I believe it would have been without Floh's sanction.'

'I'm glad you're prepared to see the possibility, at least.'

'Perhaps there was rivalry over the woman's favours,' Weiss continued, evidently warming to the idea. 'Panewski's anger at her could explain the mutilations. Or perhaps the butchery was simply intended to put us off the scent—to make the affair look like a random sex-killing.'

Blessed nodded. He had been gazing pensively at what little was left of the old Berlin skyline, recapturing his memories of the way it had been here in the heart of the city ten, fifteen, twenty years ago. Over there had been the Anhalter Station, and beyond it the clusters of ministries, dominated by the monumental façade of the Reich Chancellery, where Hitler had celebrated his conquests, and beneath which he had built his concrete bunker, the rat-hole where Germany's King Rat had chosen to die . . . And now hunger and despair haunted the daytime silence. At night, the once-brilliant city lay dark as an ancient, unlit plain. Violent impulses seethed beneath those ruins. Rage bred from itself, spread like a virus. Any atrocity was possible.

He looked at his watch. 'We'd better be going,' he said. 'Better to be early than late.'

They walked past blackened, roofless buildings, crossed the Landwehr Canal by the old hump-backed Potsdam Bridge. In '45 this area had seen fierce fighting when the Soviets had made their big push to break through across the waterway and into the heavily-defended Tiergarten. After the bridge, there seemed to be more people about. As they approached the Potsdamer Platz, Blessed and Weiss found themselves among crowds.

In Weimar days this had been a great traffic circle, teeming with buses and cars, Berlin's equivalent of Hyde Park Corner. Now the square was shabby and pot-holed; only the tramlines had been repaired to something like their pre-war condition. Most of the buildings that surrounded it lay in ruins, and the bustle, the billboards, the bright lights, were only a nostalgic memory. Because its eastern half lay in the Russian Sector, the Potsdamer Platz had become a kind of frantic no-man's land, the haunt of pimps, hustlers and other transients.

There were always people about, but the crowds in the square today were different, standing around in gangs, looking ugly, ridiculing and hurling abuse at the Red Army troops and Soviet-controlled Protection Police just a few yards away on the other side of the sector border. Nevertheless, they were letting the trams cross into Russian territory. A cumbersomely-converted woodburning bus was returning west in a puffing fog of smoke. There was apparently unhindered movement of pedestrians in both directions across the newly-established demarcation line—a simple white stripe that British MPs had painted there a couple of days ago to show the Russians that His Majesty's Government meant business in defending its sector. Germans returning from the east were carrying bags and sacks.

'The Russians have made a big play of having plenty of food in their sector,' Weiss observed. 'They must have raided the entire countryside from here to the Baltic to make such supplies available. So, they encourage us to go east to buy from these stocks, in the hope that we will think, ah, everything will be wonderful if we will stop supporting the western Allies and let the Communists have the whole of Berlin.' He laughed harshly. 'The Soviets must consider us stupid. Everyone knows that the food we can get over there is being taken from the mouths of people in the east to make a propaganda advantage in the west. The irony is that most of it will be sold through the capitalistic black market.'

87

'Berlin cynicism.'

'Berlin realism,' Weiss countered. 'And someone has just thrown a stone at a Soviet officer over there. I think it's time we got out of here. This is not our concern.'

The situation was, in truth, warming up. From among a group of youths on the western side, a small shower of missiles had been directed at a fair-haired Russian officer. The officer drew his service pistol. It was enough to send the boys diving back into the protection of the mob. British MPs were already moving through the fringes of the crowd, hunting for the troublemakers, and German police—hard to make out whose side they were on—were waving their nightsticks. It was a tragicomic mess that just one stray bullet would turn into a massacre.

'You're right,' Blessed agreed reluctantly. 'There's always a temptation to watch history being made. I'm told it can be fatal.'

They passed open-topped British and American army trucks full of armed troops being held ready between the Potsdamer Platz and the Tiergarten. A couple of minutes later they had arrived at the eastern edge of the huge park where, unless this day was really unlike any other, Berlin's biggest black market would already be in full swing.

Soon they were in the thick of it, between the Brandenburg Gate and the Soviet War Memorial, which lay several hundred yards inside the western-occupied part of the city. The memorial, always guarded by a pair of impassive, smartly-turned-out Russian infantrymen, consisted of two Soviet tanks—supposedly the first Red Army armoured vehicles to penetrate Berlin—set in concrete by the side of the busy Charlottenburger Chaussee.

There were jeerers here too, for the blockade had unleashed many powerful feelings among Berliners, but nothing got in the way of the black market. Fifty yards from the Soviet memorial, several hundred traders and their customers milled around in the mellow sunlight. Beneath the remains of ancient chestnut trees, the Tiergarten had become a modern babel, an open-air market of nations. Rangy American GIs in sun-glasses haggled over German family heirlooms; baggy-panted Russians, sturdy as steppe-ponies, examined wristwatches, shook them to check their mechanisms were sound, peered with grave curiosity through the viewfinders of Leicas and Rolliflexes. Though lookouts had been posted in case police arrived in strength for a raid, the atmosphere was relaxed, brazen. As Blessed and Weiss made their way through the mêlée, a man was selling 'Soviet' cabbages from a handcart. Another brushed against Weiss, opened his coat to reveal a huge ham fitted into a poacher's pocket, named a stupendous dollar price, then disappeared just as quickly when he found no immediate taker. Other dealers were peddling the usual packs of butter, coffee, tobacco, various clothes and household goods.

At a point about a hundred yards from the shell of the Reichstag building, Blessed stopped. He looked around casually, exchanged glances with a tall man in a ragged coat and a German army cap who was standing nearby.

'No sign of them yet, apparently,' he said quietly. 'We wait here for the connection to be made. It could be a while.'

'Of course, I should not say this, but there is something brave, even noble about these black-market dealers,' Weiss remarked after a while, keeping his voice low and conversational. 'Call it dancing on the edge of the volcano. These may be our last days of freedom, but for them a deal is still a deal!'

'As far as I know, there are no plans for us to evacuate Berlin, Manfred,' Blessed said. 'That's all I can say.'

'And the Russians?'

'I can't do anything about the sodding Russians, Manfred. Dealing with them is up to my government and the other allies. All I'm really interested in is solving this case. We're on Floh's patch now. He's in that crowd somewhere, even though we can't see him. According to our information, he's due to meet his contact here very soon.'

Several more minutes passed. Then Blessed touched Weiss's arm. 'From now on, whatever happens, don't react,' he said softly. 'The party's about to begin. I've just seen Mitchellson, the courier. And he's with Panewski. It's hard to believe our luck. Stay where you are until I tell you to move.'

Karl-Heinz Panewski was over six feet tall, broad-shouldered and flat-faced, with receding hair and big hands. He carried a small briefcase of the type often used by minor officials who wanted to look important. He was grinning, clapping the other man on the back while he drew him quickly through the milling crowd; this was presumably meant to imply bonhomie, but it looked more like a drover manœuvring a bullock into a pen. Mitchellson was small and plump and worried-looking.

The man in the cap was suddenly no longer at his post. Blessed nodded to Weiss and set off in pursuit, not too eager, not too quick. Weiss followed. They must have covered seventy or eighty yards before anything happened.

There was a cluster of figures by one of the few surviving trees in this part of the park. It looked as if a poker game was going on. Then the cluster opened and a small man in a brown herringbone overcoat and a fedora appeared. He moved quickly but with the jerky movements of old age, extended a hand towards Mitchellson, his face set in a gash of a smile.

'That's Floh all right,' Blessed murmured.

Suddenly there were more men everywhere, all in civilian clothes but shouting to each other in English. Two of them had guns, including Sergeant Kelly, who was the first to reach the old man and Mitchellson. Floh had already turned, and had run several yards surprisingly quickly, in a purposeful scuttling motion, but Kelly halted him. Waving his service revolver in one hand, with the other he seized his quarry by the shoulder. The man stumbled, then righted himself, peered around to establish that there was no escape, and said, 'What do you want with me? I am sixty-eight years old! Even old men have to eat . . .'

Blessed made no move to intervene. None of the SIB plainclothes men acknowledged him. The crowds, meanwhile, were beginning to scatter, obscuring his view. For some reason, the area seemed to be full of children—young boys of various ages. One of them gave Blessed a quick kick on his way past. He cursed under his breath. By the time they were gone he and Weiss were able to witness the first arrest.

'Floh, you're nicked,' bellowed Kelly.

'I am Gross. Ludwig Otto Gross. A simple pensioner. I have my papers . . .'

'You're Floh, you old bastard,' Kelly insisted. 'I'm taking you into custody under Ordinance Number 56 of the Allied Control Council, to wit restrictions on improper dealings between natural or juristic persons resident in the British Zone of Germany and members of the British Forces.' He paused for an instant, caught his breath. 'Now, come quietly or I'll break your fucking arm!'

Floh swore roundly in Berlin dialect. He had caught sight of a paddy-wagon belonging to the British military police waiting by the Moltkestrasse boundary of the Tiergarten, ready to take him away.

EIGHT

'LET'S GET THIS ON THE RECORD. You claim you didn't know Taffy Price was dead. You say you didn't even know the man,' Blessed said, speaking German although Floh's English was excellent. 'I think you're lying. In fact, I *know* you're lying.'

Floh's grey features were impassive. He was frightened, but he was also tough and devious, a hardened veteran of the Berlin underworld. He shook his head in apparent bewilderment.

'I am an old man. I know faces. Names I forget, sir,' he mumbled.

Blessed had stationed himself just inside the door of the darkened interrogation room in the Knesebeckstrasse military police station. The windows had been covered with thick blackout felt, and the desk-lamp—the only light available—had been placed so as to blind Floh if he tried to look in his direction. From where the old man sat, facing Kelly and Weiss across a bare table, Blessed presented an unsettlingly anonymous silhouette. Kelly and Weiss were asking most of the questions, but it was the sharp and unpredictable interventions from the darkness in his perfect, Berlin-flavoured German that had such an interestingly disturbing effect on Floh.

'But you certainly know Mitchellson. Mitchellson is a friend of his. Mitchellson also sells drugs.' Weiss picked up the interrogation. 'Price was seen with you and Mitchellson some months ago. In a bar in the Kantstrasse near the NAAFI cinema.'

'I go there sometimes, Herr Inspector. The English boys like me. They buy me drinks and give me food. And there is a good warm stove . . .'

'You were talking with Price and Mitchellson on that occasion for

91

over an hour, you old bastard,' Kelly cut in harshly, switching to English. 'We were watching you. A bit after that we pulled you all in for questioning, as you well remember.'

'Ah . . . yes . . .' Floh smiled, as if recalling some trivial incident that had slipped his mind. 'I was released a little later. An unfortunate mistake.'

'Mistake be buggered. What were you up to with Price and Mitchellson?'

'I told you. I don't know their names. Perhaps if you were to show me a recent photograph—'

'*What were you doing?*' Blessed said. 'Answer the sergeant's question!'

Floh moistened his thin, old man's lips. Strangely, his tongue was small and pinkly perfect. 'I act as . . . how shall I say . . . a tourist guide for Allied soldiers. I earn a few cigarette, or a few ounces of butter, for my services. I hardly ever learn their names. But this you already know. This I explained at the time, before I was released . . .'

Kelly clenched his fist, then appealed to the invisible Blessed. 'Sir, we all know what this wicked old pimp was up to. He was setting up a deal. I'm getting tired of this. I could have him singing his black heart out in five minutes if you'd just let me. I know how to leave no marks.'

Blessed shook his head. Kelly could see his reaction but Floh couldn't. The old man appeared untroubled, but Blessed noticed his right foot tapping nervously against the concrete floor.

A silence followed. Kelly continued to stare in Blessed's direction, apparently waiting for him to change his mind. The sergeant's face, no thing of beauty even in repose, was tense with anger and the desire to do violence.

'I never touched the package that the English soldier—what was his name?—was carrying in the Tiergarten today,' Floh said eventually. 'You have examined what was in it, sergeant. If you say penicillin, you must be right. But I never actually touched it.'

'Who are you kidding? He was handing it over to you, and you were grabbing at it as if it was your birthday present. We have at least four witnesses to that. And in your pocket you were carrying two hundred dollars in American occupation scrip.'

Floh said nothing. After a while he shrugged.

'I'll tell you something, you old bastard,' Kelly hissed. 'I can get witnesses, *reliable* witnesses, to say anything I bloody well want them to. What do you think of that? You still reckon that penicillin was nothing to do with you?'

'Take it easy, Sergeant,' Blessed warned. 'None of that while I'm around. It's not necessary, anyway. Just tell him what the law holds in store for him, will you? That should be quite persuasive enough, I think.'

While Blessed listened, and Weiss smoked a cigarette, the sergeant went into the details of the charges Floh could face, and what the English courts could do to him, even with the limited evidence at their disposal.

'Y'see, in England we have something called conspiracy law,' he said. 'Did you know that under this handy little instrument of justice, you can end up getting a heavier sentence for *thinking* about doing something than for actually *doing* it? Amazing but true. And since you were involved in dealings with a British serviceman, we can do you under English law. There's no doubt we could make a conspiracy charge stick in this case. Now let's see. How old are you?'

'I told you, Sergeant. I am sixty-eight years old. I don't know what you want with an old man like me, but I will do my best to help you,' Floh said, switching to a plaintive tone. 'All I want is to spend my old age in peace.'

Kelly laughed in his face. 'That shouldn't be hard to arrange. Moabit Prison's awful quiet, I'm told. I don't doubt we could bang you up in there for the rest of your filthy life. Unless—' The sergeant turned to Blessed again, as if seeking his approval. 'Sir? What do you think?'

Blessed sighed heavily. 'I don't know. Perhaps Mitchellson would be a better bet for turning King's Evidence. Certainly more straightforward to deal with than this slippery old eel. Or we could try Panewski when the doctors say he's ready. Quite honestly, Sergeant, they all make me sick. I'd like to hand the lot of them over to a military court and forget the whole business. If it weren't for the murders, that's exactly what I'd do.'

'Too right, sir. I'm sick of this old bastard here. I reckon we should do what you said, charge this one and concentrate on his mates.'

Before Blessed could answer Kelly, Floh leaned forward and spoke to Weiss in an urgent croak.

'Herr Inspector,' he demanded, 'please make the English gentlemen see reason. You know I am no monster. I have had a long and varied life. I know people from many professions. Please. If there is any way I can help these enquiries . . . just tell me what they want to know.'

'Speak to the sergeant,' Weiss coaxed. Tonight he had assumed the 'soft' role. 'Be frank about your dealings with Mitchellson and Price. And if you have any idea who killed Price, tell him that, too. You're not out of danger so far as the murder is concerned, Floh. Not by any means. Co-operate!'

Floh turned. 'Sergeant,' he said hoarsely, 'what do you want to know?'

Kelly took his time before he acknowledged his question.

'Know? Old bastard, I want to know what was your business with Mitchellson and Taffy—and I want to know who killed Price and why.'

Floh looked at Kelly, then at the shadow of Blessed. 'And . . . the gentlemen will excuse me, but what will you do for me if I share some of my knowledge with you in the privacy of this room?'

Blessed opened the door. 'Providing you can prove you had nothing to do with those murders, we might—I repeat, might—go easy on you. But we'll want a lot from you in return. An awful lot.' He buttoned up his tunic. 'Meanwhile, I think it's time I had a word with your friends.'

Blessed stepped out into the corridor, closed the door quietly behind him. At the door of the next room but one he stopped and looked through a spyhole. Mitchellson was slumped at the table with his head in his hands. A guard sat in the corner, reading a newspaper. He was under orders to say nothing to the prisoner, to refuse all requests, even for a smoke or a drink of water. For the past hour and a half Mitchellson had been told nothing, charged with nothing. He should be stewing nicely. Blessed continued along the corridor and began to climb the stairs.

'Any news from my people about Panewski?' he asked the sergeant on duty at the desk.

The man shook his head. 'Nothing, I'm afraid, sir.'

'Then it looks like we've lost him. For the moment, at least.'

They had lied to Floh about Panewski. He hadn't been caught. He was out there in the city somewhere. The big man had got away free—some German kid, part of a gang who happened to be hanging around the scene, had tripped up the armed SIB man before he could get in a shot—but this was not the time to let his friends know that. Usefully for Blessed, they still thought Panewski was in hospital under guard, and that he might be persuaded to give evidence against them.

'Your chaps were in trouble right from the start, by the sound of it,' the desk sergeant remarked. 'I've been on a few patrols in the Tiergarten, and I'll tell you, it's worse than a jungle. Let an old hand like Panewski give you the slip and he'll be off across the sector border like a hare from the trap.'

Blessed entered the empty office that he was borrowing for the evening, picked up the phone. When he got through to BlessForce, the man on duty there confirmed that there was still no trace of Panewski: Blessed asked if there was any other news and was told they had the written pathology report on Price and his woman—did he want that sent over to the Knesebeckstrasse now? He said he most certainly did.

Blessed returned the receiver to its cradle, looked at the clock. It was a little after nine, almost exactly fourteen hours since his day had started. At the Donaldsons' dinner party, meanwhile, they would be clearing away the remains of the fish. The main course would be roast beef or leg of lamb, perhaps wild boar if some chum of Harry's had been hunting at the weekend. One way or other, the Donaldsons kept one of the finest tables in Berlin. Their black-market contacts were of the very best. He pictured Harriet, scintillating and flirting, secretly fuming, drinking too much claret and probably exchanging I-told-you-so looks with Redman. Blessed could see it all in his mind's eye, but still he knew he must stay here until he'd done everything he could.

Ernie Mitchellson looked up with a start when his guard opened the door to admit a stranger in the uniform of a captain in the Royal Artillery. He got to his feet, came clumsily to attention. Blessed knew he had been right to change back into officer's uniform; its power over a man like this was immense.

'Easy,' Blessed said. Mitchellson was terrified and demoralised, as he had hoped. A low-key approach would probably do the job in this case. 'Sit down if you like.' He waved the guard back to his corner.

Blessed took his time placing his notepad and uncapping his pen. When he looked up, his prisoner was sitting bolt upright, staring across the table at him, as if transfixed. Mitchellson was about five feet five, plump and balding, and had been driving heavy goods vehicles for six years, including war service in North Africa and Italy. He had a sty in his left eye.

'Well?'

'Well what, sir?'

'Come on, Mitchellson. What were you doing in the park with a hundred-gram packet of penicillin? Trying to flog a bit of white gold, were you? That's a very, very serious offence according to the book.'

Mitchellson turned pale and put his head in his hands again. Unlike Floh, he was no cold, bare-faced professional. This was just an ordinary squaddie who had seen the only chance he would ever have to make some easy money. He had weakened, he would pay heavily for his weakness, and he knew it.

'It was a mistake, sir. I'd been given this little parcel by . . .'

'Taffy Price?'

'I didn't know what was in . . .' Mitchellson's feeble explanation died away and he swallowed hard. 'You been talking to Taffy?' he murmured.

'Never mind that. Just answer my questions truthfully, please,' Blessed said. 'Was it him?'

'Yes . . . sir.'

Blessed let the man's words hang. So far as he could tell, before their arrest neither Mitchellson nor Floh had known that Price was dead. Mitchellson still didn't, or so it seemed. Blessed wasn't absolutely sure about Floh, but in this case he was inclined to believe the ignorance was genuine.

Mitchellson continued after a while, because silence was worse than talk: 'Taffy asked me to go to the Tiergarten and meet this bloke, you know, and hand over the parcel. He said it was something for the bloke's family.'

'Was this Floh or Panewski?'

'I don't know them—'

'You're lying, Mitchellson!' Blessed snapped, showing some steel. 'You were with Price and Floh at the Tabasco one night in February, and then you carried on and had a drink with them in a bar in the Kantstrasse. Price and Floh were picked up later. Just because we let you go, that doesn't mean we haven't been watching you very carefully. Understand? There isn't much about you and your partners-in-crime that we don't know.'

The last claim was far from true, and Floh would never have fallen for it. If only Mitchellson knew how short of men BlessForce was, and how hard it was to keep a watch on the big criminals, let alone small fry like him.

'You Military Police, are you, sir? SIB?' Mitchellson asked anxiously. 'I know you officers can wear any uniform you like.'

'That's none of your business. All I'll tell you is, I'm here to put you in prison.' Blessed waited for the words to sink in and then leaned forward confidentially, almost tenderly. 'Maybe even to see you hang . . .'

Mitchellson half-rose, his fists clenched. His mouth was working, but no sound came out. Blessed was glad the guard had been told to stay in the room.

'Sit down, Mitchellson,' he said, still impaling him with a cold stare. 'Your associate, Corporal Price, is dead. Murdered. I have seen his body. Very badly cut up. So was his girlfriend. What do you know about that, eh?'

The man subsided back into his chair. 'Christ, sir. Dead? Taff and Suzy?'

Blessed nodded. 'The woman had been particularly horribly mutilated. Do you understand?'

'Not entirely, sir. No.'

'Come on, Mitchellson. What happened? Did they get in your way? Rub you up the wrong way, did he, poor old Taffy?'

'Sir, please. You must understand I had no grudge against Taff—Corporal Price. I mean, we met just yesterday and everything was apples. We had a beer at the Winston. Suzy couldn't come along, of course—'

The Winston was the Other Ranks' club in the Ku-Damm. No Germans admitted. 'She was German, then?' Blessed said.

Mitchellson realised that Blessed hadn't known much about the woman. He also realised it was too late to take advantage of the fact.

'Yes,' he answered sullenly. 'That's all I knew about her. That and the name "Suzy". She was some bird Taff went with when he was in Berlin. She didn't say much, like. Not to me, anyway. But a looker. For her age.'

'How old? Was she married? Children?'

Mitchellson was not taking the news well. Like many weak men, his response to a crisis was to retreat into himself.

'I . . . dunno . . .' he said, forcing himself to answer the question. 'I don't think so. Maybe her old man was killed in the war. She was just . . . around. You know how it is with German birds. They're available and you take 'em. You don't ask for details, do you? Christ. Old Taff. Dead. Christ.'

'Why should anyone want to kill them? Think hard, because if your answers are not satisfactory, you could face a charge of capital murder.'

Mitchellson shook his head. 'No, no. Taff was sharp, but I can't think why anyone would do him in. Except for the money he carried. He always had a few quid or a few dollars on him, to flash around, like. But he never did anyone down . . .'

'Except for the Royal Army Medical Corps.'

'Yeah, well . . . I mean, he was honest in his dealings, considering the fact that he was a thief. You got your percentage. Compared with some of the shysters you meet in Berlin, he was a bleedin' saint, if you ask me.'

'Saint Taffy, eh? Did he try to steal other men's women?'

'That wasn't his style,' Mitchellson said without equivocation. 'I mean, I won't say he was a hundred per cent faithful to Suzy, but . . . well, there are enough spare birds around, all willing to drop their drawers for a packet of ciggies, aren't there? Why bother pinching them from other blokes?'

'All right. What was this Suzy's other name?'

'Dunno. She wasn't even really called Suzy. That was just Taff's name for her; he called her "Susannah" when he'd been drinking and was feeling playful, like. He told me her German name once . . . oh, bleedin' hell, I can't remember.'

'Try. Try hard.'

'I can't,' Mitchellson moaned. 'Suzy shared a flat with some girl. She brought her to some of Taffy's knees-ups.' He brightened. 'This friend's name was Anna, a real cracker. I remember that . . .'

'What was her other name?'

Mitchellson's face fell. 'I . . . I dunno. Just Anna.'

'Where did they live? Where was this flat?'

'Um, Moabit, I think. Somewhere up there.'

'There are about twenty thousand people in Moabit, Mitchellson. Can't you be more specific? Not even to save your life?'

'Oh Christ. I swear to God, I didn't do it. I'm so tired. So fucking tired . . .'

'Wake up! How did Suzy live? Did she go with soldiers for money?' Blessed pressed him mercilessly. 'You don't want to hang, you'd better stay awake.'

'Um, she wasn't like the others. She had a proper job. She worked for a doctor.'

'Did this doctor buy penicillin from Price, then? Is that how Price met Suzy?'

Mitchellson nodded miserably.

'Answer both questions. Yes or no.'

'Yes and yes. He met her through the quack.' Mitchellson's answer came in a low, choked whisper. 'This quack was an abortionist. He used to cure the clap, too. Worth a fortune to that doctor, it was, the penicillin.'

'A back-street abortionist, eh? What was his name?'

'Schmidt. I know you're not going to believe me, but it's true. I never saw him or dealt with him, Taffy did. I only knew his name.'

'Ignorance is bliss. So what exactly was your job, then?'

'I organised the transport between the Zone and here. Sometimes I'd drop stuff off, like with Floh today in the Tiergarten.' Mitchellson's voice had turned dreamy, slightly slurred. Blessed sensed he might slip away from him.

'The more you tell us, the easier it will be for us to recommend that the court treat you leniently,' he reminded him. 'Don't hold anything back. We'll get it out of you in the end.'

'Honest, sir. I didn't know nothing much about that side of the business. Taff had his own contacts and he kept them to himself. He was waiting for the big one, he said. Maybe he'd landed the big one . . . the last time I saw him, he told me he felt like he'd broke the bank at Monte Carlo. Mind you, he said that plenty of other times. Taff used to love that old song. You know the one . . .'

Quietly Mitchellson began to mouth the words of the old music-hall number, swaying in time to the tune:

> 'Oh-oh-oh . . . he-e-e-e . . . strolls along
> The Bois de Boulogne
> With an independent air
> You can hear the girls declare
> He must be a millionaire . . .'

Back upstairs, the desk sergeant handed Blessed a sealed brown envelope that had arrived from BlessForce. He walked back into his borrowed office along the corridor, sat down at the the desk and lit up a cheroot.

The pathology report consisted of three handwritten sheets in German, then another three-quarters of a page in English. The German part was signed by Dr. Med. Adalbert Schwinck, the Kripo pathologist. The English bit had been approved by his British colleague, Major Gilbert-Hadley of the Medical Corps. It

99

confirmed and expanded on the information that Blessed had gleaned over the phone that afternoon. The captain's tired eyes drifted across the pages, noting 'hypostasis indicates that the bodies were not moved after death . . . the condition of the cadavers indicates that death occurred sometime between ten and eleven pm the previous night . . .' It was all valuable, if mundane, information. Then Blessed came across a scrawled note in the English MO's handwriting, headed 'Other Observations'.

'There are clear indications,' it said, 'that the male victim suffered from relatively advanced symptoms of syphilis. The female had almost certainly also been infected, although because of the extensive mutilation of the tissue around the genital area, it is difficult to be completely sure of this.'

Blessed sat rigidly at the desk for a long time, staring at those baldly expressed facts, re-reading them without knowing why. This was not remarkable, he said to himself. Soldiers caught venereal diseases, and spread them. This information was not at all special. But his heart was pounding in him until it pained him. He was sweating hard. Somewhere inside himself, he was gripped by such loathing, but also such fascination, when he was brought close to that disease, that death.

'Sir?' A cough.

Blessed realised that Kelly was standing in the doorway, looking at him.

'Sorry to disturb you, sir,' the sergeant said with an embarrassed smile. 'I was wondering if you'd mind coming back and helping out again for a sec.'

'I thought Floh was preparing to sing his heart out, Sergeant.'

'Didn't we all?' Kelly laughed painfully. 'You think you're making progress, then you find he's done some fancy footwork and everyone's back where they bleedin' well started. Perhaps if you could pop back and get a bit fierce with him . . . You know how these Jerries are when it comes to respecting officers—even an old ginger like Floh.'

'Very well.' Blessed pulled himself together. 'Sergeant Brownlow is taking a statement from Mitchellson, by the way. He's admitted his involvement, and incriminated Panewski and Floh. I also got some pointers to the dead woman's identity, and the names and addresses of a couple of Price's customers.'

'That's very good news, sir. Let's hope Floh'll crack now that Mitchellson's started to spill the beans.'

100

'Yes. Let's hope. I'll be with you in a moment or two.'

He'd give himself fifteen minutes or so with Floh. Afterwards he would rouse his driver Thwaite and make for the Donaldsons'. Something told Blessed he should be there, among Berlin's privileged revellers, this night of all nights. And anyway—for God's sake—he had promised.

NINE

'HOW ARE POTATOES DOING at the moment?' Blessed asked Thwaite. He settled into the leather interior of the Horch and made an effort to relax as the car sped southwestwards through the darkness towards Dahlem and the tail-end of the Donaldsons' dinner party.

'Well, the latest word has spuds easing a bit, sir,' his driver said. 'The markets were nervous about the wet weather causing disease, but in the past day or two the sunshine has allayed fears somewhat. The trouble is this bloody Roossian blockade, which makes folk scared.'

'Of course. The situation's very unstable. How about cigarettes?'

'Still dropping, sir. You know, on the Elsässer Strasse in Cologne the price of a packet of Luckies has gone right down from sixty old marks to five new ones in a matter of a week! Amazing! It'll kill the *Schwarzmarkt* over there in no time. Here in Berlin, of course, it'll depend on the political situation, and on sorting out the currency mess.'

Thwaite, a talkative Yorkshireman, was an excellent driver and could also, at any time, quote you the going rate on the black market for anything from Lucky Strikes to lubricating oil, Budweiser to beachballs. He insisted to Blessed that his fascination was harmless, just one of those vaguely self-improving hobbies, like bird-watching or collecting beer-mats.

'The *Schwarzmarkt*? Aye, I go down to the Tiergarten and keep me eyes and ears open, don't I? I mean, it's living history, something to tell me kids about in years to come . . . Have I ever dabbled?' Here he would chortle modestly. 'Well, it's like this: no matter how fond

102

you are of horseflesh, can you really enjoy a day at the races unless you've got a few bob riding on the results?'

After some soul-searching, the captain had decided to turn a blind eye. The soldiers of the occupation forces were ordinary, fallible men who had been made into little kings by their access to items such as cigarettes, nylons, chocolate, coffee, even humble cheese sandwiches, which to the German population were unattainable luxuries. Inevitably, most soldiers dabbled in the black market, exploiting this advantage to tempt Fräuleins, to lay up small and large fortunes, or—surprisingly often—to help German families of whom they had become fond. It wasn't small-scale black-marketeers that attracted Blessed's loathing, but the stealers of morphine and penicillin, the traders in human flesh, the hoarders of urgently-needed foods, the corrupt military office-holders who used their power over the German population to make fortunes. Despite his contacts, Thwaite was small-fry. In any case, there were a lot of advantages for Blessed in having the basic black-market information on tap without the need to employ agents, constantly consult the German police. He could just ask Thwaite, because, as experience had proved, his driver was rarely wrong.

'Thanks,' Blessed said. 'Admirably concise. Anything else of note? Is the Russian blockade causing any especially interesting problems?'

'Oh, aye, sir,' Thwaite said with a chuckle. 'There's bin the water sharks. See, some of the sharp operators thought there'd be a water panic, what with the prospect of no fuel for the pumpin' stations. So they started hoarding the H_2O. Rumours of the city running dry was spreading fast, so it looked like a good bet.'

Thwaite broke off to hurl routine army-of-occupation abuse at an old lady who appeared from out of the darkness, pushing a handcart piled high with belongings down the middle of the road. He hated having to slow down for anything, especially Germans.

'Anyway, then the Kommandatura puts a lot of blather in the papers,' he picked up his story once more. 'Y'know, about there being enough coal to pump up the water from here till doomsday, and blah-blah . . . Hey presto, your Berliners calm down, and our criminal masterminds are left holding bloody thousands of forty-gallon drums of Adam's Ale that's stopped being liquid gold and is just bloody water again!'

'It's good the public trusts the military authorities, of course.'

'Trust, be buggered!' Thwaite scoffed. 'The water sharks was right. There isn't any bloody fuel. The Kommandatura was lying.

103

If summat doesn't happen quick, there'll be no bloody water—not for the factories, not even for drinking. But the silly sod on the street believes the load of bollocks put out by the Kommandatura, so, far from getting rich, the water sharks get very, very wet.'

Blessed laughed. 'I hope you didn't get wet too.'

'Sir, you know me better than to think such a thing,' Thwaite said indignantly, with his usual magnificent ambiguity.

The Horch turned into the Donaldsons' driveway at four minutes past eleven. It was pretty late to turn up for a drink, but his hosts were well-known night-owls, so Blessed felt on safe ground. Dinners here never broke up before midnight, and were often still going strong at one or two in the morning. His expectation was proved right: several cars were parked outside the front door, and every light in the house seemed to be blazing, despite the blockade and the supposed electricity shortage. He wondered how the Berliners felt about such extravagance: the electricity being wasted by these expatriates on this night alone would enable a German family to cook meals for a month, perhaps more.

'Just picking up Mrs Blessed, are we, sir?' Thwaite asked.

'I'll be having a drink, for form's sake. I won't be too long. You must be tired.'

'Oh, no tireder than yourself, sir. But perhaps I'll get me head down for a while now, have a bit of a doze while I'm waiting.'

Blessed rang the bell. While he waited on the doorstep, an inspection of the parked cars confirmed that Redman's official Bentley was not among them. Perhaps he was still out somewhere, 'fact-finding'.

The door was opened by the Donaldsons' German butler, a corpulent, lizard-faced man named Guenther. Harry, who was fond of freaks, refused to sack him, though Guenther was famously rude to guests and usually got drunk during dinner along with everyone else. Tonight he was relatively sober, but still none too welcoming. Fortunately Donaldson was hovering behind him in the hall.

'Jim,' he said. 'Come in. What a wonderful surprise.'

'Surprise? Didn't Harriet tell you I'd promised to make it?'

Donaldson shrugged. He was wearing a dinner jacket with the bow tie loosened, holding a brandy-balloon. As usual, he had been drinking heavily, but—as was also usual—there was still a shrewd glint in his eyes.

'Well, yes, Jim. But Harriet also said you send messages these days and still don't turn up. I mean, I'm delighted she was wrong.

104

Have a good stiff drink, old boy. Got some catching up to do, eh?'

'I think I'll have a stern word with Harriet, too,' Blessed said, only half joking. 'Putting about rumours like that.'

The news agency man smiled sympathetically. 'You'll have to save the chastisement for later, though,' he said. 'Your missus has gorn orff home. Left about half an hour ago.'

'Did your chauffeur drive her?'

'No. Redman said he'd drop her off. He'd spent the evening charming the pants off the assembled company, especially the women, and regaling us all with the latest Westminster gossip. Then, typical bloody politician, he announces he has some paperwork to catch up on back at his hotel and an early start in the morning, so thank you and goodnight. Harriet said she was not feeling so good, and there was no point in waiting for you to turn up—' Donaldson wiggled his brandy glass expressively to show how it had been.

'I see. Oh, well,' Blessed said.

'You'll still have a drink with us, though, won't you? I want to hear some stories about *vice*, Jim. London desperately wants a piece on how vice and degeneracy continue to flourish in Berlin despite the blockade, to add colour to the political stuff, and you're the man to ask about that, aren't you?'

Blessed didn't answer that question, but he agreed to stay for a drink, because not to do so would have been to lose an impossible amount of face. To have chased off home after his wife would have been extremely un-Berlin. And so Guenther, smelling strongly of dry sherry, arm-wrestled him out of his coat, and into the dining room Blessed went.

As he came through the door, Gillie Donaldson, a busy redhead, was sailing towards him in imposing billows of tangerine silk. She kissed him on both cheeks. 'That lively wife of yours has gone, Jim, I'm afraid. Bailed out early,' she babbled. 'So we'll get you a glass of something lively instead. It's wonderful that you turned up at all. You'll get your reward in heaven. Now, you know everyone, don't you?'

Of course, Blessed did. He had a couple of drinks to quell his unease, and gossiped amusingly about the black market, and tarts, and nightclubs. He played the dashing SIB officer. He dished out a bit of harmless dirt of the kind that oiled the social wheels of occupation Berlin, until he could decently plead tiredness and leave. He didn't once mention Taffy Price and his Suzy.

When Blessed arrived back at the Villa Hellman, the place was in darkness except for the security light by the front door. He let himself in, stood in the hall, listening to the silence and feeling his exhaustion. Then a sound at the top of the stairs made him start, glance towards the first-floor landing.

His daughter, Daphne, was standing up there, wearing a cotton night-dress, gazing at him through the carved oak balustrades.

'Hello, Daddy,' she said. 'It's my birthday tomorrow.'

'I know it is,' Blessed said. 'Good evening to you, Daff. Or should I say good morning. Do you know what time it is, my girl?'

'Time for a kiss, of course.'

It was one of the private jokes that they had developed when he taught her to read the hands of a clock, count the seconds, minutes and hours. When she got bored of the lesson, she would simply answer his question, 'What time is it?', with 'Time for a kiss'.

Blessed laughed, climbed the stairs in his coat and hat and planted a kiss on her forehead, swept her into his arms and held her there. He could feel her breath on his shoulder, her small body against his chest. Here was his other world, the world that made it possible for him to deal with Floh and Mitchellson, the medical reports and the unimaginable wickedness of everything.

Daphne giggled. 'You smell of whisky and cigars, Dad. Have you been working?'

'Mostly. I went to Mr and Mrs Donaldson's house to fetch Mummy, but they told me she had come home.'

'She's not home yet. I know, because I've been awake, reading *Swallows and Amazons*, and I would've heard her. She always makes a lot of noise when she comes home from a dinner party.' Daphne paused thoughtfully. 'I wonder where Mummy has gone?'

Blessed didn't look at her. 'I expect she was delayed, sweetheart. Grownups have to be polite, you know. If people ask you in for a drink on the way home, you can't always refuse, no matter how much you'd like to.'

'I should say no, and I wouldn't care what they thought of me, if I was tired and I wanted to go home and have my dad tuck me into bed.'

Blessed kissed her again. 'Well, you're not a grownup, thank goodness,' he said. 'Now, I think you should be in bed at last. I'll tuck you in.'

Gisela appeared at the bottom of the attic stairs, pale with sleep.

'Hello, Captain Blessed,' she said, then frowned at Daphne. 'You are a very naughty girl. You promised me you would go straight to dreamland. This is not dreamland. This is your father and it is the middle of the night.'

Daphne looked defiant, then slightly shamed. 'I couldn't sleep.' She turned pleadingly to her father. 'I had a nightmare. About the little German boy who followed me home from ballet class.'

'This afternoon, was it?' Blessed said, smiling to hide his concern. 'Did he say something nasty?'

Daphne shook her head. 'No. But he was scruffy. And he *stared* at me.'

'I think he was just a beggar boy,' Gisela said quickly. 'I shooed him away, because we had nothing to give him. Then later, as we reached home, we noticed that he had returned. After we had entered the house I checked the street once more, but he was nowhere to be seen. Daphne lives a very sheltered life. Elsewhere in Berlin this happens all the time, and no one thinks twice about it.'

'Yes. Well, thanks, Gisela. I'll tuck Daff in. You go back to bed.'

'And so how was your day, Captain?' Gisela asked.

Blessed could not help but smile. It was a quite surprising question, expressed with an unexpected element of warmth.

'It was hard,' he said. 'Long and not very pleasant. A difficult case. I can't really . . .' Blessed shrugged, tried to indicate that he couldn't discuss things with Daphne present.

'I understand. Would you like a cup of tea or some cocoa? I can make you some while you are putting Daphne to bed.'

He shook his head. 'No thanks. I don't think Mrs Blessed is back yet, by the way, so don't worry if you hear someone come in later. It will be her.'

Gisela nodded unfathomably. 'Then goodnight, Captain.'

Blessed shooed Daphne up the stairs and along the hall, pausing to toss his coat and cap into the bedroom he shared with Harriet. Daphne's bedroom was no longer tidy, of course, despite Gisela's efforts that morning. Since then his daughter had managed to strew books on the floor, and leave her clothes in a heap.

'Daff, just tidy up the books and clothes,' Blessed said. 'Come on, I'll help you. Gisela went to a lot of trouble this morning making your room nice, you know.'

'Mummy says that's Gisela's job, though,' Daphne said.

'Well, it's not her only job,' Blessed said, ignoring the implications of his wife's casual snobbery. 'Do you like Gisela?'

'Yes. She's my friend, actually. She's the best nanny I ever had in my whole life ever.'

'Well, if she's your friend, you should remember that it helps her if you keep your room tidy. Then she doesn't get so flustered and tired.'

Daphne nodded, sighed, began to pick up the books.

'Beryl Watson says Gisela can't be my friend because she's German. Beryl says we have to be horrible to the Germans, because they're wicked. Because they were really, really beastly to the Jews and everybody.'

'Not all Germans are wicked, Daff,' Blessed said. 'Some were very wicked, and the rest of them are paying for that. But most, including Gisela, are just ordinary people. Your granny was German, for instance. Did you tell Beryl Watson that?'

'No.' Daphne looked down at her hands. 'I didn't want to tell her that. She's so horrible and so stupid she would have told the other girls and then . . . I don't know what then.'

They would have to talk about this one day, Blessed thought, but not now. He was too tired. 'Your granny was a good woman, Daff. You don't have to be ashamed of her, and I know you're not. One day the British and the Germans will be friends again, don't worry. Do you remember your granny?'

'I think so,' Daphne said vaguely, in the way children do when they can't really remember, but don't want to hurt anyone's feelings. 'I've seen the photograph of her holding me when I was little. But didn't the Germans kill her, Daddy?'

How did you explain all those layers of irony to an adult, let alone a child? Blessed said: 'In a way. But it was a war. They didn't mean to kill her. That's the trouble with war. That's why it's a bad thing.'

Daphne got under the sheets, paused, then pushed out her arms towards her father. They embraced, exchanged goodnight kisses.

'God bless Daddy and Mummy, and Gisela, and Grandpa Fiske,' she said, going through the list of the living before she started on the dead. 'Then bless Granny Fiske, and Granny Blessed and Grandpa Blessed. Did the Germans kill him too, Dad?'

'No. They didn't. He died when I was little.' Why was everything going wrong today? Why was even Daff asking the most awkward questions?

'Why did he die?'

'He got very ill. Look—'

'Promise you won't die when I'm little.'

108

'I'll try. I don't think I will.'

'Promise you won't die like Grandpa Blessed.'

'That I will promise you,' he said. 'I won't die like Grandpa Blessed.'

'Goodnight. It's my birthday very, very soon.'

'So it is. Goodnight, Daff.'

Blessed walked back towards his bedroom, decided he couldn't face it yet. He was exhausted but also oddly restless. He slipped off his shoes and padded cautiously down the stairs, so that Daphne had no excuse to get out of bed again to see what he was doing.

In the dining room, he found a tumbler, got out the bottle of White Horse from the drinks cupboard. He started by pouring a double, then topped it up to a treble, completed the recipe with Malvern water. As usual, the first sip tasted terrible, the second not so bad, the third absolutely wonderful.

He had just fetched himself another whisky into the drawing room when he heard a key turn in the latch. He could see his wife for some time before she saw him. As she came through the door she looked preoccupied. She closed the door, moved into the room, took off one red silk evening glove and slapped it against the other. Then she saw him and stopped. She was swaying visibly.

'Ah,' she said wryly. 'The hero has returned! Better late than never, as they say . . . Well, "Operation Stiffs" must have been *quite* gripping.'

'It didn't go all that well, actually. One of the villains got away. That's why I had to stay so late at the Knesebeckstrasse.' He swallowed some scotch. 'You're not exactly early yourself. Tell me about the dinner party.'

Harriet kicked off her shoes, made a sour-amused face. 'So-so,' she said. 'You know how the Donaldsons are. They do go on a bit. Once the brandy's come out, it's very hard to get away . . .'

'I arrived at the Donaldsons' just after eleven, Harriet. You weren't there.'

The blood seemed to drain from her face. Then she smiled in a strange, painful way. 'So . . . Blessed of the SIB strikes again. You led me on, you bastard, didn't you? Is that standard interrogation procedure, or what?'

'What do you think? You didn't have to lie.'

'I need a drink.' Harriet strode through to the dining room, banged around the cupboards and came up with a half-empty bottle of gin. 'This,' she said as she came into the drawing room again, 'is what I bloody well need. Short of a divorce, this is what I need, James Walter Blessed.'

She gave herself a large gin, mixed it with a small tonic. Blessed waited until she took a gulp, and then said: 'Did you go home with Redman, then?'

'Well, they obviously told you we left together.'

'Yes. But I want to hear it from you.'

Harriet met Blessed's eye and held it, then nodded slowly, as if she had come to a decision. 'You want to hear it from me that I'm fooling around with Larry,' she said. 'Well, it so happens that I am.'

Blessed felt surprisingly calm. Perhaps he had always known that this would happen sometime.

'Why?' he asked.

'That's the first thing anyone would want to know, I suppose. I don't know how to answer you.'

'Try.'

'OK. Because . . .' Harriet swallowed hard '. . . because I needed to remember what it was like to be excited. And actually it felt very good . . . When were you last really excited by something, Jim?' she asked. 'Apart, that is, from a pathetic black-marketeer caught in your headlights, or a corpse discovered on a bomb-site. That's how you get your jollies these days, is it?'

'No. It's my job.'

'Oh, for God's sake, who are you trying to fool? You love it!'

There was nothing much he could say to that, because really she was right. He loved his work. Or perhaps more accurately, he was in thrall to it—the same way he was to Harriet.

'You're bored, then,' he said.

'Frustrated would be closer to it, I think.'

'And are you in love with Larry Redman?'

Harriet shook her head. 'Not yet.'

'So do you want a divorce? Or will gin and adultery do for now?'

She giggled. 'You can be amusing when you want to,' she said, and to his surprise, sat down on the sofa next to him. 'I can only really be clear about the gin,' she said. 'There's nothing in the way between me and the gin. But between me and the other thing . . . well . . .' She held up the fingers of her left hand and began shakily to tick off the points with her right, the one that held the gin tumbler. 'There's . . . let's see . . . the marriage licence . . . and our daughter, Daphne . . . and there's, yes, I suppose there's still you . . .'

'None of those things seems to have deterred you in the end,' Blessed said.

'I'm sick of being an SIB widow, and I'm sick of endless cups of this and glasses of that with the other officers' ladies. I need a man to show me a good time. It's like medicine. Like fresh air.'

For the first time, Blessed felt the numbness within him give way to anger. 'I'm sorry,' he said. 'I'm almost middle-aged, you know. I have a job, I care a great deal about it. It takes a lot out of me. If you wanted a playboy, why didn't you marry one?'

'Ouch,' Harriet said, and laid her head back on the sofa frame until she was staring at the ceiling. She sighed: 'We didn't go to bed tonight, Larry and I. I just couldn't.'

'Have you slept with him before now?'

'A few times. When you were in Hamburg for that conference a few weeks ago. Larry doesn't feel especially marvellous about it,' she continued inexorably. 'I suppose that's why he wants me to leave you. So everything's more above-board.'

There were a lot of things Blessed could have said to that, but instead he sat still for some time with his eyes closed. His wife was very drunk, drunker than he had thought she was. He knew he should storm out, tell her he intended to ring his solicitor in the morning, or go round to Redman's hotel and horsewhip the man there and then. But his surge of anger was over. Now Blessed felt tired, and very old, and to blame for everything that had gone wrong. It was a familiar feeling.

At first when he felt her head on his lap, he thought she had rolled over and passed out. Then there was movement. He felt her fingers playing over his crotch, his thigh.

'I remember,' Harriet was saying. 'I remember in London, that last summer before the war, just after you'd qualified, before you decided to do your patriotic bloody duty and join the military bloody police. We were in bed all the time, couldn't help ourselves. How we fucked, Jim, how we fucked.' She ran the word over her tongue. 'I liked the secret, sexy life we led. I liked the way everyone else thought you were so solid and responsible, yet when we got our clothes off, my oh my . . .'

'Things were different then, Harriet,' he murmured. 'We were young. We had no responsibilities to anyone but ourselves—'

'Perhaps that's the sad truth. But I gave no false prospectus, Jim. You knew I was a handful. The difference was, a handful was what you wanted.'

This was another familiar feeling, independent of circumstance, amoral. Blessed laid his hand on her hair, gently holding her just where she was.

'Oh . . .' Harriet continued, and stroked his hardening penis. 'I wanted a handful as well, in my own way, and I got it. I still like to inspect it now and again.' She laughed throatily. One long-nailed finger and a thumb slid between the buttons of his trousers and deftly undid one, then a second and a third, continued until they were all opened and she could slide him out and circle him with her grasp. She kissed the tip of the shaft, cupped his balls in her other hand. 'I'd never have believed I could want anything else. And, in fact, you see there's still no one quite like you. Not Larry, not anyone . . .'

Without thinking, Blessed was unzipping the back of her dress, stroking the warm skin of her back, pulling the straps over her arms until she was naked from the waist up, pressed against his chest, her lips searching for his. He kissed her bruisingly hard, felt her excitement leap, knew that this was what she had wanted all along, and he just didn't care. He pulled her astraddle him, heedless of the precious nylons she was wearing, the danger that at any moment someone might come out onto the landing. They were back in that little room in Bayswater, in the summer of '39, Jim and Harriet. He touched her clitoris and she moaned, pushed him away for the moment. 'Come inside . . . hard . . .' Jim and Harriet . . .

When Harriet rolled off him, lay with her eyes open, staring into space, she was smiling.

She was still smiling when she padded over to where her bag lay, fished out two cigarettes and lit one for each of them. Jim and Harriet.

'I have a feeling we shouldn't have done that,' said Blessed, suddenly ashamed of himself.

'Why not?'

'We should have been considering what to do next. This is serious.'

'We did consider what to do next,' she said drily. 'And what is more, we darned well did it. And very nice it was too.'

'I meant, what to do about our marriage.'

'Ah. *That.*' Harriet took a long puff on her cigarette, shrugged herself back into her bra. 'A question: Will you leave the army?'

'No. Not yet.'

'That's what I thought you'd say.' Harriet got to her feet, took a couple of steps, then turned and faced him. 'I've booked myself on a plane to London,' she said. 'I did it this afternoon, and I intended

112

to tell you in the morning. Before you caught me out over the dinner party and left me no alternative but . . . as they say . . . immediate full disclosure.'

'Harriet, for God's sake—'

'Obviously I can't miss Daphne's birthday, so I'm going the day after tomorrow. And no, not with Larry, though doubtless I'll see him over there.' Harriet gestured impatiently with her cigarette. 'I'm not leaving you for him, you know. I just want time to think.'

Blessed realised that for all Harriet's addiction to the grand gesture, she was serious. There was a hard edge to her voice, a determination that would outweigh her guilt, probably overrule any objection he could think of.

'What about Daphne?' he said.

'Is that all you can think of? Well, your question's easily answered: You and Gisela can look after her. She'll be perfectly all right. Other mothers I know leave their children with German nannies, sometimes for weeks on end. Daff doesn't need to be told why I'm going away. Not yet.'

'There's a crisis on here. Maybe she'd be better off in England.'

'I spoke to Larry about that, and to a heavyweight staff colonel. They both say there are no immediate plans to evacuate the children of British servicemen. Contrary to all the hysteria in the press, those who know consider a shooting war with Russia to be extremely unlikely.' She met his gaze. 'I'm not so irresponsible as you'd like to think, you know.'

'You seem to have it all worked out.' He was damned if he was going to beg. And damned if he was going to explode, either. 'Sewn up tight.'

'I suppose so. The fact remains, I've got a seat—it took some arm-twisting to get it, I can tell you—and I'm darned well going. Alone.'

'This isn't the right time.'

'It'll never be the right time.'

'Then damned well go, then!'

'Try stopping me!'

Blessed knew they could go on and have one of those desperate, ridiculous, back-and-forth conversations that ended either in tears or violence. What weakness, what old internal injury, kept him wanting her, made him always come back for more? Find the wound, you find the truth. Find the disease . . . He wanted to tell her about the pathologist's report on Price and the woman. He wanted to confess about his father and his mother, but instead he forced himself to calm down and to say, stiffly and coldly, 'Listen, there's obviously nothing more to discuss. For the meantime, we'll keep up appearances, for Daff's sake. Until we know exactly where we stand.'

Harriet nodded. 'All right by me, I suppose.'

Blessed looked at the time. 'Christ. It's after two. I'm due at the Knesebeckstrasse in a few hours to continue with those interrogations —*and* I've an important call to make on the way there.'

His job was like an iron chain that tugged at him, and he always had to go where it demanded. His job was his self-justification, and his defence against his secret inner demon. Inspector Weiss summoned him, flanked by Kelly, and could not wait; and Mitchellson and Floh; and the mysterious Dr Schmidt: None of them could wait for Captain Blessed to tidy up his life.

'Well, that's that then, isn't it, Captain?' Harriet said. 'We wouldn't want to let any of your professional colleagues down, would we?' She moved to the foot of the stairs. 'Meanwhile, I'm not at all sure about the marriage, but thanks awfully for the fuck.'

The little watcher outside the window shifted his weight very carefully from one foot to the other, anxious not to make a sound among the woody undergrowth. He was sweating, still excited after having witnessed the coupling on the sofa. He continued to stare into the brightly-lit room. The man was sitting there alone now, nursing another whisky.

The man's clothes were still unbuttoned, his neat officer's hair mussed; he didn't seem to care about any of that any more. Mummypie had gone upstairs—the tall, drunk woman with the fair hair and the white naked skin, who had climbed onto this man, had fucked, oh yes, fucked—this was one English word the watcher knew only too well!—and then afterwards had *scolded* him. So, this woman was the mother of Daff-nee, the girlie he had followed home from her school on Boss-Kind's orders. And the man left downstairs, Kepten Blessed, was the girlie's father. He was also the Tommy officer Boss-Kind had told him to watch, because he was a danger to the safety of the Kinder. He must be *dealt with* somehow, Boss-Kind said . . .

The three of them—Kepten Blessed, Mummypie and girlie Daff-nee—were what Hats called 'a family'. So many fine things they had in this house of theirs. Benno longed to touch and . . . yes, *take* what he saw. Eck, but their life seemed frightening at the same time it was fascinating.

From the way Kepten Blessed kept looking at his watch and then at the remains of his whisky, the watcher knew that soon the Kepten would follow Mummypie to bed. Benno himself was weary, sore from walking and stiff from keeping still. It was time for him to find his way back to the Bernauer Strasse, to the Kinder Garden. It was time to report what he had seen to the Boss.

TEN

IT WAS VERY LATE—somewhere around half-past three in the morning—when Benno arrived back at the Kinder Garden. This was despite
the fact that some friendly-drunk Hersheys returning from a party out
on the Havel had given him a lift as far as the Grossmarkt in their jeep.
In their atrocious dance-bar German, they'd called him a 'little sausage'
(*hey, komm-ah hay-er, kline worst-shayne* . . .), and treated him like a
pet, passing him from lap to lap, plying him with cigarettes and slabs of
chocolate. Benno was still exhilarated from all that contact, still hearing
the Americans' slow, well-fed voices. He was still humming tunes
from their car radio, courtesy of the American Forces Network—its
fast-talking, gloriously incomprehensible DJs had played some of
his favourites, including Hoagy Carmichael's 'Stardust', and Glenn
Miller's 'Pennsylvania Six-Five-Thousand', and the one on his lips this
very moment, the Andrews Sisters' 'Rum and Coca Cola' . . .

> 'Singin' rum and co-ca co-la
> For both mu-thah and daw-dah . . .'

'Hey, Benno!'

'The Wonder?'

Benno had just closed the street door behind him when he heard the
familiar voice. He could make out the faint halo of an electric light at
the top of the cellar stairs. It must be the time for the Bernauer Strasse's
electricity to be switched on, its pathetic hour or two of rationed power.
Maybe for once the lung-soup would be hot.

'You beddabelieve it is the Wonder, oh yes.'

They ran together and collided in the hallway. Benno smacked the
Wonder hard in the chest, even though his friend was so small and

116

skinny, and the Wonder smacked him back. They staggered around the hallway for some time, arms on each other's shoulders, laughing wheezily. As soon as he had recovered his breath, Benno launched into an account of his evening's watching work.

'Well, first I follow Kepten Blessed's little girlie home through those neat Spandau streets, just like Boss-Kind told me to,' he said with a grin. 'Girlie and Nannypie . . .' He mimicked Blessed's daughter and Gisela coming home from Daphne's ballet class. He made the girl skip, the woman wiggle in an exaggeratedly sexual fashion, to show that Gisela was attractive. 'After dark I find a per-fect hideout yes *Versteck* in some bushes near that Kepten's big villa. I see those Hats, I watch them come, I watch them go . . . Late at night, home comes the Kepten. Whisky-walk!' Benno made like a flat-footed Englishman, rolling slightly. 'Later still, *nach Mitternacht*,' he continued, 'we see little Mummy's gin-walk.' Harriet was re-created for the Wonder, tottering on her high heels. Benno dropped his voice, leered. 'And now I tell you what happened when they got together—fighting . . . *ach scheiss* and fucking . . .'

Benno opened his palms to receive the applause. To his disappointment, the Wonder merely nodded his head in a superior kind of way.

'Wassamatter, Wonder? You don't wanna hear what Kepten and Mummypie get up to when their little English girlie is fast asleep?'

The general principle of what James and Harriet Blessed had got up to on the sofa at the Villa Hellman was no mystery to Benno or the Wonder; neither of them could remember a time when they hadn't known what men do with women—or, for that matter, with other men. The Kinder recalled vividly incidents from the Red Army's infamous rape of Berlin—the time they called 'Point Null', or 'the *Frau, komm!* Russkie-terror' from the Ivans' cry when they came looking for women—and since then they had seen soldiers and girls doing it in cellars, on bomb-sites, in backrooms where they could be observed through slits and cracks. Ruins provide little privacy. All the same, Benno was surprised that his friend showed quite as little interest as he did.

'You getting like Boss-Kind? You don' wanna hear 'bout that kind of stuff?' he repeated.

'Nah. But you know we had such a *big* time with Boss-Kind,' the Wonder said. He grinned lazily. 'Wait till I tell you about the Tiergarten operation. Ready to listen?'

'Any time. You know me,' said Benno, hiding his irritation.

'OK . . . What happens in the Tiergarten is like this: there is an ambush by undercover Tommies,' the Wonder drawled. 'Two Hats are captured. But a third Hat, he runs away, and in the end he escapes—because Boss-Kind himself tripped up the Tommy who was after him with his pistol, getting ready to shoot him . . .' The Wonder tensed his fingers into the shape of a cocked gun, clicked tongue against palate to simulate its firing, and winked one little eye. 'You wanna know what happened next, eh, Benno?' he asked slyly.

'Sure. Fine. OK.'

'The Hat who escaped from Kepten Blessed and his Tommies is staying *here*, Benno,' the Wonder whispered. 'Here in the Kinder Garden!'

'A Hat?' Benno repeated. 'Staying in our Kinder Garden?' He was lost for words. Hats were never allowed in the Kinder Garden. Upstairs, maybe. That was where Boss-Kind met adults, including the gangster, Riese, who had become his great ally. But in the Garden itself? Only Doktor Barnhelm, who didn't count.

'Not right in with all of us,' the Wonder admitted. 'This Hat—the Boss calls him Bigman—will sleep in Boss-Kind's Lair. His Hat name is Panewski. But the name that Boss-Kind has given him is right, because big is what he is. Eck, this Bigman-Panewski is also an ugly asshole, I tell you, Benno . . .'

'And . . . what do the other Kinder think, Wonder?'

'Boss-Kind says this Hat is special,' the Wonder answered evasively. 'So it is all right. He tol' me to wait here for you, bring you straight to the Lair. He wants to hear you report on your work in Spandau, watching Kepten Blessed and all.'

Benno was hurt by the realisation that the Wonder had waited up for him only on Boss-Kind's orders. Benno suddenly felt very, very alone.

He shrugged and smiled. What else was there to do? He tramped obediently down the stairs after the Wonder, who was still burbling on about the events in the Tiergarten, about all those undercover Tommies, and all the rest of the action, beside which Benno's achievement was that of a pathetic Peeping-Tom. *Best of all*, the Wonder kept reminding him, his voice honey-thick with hero worship, as they picked their way through the trash in the cellar, ducked inside the cupboard and waited at the thick shelter-doors for the guards to answer their knock, *Ach scheiss the best of all, how Boss-Kind himself tripped the Tommy who had aimed his pistol at the fugitive, and helped this Bigman-Panewski to flee, and finally to reach the haven of the Kinder Garden . . .*

As they passed through the guardroom, Benno heard Kinder laughing, the radio playing swing, and smelled soup simmering on the stove—everyone getting maximum advantage from the power-supply before the authorities shut it off again. He would have lingered, but the Wonder dragged him on, kept them moving to Benno's appointment with the Boss and his dangerous guest.

Boss-Kind's Lair was set apart from the rest of the Kinder Garden, along a narrow corridor off the guardroom. It was a bare cube of a room, in wartime a storage area for gas masks and other lifesaving equipment. The corridor had once led past it and up to a separate entrance on the street, through which Berliners caught in the Bernauer Strasse by an air raid had been able to enter the shelter. This access had been bricked over shortly after the war, leaving a concrete cul-de-sac.

Along the corridor Benno and the Wonder trotted, oblivious to the damp, unhealthy air, because after all this was home to them. A weak bulb shining from a fixture in the ceiling revealed their way; at the very limit of its light, they arrived outside Boss-Kind's Lair. The Wonder glanced for an instant at Benno in that peculiar, wide-eyed way he had. Then, taking a deep breath, he knocked slowly on the narrow steel door, twice.

They waited. After a while, the door opened, and Granit was there on the threshold, filling the narrow entrance with his bulk.

'Eck, Wonder, you brought Benno at last,' he said.

As Granit turned back into the smoke-filled Lair, Boss-Kind's voice declared from somewhere inside and out of sight: 'Oh yes, Granit, you bring that Kind Benno in here to see me and Bigman. You do that *now*!'

The Lair was eight feet by six, with a bed in the corner covered by a sheet and a blanket. On a tiny table sat Boss-Kind's wind-up phonograph, to give him music when the electricity was off. A much-repaired armchair and another, larger, table filled the rest of the room—literally, so that when the Wonder and Benno stepped inside there was nowhere to go.

The Bigman character was sitting on the bed. Boss-Kind was sprawled in the armchair. He got to his feet, gave everyone his captive cat's stare, then snapped his fingers. 'Out, Granit!' he commanded. 'The Lair is too full.'

Granit looked resentful, but he took the hint and ducked out. In the brief silence that followed, he could be heard plodding off down the corridor.

'You go too, Wonder,' Boss-Kind said. 'The room is still too crowded, and I don't need you for now.' Because the Wonder looked so sad, he added quietly, almost kindly: 'Our days are always busy, so maybe yes maybe you should get some sleep. I think tomorrow we gotta start early again.'

So the Wonder also disappeared. This left Benno alone with the stranger and Boss-Kind, who promptly sat down again in his wreck of an armchair. Benno squatted down on his haunches on the damp floor.

'This is Bigman,' Boss-Kind said, indicating the man on the bed.

Getting his first proper look at Panewski through the swirling clouds of cigarette smoke, Benno saw a flat face unimproved by a broken nose, hard eyes—the left one slightly wandering—a torn black windcheater tossed over almost freakishly broad shoulders.

'Bigman,' Boss-Kind continued, 'Bigman is staying here for just one night. We helped him out of a little trouble in the Tiergarten. Riese knows him, and also the man, his partner, who was captured by the undercover Tommies—this I am sure the Wonder tol' you . . .' He flashed an ingratiating grin at the man on the bed, something Benno had never seen him do before. 'Any friend of Riese's is a friend of ours, that is true! Eh, Benno? Eh?'

Benno let the Boss wait for just a second and then grunted, 'Eck . . . oh yes, Boss-Kind. One-hundred-per-cent, yes.'

His reason told him to trust the Boss on this one: Dealing with the world of Hats like this was best left to the Boss.

'So tell me 'bout Spandau, 'bout this Kepten Blessed, Benno.'

Benno went through his routine. Boss-Kind watched him carefully, sitting like a statue with only his eyes alive. Bigman-Panewski also listened.

When Benno had finished, he waited. Panewski seemed amused by the story of the sexual encounter, but Boss-Kind was staring into space, like he was lost in a dream, far away. Recently the Boss had become so changeable, sometimes coldly efficient and level-headed, other times impossible to reckon on, capable of anything, truly terrifying.

'You finished with me now, Boss-Kind?' Benno asked finally. 'I am hungry and tired. The soup is hot, it smells good, and the electric power is on . . .'

No answer. Even Bigman-Panewski was starting to look a little confused. Finally he spoke. 'The kid's asleep on his feet, Boss-Kind,' he said. 'And to be honest, I could do with some shut-eye too.' He ground his cigarette out on the floor with one hefty foot as if liquidating a small but dangerous animal. 'For Christ's sake, he told you what you wanted to know, didn't he?'

Bigman's accent was pure Berlin street-Deutsch, Benno heard. A ton of gravel had been raked into his voice by thirty years' heavy smoking, which had also turned his teeth to brown pointed palings.

Boss-Kind nodded. Then he began to recite, beating time with one hand on his thigh:

> Russkie Froggie Yank and Tommy bet
> You can have that Fräulein for a cigarette
> But just watch out while you dip your prick
> 'Cos my knife is sharp and my arm is quick . . .

'You gotta knife, Bigman?' he asked suddenly, uncoiling from his chair and getting to his feet. 'You use a knife?'

Panewski was on his criminal mettle now, with his reputation to think of. 'I can handle myself,' he said. 'I can use a knife as well as a gun, or my fists . . .' He held up his big hams of hands and flexed them, then clenched them menacingly.

'You got a weapon *now*, Bigman?' Boss-Kind continued in the deceptively conversational tone he had adopted. ''Cos you know, it's good, even vital for you to be able to defend yourself. This world is a *terrible* place for an unarmed man.'

Panewski's eyes narrowed with suspicion. He looked dangerous. And very big. Benno hoped Boss-Kind knew what he was doing. Maybe he was playing some game of his own, or maybe he was on orders from Riese. In either case, Benno wished himself away from here, in the bunker with the banter and the company and—most especially—the hot soup. The electricity would soon die. He was wondering whether to feign a fainting-fit when Boss-Kind ducked, reached under his chair and pulled out a large cloth. From the way he handled it, it contained precious and weighty goods.

'Well, Bigman?' he said. 'You can tell me. You gotta weapon?'

Panewski shook his head. 'No weapon,' he admitted.

'I knew this already,' said Boss-Kind with a grin. 'I saw you throw away a knife in the Tiergarten, because you were scared the Tommies would catch you, and if you carried that knife and they found it, then there would be many oh so many years in jail just for that offence alone . . .'

Suddenly he plonked the cloth down in Panewski's large lap, and

121

stepped back. Boss-Kind gestured at the cloth, like a parent encouraging a child to open a Christmas present.

Panewski looked at him once more with suspicion, then shrugged his shoulders and carefully opened up the cloth. Benno recognised the weapons immediately. He snatched his breath in his amazement. They were the Boss's two most valued treasures. These were solid brass knuckledusters, but their peculiarity was that each had been fitted with a sharp blade that closed in like a jacknife. The weapons were savage enough when wielded with the blade closed; with it unclasped they were lethal. Benno had seen several criminals with them—they were popular among the wild Polish and Russian DPs, war-brutalised refugees who had taken to crime in Berlin rather than be sent back to a future under Stalin. In fact, as he recalled, it was from a Pole or a Ukrainian that Boss-Kind had first acquired them shortly after Point Null. Benno had only ever seen him use them with the blade closed—during one of the quick, vicious robberies known as *Spritzen* which had sustained the Kinder Garden in the early years—and even then they had wreaked terrible, bloody damage. All the rumours said that Boss-Kind opened up the blade when he was out on Riese's business, but the main point was, these knuckleduster-blades were oh-so precious to the Boss. This must be Riese's orders, Benno told himself. What else could explain such an extreme act of sacrifice?

Panewski was still staring at the weapons when Boss-Kind said: 'You choose, Bigman. I give you one of these. Pick them up,' he urged. 'See which you like best . . .'

Panewski obeyed. He examined each blade, tested each clasp, carefully and thoughtfully, like the professional he was.

'I don't know,' he said doubtfully. 'If I get caught with a weapon . . . I'm well-known. My record's on the police files. They got a mug-shot, dabs, everything . . . You're young,' Panewski muttered. 'What do *you* know about being on the run?'

'Well no, we never got caught yet, it's true, Bigman,' Boss-Kind said in a double-edged fashion that passed way over Panewski's head. 'But the offer of the special blade is real. It's up to you, yes up to you . . .'

'You got a gun? With a piece, maybe it would be worth it, because I could shoot my way out of trouble, even against a patrol . . .'

Boss-Kind shook his head.

Panewski thought for a moment. 'Then no,' he said. 'Thanks, but no. And thanks to Riese too. Why Riese and you are helping me, I don't know, but I'm glad you got me out of the Tiergarten. Those Brits meant business.'

With a shrug, then with a butler's flourish and a craftsman's care, Boss-Kind leaned down and folded the cloths back over the knuckleduster-blades. 'Up to you,' he said. 'Bigman, you are experienced.' He put the bundle back where he had found it, his manner still respectful and calm.

'Yeah. And the other thing I know is, I'm going to be knackered if I don't get some shut-eye, kids. What's the plan for the morning? Where am I supposed to meet Riese's boys?'

'You leave at seven-thirty. For a secret place on the far outer side of the Russkie-Sector. There Riese's boys will pick you up and escort you to the complete safety of the Russkie-Zone itself. This secret place is on a lake. We can use it whenever we like . . . Benno knows it, eh, Benno?'

The sound of his name brought Benno back to consciousness. After the initial excitement of seeing the knuckleduster-blades produced, he had become bored and had given into his exhaustion.

'Eck,' he drawled. 'You know, Boss-Kind, I just dozed off, oh yes. No sleep, no soup, *ach scheiss* you surprised?'

Boss-Kind smiled, sat back down in his armchair. 'Maybe not, Benno. But you know I was telling Bigman 'bout the lake, and I told him you—especially you, 'cos you are a long-time Kind—you know where it is, also how to get there. I told him the Kinder-truth, eh?'

Benno nodded. 'Oh yes, I know that old house by the Grosser Müggelsee.'

'You see?' Boss-Kind said with a grin. 'You see, Bigman? Good, eh?'

'I don't care, kid. I don't care if he knows the fuckin' way or his three-times table, so long as I get where I need to go.'

'Just the two of you,' Boss-Kind said, ignoring Panewski's irritation. 'Father and son go to the lake! No patrol, no Russkie or Froggie Hi-Hat, will stop you at the sector border or on the way eastwards, because you know *ach scheiss* daddy and his boy will look so *in-no-cent!*' Boss-Kind cackled loudly, so neat and hilarious did he find his solution to tomorrow's problem. 'Just the two of you. Benno will guide you to the lake to meet Riese's boys, Bigman! Better, far better than a big gang!'

'Me . . . with Bigman? Are you crazy, Boss-Kind?'

'This you will do, Benno. This you will do for the Kinder Garden,' Boss-Kind snarled, snapping into dictatorial mood. 'We all live for the

Kinder Garden. You, Benno, you live for the Kinder Garden too.'

There was a moment's silence. Benno felt sick. His stomach was turbulent with hunger and fear.

'Eck, Boss-Kind, you're right. I do everything for the Kinder Garden. *Live* for it?' Benno pulled the nastiest face he could manage in his depleted condition. 'Soon,' he said, 'soon, I think, I *die* for the gadawlmighdy Kinder Garden, or *what*?'

ELEVEN

HIS DEAD FATHER'S FACE, last seen when Blessed was eight years old, was collapsed, eaten by sores. A worm reared out of his open mouth. The whore was pictured as blonde and blowsy like the popular fantasy, though of course he had never seen her at all. Her belly and breasts crudely and temptingly sculpted by a tight red dress, she sat astride a chair and watched his father suffer, laughing fit to die. But then she lifted her skirt, revealing that *the female had almost certainly also been infected* . . .

Still trapped in his dreaming world, James began to run. From his father, from the woman . . . faster . . . faster . . .

Then he was leaping down that wooded hillside in Lebanon. Jamail's men were firing from the heights, but their missiles were arrows with rubber tips, and Blessed felt all-conquering as he tumbled towards the Dodge truck. And there behind the truck stood Harriet and Daphne, waving and smiling, dressed in white frocks and gloves. He kept running, feeling the arrows bouncing off his shoulder-blades. Nothing could harm him. Only when he got closer did he realise that Harriet was turning away with an expression of disgust. So, Daphne was waiting for him alone. She, at least, was still smiling in welcome. *What did he care about Harriet when such a pure, unconditional love was his?* Blessed arrived by the truck, was reaching out for his daughter. But now *Daphne was looking up at him and screaming in terror* . . .

The first nightmare was recurring; it had haunted Blessed's sleep since childhood. The second had never visited him before last night. It was the more harrowing by far, and was still disturbingly fresh in his mind the next morning as, with the time approaching eight o'clock, Thwaite drove him towards Mariendorf, in the American sector, to call on his aunt and cousin.

They were following the perimeter of the American airfield at Tempelhof. The only visible evidence of the famous air-lift was a larger than usual number of covered trucks on the service roads, and on the apron groups of German labourers in blue overalls.

Blessed sighed. It must, he told himself, have been the revelation of his wife's adultery that had lent the dream such awful vividness. And maybe the effect of those whiskies. He had made quite a dent in the bottle of White Horse before finally staggering upstairs to the newly-delineated no-man's-land of his marriage bed.

Daphne had bounced onto that same bed at six-thirty, happy and full of beans, despite her own late bedtime the previous night. And why not, when she had a nurse's outfit and a dolls' hospital sent specially from England? Even when Harriet had broken the news that she was going to England 'for a week or two', their daughter had simply nodded and said, 'Gisela will look after me. And Dad, of course.' Harriet had acted entirely according to their agreement, smiling and laughing and giving no hint that there was anything wrong.

The Horch took a right-hand turn. Blessed's German aunt, his *Tante Lotte*, had been a central and beloved fixture in his life ever since he could remember. Her old flat had been comfortable in the rather fussy Biedermeier style, filled with accumulated family treasures and furniture. Her sister, Blessed's mother, had been exiled by her foreign marriage, then both Plenzendorf parents had died, and finally her husband had been killed, leaving Lotte alone there to bring up her little son, Gerhard. Somehow she had managed to keep the flat on; its rooms had housed a homely little museum of family memorabilia, with Lotte as its fiercely protective curator. That comfortingly familiar place was where Blessed had stayed during many visits with his mother, and where he had lodged during the year he spent in Berlin as a young man. The flat had been destroyed during an Allied air raid in the spring of 1944, along with almost everything it contained. Of course, Lotte's story was not unique. Resilient and cheerful, thrifty and tough, she had preserved her world and her family's treasures against the ravages of war, revolution, inflation, slump and Nazism. History's last, cruel joke on her (and the rest of the old German middle class) had been for every priceless thing to be blown away one night, at the whim of some terrified boy bomb-aimer from Barnsley or Baltimore whose only concern had been to jettison his explosive load and get back safely to his best girl.

And so Lotte moved to the unfamiliar district of Mariendorf, where the hard-pressed municipal authorities had offered what she always described as 'simple but perfectly adequate accommodation'. Actually, her new home was a cramped, poorly-heated cellar, underneath a patched-up tenement block backed by factories and gas-holders. On his return from the an American POW cage a year previously, Gerhard had joined her there. Blessed and his cousin had never liked each other, though of course they had been forced to play together as children. After Gerhard had become an ardent Nazi—which he remained to this day—the relationship had cooled even further. If it hadn't been for the fact that Blessed loved Tante Lotte, and that this love manifested itself in a regular supply of food parcels, there would have been no need for the cousins to meet at all. Today was different, though. Today the captain had brought a kilo of coffee for Lotte, but his real business was with cousin Gerhard.

As usual, it was Lotte who answered his knock on the peeling, plywood cellar door. She was sixty-four, but despite that, and all the hardships of recent years, her eye was still bright and her movements brisk and lively. The elder by five years, his aunt had always been rounder, heavier than her sister, but postwar privations had slimmed her down, caused her fatty disguise to drop away and the family resemblance to reassert itself. There were the same proud Plenzendorf cheekbones that Blessed had inherited, the same even features, dominated by startling violet-blue eyes, that must have attracted his father to his mother in that drawing-room in long-ago Imperial Berlin. Now when Blessed saw Lotte, it was almost as if his mother had come back to life.

'*Chames*,' she greeted him, beaming with pleasure. '*Chames*, how *wonderful* to see you.'

Blessed submitted to Lotte's embrace and a kiss on each cheek, then was led inside into the first of the two dark cellar rooms. As with hundreds of thousands of Berliners, this was what his aunt's and Gerhard's once-comfortable world had come to. Of course, everything was impeccably clean. Lotte's bed was in the front room, and Gerhard's 'room' was marked off by a bead curtain that Blessed had known since his childhood visits. (How and why had she saved it from her apartment when so many other, more wonderful things had been reduced to ashes? And when would he ever pluck up the courage to ask her?)

127

When the coffee was formally presented, Lotte said, 'Oh you shouldn't, it is not necessary,' but she clapped her hands together delightedly, like a young girl. Then her face fell. 'Chames, it is not possible to have electric light or make coffee for your breakfast. Since this Russian blockade, we are back to how it was in forty-five. The electricity and gas now come on in the middle of the night. We have to get up from bed and cook our potatoes and do our ironing and our everything, and it is two o'clock in the morning. Imagine.'

'I've already had some breakfast, Lotte. You know there are no problems where we are. Soon . . . well, eventually things will get better.'

Lotte nodded. 'I have been saving candles. I will fetch one . . .'

'Please, no. I can see perfectly well. I know how hard it is to get candles. Don't waste them.'

'Then what can I do to make this morning special, Chames? You are here. How long has it been since the last time?'

'Easter, I think it was. I'm sorry, Lotte. I've been so damned busy, and there's been conferences, including a trip to Hamburg . . .' *While I was away on that one, my wife had sex with a member of the British government, by the way,* a voice inside his head persisted, supplying Blessed with the truth he could never share, or at least not with Lotte. 'There'll be more time when the crisis is over,' he said, hardly hesitating at all. 'Today, all I want is the pleasure of your company for a few minutes. And a chat with Gerhard. I need his help.'

'Ach. He is still asleep. It is always the same with him,' Lotte said, glancing towards the curtain. 'Ger-hard!' she called out. 'It's your cousin, Chames! He has come to visit us, so get yourself out of bed!' She turned back to Blessed with a sigh. 'And how is Harriet, and how is little Daphne?'

As usual, Blessed's aunt pronounced his daughter's name as 'Deff-nee'. He and Daff made a joke of that.

'Fine,' he said. 'Flourishing,' he added, compounding the falsehood.

'Harriet still hates Berlin?'

'She's going to England tomorrow, in fact. For a week or two. She needs a break.'

Lotte looked him over with the shrewdness born of simplicity. 'You be careful how you treat Harriet, Chames. All she really wants, you know, is a nice house, some money, a few comforts . . . So why do you still play soldiers like this? You could go back to the law, become a successful advocator . . .'

128

'Solicitor. I was trained as a solicitor, just like my uncle. It was his idea, remember?'

Lotte nodded, either oblivious to Blessed's touch of sarcasm or choosing to ignore it. 'Yes. A lawyer is a figure in society. Harriet, she needs a position. It is something she was born to, Chames. You are . . . just a *policeman*,' she said, as if still incredulous at the humble career he had chosen. 'If you were a captain in the Royal King's Life Guards—better still, a major or a colonel—of course, it might be different.'

'Perhaps.' Blessed glanced furtively at his watch. He hated to cut short his time with Lotte, but he had a full day, including, he hoped, an appearance at Daphne's birthday tea, and the talk with Gerhard might take a while, because Gerhard could be very difficult.

'You have not changed since you lived with me. Always so secret, so impossible to know what you were really thinking. I never understood the reasons why you did things . . .'

'I'm not denying you're probably right about Harriet, Tante Lotte.'

'Ach, you are your father's son!' Lotte scolded him affectionately. 'Your dear father also had no ambition. Then he died so young, leaving your mother with so little . . .'

Blessed wondered if Lotte had ever heard the truth about his father's death. Probably not. She was a kindly woman, but even she would not have been able to summon up that vestigial 'dear' if she had known. Of course, she needn't worry that Daphne would be left destitute if he died suddenly, as his father had; Harriet's trust fund, and Sir Hugh Fiske's will, would leave her very comfortable. That was the big difference in the situations. Not the only difference, but the main practical one.

'I'm sorry, Tante Lotte,' he said with an impatient glance at the bead curtain. 'If that cousin of mine won't come out of there, I'll have to go in and get him . . . England needs Gerhard, I'm afraid.'

'If you tell him that, he will run a mile. He is in an English-hating mood at the moment, I don't know why.'

'All right, then *I* need him.'

'Nevertheless, Chames, it's better you leave him to me. I know how to handle Gerhard,' Lotte said with a sigh. She turned again and called in a loud, commanding voice: 'Ger-hard! Jump up, boy!'

The 'boy' appeared five minutes later out of the gloom at the far rear of the cellar. Gerhard was thirty-three, once flaxen-haired but now prematurely grey; once a fine-featured, almost beautiful youth, now petulant and worn. He had been an enthusiastic Nazi since the

129

age of seventeen, right through medical school and on into his war service, mostly on the Eastern Front but, luckily for him, with an armoured division in the Ardennes during the war's last months. He had been captured during the fighting around Aachen, and had been suspected, though never convicted, of participating in 'flying court-martials' that had carried out on-the-spot trials and executions of civilians and soldiers suspected of 'defeatism'. As a result the Americans had interrogated him thoroughly and kept hold of him for more than two years. But in the end their righteous anger, so intense and all-condemning in the hour of victory, had died down, as righteous anger does—especially when there are other things to worry about, like the Russian threat. So they had released Gerhard to go home to his mother, with whom he was now living for the first time since leaving home to begin his medical studies.

Blessed extended his right hand. Gerhard, being at heart still a well-brought-up boy of the pre-war German middle class, shook it.

'Good morning, Gerhard.'

'Good morning, James.'

Gerhard prided himself on his correct pronunciation of Blessed's Christian name, which was difficult for most Germans. Not for Gerhard the cosy 'Chames' by which Lotte always addressed him.

'You are on another charity visit to the poor, starving Germans, I see.' Gerhard patted his pockets, waited until Blessed supplied him with a Senior Service from a freshly-opened packet of twenty and lit it for him. He dragged hungrily at the precious Virginia tobacco without more than a cursory nod of thanks. 'You want to talk to me, I hear. What about?'

'And we thought you were asleep in there . . . We'll discuss it a bit later. How are you, anyway?'

Gerhard smiled crookedly to indicate suffering bravely borne. He wore an old ski-sweater that carried a faint aroma of sweat, and a patched pair of corduroy slacks. His hair was long and dirty. Few would have believed that this man was a qualified Doctor of Medicine from the University of Marburg.

'Life was maybe getting gradually better until this last week and this blockade. Now—but at least we have our nice new money,' Gerhard said sarcastically. He scrabbled in his pocket and fished out a new but already heavily-crinkled one Deutschmark note. 'We have lost all our old, worthless savings yet again. This is the fate of us Germans, just like the inflation in the twenties, except now it is by order of the western allies, not the Reichsbank.'

130

'That is unfair, Gerhard,' Lotte protested. 'This trouble in the past few years was Hitler's and Germany's fault. Now the Allies are trying to help us—don't you see those aeroplanes flying over us, day and night, coming in to land at Tempelhof? They are filled with food and fuel for us, the people of Berlin. You should be ashamed of yourself, talking to your cousin like that.'

Although his aunt was saying all this mostly for Blessed's benefit, she was actually right about the currency, and right about the airlift. In the parts of Germany occupied by the three western powers, a currency reform had been carried through the previous week. In an overnight coup the old, virtually valueless Reichsmark (which was also valid in the Russian Zone) had been declared invalid and a new Deutschmark introduced. The reform hadn't extended to the Russian Zone. The Soviets had called it a 'provocation' and had hastily printed their own, separate 'reformed' currency, but in the West everyone was able to exchange sixty old for sixty new marks, whose value was guaranteed by the Allies.

Money was worth something again, at least in the 'Trizone' of West Germany. The problem was, with the country dividing into a capitalist west and a communist east, what would happen in its old capital city? The Soviets were insisting that only the new East-Mark was valid there. Would the western powers have the courage to make the Deutschmark (West) the only valid currency in their sectors of Berlin, tying West Berlin's economic system to West Germany's, or would they back down under Russian pressure? This, in effect, was what the blockade was really about.

'Your mother's right. We're trying to put this country back on its feet,' Blessed said. Whining, sour-minded little shit, was what he thought.

'He should drop his charity packages by anonymously, Mutti, so we don't have to grovel,' Gerhard said to Lotte, as if his cousin had never spoken.

'Perhaps Chames was moved to come by because it is Daphne's birthday,' Lotte said. 'His immediate family makes him think of his wider family, like us.' She shook her head sadly. 'Ach, why did you never get married, Gerhard? There were always plenty of girls after you when you were younger. If you had children, you would not be so cynical.'

'I was too busy fighting, Mutti.' Gerhard grinned. 'And a man did not necessarily have to get married to enjoy himself in those days.'

131

Lotte frowned and turned to Blessed. 'Hitler turned all these boys into monsters. No manners, no morals. What will the next generation be like, I ask you? There are children who have never known love, or a family, or religion . . .'

'Or a good cup of coffee,' Gerhard said.

Of course, this visit couldn't really be hurried, and Blessed had known it. Next his aunt pleaded with him to explain the international situation, and the blockade, and how the West expected to feed and fuel Berlin entirely by air. So he did his best with her, while Gerhard brooded silently. Blessed didn't bother including his cousin, because he knew Gerhard wasn't much interested. Gerhard's main interest in life these days was getting drunk. He made some deals on the black market, sometimes good ones that more clear-thinking men could have turned into the basis of a fortune, but he used the profits to have girls, and to buy cheap schnapps, but mainly—especially lately—to buy cheap schnapps. Gerhard's adolescent dream, of power and glamour and life as a member of a master race, may have been a tawdry one, but the pain of its loss was none the less. Even when reason tells you how worthless was the dream, like Gerhard's, it still hurts.

'I have to be at the office, Tante Lotte. I'd like to stay longer, but I can't.'

'Kiss me. And give Daphne and Harriet my love.'

'Of course, of course.' He leaned over and brushed her cheek with his lips. He heard her sigh as he straightened up again.

'You must bring them to see me soon, please,' she murmured.

It was this indirect reproach that Blessed dreaded. 'Perhaps later this summer. When I can take some time off.' He looked at his watch yet again, then at Gerhard. 'I'd like you to come outside, please.'

'Yes?'

'Yes. Business.'

Gerhard got to his feet. 'The victor speaks. I obey,' he said. 'Got another cigarette?'

Yesterday's sunny spell had been short-lived. The morning was dull and damp. A policeman pedalled by on an old bicycle that rattled over the wet cobbles like a stick played along iron railings. A housewife hurried past with an empty shopping-bag, heading for the early-morning grocery queues. The determination on her careworn face let the world know that, however long it took, by tonight she would have something to set on her family's table, even if it was only a dish of turnips. The women, Blessed had soon decided, were the real heroes of this city; the men had lost the war, but it would be they—the middle-aged mother who spent her days clearing rubble and her evenings caring for her family, the young Fräulein, the 'bit of frat' who hooked her Tommy or her GI and made sure he stayed hooked—who would win the peace.

Blessed led Gerhard into a doorway for shelter from the steady drizzle.

'Quick,' Gerhard said. 'If my friends see me with you, I'll never hear the last of it.'

'Still involved with dirty politics?'

'I stand by my friends from the old days. Our loyalty to each other is all we have left. Surely even our new Allied masters cannot forbid us that?'

Blessed shrugged, gave Gerhard the cigarette he had been waiting for.

'It's because of your friends that I want to talk to you,' he said then. 'None of them will be placed in any danger if they help me, I promise.'

'Such promises I have heard before,' Gerhard retorted sceptically.

'Suit yourself. All I need is some information. Or a short cut to some information. I shall find out what I need to know anyway, but I thought . . . well, why not give dear cousin Gerhard the chance to be of service? Oh, and I almost forgot . . . You also get two packets of these . . .' Blessed indicated the cigarettes they were smoking.

Gerhard looked up and down the shabby street. Blessed knew that his cousin was too ineffectual, too lazy, and a lot of the time too drunk, to really cut a figure in any of the seedy little neo-Nazi groups that had arisen in the past year or two. Nevertheless, he did have friends, and some of them were neither ineffectual nor lazy. They were who Blessed was aiming for, through the medium of Gerhard's greed. It was important to make the bribe seem big and the favour small, even when the reverse was true.

'What's this information, James? It depends what it is.'

'I have a name. The name of a doctor. His name is Schmidt.'

Blessed waited while Gerhard recovered. His cousin found this name so funny, he laughed so hard that he was soon convulsed by a coughing fit.

'This Schmidt—yes, that's his real name apparently—is involved in the therapeutic drugs black market in a big way,' Blessed continued calmly.

'Schmidt?' Gerhard cackled. 'Why could he not have called himself Mayer? Or perhaps Braun? Why make things easy for us?'

'He's an abortionist, plies his trade around the Ku-Damm somewhere.'

'OK, OK . . . that reduces the field to about five hundred, of whom perhaps only twenty are called Schmidt . . . James, I don't go down to the Ku-Damm much. I'm a German, one of the losers. The Ku-Damm is for the victors, the girls only go for the hard-currency hard-ons. You know? I stay around here, where things are familiar and the people can be trusted. But . . .'

'*But what?* Don't think you can play me for a fool, Gerhard. My car's waiting just down the street. It's warm and dry. I could just leave you standing here in the rain if I wanted to.'

'I don't think you will, though. You see—as I was about to tell you—I have a friend who runs a little clinic there, who knows almost everybody.'

'A doctor, like you?'

Gerhard smiled coyly. 'Two packets? Maybe three, I think. And one packet in advance. To go hunting around the Ku-Damm is expensive, James. In fact, even breathing the air there costs an arm and a leg . . .'

'Ten cigarettes now, the rest when you come up with something more substantial.'

'What about my friend? My friend is not going to help out of simple love for the Allies, I can tell you that.'

'A packet for your friend.'

'It will also take at least two. Two packets will certainly reveal this Doktor Schmidt you are seeking.'

'All right.' For Blessed the information would be cheaply bought. He knew that Gerhard would probably steal most of the cigarettes intended for his friend, but that was the friend's problem. Or possibly Gerhard's. One day Gerhard might let someone down so badly that they would decide the world was better off without him. It was a thought that had occupied Blessed's own mind from time to time since Gerhard had hit him with a mallet at the age of four, then burst into tears and tried to plead self-defence.

'Ring me this afternoon here,' he said, handing over a slip of paper with the number of his direct line at BlessForce, the one he always gave to informers. 'If I'm not there, tell whoever answers where I can contact you, and I'll ring you as soon as possible.'

'OK.'

Blessed reached into his pocket and tossed Gerhard a whole packet of Senior Service. 'A bonus, so you can't tell everyone your cousin is mean. But be quick. I can't wait. Put on some good shoes and a jacket, and hit the Ku-Damm. Now. And don't start drinking until you've got something to tell me.'

'Nasty weather out there, sir,' Thwaite commented after Blessed had returned to the comfort of the Horch. 'While you were busy, there was a radio message from Sergeant Kelly. Mrs Price should be leaving Hendon Aerodrome for Berlin in the next hour or two. He wants to know if you'd like to interview her. If you do, he'll get Welfare to fix her up with overnight accommodation.'

Before he went home last night, Blessed had decided there was no postponing the formal identification for any longer. It would be up to him to ensure Mrs Price didn't make a fuss.

'Get him back on the air, will you?'

Kelly came on a couple of minutes later, repeated that he thought the widow would be arriving sometime this evening—exactly when depended on the RAF. Did Blessed want him to arrange a meeting?

'I suppose it might help for me to have a word with her. Any other developments this morning?'

'We're following up on the four drug-dealers Floh named. But this morning the sly old sod says there's others who are too "protected" to be touched. He can't identify them because if he did it would endanger his life, or so he says. If you ask me, he's hoping he'll be able to wriggle out of things like he did over that pimping charge, by threatening to name some important army and government names. He says he wants a private interview with you.'

'That's the trouble with allowing an experienced criminal a good night's rest. It gives him ideas. What about Ernie Mitchellson?'

'Him? He just keeps falling asleep.'

'Have Weiss's men found Doktor Schmidt?'

'No, sir. This is a big city. Our Kripo chums have really got their hands full. Lots of government papers were destroyed in the war, including public health records. Add to this the fact that many doctors lost their surgeries in the bombing . . . Most are practising in rat-holes, if they're practising at all.'

Blessed grunted sceptically. If there was one thing he was pretty sure of, it was that the Dr Schmidt they were looking for wasn't

135

going to be found in anything resembling a rat-hole, except perhaps metaphorically.

'Well, I don't care how big Berlin is,' he said. 'We've got to find Schmidt the abortionist. Because it's vital that we identify Suzy, Kelly. I feel it in my bones. We must know exactly who she was.'

TWELVE

BENNO WAS DOOMED to fail in today's mission, which was maybe why he had never wanted it.

He and Panewski were up painfully early after just a snatch of sleep, hollow-eyed and terse with each other. Not so Boss-kind, who seemed utterly refreshed. He arose from the wrecked chair he'd been sleeping in as if from a feather-bed, dished out the Soviet Zone money they would need for the trip east, and issued his final instructions with the tireless verve of a young general who is already anticipating victory.

When they emerged into the Bernauer Strasse, they were greeted by a drifting drizzle, cloying and dull as fog. This was excellent border-crossing weather, as Benno assured Panewski; weather that encouraged sentries to stay incurious in their dry guardposts, that inclined mobile patrols to stay in their cosy vehicles. As if to prove Benno's point, a pair of Froggie conscripts had stared at them with damp indifference from their chilly perches in a covered jeep parked just short of the sector border. On the Soviet side, blockade or no blockade, there were no soldiers or police in sight. So Benno and Panewski, 'father and son', crossed with ease into the Russkie-territory of 'Democratic Berlin'. (By now Benno was so used to this staggeringly mendacious description, he didn't laugh, but Panewski, a habitué of the West who only ventured into the preserves of the Reds when he had to, couldn't stop himself from cracking a twisted grin, thus becoming one of the rare few who during the year of 1948 entered Russian-occupied Europe with a smile on his face.)

Boss-Kind had told them to keep on walking once they were in the East. And they did, hand in hand, as instructed. All along the route, as usual, giant Marxes and Engelses, Lenins and Stalins, Piecks and Grotewohls glowered into the middle distance from up on their lofty billboards, their gimlet prophets' eyes fixed firmly on a future that was altogether more palatable than the dirty, devastated streets below. Scuttling by this way on the home stretch from a mission in the East, Benno had often fantasised that maybe, when no one was looking, these icons communed with each other across the eerie, graveyard quiet of the Russkie-sector. Certainly they said nothing, literally or figuratively, to him or Panewski as the pair made their way through the soft, persistent rain to the Prenzlauer Allee S-bahn station to catch a train to Karlshorst.

This was another thing you had to know about the East: to Karlshorst there were always trains, whatever the situation. The reason was that there, in a former Wehrmacht barracks, was the Red Army's headquarters, seat of General Kaltikov, the Soviet military commandant. The Russians had to ensure that their officers could get from there into the centre of Berlin to their offices and their various tasks, then back again. And so the line between Karlshorst and the city was guaranteed to be running. Then from Karlshorst they were to take a further train down to Köpenick, where Berlin began to enjoy a genuine whiff of country air, and where a boy and his father could wander unsuspected along the decrepit lakeside promenades towards the Grosser Müggelsee, where Riese's emissaries would be waiting to guide Panewski-Bigman to the haven they had planned for him in the depths of the Soviet Zone, out of the reach of any Tommy—even of that Kepten Blessed, whose pretty daughter trotted home from school with Nannypie like a well-trained and well-fed pony.

That was the travel plan. Trains were not frequent this morning, and they were crowded. Nevertheless, the fugitive and his solemn little keeper managed to jostle their way into an open-doored S-bahn car just before the train rattled off, following ill-repaired, rusting tracks into the rising sun. More luck: They didn't even have to change trains at Ostkreuz.

As they got to each station, Benno leaned out, checked that there were no bands of Soviet watchdogs or uniformed German police preparing to board the train and do a spot check. Travelling against the commuter-traffic as they were, the initially crowded car gradually lost its population. The S-bahn jolted its way through increasingly shabby suburbs, some less badly bomb-damaged than the city centre but disfigured instead by neglect and poverty and ancient industrial grime. Surprising amounts of sad washing hung between the sooty tenements by the railway tracks; lines of patched sheets and shirts, threadbare dresses and underwear, left out in the rain. By the time the train swung out the other side of the knot of junctions around the Ostkreuz, they had managed to sit down together on wooden bench-seats polished and shaped by the spines and behinds of a generation of commuters; in fact, the car was all but empty. There was a sprinkling of older women with the inevitable string bags, and a couple of gaunt middle-aged men at the far end carrying large knapsacks; from their conversation it was clear that they had come from the West and were risking a foray out into the market-gardening areas beyond the city fringes to 'organise' some fresh vegetables. Immediately opposite Benno and Panewski, a young Russian lieutenant sat round-shouldered and collapsed, expressionless, with one hand resting limply on a cardboard briefcase in his lap, the other slid inside his olive-green tunic and clutching his heart, as if some terrible hurt had immobilised him. He reminded Benno of a tragic statue he'd seen among the ruins of the old royal palace in the city centre, before the Reds had started to clear all that uncomfortable historical mess away and turn the site into an open square named after both Marx *and* Engels, a nice *new* place where they could hold party rallies and parade in the fancy, Russian-style uniforms that were creeping into vogue among certain natives in the Soviet Zone and the Soviet sector of Berlin.

'I don't know these places,' Panewski muttered. 'I'm a Ku-Damm man. Friedrichstrasse. For me, the sticks start on the eastern side of the Alexanderplatz.' He had been silent for most of the trip so far, hiding behind a copy of *Neues Deutschland*, the communist daily paper. 'How far we still got to go, kid?'

'A kilometre and a half. Maybe two.'

'Right . . . Kid, I want to ask you another little question.' Panewski's rasping voice was now so quiet as to be barely audible. 'OK?'

Benno shrugged wordlessly. Like him, Panewski had been watching the heartbroken—or maybe hungover—Russkie carefully. When Panewski spoke, the man made no reaction at all, not a flicker of an eyelid: either he was totally gone in self-absorption, or he spoke no German, or both.

'That kid you call the Boss, he's planning to go to the West, to Frankfurt,' Panewski continued, as if Benno should know what he was talking about. 'I want to know, is Riese going west too?'

Benno had no idea what plan Panewski was referring to. It was the first he had heard of it, this trip to the Hershey-Zone. As for Riese, Benno had never even spoken to him, though he had seen him twice. The first time, he had glimpsed the gangster's compact form hurrying up the orphanage stairs in the company of an impressively large bodyguard. Then, sometime during the last winter, Riese had been standing in the corner of the outer cellar, stamping his well-shod feet among the garbage to keep warm, deeply and seriously in conference with Boss-Kind and another Hat. Riese had looked round and seen Benno watching them, had frowned, pursed his thick lips. Immediately the Boss had looked at Benno in a way that told him to make himself scarce. All this flashed through Benno's mind. He waited a long moment, then answered Panewski with a question: 'He tells you all his plans, Boss-Kind, does he?'

Panewski chuckled drily. 'We were whiling away the night. He let it slip, you know how it is, kid.'

A nod was all the response that Panewski got out of Benno this time.

The big man had his left arm draped over the back of the wooden seat, with the beefy hand settling on Benno's left shoulder. It was a deliberate, disarmingly paternal gesture. Suddenly Benno was aware of the silent pressure of Panewski's muscular fingers on his shoulder, kneading cruelly. He winced, then bit back further reaction. He was determined not to show his feelings. Let these Hats know they scared you, and you were lost.

'I need to know if you know, son,' Panewski insisted.

'No.' The hurt was not yet unbearable, though it could quickly get that way. But why should Benno play games? All he must do was deliver Panewski to Riese's people and go back to the Kinder Garden for a well-deserved bowl of soup. That was his mission, not keeping non-existent secrets from this *Drecksack* of a Hat. 'No,' Benno continued, 'I don't know. That's the truth.'

'Sure?' Panewski's voice was ominously soft. '*Kinder-sure?*'

The pressure was becoming in-tol-er-able . . . Benno swallowed hard, clenched his teeth, resisting letting out his anger as well as his pain. This Hat was mocking Kinder-talk . . . 'Sure,' he said finally, through his locked jaws. 'I mean, I don' know. I didn' even know Boss-Kind's plan.'

Just before it felt like a muscle would pop, Panewski's fingers stopped working. The pain was quickly gone, leaving only a dull, bruised after-ache.

'I think Riese is going. Going west, I mean,' Panewski said, looking away. 'I was just curious to get some confirmation,' he added. 'When

140

you're deciding if you want to do business with someone you need to check every angle. You understand that, eh, *son*?'

'Oh yeah, *dad*. But you are *already* doing business with Boss-Kind—and with Riese—you beddabelieve. You been doing it since you let them get you away from the Tiergarten . . .'

A laugh, slightly forced. Panewski patted Benno's knee. 'I like you, kid. You're smart. Anyone ever tell you that?'

They were entering a canyon of repair sheds. This was Benno's excuse to rise from his seat and cross to the window, stick his head out to ensure that there was no trouble ahead. But the train was not slowing down; this one obviously by-passed the Rummelsburg works station and went directly down the long straight to Karlshorst. As Benno turned back into the car, the tragic-statue Russian let out a long, deep sigh and unfroze. The hand went down from his heart and joined the other on the cardboard briefcase. He yawned, peered at the passing scenery. Batches of old rolling-stock huddled together like bulky animals grazing at the coarse grass between the sleepers. Goods-wagons—probably filled with German machines and manufactured items being taken by the Russians as part of their ruthless programme of enforced reparations—were waiting for a locomotive to pull them away. Then the Russian got to his feet, swaying with the train's motion, stood waiting for Karlshorst. To him Benno, only a few feet away, simply did not exist.

The boy was grateful that the tragic-statue Russian did not see him. Invisible was the way he and the other Kinder liked to be. To be a Kind—if you knew how to do it right—was to be as invisible as a stray dog, as a tree, as a fence, as washing left out in the rain; it was to be *scenery*. This was very useful, a strength, almost a magic power. Benno looked back into the car. Panewski was still sitting on his big arse, waiting for the train to stop before he moved. His gaze was empty, even though his eyes were directed at Benno. *Panewski is looking through me*, Benno thought. *Most of the time, even now, to him I am unseen, unheard, because I represent no threat. Like most Hats he notices only what is his own size, and noisy, and obviously dangerous. This is also why Panewski is more interested in Boss-Kind than me, and far more interested in Riese than in either of us . . .*

Karlshorst station was coming into view. The train slowed to a walking pace, its ageing brakes slipping squeakily against the drive-wheels. The up platform was busy but the side of the tracks where they would leave the train seemed pretty much deserted. Some civilians,

141

a female station employee in a shapeless blue uniform, a couple of Russkies with no obvious function, but then there was nothing unusual in that; nothing that to Benno's practised eye looked like it would mean a search, awkward questions.

The train stopped abruptly, with their compartment opposite the rusty sign that announced Karlshorst in peeling black gothic letters.

The tragic-statue Russian wearily grasped the handle of the door, swung it open and launched himself out of the train. The last Benno saw of him, he was trudging towards the exit, swinging his briefcase gloomily, a man in a dream on his way to work. Brutal one moment, delicate fantasists the next, that was the Russkies all over, Benno decided. Hard people to rely on. The Hersheys and the Tommies, even the Froggies, were more predictable, therefore easier to manipulate.

This train terminated here. At a nod from Benno, Panewski followed him out onto the platform. This part was not covered, so the drizzle, which had become harder, more like real rain, was falling straight on them, but nevertheless Bigman paused deliberately, looked around.

Trust an arrogant shit of a Hat like this to pretend he was in control, when really he knew nothing, Benno thought. 'You know, it's OK—' he started to say.

But it was not OK for Panewski, apparently. He stiffened, grabbed Benno by the arm, hissed at him to be quiet.

'There's something going on,' he whispered. 'See that fat Ivan over there?'

About twenty yards away Benno saw a well-padded Russian sergeant lounging against a disused kiosk on the covered part of the platform, apparently engrossed in some early-morning reading-matter. There was nothing especially strange about him as far as Benno could see.

Panewski drew Benno away, began to look pointedly in the other direction. Benno checked, saw that the Russian was still absorbed in his reading. It was a broadsheet newspaper with a lurid, commie-red mast-head.

'*What*, Bigman?' Benno hissed angrily. 'You keep up that pointing and grabbing, and you will have that Russkie on our *asses*, whoever he is!'

Benno was trying to keep his own movements inconspicuous, at the same time running an eye over this end of the platform for possible emergency exits. There was a low wall to their right. The drop to the street beyond could be five feet or twenty-five; it was hard to tell without shinning up it and taking a look. On the scarred brickwork of a building opposite the station, at about the same height as this platform, was a big hammer-and-sickle daubed roughly in red paint, and in letters several feet high: 'SAY NO TO FASCISM: VOTE SED'. Unless they'd actually erected scaffolding to paint that communist slogan over there, it couldn't be too far above ground level.

'Pay attention,' Panewski snarled. He looked scared, his eyes were hunted. 'That fat Ivan is a man called Andreyev. He's a cop. I had a run-in with him last winter. If he spots me out here, I could just disappear into one of their prisons and never come out—' Panewski shivered at the thought.

Benno looked sceptically in the direction of the supposed 'Andreyev'. 'Eck, he don' seem interested in you, Bigman,' he said. 'Relax.'

'Listen. Maybe he hasn't recognised me yet. But if we go through that exit, we'll have to walk right past him. Then maybe he'll realise who I am.'

'Sure, sure. So what are you going to do, Bigman? Pray? Steal an old lady's fur coat and pretend to be a babushka, eh?'

'No. You're going to help me.'

'Ah.' Benno smiled resignedly. '*Und?*'

Panewski fished in his coat pockets, pulled out a battered electro-plated cigarette lighter. Benno had never seen him use it. Probably it didn't work.

'See this?' Panewski pressed the lighter into his hand. 'You go over to fat Ivan, say you want to sell it to him, and don't take no for an answer. Tell him it's Hitler's personal lighter. Tell him *anything*, kid, so long as you keep him occupied for a couple of minutes with his back to the exit. That'll give me plenty of time to nip through to the street. I'll meet you out there and we'll plan our next move.'

As such, this operation should have been straightforward for a Kind like Benno. For all their Slavic unpredictability, working the Ivans like this was usually not so bad. Provided the Russkie so-called cop wasn't too clever, and provided there weren't other Russkie cops around. Even if the Soviets hated you, Benno consoled himself as he steeled himself for the approach, even if they hated all Germans, the worst you got at his age was an absent-minded, grizzly-bear cuff round the ear. Again, there were advantages to being a Kind.

Panewski stuck his hands in his pockets, shrugged at Benno meaningfully, made a get-over-there-and-get-started motion with his eyes.

So Benno weighed up the cheap artefact, put it in his pocket. Soon he was out of the drizzle and under cover, homing in on the Russkie. He got within range of the man's borscht-breath, stood there for a moment or two, shuffling from foot to foot and making a little clicking sound with his tongue. Fat Ivan was not responding. Gripped by thrilling production figures for tractors in the paper, maybe, or Comrade Stalin's latest speech about how the evil capitalist West was trying to provoke a war over Berlin.

'Hey, friend!' Benno began then, in a low, throaty murmur. '*Russkisoldat*, friend!'

Fat Ivan lowered his paper, peered at this little interloper. He had sad eyes, close up, and gappy teeth. He didn't look either especially soft or especially cruel, more neutral, like a curious animal.

'Bargain. Ten cigarettes?' Benno said.

The Russian raised an eyebrow. '*Wass iss dass?*'

Benno darted round the other side of him, beckoning over his shoulder. 'Come, friend. I show you . . .'

One quick glance around to make sure no one was watching, and Fat Ivan was hooked. He followed Benno, turning his back on Panewski. Slowly Benno produced the lighter, nodding and winking, really spinning it out. He must have held the Russian's attention for thirty seconds that way. Then out came the lighter with a flourish. The potential client's face fell, but Benno was ready for that.

'Wait, friend!' he muttered intensely. 'This lighter, this lighter belong Gitler. Nazi Führer!' He was mimicking the Russian inability to say their 'h's, but the Russkie didn't seem to notice. 'Very valuable. You take this gome to Ross-y-a, it will be oh yes worth *millions*!'

The Russian wasn't convinced, but he was having a good time anyway. He grinned slowly, pointed at the initials that could just be made out on the casing. Benno also looked closely for some moments, to encourage him. The engraved initials were only too obviously 'J.S.'.

'Hah!' his victim exclaimed. 'No Gitler. But maybe Josef Stalin, eh?'

So tickled by his own wit was Fat Ivan that he threw back his head and laughed and laughed. Meanwhile, Benno glanced past him and saw Panewski. Ashen and determined, walking so fast it was almost a trot, Bigman was heading through the exit in the direction of the street. He wasn't looking to the left or to the right—he was just *moving* . . .

Benno gave it thirty seconds more, to be on the safe side. He dropped his price to five cigarettes. Fat Ivan was still haggling, demanding petrol for the lighter so he could see if it worked. *OK*, Benno muttered under his breath, *five-four-three-two-one* . . .

'Eck,' he said then, prising the thing from the Russian's grasp and holding it up as close as he could get to the man's looming moon-face. 'Eck, Russkie-friend, you want this Gitler-lighter?' he demanded sternly.

Fat Ivan grinned, made a twiddly maybe-yes, maybe-no gesture with his thick hands.

'*Scheiss-drauf*, and I shit on you too,' Benno growled, and popped the lighter into the pocket in the front of the Russian's tunic. 'For Soviet-German friendship, I give you this. Josef Stalin! You beddabelieve! Oh yes, *auf Wiedersehen, tovaritsch!*'

And with a quick farewell tap on Fat Ivan's arm and a friendly chuckle, Benno turned tail and ran off through the exit, leaving a very bemused Russian anxiously searching in his tunic pocket as if the lighter were maybe a grenade or a tarantula spider that had been planted there.

Benno laughed as he ran through the echoing tunnel that led to the street. If that had been a Russian cop, he thought, then Russian cops were *nothing*. But Bigman had better be grateful. He owed Benno a cigarette for this one. Right now, during the trip down to the Müggelsee . . .

Here was the street. Here—up on the wall across the way—was the red hammer-and-sickle. Here was a young woman pushing a handcart piled with junk furniture over the glistening-wet cobbles, with a three-year-old kid trailing listlessly behind her. Here was a white-whiskered old man in a torn waterproof cape and a blue worker's cap selling newspapers and drab, Soviet-licensed magazines. Here was a scrawny mongrel dog crouched at the old man's feet. Here was everything, just as Benno had expected it. Except there was no sign—not a trace, *keine Spur*—of Bigman-Panewski.

Benno was thinking fast, too busy to be afraid. Maybe, he told himself, there had been a cop, or something else suspicious, and so Panewski had panicked and taken cover nearby. Benno tried to put himself in Bigman's shoes, looked around for possible bolt-holes. The only real possibility, he decided, was a dead-looking corner-pub across the street. The pre-war sign advertising Schultheiss beer was cracked, almost illegible. The place itself didn't seem to have a name, but the door was half open. Traditionally, bars in Berlin, even suburban ones, were open pretty much round the clock. Benno legged it across the street, stuck his head through the door of the taproom. It was a mausoleum. A barman was staring gloomily into space. Two silent workers in overalls sat at a table nursing half-empty glasses of beer. No Bigman.

Benno darted back into the street. To the left of the old newspaper-seller was a bridge where a cross-street ran under the S-bahn. Benno wondered whether to wait a little longer for Bigman to show. Then he made a snap decision, splashed his way over to the old man's portable wooden stall. The dog started yapping. A city-bound train boomed over the bridge, preparing to stop at the station. At first Benno couldn't even make the newspaper-seller understand him.

'Big . . . man! Big . . . man!' he repeated. 'Came out of the station two, three minutes ago.' Benno pointed upward to show how tall Panewski was.

The old man stared at him suspiciously. The dog, a ratty little dachshund cross, was still yelping and snapping frantically. Finally the train squealed to a halt, making Benno's voice audible. The old man kicked the dog, which settled down into a whimpering crouch. Then, cupping his hand to indicate that he was slightly deaf, he waited for Benno to repeat his question.

'*I am looking for my father!*' Benno lied at top volume in the temporary quiet. '*He was out here in the street just a few minutes ago!*'

'*Ach so, ach so . . .*' the old man said in the careful way of the hard of hearing. 'Yes. Such a man I saw. He stopped to ask me something.'

'What did he ask you?'

The old man thought for a moment. 'He asked me,' he said, 'he asked me if, by going under that bridge, one could reach the other platform and catch a city-bound train. I told him, yes, and that one was due very soon . . .'

Benno swore. Without pausing to thank the old man, he raced towards the bridge. But already the S-bahn train was leaving rain-swept Karlshorst, gathering speed along the line that led back into the heart of Berlin—with that oh-so-*schlau*-smart Hat Panewski on board.

Yes, Panewski had been clever in the way he had lost Benno, duping him into believing that the innocent Fat Ivan was a cop called Andreyev. But why? Why had he fled? Benno stood on the empty platform, oblivious now to the soaking downpour, and watched the train receding slowly into the distance. Such frustration as he felt, such rage and shame at his own stupidity, would have reduced a weaker Kind to tears.

So, why had Panewski run away like this, when Boss-Kind and Riese had done him such a huge favour, and when they had gone

146

to so much trouble to save his hide from the Tommy Kepten Blessed?

How could Benno have been so trusting, yes so *dumm*?

And what would Boss-Kind think of Benno's stupidity? And how terrible would be the Boss's wrath when Benno dragged his weary, beaten carcass back to the Kinder Garden?

THIRTEEN

'HABEAS CORPUS. I have read about this thing in the newspapers,' Floh said carefully, proud of his knowledge. 'It is the foundation of British justice. Essential to the British democratic way of life which you say you want to introduce here in Germany. So I ask you for a lawyer. I ask to be charged. But always you refuse, Captain. Still no lawyer, still no charge.' The old man's eyes glinted cunningly. 'Tell me,' he demanded. 'Tell me where, in all this, is your famous habeas corpus?'

Their worst suspicions had been proved accurate. Blessed should have known better than to allow a man like Floh time to recover his nerve. This morning, alone in the cell, the prisoner was keen-witted, defiant, as he faced Blessed across the interview table.

'You're just wasting my time, Floh,' Blessed said. 'Berlin is a city under military rule, where crime, violence and corruption are rife—and to cap it all, there's the threat of imminent invasion. Do you think we can afford to care about all that habeas corpus rubbish?'

'In England—'

'This isn't bloody England!'

Floh raised his eyebrows, leaned back in his chair, with the long-suffering look of a philosophy professor who has tried and failed to hold an intelligent conversation with an especially persistent bar-room bore.

'Did you kill Corporal Price and his girlfriend?' Blessed asked in an altogether quieter voice after a while.

Floh shook his head firmly, meeting Blessed's eye in the determined way of the professional liar. 'No, Captain.'

'Did Panewski?'

'No, Captain.'

'How can you be so certain of that?'

'I know Panewski very well. That kind of violence is not in his character.'

'Is that all you can say?' Blessed retorted.

'Captain, Panewski and I have no secrets from each other, I assure you.'

'Let's try another way of putting it: Do you know who killed Price and the woman?'

'Well . . . no . . . but . . .'

Floh was preparing his pitch, Blessed knew. Let him take his time. Up to a point. 'Yes?'

'Captain, I know of Price's contacts with some particularly ruthless businessmen, very strange people . . . Whether they were definitely responsible for the killings, I cannot say, of course . . .'

The only important overnight development, in response to Mitchellson's confession, had been Floh's admission to dealings with the driver and Price, though naturally these had been completely legal (so far as he was aware). Floh stoutly maintained that he had no idea why Mitchellson should be trying to incriminate him in this despicable way, first by appearing to pass over illegal substances, then by fabricating such a malicious story. Of course, Floh admitted, after years of dabbling in many areas of entrepreneurial activity, one made enemies . . .

So far as his reference to 'particularly ruthless businessmen' was concerned, it was impossible to tell if Floh was merely spinning a yarn, or whether he really had something—or thought he might have something—that could be parlayed into a deal. It was clear that his aim was a light sentence, perhaps even immunity from all punishment, if he disclosed his hand gradually and skilfully. The old villain was actually in quite a strong position. His flat had been searched during the night without any incriminating items coming to light. There was nothing whatsoever to link him with the murders except an acquaintance with Taffy Price, and it might prove difficult to make the drug-dealing charge stand up on Mitchellson's evidence alone. Meanwhile, Floh was getting a couple of square meals a day and a roof over his head, all at the expense of the British Military Government. He had everything to gain by sticking to his story, and nothing much to lose.

Blessed sipped at the mug of hot, sweet tea that one of the Knesebeckstrasse staff had brought him a few minutes earlier. Then he put the tea down and lit a cheroot, taking his time, offering Floh nothing.

'Am I to understand that you are prepared to provide certain information,' he said deliberately, switching to a formal, bureaucratic manner. 'And that, furthermore, you believe this information might lead to the apprehension of the person or persons who committed these murders?'

'It is dangerous information. I'm sure you understand that the more valuable it proves to be, the more danger I could be placed in, Captain.'

The gentle answer that turneth away wrath—and telleth nothing. Floh was a past-master at such evasion. Blessed recognised the skill, because he was pretty talented in that direction himself.

'OK,' he said. 'Let's be brutally direct. Unlike you, I don't have all day. Now, let's suppose you really can supply me with this precious information. What do you expect from me in exchange?'

'Freedom. For me and Panewski. And we would need to go somewhere until the heat died down, you understand. That takes money.'

'You realise you're making an impossible demand. Be realistic, Floh.'

The old man made a tiny, open-handed gesture that clearly implied that his demand was nothing of the kind.

'There's nothing to stop me from concentrating on Panewski,' Blessed said. Of course, Floh still believed that Panewski was also in prison. 'It may be true that you were not directly involved in these murders, but I'm not at all convinced about him. Candidates for the gallows tend to become talkative—'

'I told you, Panewski has murdered no one,' Floh sneered coolly. 'As for trying to get him to help you, you would be wasting your time. He wouldn't dream of grassing. And he doesn't know all the things I know.'

This claim had the ring of truth. Although Floh didn't yet know that Panewski had got away in the Tiergarten, he didn't seem at all worried that the big man might give away information. The degree of control he exercised over Panewski was interesting. Weiss had been right to assert that the old man was in charge: whatever Panewski had done, Floh had probably ordered.

'Then perhaps I'll just proceed with the drugs charge,' Blessed said. 'Mitchellson's confession alone gives us enough evidence to put you away for years . . .'

Floh shrugged his bony shoulders. 'Ah well. These days, there are those who say we are better off in jail than out. You get regular meals, tobacco . . . Certainly better than a bullet in your head, or a knife across your throat,' he added. 'And as I have already told you, I should insist on having some of your Military Government people—ones with whom I have had dealings—called as witnesses if it ever came to a trial. Especially if I were to ask for the court to take certain other offences into account . . .'

The devious old sod knew perfectly well that his threat to name names had helped get him off the procurement charge last year, Blessed thought. He was quite prepared to pull the same trick again. The appalling thing was, if word of this got through to some of the more nervous Mil. Gov. bureaucrats, Floh might—just might—manage to get this charge dropped, too. Blessed was also recalling yesterday morning's ominous little chat with Harrison, and wondering whether the disturbance of such a hornet's nest might have given him and the others an excuse to disband BlessForce and boot its commander out of Berlin with even more indecent haste than they already had planned.

Blessed felt a surge of anger, and also the makings of a wild idea, a notion that the only way to beat the hand Floh was holding might be to change the game . . .

'So that's your offer, so-called?' he asked quietly. 'That's what I came rushing in here for this morning?'

'Why yes, Captain. It is very valuable but also very dangerous information. Like everything else, it has its price.'

Blessed got to his feet. 'Ah well, Floh. That's just a pity.' He strode over to the door of the interview room, opened it and called in the military policeman who was waiting in the corridor. 'You can release this man,' he said. 'Send him home in a police car with all the lights flashing. Behave as if he's an honoured friend of the authorities. Have the paperwork sent along to me at my office.'

He savoured the look of dismay on Floh's face, the panic in his eyes.

'Goodbye,' the captain said. 'I'm tired of talking to you. I'm tired of feeding and housing . . . and protecting . . . you. We'll probably pick up the people you named, just to stir things up a bit. Meanwhile, you toddle off home . . . no, I insist, we'll escort you right to your door . . .'

Blessed walked out of the cell without looking back. He kept going up the stairs, past the station desk and into the street. In fact, he didn't stop until he arrived back in his own office at BlessForce.

Blessed's personal phone rang. Just as he had expected, it was 248 Company on the line.

'Floh doesn't want to go home, sir,' said the MP at the Knesebeck-strasse who had been told to organise the prisoner's release. 'Not on those terms.'

Blessed laughed unkindly. 'He wouldn't, would he? But it's compulsory. No matter what he says or does, he leaves that police station and is delivered right to his own front door. You have the address. All right? I don't care if he wants to tell us *everything*. I don't want to hear it. I want to get *rid* of Floh, and in exactly the way stated. Are we clear?'

He put down the phone, buzzed for Kelly to come through into the office.

'Floh will very soon be on his way home,' he told the sergeant. 'His flat is to be watched by pairs of plain clothes men working in eight-hour shifts, starting from the moment he goes through his front door.'

Kelly impassively noted this in his pad.

'Those plain clothes boys are to be issued with a description of Karl-Heinz Panewski, and copies of the old mugshots from Kripo files. If he is seen in the vicinity of Floh's flat, he is to be apprehended. All necessary force may be used, but I want him alive.'

'Very well, sir.'

'Also, I'd like you to get hold of Inspector Weiss. I need to know how he's getting on with the search for Dr Schmidt.'

'I'll try to get hold of him.'

'And I'll be unavailable for a couple of hours this afternoon. Urgent family business.'

'Oh, right, sir.'

Kelly smiled, enquired no further. He knew that this 'urgent business' was code for Daphne's birthday tea. Trust a policeman, even one as inept in most of the human skills as Kelly, to know how common it is for love to masquerade as duty—almost as often as duty masquerades as love.

FOURTEEN

IT WAS AROUND MIDDAY when Benno slipped furtively back over the sector border. With understandable reluctance he set off on the home stretch. By now the rain had drifted off west towards the safety of the British Zone, and here in the huge mantrap that was Berlin, the sun had burst out with a noon vengeance, as if it was eager to burn the moisture off the humid streets and ruins, dry the besieged city's aching bones.

The gloom of the cellar matched Benno's mood more accurately than sunlight. Never before had he returned home with such a heavy heart. And the Kinder's underground stronghold was even danker and damper than usual.

There was no one about. All the Kinder must be out on the streets now. When he got through into the guardroom, though, there was a solitary Kind on duty there. He told Benno that a blocked gutter had led to flooding from the street into the Kinder Garden. This had necessitated much bailing out, until the leaking channel was finally cleared from above.

'That was hard, wet work,' the guard said. 'You know, Benno, you were so lucky to be away on that mission with Bigman-Panewski . . .' Then he looked at the battered alarm clock on his table. 'Hey, Benno, how did you get to the Lake and back so quickly? Eck, but did you steal a Mercedes racer, or what?'

Benno did not explain. 'I gotta see Boss-Kind. Report,' he said, though he would have done anything to avoid seeing the Boss at this particular moment.

'He went out, just like everybody else. He said he'd be back soon, though.' The guard lowered his voice confidingly. 'You know, suddenly we hear Boss-Kind talking of Frankfurt and the whole wide rest of the Hershey-Zone. That's Mainz and Mannheim, Heidelberg and Wiesbaden—Boss-Kind says compared with Berlin they're fat, sunny cities. No Russkies, no sector borders, just rivers and green fields and dumb-friendly Hersheys with money to burn . . .'

'I'll take a rest, yes,' Benno interrupted. 'Tired. You beddabelieve how much . . .'

Benno was telling the truth. He could no longer absorb gossip, no matter how juicy. After such a long day and such a long night, exhaustion had overcome him. Suddenly he felt as weary as a refugee who'd walked a thousand miles and still had another thousand to go.

The dormitory was empty. Benno couldn't even bring himself to grab some food, he was so intent on rest. He didn't care if the place was still damp from the morning's flooding. Still dressed in his wet street-clothes, he dropped onto his familiar iron cot. He didn't even pull back his blanket, just keeled over and slid down that soft, dark tunnel into unconsciousness.

Benno was dreaming about the old room again. Nothing extraordinary about it. In fact, all the scene ever consisted of was a window with moonlight streaming in, and close to the window, a highbacked chair. Everything in the old room was giant-sized. He was looking up at it. But mingled with all this enormity was also a kind of familiarity, a safety. There was always the same figure in the chair, though he never saw its face. And usually, after a while, there would be a terrible explosion, and everything would go black. The times he really loved, though, were the rare peaceful ones, when the dream simply consisted of his inhabiting that magic place, and . . . slowly . . . unbelievably . . . feeling . . . happy. That last bit was one thing he *never* told the other Kinder about . . .

Suddenly, he was back in his iron cot, back at the Kinder Garden. Someone had him by the shoulders and was shaking him. The magic of the old room disintegrated. Benno's eyes tore open so quickly that it hurt, but for a moment he could make out nothing in the darkness. He let out a yell, but already he was feeling foolish, because he could hear a peculiar, barking laugh that he recognised only too well.

'Dreamtime over! Dreamtime over!' Boss-Kind was chuckling as he shook him. 'Good! Good!' he exclaimed when he saw that Benno's eyes were wide open. Then he released his grip on Benno's shoulders and let him sink back down onto the cot.

Wheezing with shock, Benno just lay there. The Boss was grinning down at him in a way that Benno knew did not necessarily represent good humour.

'You don' do . . . oh no . . .' Benno hissed at last. 'You don' do that again, Boss-Kind. You Kinder-promise me . . .'

Boss-Kind switched off his smirk and made an apologetic face. 'You beddabelieve. Kinder-sorry, Benno. Just got back, and I need to talk to you 'bout your mission.' The ambiguous grin crept back. 'Your *failed mission.*'

What could Benno say? Boss-Kind would easily have worked out that in the time they had, Benno and Panewski could never have made it to the Lake. Or maybe Riese's boys had already reported that there was no one at the house on the Müggelsee.

His eventual reply was feeble but factual. 'Karlshorst,' Benno stuttered. 'Bigman got away there. I was stupid—'

'It was not your fault,' Boss-Kind cut in calmly and decisively. 'And you know, it don' matter all that much. Riese and me, we were doing that shitfaced Hat a *big* favour. If he so dumb, he don' want the Kinder and Riese's boys to help him escape from the Tommy Kep-ten Bless-ed, that is *his* problem.'

Benno was hardly able to believe his ears. The Boss so reasonable! Benno saved from disgrace and worse!

Boss-Kind nodded. 'You are a guide, not a guard, Benno. You are a watcher, not a puncher.' He picked a pack of Larks from the breast pocket of his shirt, flicked one out and offered it to Benno. This was honour indeed. Or something. 'If I wanted to *guard* that Bigman, I send big Kinder—maybe Granit, Banana . . .'

'Eck, Boss-Kind, that is good news,' Benno said, taking the cigarette and accepting a light. Such extravagance! The thought of smoking a whole Lark, just like that! 'I got back,' he explained with a nervous titter, '*ach scheiss* I got back, and I was crapping in my boots, and so ex-hausted . . .'

'You got some sleep already. An hour maybe. Now you gotta get up, Benno. Oh yes,' Boss-Kind insisted softly. 'I got watcher work for you.'

Benno groaned. Then Boss-Kind flashed him a demon-look, the one where his cat's eyes burned and the skin pulled back tight on his face like a frightening mask.

'The Kepten, Benno. You will watch the Kepten this afternoon,' he said. 'Ku-Damm and anywhere west of there. *No argument.*'

'OK, OK . . . But first I wanna know: Are you leaving Berlin, Boss?' Benno demanded on impulse, sick of just listening to orders, never asking any questions. 'Me and Bigman, we were talking on the S-bahn before he ran away, and he said you were going to the Hershey-Zone. Soon.'

Boss-Kind's expression was impassive now. 'Maybe.'

'This means you are going, I think, Boss-Kind.'

'Maybe soon, Benno,' Boss-Kind admitted. 'A short trip. No, not for long . . .' The Boss reached down and tugged affectionately but also somehow very intimidatingly at Benno's thick mop of dark hair. As he leaned over, his coat swung down and brushed against the younger boy's legs. Benno felt a heavy object in its pocket and knew that it was a knuckle-blade, one of the pair that Boss-Kind had offered to Panewski last night. 'There is so much business to be arranged,' the Boss murmured to Benno. 'One big, special piece of business before we can all be safe.' He smiled encouragingly. 'Your part in this business, Benno, your part is you gotta watch that enemy of ours, that Kepten Blessed . . . Such big, special business . . .'

How big? How special that it meant sending Benno down the Ku-Damm to watch that Tommy when he was already half-dead with tiredness? Why was Boss-Kind off to the West?

These thoughts tumbled through Benno's resentful mind as he lay there looking up at Boss-Kind in the gloom of the empty dormitory. Then, of course, there was another line of reasoning, perhaps the most important and disturbing one: Why did they still have to bother with Kepten Blessed now that Panewski had got clean away? Boss-Kind shouldn't be interested in the Tommy Kepten any more. So what was going on *now*? What did Boss-Kind want with Blessed *now*? And where, *ach scheiss*, where would it all *end*?

FIFTEEN

IT WAS FIVE TO THREE in the afternoon. Blessed had briefed Kelly to deputise for him during his absence at Daphne's birthday tea. Thwaite would have the car waiting outside at three o'clock, giving them just enough time to make it to the Villa Hellman for the party, due to start at half-past.

When the phone rang, Blessed thought it might be Harriet with a last-minute request for him to pick up some extra cakes or a couple more bottles of lemonade from the Club on his way home. In fact, it was his cousin, Gerhard. He was calling from a bar, judging by the sounds of laughter and tinny music in the background. Gerhard wasn't yet drunk, but Blessed heard a vigour in his voice that wasn't usually there. His cousin was enjoying that initial shot of energy alcohol gives you, the feeling that life's not so bad and anything's possible, before the depressive effect sets in.

'Hallo, James. I have a friend here who knows about a Doktor Schmidt. This Doktor Schmidt fits your requirements in every way, I think.'

'Where are you, Gerhard?'

'I am in a hard-currency dive called Johnny's, opposite the Rio Rita. Maybe five minutes' walk from you.'

'Bring your friend here, then.'

'Impossible. My friend is distrustful by nature. My friend will only do a deal with you in person, James, and on neutral ground. Now. With me present as an intermediary. Well?' Gerhard was enjoying himself. Gerhard had cousin James by the balls for once, and he didn't intend to let go easily.

Blessed cursed under his breath. 'I'll be over in ten minutes.'

'James?'

'Yes.'

'Please wear civilian clothes.'

'Of course.'

'And James?'

'Yes. I'm still here.'

'Bring plenty, plenty cigarettes. This friend doesn't come cheap, even for my relatives.'

Blessed put down the receiver, said something obscene. Then he phoned the Villa Hellman. He heard Gisela's voice.

'Hello? Gisela?' he said. 'Is Mrs Blessed there?'

'I'm afraid not, Captain Blessed. Because of Daphne's birthday, and because she is going to England tomorrow, Mrs Blessed decided to pick Daphne up from school today. Should she ring you back, or will you phone again?'

'I . . . can't. I'll have to ask you to give her . . . give them both . . . a message.'

'Yes. Of course.'

'I have—I mean that—I *have* to go and see someone. Now. So I'll be late, but I'll try to make it home before the party's over. All right?'

'Yes. I think Daphne will be disappointed, but also there is plenty for her to do here.'

'Yes. As I said, I'll *try* . . .'

When Blessed emerged into the street, he almost collided with a small, very dirty boy who seemed to be waiting for something or someone in the middle of the pavement. He scolded the youngster, more in frustration than in anger, and set off on the short walk to the Kurfürstendamm. Blessed had on the suit he habitually wore for plain-clothes work, an old German-made wool outfit that he had bought on a visit here just before the war. It made him indistinguishable from the vast majority of German civilians, who were also wearing aged clothes. At present estimates of production in the British Zone, an adult German male would be able to buy a new pair of shoes every five years, a suit every twelve. Another convenience of wearing civilian clothes was that you didn't have to fight off the attentions of racketeers and prostitutes, who were drawn to an Allied uniform but treated their fellow-Germans (unless they were known black-market barons) with contemptuous indifference.

Johnny's was a hole in the wall, advertised by a crude painted board depicting a bare-breasted brown girl in a hula skirt. It said, *We speak English! Nous parlons francais!—WE ARE ALWAYS FRIENDLY.* Blessed picked his way down the winding stairs, skirting a pool of fresh vomit, and pushed through a curtain into the place.

Apart from the usual Fräuleins, Gerhard and his friend were just about the only natives in the bar, and they were under siege. A group of American soldiers were offering to buy a drink for Gerhard's companion. The two Germans greeted Blessed's arrival with relief.

'James, this is Dr Hallgarten,' Gerhard said nervously.

'Pleased to meet you,' said Blessed. He turned to the nearest American, said, 'I'm British. I'm military police, and if you don't bloody well clear off, I'll have you arrested.'

The man shrugged. 'Hey,' he said, and turned away.

Dr Hallgarten was a woman in her late thirties, dark and slim, almost Italian-looking. She wore a gabardine coat and a black beret.

'Good afternoon,' she said. 'And thank you. It was just high spirits, but those American boys were becoming a little wearisome.'

Gerhard had caught a waiter's eye and was beckoning him over. 'You see, I thought it would be safer if we met here, because no one I know could come here in the usual way. Johnny's is a bar where they accept hard currency only.' This was Gerhard-language for a bar where James had to pay the bill.

Blessed was still studying Dr Hallgarten. 'I was expecting a man, and somebody different. I didn't think Gerhard knew people like you,' he said.

Gerhard was busy ordering a beer with a schnapps chaser. 'James?' he asked. Blessed said he would have a beer too, but no schnapps. Eva Hallgarten ordered a second glass of tea. Her first had gone cold.

'Eva . . . Dr Hallgarten was the wife of my old university friend, Erich. She also qualified as a doctor . . . one of the last to do so before Hitler stopped our women from going to university and studying such things . . . What did you expect, James?'

'I expected one of your Nazi friends.'

'Eva is no Nazi. Neither was Erich. You see, Nazis are not the only people I know. Do you think there is hope for me?'

Eva Hallgarten continued to look directly at Blessed; it was as if Gerhard was a form of unavoidable noise, like a drill working in the street.

'My husband was drafted in 1942 and killed in Russia a year later,' she said when Gerhard shut up for long enough. 'He never wanted to have anything to do with those bastards, but they gave him no choice.'

'I'm sorry,' Blessed said.

She thanked the waiter as he set down her glass of tea.

'Whose bill is this going on?' The waiter was a man in his fifties with a pugilist's face. 'No German marks here. I want to see real money.'

Blessed took out two British pound notes and laid them on the table. 'When we've finished, you can have this,' he said. 'And I don't want you interrupting the conversation again. I'm discussing business with my friends.'

'Just making sure, mister. It's part of my job,' the waiter said matter-of-factly. It took a lot to embarrass a Ku-Damm veteran. He put down the drinks and turned away. Two tables away, a group of young Americans were banging their empty beer-steins on the table, bawling the universal demand of the GI out for a good time, *'Mak snell! Mak snell!'*

'So do you still practise?' Blessed asked Eva Hallgarten.

'Yes. I practised quietly for years, all during the Hitler time, though it was not easy. After the Russians came in 1945, there were many women with special physical and mental problems. Since then I have tried to help them. I run a small unofficial clinic.'

'And Dr Schmidt?'

'Five packs of cigarettes,' she said coolly.

'Dr Hallgarten . . .'

'Five packs. It will buy black market medicines. The legitimate pharmacists have a little more than they did last year, but mostly all we can get is skin cream, talcum powder and, if we are really in luck, aspirin. None of these cure venereal diseases or clear up post-partum infections.'

'Five packs,' Blessed agreed quickly. 'Now tell me about Schmidt.'

'If this is the right man, and I think it is, he practises two doors from me, does a lively trade in abortion and curing VD—for a price, a high price. His clients are mainly the mistresses of black-marketeers or Allied officers. They are the only people who can pay his prices.'

'Why are you prepared to turn him in?'

'He used to hand on to me some of the drugs he obtained illegally. He would also, from time to time, perform abortions for women patients of mine—usually those who had become pregnant after rape.'

'So he wasn't such a bad man, then?'

'He was susceptible to blackmail. Let us not be naïve, Mr Blessed. But these past few months he has become greedy. He says he has no drugs, and the abortions have become too risky, but I know this is not true. So . . . you can have him. He is of no use to me any more. To be honest, if you arrest Schmidt, I may be able to take over his surgery, which is far better equipped than mine. I have good friends in the Health Bureau. It could be managed.'

She spoke so calmly and coldly that Blessed was chilled as he sat there listening to the fun-loving GIs still guffawing their '*Mak snell!*'

'I don't know whether I shall have him arrested at this stage,' he said. 'Or ever. And I don't want any gossip. You understand?'

'Yes. That's why I want the packets of cigarettes. There has to be some recompense just in case Schmidt gets away clean.'

'You don't like men much, do you?'

'Is that any of your business, Mr Blessed?' Eva Hallgarten retorted sharply. Then she took a sip of tea, seemed to relent. 'Let's . . . let's say I've given up on them. I've seen too much of what they can do.'

'Fair enough. So what's this Dr Schmidt's address?'

'The cigarettes?'

'I brought two packets with me for Gerhard, two for you. That was the original agreement. I'll give you all four. Gerhard will have to collect his share, plus the rest of yours, later.' Blessed looked at Gerhard, who had finished his beer and his schnapps and seemed restless. 'Any problems, just ring me, Dr Hallgarten. Especially if Gerhard doesn't bring the packet you're owed.' He wrote down the direct line number on a piece of paper.

'I will. Even better, you arrest Dr Schmidt.'

'This is part of something larger. I can't arrest him now without upsetting the rest of our plans.' Blessed paused. 'By the way, do you know his receptionist?' he asked, as if it were an unimportant afterthought.

Dr Hallgarten smiled. 'I don't know her at all well. She has an English boyfriend, and why not? She is in her early thirties, quite pretty, perfectly nice. A . . . a good-time girl, I think you would say, but not a prostitute. I believe she was Dr Schmidt's girlfriend at one time, until the English soldier came along. He has supplied Schmidt with penicillin this last year.' Dr Hallgarten frowned. 'I only agreed to tell you about Schmidt. I think this must be counted as extra, Mr Blessed.'

'OK. Two packets more. Gerhard owes you three from me. Just keep talking.' The really virtuous and the really wicked had one thing in common, Blessed thought. They drove very hard bargains.

'I think the Englishman also dealt in narcotics. I saw him in the street outside Schmidt's sometimes. With Americans, especially, but also with others. Black-market types. Young thugs. Some were frighteningly young. There was a wild German boy, I remember, maybe seventeen, eighteen . . . this was last week. He and the Englishman, I don't know his name, and Heidemarie—'

'That was her name? What was her surname?'

'I don't know.'

'All right. They were doing what?'

'Arguing.'

'About what, Dr Hallgarten?'

She shrugged. 'I don't know. The young boy was being very passionate. To tell you the truth, I think neither of the two adults took him seriously. Finally he walked away in disgust. I remember he talked very fast, used many American words in a strange way. The next day they were all friends again though, I think.'

'Fine. Let's get back to Dr Schmidt. Do you think he was jealous of Heidemarie and . . . this Englishman of hers?' He decided not to mention Price's name.

'Why are you asking me all this?'

'Please, just answer my question.'

'The answer is, I don't know. It's unlikely. Schmidt has never been short of girlfriends. He earns hard currency, and so in Berlin these days girlfriends are not hard to find. I don't think he's the jealous type, anyway.' Eva Hallgarten glanced at her watch. 'Now, if you will excuse me, I must get back for my appointments . . .'

'Dr Schmidt's address?'

'Joachim-Friedrichstrasse, number 27. Fourth storey. I don't remember the apartment number but it's the one at the back.'

'And yours?'

'Number 22 in the same street. Why do you want to know? I am allowed to ask why this time, am I?'

'There might be things to send there.'

Eva Hallgarten nodded coolly, got to her feet. 'Feel free to make any contribution you like. I am utterly without shame or scruples when it comes to keeping the clinic going,' she said, and added, 'Nowadays I don't know who to dislike most, you or the Russians. In the East, there is nothing, whatever you do, while in the West there is everything—at a price.'

'Are we at least better than Hitler?' Blessed asked quietly. He put the four packets of cigarettes on the table.

She picked them up and distributed them quickly through the pockets of her coat. 'Anything is better than Hitler,' she said. Then Dr Eva Hallgarten made her way past the noisy GIs, to the curtain, and was gone.

'Another drink to celebrate?' Gerhard suggested hopefully. 'You got some good information there, eh, James?'

'I have a Dr Schmidt. Perhaps even *the* Dr Schmidt.' Blessed gave Gerhard a white English five-pound note. 'Do what you like with that,' he said. 'I'll have the rest of what's due delivered to your apartment. If you don't pass on the other packets of cigarettes to Dr Hallgarten, I'll want to know why.'

Outside on the pavement, Blessed took several deep breaths, thanked the Lord to be free of Gerhard. At the same time, he couldn't stop thinking of Daphne and feeling guilty because he knew he had no choice but to go and seek out this Dr Schmidt immediately. One could never risk a key witness disappearing. The success of his meeting with Dr Hallgarten had ruined his chances of spending even a few minutes at his daughter's party.

He found himself focusing on a scruffy German boy who was staring at him from the service doorway of the Rio Rita. Perhaps it was his tormenting thoughts of Daphne that made him notice the kid, made him itemise to himself the sad details: ten, eleven years old, wearing a dirty, moth-eaten sweater and baggy shorts, boots too big for him, a mop of unkempt, dark hair.

When Blessed saw this boy, he was looking at nothing more than a typical postwar street urchin. Here was a street-survivor, serious beyond his years, given even more of an adult look by his world-weary, fatigued expression. German adults had dubbed such war orphans *Kellerkinder*, 'children of the cellars'. Often living off their wits, sleeping in deserted basements and sewage tunnels, these kids were seen less often now than just after the war, but were still far too common a feature of Berlin and other German cities. At least Daphne was safe and well-fed. Her mother would be at her birthday party, and so would a German conjuror whom Blessed had arranged through an acquaintance on the entertainments committee of the officers' club. He told himself that Daphne would only miss him for a minute, for as long as it took for the magician to begin a new trick. And he would make it up to her soon . . . By now the urchin had looked away and was staring in his same, unnervingly neutral fashion in another direction entirely. It was time to get back to the office.

Only when Blessed reached the street entrance to BlessForce did the penny drop. Only then did he understand why he had been drawn to the boy who had been watching from the service doorway of the Rio Rita. On the threshold he stopped dead for a moment, glanced around him, disturbed by his realisation that the urchin was the very same one he had almost collided with three-quarters of an hour before, on this exact spot, while hurrying off for his extremely important and confidential meeting with cousin Gerhard and Dr Eva Hallgarten.

SIXTEEN

WHEN BLESSED GOT BACK to his office, Inspector Weiss was waiting for him, drinking tea and reading a copy of the Berlin *Tagesspiegel*. He rose to welcome the captain, showed him the newspaper. There was a modest single-paragraph report at the bottom of page two announcing that a couple of bodies had been found on waste ground behind the Potsdamer Strasse and that the British Military Police had joined the investigation into the deaths. It said that robbery was suspected as the motive.

'We're lucky the airlift is such big news,' Weiss commented. 'So long as it stays that way, we should be able to keep the case off the front page.'

'I don't want to involve our Press Liaison people. Can you deal with that side of things, Manfred?'

'Of course. I know all the boys on the crime desks. If the worst comes to the worst, I can always apply some gentle pressure. They won't like it, but they'll fall into line eventually. They need my cooperation more than I need theirs, and they know it.'

'Word may get around anyway. Floh may tell people.'

'Ah yes,' Weiss said, poker-faced. 'I heard you decided to take a chance with him.'

'You look as if you don't approve.'

'Perhaps I'm still a Prussian civil servant at heart, James. And Floh could have been very useful, even if he had nothing to do with the murders.'

'Certainly,' Blessed said with a shrug. 'But his price was too high. Now he's back at liberty, a provocation to the other drug-dealers, and, I hope, a target for whoever murdered Price and his girl.'

'Yes. If you are right, that could provide a breakthrough in the case. What about Price's other associates?'

'Floh gave us a few names. I'm having the villains concerned pulled in for interrogation, of course, but personally I think he was just using this opportunity to settle some old scores. And the very fact that he felt free to grass on these people probably guarantees they're small fry.' Blessed lit a cheroot. It was just after four. At the Villa Hellman, his daughter and her schoolfriends would be sitting down to their cakes and sandwiches and fizzy pop about now. Perhaps Daphne had already blown out the eight carefully-hoarded candles on her birthday cake. He exhaled some smoke, put his feet on the desk. 'Brownlow and Co. can deal with them. We might get a confession or two if we play our cards right. It won't help with our murders, but it never does any harm to bump up the conviction figures, does it?'

'Does Floh know yet that Panewski's still on the loose?'

'He didn't when he left here. I thought it might be more interesting if he found out for himself. Also, if Panewski realises that Floh grassed on several other drug-dealers, he may change his mind about what a wonderful fellow the old man is. In fact, I'm hoping he may decide to pay Floh a visit to discuss his views on the matter . . .'

Weiss still looked doubtful. 'You are having Floh's apartment watched?'

'Come on, Manfred. What do you think?'

'Yes, of course. A foolish question. And by the way, my men are still working their way through the lists, the phone directories, for a Dr Schmidt. So far, they have found several possible candidates and—'

'Actually, we may well have our Dr Schmidt,' Blessed said. 'I still have to interview him, but I don't think there can be much doubt.'

'I see. I'm impressed. How did you find him?'

'I have family here, as you know. For once that turned out to be an advantage.'

'So shall I call my boys off and give them something else to do?'

'Get them to check around Panewski's old haunts, talk to known associates, the usual routine. They might turn up something. Can you just issue new orders over the phone and trust them to get on with it?'

'Of course. They're experienced detectives.'

'Good,' Blessed said. 'Because I'd like you to come with me when I talk to our supposed Dr Schmidt. His surgery's just a short walk from here.'

First Kelly brought Blessed up to date on the routine BlessForce work that was still going on. A British officer had been caught passing on forged new Deutschmark notes. Astonishing that fakes had been produced so quickly. An anonymous letter had been received, detailing massive fraud in the military administration's ration office. Someone would have to follow it up and see if there were grounds for an investigation. And there was a memo from the Acting Provost-Marshal saying that help had been requested with security arrangements at the airfields being used for the airlift. Large-scale theft by German employees and Allied groundstaff was reckoned to be inevitable. Harrison had scrawled, *'Seems up your alley, James'* across the top of the letter. Blessed told Kelly that it was not up his alley and could safely be put up something else entirely. Lastly, Kelly told him that he had checked with the Air Force. Price's widow had taken off from RAF Wunstorf and, barring disasters, should be here at BlessForce by the late afternoon.

Blessed and Weiss left the building, looped north through the Savignyplatz, following the S-bahn viaduct down streets of patched-up apartment blocks, queues outside every shop. The food lines were longer than he had seen for a year or more.

At present rates, Blessed had heard, the city would be able to feed itself for less than a month without massive importing of fuel and foodstuffs. He wondered if he shouldn't have pushed Harriet harder to take Daphne with her to England. He wondered, as he so often had this year, if he should get the girl into an English school for the start of the autumn term in September. Was he keeping her here in Berlin because he couldn't bear the prospect of waking up on a Sunday morning, or of coming home from the office early, and not finding a little round face with its gap-toothed smile beaming at him in the hall, or peering round the door?

'I saw this child today, twice, in different places, an hour apart. I could have sworn he was following me,' Blessed told Weiss as they passed the Stuttgarter Platz S-bahn station.

'Really? Did he approach you?'

'No. But he had his eye on me. If I'd just seen him going about his business, that would have been a coincidence, and fine. The Ku-Damm and the neighbouring streets are a small world of their own. Once you've been around for a while, you keep seeing the same people.'

'So? It's possible he was hanging back, wondering whether to proposition you or—'

'Christ, do I look like the type who likes little boys?'

Weiss laughed. 'What type? One can never tell, believe me. Or he may have been hoping you would be a candidate for a black-market deal, or for this thing they call *spritzen*.'

Blessed nodded. Young kids would act as agents for a gang of thieves. They would lure a promising-looking sucker into some waste ground on the pretext of a currency deal or a black-market bargain. There the others would overwhelm him, beat him up and steal everything he owned, even his gold fillings.

'It's possible,' he conceded. 'But why me? Especially as I'm dressed in German civilian clothes.'

'I don't know, James. Perhaps the child had seen you in uniform on some previous occasion. Perhaps it was a simple case of mistaken identity.' Weiss glanced behind them. 'Do you see him now?' he asked.

Blessed shook his head. 'I've been watching out for him, but I'm pretty sure he's gone. You know, Manfred, it's what's happened to the children here that really depresses me.'

'It is terrible,' Weiss sighed. 'I am very lucky that I have managed to feed my own children, to keep them off the streets. This is all one can do. Soon things will be better.'

'You think so?'

'All right, maybe I should say I *hope* so,' Weiss said with mild irritation. Few Germans were eager to discuss such matters with foreigners.

The building in which the supposed Dr Schmidt practised was well preserved compared with most of the centre of Berlin. Some chance had saved this particular block of buildings from the Allied bombers. Blessed looked across the street to Eva Hallgarten's place, saw that it too was in good condition, apart from some bullet-holes just below the first-floor windows. Providence preserved the good and the wicked alike, that was another thing they had in common.

The lift was out of order and obviously had been for years. Blessed and Weiss climbed the four flights of stairs, on the landings catching glimpses of backyards, facing windows, wrought-iron balconies festooned with washing. On the fourth floor there were three doors, one freshly-painted and with a brass plate inscribed, 'Schmidt. Dr. Med.'

'You ring,' said Blessed. 'And you show your identification. But leave the questions to me. All right?'

Weiss turned the bell-handle, an old Victorian arrangement that produced a faint, grinding echo on the other side of the door.

There was a delay. Then the click-clack of high-heeled shoes approaching over a wooden floor. A spyhole opened at eye level.

'Yes?' a female voice asked. 'Dr Schmidt is busy with a patient at the moment. Would you like to make an appointment?'

Weiss leaned close to the spyhole. 'I am Inspector Weiss of the Kripo. My colleague and I wish to ask Dr Schmidt some questions on a matter of urgency.'

'Just a moment.' The woman ducked away.

They waited. Eventually she reappeared at the spyhole. 'What is this matter, please?'

'We wish to discuss Heidemarie,' Blessed put in. '*Now.*'

Click-clack away again. Another minute passed before the door swung open and they were faced with a beautiful, brown-haired woman of about twenty-five, dressed to kill in high heels and the latest creation by Gieriger and Gipp, an all-German copy of the Christian Dior 'New Look'.

'Come in, Herr Inspector and Herr colleague,' she said. 'Dr Schmidt will see you just as soon as he is free. He asks the gentlemen to understand that he is an *extremely* busy man.'

'To pay for all this, he must be,' Weiss growled.

They were shown into a small waiting-room containing two elegant sofas and some armchairs. There were German and English-language women's magazines, plus a couple of dog-eared copies of *Time*. The feeling was comfortable, discreetly luxurious and—because of the time and the place—completely unreal. Everything was as if ten years in the past or ten years in the future. No Berlin doctor in 1948 could keep this place going by treating Germans.

Blessed and Weiss sat in silence. Five minutes later, the door opened and a blonde young woman of twenty or so, slightly less pretty than the siren at the reception desk, but even more expensively dressed, emerged from the consulting room. Behind her waddled a portly, crew-cut American colonel, patting the girl out by the ass and saying, 'Don't worry. It'll be all right. A few days and we'll be just fine.' He turned to the figure behind him. 'Send the bill to me, ah, care of the club, as usual. OK?'

In the wake of this couple appeared a handsome, silver-haired man in late middle-age. He wore a double-breasted check suit and a professionally paternal smile. 'Herr Colonel,' he said in charming, fractured English, 'I shall do whatever is most convenient. I'm sure a short stay in our clinic will solve the Fräulein's little problem.'

When the pair had been ushered out, he turned to the two policemen. Suddenly his eyes were hard, his look steady but guarded.

'Gentlemen,' he said. 'What can I do for you? I have another important patient—a senior Allied officer—due in fifteen minutes.'

It was an outrageous piece of rank-pulling. Schmidt thought they were two ordinary Kripo operatives who would back off when faced with a man who was under the protection of the Allied military establishment. Here was the doctor who performed abortions for the mistresses of Berlin's military rulers, and who cured their doses of the clap. The way the political realities stood, that put him a cut above any other German, even a German policeman.

'Sit down,' Blessed said in German.

Schmidt was placing an American cigarette in a long silver holder. 'In a moment,' he said testily. 'This isn't the old days, you know. Five years ago you could order an ordinary civilian around like that, but . . .'

'I still can,' Blessed said, and pulled out his SIB warrant card. Schmidt did pretty well considering. He finished lighting his cigarette.

'Well, Captain. You speak good German. I congratulate you.' He smiled glassily, clearly appalled. 'Anything to help, of course. Claudia said you are seeking information about my former receptionist, Fräulein Sanders.'

'Ah. Sanders. Heidemarie Sanders.' Blessed made a note of the surname. 'You describe her as your former receptionist. I was under the impression she still worked here.'

Schmidt threw up his slim hands. 'She had been working for me full time, and then on and off, as she wished. The last time she came in was three days ago, but then she disappeared without warning. I must confess that I haven't seen her from that hour to this. Luckily, Claudia—Fräulein Albrecht, that is—was able to step into the breach.' He tapped some ash out into an onyx ashtray. 'Marvellous girl, Claudia. So has Heide got herself into trouble with the British Army, Captain Blessed?'

'In a way. More her boyfriend, Dr Schmidt.'

'Ah, of course. He is a British soldier, I believe. I met him sometimes when he would come to pick Heide up from the surgery.

A vulgar fellow. We had little in common. His name was Prace, or Prize, something like that . . .'

'Price.'

'Ah, yes. Excuse me, but my knowledge of English is not so very good,' Schmidt said with an apologetic smile. 'So tell me, Captain, what has this soldier Price actually done to bring your attentions upon himself?'

'You want to know what Price has done, Doctor?' Blessed asked. 'Well, he's been murdered. The night before last. Along with your Fräulein Sanders.'

He watched Schmidt carefully. This man didn't seem the jealous type, Eva Hallgarten had been right about that, but he was certainly capable of killing for gain, or of hiring someone to do his killing for him.

Schmidt's eyes flicked away. Then he put his cigarette down to rest on the ashtray and crossed his legs, clasped his hands on his knees, raised an eyebrow. If he really did have something to hide, this was a superbly-judged performance. A little disturbance, but not too much, and mixed with just enough genuine fear to carry conviction.

'My God,' he murmured. 'I warned her about getting mixed up with Allied soldiers of that type.'

'What type?'

'Price seemed . . . seemed like a confidence trickster. How can I describe the feeling . . .'

'I think,' Weiss growled, 'that it's very much like the feeling I get when I'm sitting in the room with you, Dr Schmidt. The fact is, we have witnesses who will swear you've been buying stolen penicillin, and possibly morphine, from Price for the past year, at least. You know him well.'

'Really, Inspector. Who has been telling these lies about me? I know I have enemies, but this is absurd. And what can this possibly have to do with the unfortunate death of Fräulein Sanders?'

'We don't know,' said Blessed. 'That's why we're here.' He glanced towards the open door to Schmidt's consulting-room. 'I'm going to take a look in there. You can come with me, if you like, to make sure I don't do anything I shouldn't.'

Schmidt looked at his watch. 'Perhaps . . . could we postpone this interview until just a little later, gentlemen? You may wait in my apartment with a drink or some coffee. As I said, I have an important patient due in just a few minutes, and—'

171

'No.' Blessed was already standing in Schmidt's office, staring around. There was a high leather chair behind the mahogany desk, the usual instruments waiting ready, a filing cabinet, a couch for examinations, and an adjustable chair in the corner with stirrups to each side.

'You do a lot of gynaecological examinations, Dr Schmidt?'

'I am a qualified gynaecologist. After I was awarded my doctorate of medicine, I specialised in that subject.'

'You're very much in demand.'

Schmidt did not answer. He was eyeing the waiting-room nervously. Finally he could stay calm no longer. He took three strides and was at the double doors that separated the two rooms.

'Claudia,' he said. 'I am forced to delay the next appointment. If the brigadier will kindly consent to wait, take him through to the apartment and give him some refreshment.'

Schmidt closed the doors and turned back into the room. 'Gentlemen, just tell me what you want of me,' he said. 'Penicillin is one thing, but murder is another. I can assure you categorically that I had nothing whatsoever to do with the deaths of Heide and her dreadful boyfriend.'

Blessed and Weiss exchanged glances. It was possible to dislike this man but still admire his nerve. Whatever else he might be, Schmidt was no coward.

'Did Price sell a lot to you?' Blessed asked.

'Sell what?'

'Don't irritate me, Schmidt. You can't afford to. I think you need to understand that if we wanted to we could arrest you without even searching the premises. Now. While your next patient is waiting outside.'

'Very well,' Schmidt said slowly. 'I will admit that at certain times a physician . . . I say this as a moral supposition . . . may be forced to exploit dubious sources of supply in his search for the healing substances he needs. If this is universally true, then how much more so for us in Germany during these tragic and chaotic times? I have helped many people, Allied and German, from all levels of society, as my colleagues will bear witness . . .'

'I'm not all that interested in "moral suppositions" at the moment, Dr Schmidt. So I'll ask again, very directly, and this time maybe I'll get a straight answer: Did you buy a lot of stolen drugs from Corporal Price?'

172

Schmidt pursed his lips. 'Yes. A little morphine and cocaine,' he said. 'A lot of penicillin. It's the new miracle drug, isn't it? You, the Allies, have penicillin. We, the Germans, do not. It can mean the difference between life and death.' He shrugged. 'That's why people are willing to kill for it, and will pay whatever it costs—without enquiring where it came from.'

'Did Price cheat his clients by mixing the penicillin with other substances, so that it crippled or killed patients, or by diluting it so that it was ineffective?'

'Not with me he didn't!' Schmidt was fiercely certain of his ground. Now that he had decided to talk, he was clear and direct, a professional discussing with other professionals. 'With my clientele, I couldn't afford any of that nonsense. I can't speak for his other customers, but . . . well, I keep my ear close to the ground, and I never heard mention of such fraudulent dealing in connection with Price. That was one of the reasons I continued to buy from him.'

'Which is also why,' Blessed said, 'I'm mystified as to why anyone should have wanted to kill him. Was he good to Heidemarie, would you say?'

'Good? He took her out. He spent money on her. He didn't beat her up. To a girl like Heide, he must have seemed heaven-sent.'

'What did Taffy see in her?'

'Who knows what men see in women and vice-versa? She was still pretty. She was likeable, amusing though uneducated.'

'Was it what you'd call a regular sort of arrangement that they had?'

Schmidt nodded. 'Their relationship was strangely domestic, although I'm sure both of them continued to sleep around. They were fond of each other. Unusual these days. Captain, it was very sad that they had to die like that.'

Blessed looked towards the window. There was a pair of prints of coy, prancing Maxwell Parrish nudes on the wall, presumably to please the American clients. Their bodies were glowing with antiseptic, scrubbed health, asexual vitality. How curious in the office of a specialist in abortion and venereal diseases. Or how clever.

'This is a question I have to discuss, Dr Schmidt,' he said calmly, working to conceal the nausea and panic he felt. 'You indicated that Fräulein Sanders was sexually promiscuous. Did she tell you she had syphilis?'

Schmidt looked genuinely shocked for the first time. 'No. She didn't.'

'Would you have expected her to have told you?'

'Not necessarily. She may not have wanted me to know, because . . . well, there's a chance I might have dismissed her,' Schmidt admitted. 'In any case, Price had the drugs to cure both of them. In that way, she was lucky. Unlike your Allied soldiers, for whom penicillin treatment ensures a reliable, almost instantaneous cure, and to whom sex has become a game without risks, most German girls who catch VD can't even get the old-fashioned sulphur treatment, never mind penicillin. Like earlier generations we shall face long-term physical suffering, even madness and death, on a massive scale unless this drug becomes generally available. If we had legal supplies of penicillin, this epidemic of sexually-transmitted disease could be cleared up just like that!' Schmidt snapped his well-manicured fingers.

'I daresay,' Blessed agreed.

'Was Price infected too, Captain?'

'Yes. He probably gave it to her.'

Schmidt made a dismissive gesture. 'Typical. But it's a risk these days. What statistics I have managed to collate indicate that something like a third of the single female population of Berlin under the age of thirty have VD. You can work the odds out for yourself.'

'Might she have gone to another doctor?'

'Not one who knew me, I don't think. Presuming she didn't want me to find out, she would have been frightened that if she went to a friend of mine, he would tell me anyway.'

'Fair enough. Heide was single?'

'There was a husband, who was killed in the early part of the war. After that, plenty of boyfriends. She shares . . . shared . . . rooms with Anna, a German girl from Poland who is also promiscuous—a prostitute, in fact. They were firm friends, but Heide was very proud of having a proper job here at my surgery, instead of living like Anna and so many other young women these days.'

Blessed asked Schmidt for the address of Heide's apartment and the doctor gave it to him. Two rooms in Moabit somewhere.

'You're sure Heidemarie wasn't involved in prostitution as well?' he asked then.

'She gave herself often, Captain, but not for money—at least, not directly.' Schmidt smiled a slit-thin, cynical smile. 'There is a traditional but nevertheless fine distinction between the girl who

174

expects presents, and the girl who demands cash in advance, is there not?'

'Quite. How did she see the relationship with Price, anyway?'

'I am sure she believed that eventually Price would divorce his wife and marry her. She saw him as her escape route from the misery of occupied Germany. And . . . well, I think she realised that she was getting a little too old for the sexual merry-go-round.'

'And what do you think Price's intentions were?'

'I don't think he would have left his family for her. Price was fond of his son. He talked about him sometimes, especially when Heide wasn't around. He hadn't seen him for a long time—every leave, Price came to Berlin to set up deals and have his fun with Heide—but the child was nevertheless important to him.' Schmidt shrugged his elegantly-tailored shoulders. ' "My son and heir", he used to call the boy. Like so many men of that class, he spent little actual time with the child. All that mattered was that the boy *existed*.'

'Did Heide have any family or dependents?'

'She never mentioned any. She came from the March of Brandenburg, about twenty miles from the city, but she had been in Berlin since she was sixteen or seventeen. Perhaps as a young girl she got into trouble and was disowned by her parents. I think that's the most likely thing, personally.'

'Any former boyfriends still in Berlin? One who might have held a grudge against her?'

'The festering jealousy of the rejected suitor, eh?'

'Something like that. I want to know if she ever seemed afraid.'

'No, Captain. She was a happy-go-lucky woman who lived very much for the moment. Of course, one never knows how much she may have been hiding . . .'

'No. Now, she met Price through you. But how did you get to know Price? Did he offer himself or was he recommended by a colleague?'

'The latter.' Schmidt sensed that he was getting into deep water. 'I would never take a chance with such a person unless I knew he was reliable.'

'I see I'm going to have to ask you outright, Dr Schmidt. Who provided the introduction? Who recommended Price to you?'

'Another doctor,' Schmidt said with an airy wave. 'He has now left Berlin. He is, I believe, practising in Kiel, so you will realise he could have had nothing to do with this dreadful business . . .'

'His *name*, please!'

'Bennigsen,' Schmidt admitted. 'Dr Rainer Bennigsen. I told you, Captain, I don't know his address, only that he moved to Kiel four or five months ago.'

'Thank you, Dr Schmidt. I'm sure we'll be able to find him if we need to.' Blessed noted the name in his book. 'Speaking of boyfriends, you and she were lovers for a while, I hear,' he said. 'Is that correct?'

'Ah . . . yes, it is true. A very pleasant interlude in both our lives. For a few weeks. Until I met someone else, and she met Price, and . . .' Schmidt gave an amused shrug. 'No problems on either side, I assure you.'

'Yes. Did Price give her the name "Suzy"?'

'He did. I don't know why.'

'All right then. Was there anything, anything at all, recently that struck you as odd or disturbing?'

'Captain, I hadn't seen her for several days. She had started working part-time. As for Price, I saw him ten days ago, to do some business. I think he wanted to set her up in her own little apartment and so on, just like a gentleman's concubine, but Heide insisted on coming in for two and a half days a week. In case anything happened to him, she said.'

'In case anything happened to him?'

'Crime is a dangerous business, Captain Blessed. You know the profits that can be made. People become greedy.'

The door outside had opened. There was the sound of voices. Claudia's and a man speaking halting German with a British accent. Schmidt glanced at his watch. His manner was still unconcerned, but Blessed noticed that his Adam's apple was twitching slightly and that there was sweat on his fine, high forehead.

'Well, did you see anyone around here lately? One of our informants has mentioned that some associates of Price would come here to meet him. Did you see any? Especially, did you see a tall, well-built man, a metre ninety or so, in his late forties, with a pugilist's face?'

'There was a big man in the street with Price a few weeks ago. I didn't see his face. There were others. British servicemen. Germans of a more normal height and build.'

'The big man. You're sure you never saw his face or anything else about him? Didn't you notice any distinguishing features?'

'I don't recall any. Please understand: either I am up here on the fourth floor with my patients, or I am hurrying off to the clinic. I don't sit around watching the street, Captain. Try the neighbours. I believe some of them have nothing better to do.'

'Have you ever met or heard of a man named Karl-Heinz Panewski? Or a man named Ludwig Gross, *alias* Floh?'

'No, Captain.'

Blessed snapped his notebook shut. 'That'll do for now,' he said. 'We're not releasing many details to the press yet, so if you talk to anyone about these murders, you could end up in big trouble. Is that clear?'

'Absolutely. In any case, my clientele demands discretion. Any publicity would do my practice nothing but harm.' Schmidt made an ironic little bow and moved towards the door. 'Anyway, I hope you catch the culprit or culprits quickly,' he said.

The double doors opened. In the waiting-room, a tall man with a dark moustache was sitting half-hidden behind a copy of *Time*. He tried to cover himself completely when he saw the two visitors, but he wasn't quick enough.

'Ah, Brigadier. Afternoon, sir,' Blessed said, and saluted. Brigadier Bratby, president of the officers' club he used, and a vigorous opponent of 'being too chummy with the Germans', was caught in the waiting-room of a Dr Schmidt, the notorious pox-doctor and abortionist. 'Nice day for it,' Blessed added with a pitiless smile. He marched out, with Weiss following on his heels.

Blessed paused in the ground-floor hallway, peered around. He pointed to a door with a bellpush bearing the name 'Pless'. 'This flat looks directly out onto the street,' he said. 'These people would stand a pretty good chance of seeing and hearing anything that went on out there, wouldn't they?'

'I suppose you're right,' Weiss said. 'You want to talk to them?'

Blessed nodded. 'You introduce us again. Flash your warrant card.'

Weiss rang the bell. A minute or more passed. They were about to give up when the door opened slightly on a chain. There was a glimpse of silver hair and spectacles. A frail old lady's voice asked them who they were and what they wanted.

'Frau Pless? We're police,' Weiss said, flipping out his warrant card. 'I am Kriminalinspektor Weiss. This is my associate. We would like to speak to you, and to any other members of your family who are home.'

The old lady didn't look down at Weiss's card, and she stayed behind her chain. 'I am alone here, Herr Inspector . . . but what can I do for you?'

'Do you know Frau Heidemarie Sanders?' Blessed intervened. This woman was alone, probably housebound. The lonely and the

177

invalid make wonderful observers. They are hungry for incident, entertainment. 'She works as an assistant to Dr Schmidt upstairs.'

'Heide, yes. A nice young woman. Sometimes she helps me across the street. She and her young man, the English soldier.'

'That's right. Do she and her soldier often meet people outside here?'

'We are near the Kurfürstendamm, officer. All day and all night, British and French and American and Russian and I don't know what, with their girls, shouting and screaming and singing.' She clucked angrily. 'They told us "Enjoy the war, because the peace will be terrible." Pah! They were right!'

'We are interested in a particular friend of theirs. Maybe in the last few days—'

'Ah, those girls of Dr Schmidt, they come and they go! They smile and laugh and tease their Tommies, their Yanks. Sometimes negroes, you know. Some of them prefer negroes. Isn't that disgusting?'

'This friend, the one I want to know about, was German, Frau Pless,' Blessed persisted. 'Tall and strong, in his forties.'

'In his forties? No, officer. The one I am thinking of must have been younger than that.'

'Who was this, Frau Pless?' Weiss took over.

'A German. Outside. You wanted to hear about a German, and I'm telling you, officer. Let me see . . . this was a few days ago. Heide and her Englishman were outside. It was early in the evening. A German was complaining loudly, saying they had something, they would not give it to him . . .'

'Did anyone mention his name?'

'No. Though I think the Englishman called him in English "boy".' The old lady pronounced it 'poy'.

Blessed and Weiss exchanged disappointed glances.

'This "boy",' she continued happily. 'This boy, he was so angry he said he would kill them. I tell you, such dreadful things happen out there—'

'And what did the boy look like?' Blessed asked quickly. 'Please. This is very, very important.'

There was a silence. 'I don't know, officer,' Frau Pless said. 'I'm sorry. I thought you realised. I have cataracts in both my eyes and have been blind for the past five years.'

As they walked back along the Joachim-Friedrichstrasse, Blessed checked the time. It was after five. Taffy Price's widow should be at the station now. There was also this Anna to see, and Heidemarie Sanders' room in Moabit. Best that he and Weiss went back to the office and caught up on the situation there, then took a car to Moabit. That way, he would make it home before Daphne's bedtime. He couldn't leave it to Weiss or Kelly to check the address in the Huttenstrasse and interview Anna, if she could be found. Blessed longed to go home, but he couldn't resist the prospect of going fresh into the room where Heidemarie Sanders, also known as 'Suzy' had lived, and of being the first to feel its signals, interpret its silent language.

'Mrs Price is here,' Kelly told them when they got back to BlessForce. 'Took her no time at all to identify the body. Once she'd signed the papers, I parked her in the interview room. Want to have a word, sir?'

'All right. I suppose I should.'

Blessed was shown into the tiny interview room at the end of the corridor. It was thick with cigarette smoke. Sitting at the table in the middle was a small, round woman in her early thirties with a putty-coloured smoker's face and too much lipstick. At seventeen she had probably been kittenishly pretty; now she was simply a sharp-featured, slightly overweight housewife. The eyes, though, when they fixed on Blessed through the fug of nicotine, were watchful and intelligent.

'Mrs Price?' he said. 'Captain Blessed, SIB. I'm in charge of this investigation. I'm very sorry to have to bring you all this way to perform such a sad duty.'

Clarice Price nodded mutely.

'Anyway, thank you for your help,' he continued. 'It can't have been easy.' Blessed was aware that Mrs Price was staring in a puzzled, slightly offended sort of way at his shabby German suit. He had forgotten that he was still in civilian clothes. To her eyes he must look more like a brush salesman than a military police officer. 'Can we get you a cup of tea?' he asked.

She lit a cigarette from the end of her previous one. 'No, ta,' she said at last in a firm voice, with just the strong Welsh accent Kelly had mimicked. 'Since this morning I've had so much bloody tea, I feel like I'm turning into a tea leaf. You know? Whenever there's a crisis, everyone reaches for the tea. You can't stop 'em pouring the stuff down you.'

'Yes. That's true.' Blessed took out a cheroot. 'This must have come as a shock,' he said.

She nodded. 'And him having that girl as well.'

179

'Such things are an unfortunate fact of life. I'm afraid many married servicemen do take up with German girls while they're stationed over here.'

'They don't end up murdered, though, do they?'

'No, they don't. I'm sorry.'

'Not half as sorry as I am. I know I hadn't seen him for the best part of a year, but we were still husband and wife. And he was Caradoc's dad. You can't change that.'

'No.'

'Oh, I suppose I knew, sort of,' she said with a sigh. 'I kept the job at the colliery, I didn't want to give it up, and the boy was so little, and I wanted him to be near his grandparents and that. But there was something else that made me keep me financial independence. I knew Ronnie would start skirt-chasing when he left home, see. He could turn any girl's head—' She breathed in hard, fighting back tears. 'Was he . . . was he up to no good here, then?'

'He had dealings in Berlin, Mrs Price. He came here quite often before the blockade.'

'What kind of dealings?'

Blessed looked at her sitting there, so tight and so desolate and so angry, and he felt that there was no point, and no virtue, in telling her precisely what her husband had been up to.

'He was somewhere he shouldn't have been, and he was murdered, Mrs Price,' Blessed said. 'That's all that really matters, isn't it? I'll do my best to catch the murderer, I promise you that.'

'Oh, don't you think I didn't know my Ronnie,' she said, and laughed harshly. 'He was always keeping bad company. And he was always on the fiddle.' Then her voice turned vehement. 'But I didn't want to lose him. And neither did his son. Dear God, what shall I tell his son? His da was out with some little German tart and got murdered, is that the story?'

'I don't really know the story yet, Mrs Price. We're working hard to establish the facts.'

'It's lucky I kept the job in the colliery, that's all I can say. At least we can live. If I'd given it up, and come out here to this godforsaken bloody country, then where should we have been, I ask you?'

'I'm sure the army's welfare people will do everything they can to help you and your son, Mrs Price.'

'But . . . for Ronnie to die like that . . . you know, I still can't believe it,' she said, lighting yet another cigarette from its predecessor.

'I'm very sorry.' Blessed pushed back his chair and stood up. 'I really am. But now I'm afraid you'll have to excuse me. We're working very hard on solving this case, and I must get on. I hope you're being well looked after for tonight, Mrs Price.'

In a moment she was on her feet too, and had gripped his arm. She didn't want him to go. Perhaps she felt that for as long as Blessed stayed, she was not yet officially a widow, not yet officially alone . . .

'Oh, they're going to put me in some hostel, so they tell me,' she said. 'I don't mind, I'm sure. They're flying me back tomorrow. My first time up in an aeroplane, this has been. Christ, would you believe it? Someone said I can't bring Ronnie's body home. Is that right? You're keeping him?'

'Yes. We have to keep him. For a while. It's usual in these cases.'

'When it's murder, you mean.'

Blessed nodded. 'We have to be sure how it happened. Establishing the facts can take some time, I'm afraid.'

She nodded absently, drawing hard on her cigarette. Her eyes were clouding, their corners glistening with unborn tears. Her face was puffy, ugly with misery. He prised her fingers from his arm as kindly as he could, patted her hand and released it.

'Just one more thing,' she said. 'Was it quick? I mean, when Ronnie went, did he linger, do you think, or did he just . . . go?'

'It looks like he would have . . . gone . . . quickly, Mrs Price.'

She blew her nose with a little green cotton handkerchief that she produced from her handbag. 'And . . . she . . . ?'

'I think she had a much less easy time of it, Mrs Price, to be honest,' Blessed told her.

Clarice Price nodded. She drew in a long, deep breath and stubbed out the cigarette in the ashtray. She stood up to her full height, such as it was, and shook herself, as if preparing for the rest of her life.

'Ah well,' she said softly. 'So there's justice in this world. At least the bitch suffered.'

SEVENTEEN

BLESSED TOOK KELLY AND WEISS with him in the Horch to Heidemarie Sanders's flat in the Huttenstrasse. It was getting late. Still, he had to make sure he got in first with this Anna, and with Heidemarie-Suzy's room. Then he could go home with a clear conscience, leaving the others to do a routine search and take a statement.

They almost missed the building, or what was left of it. Most of the dwellings in Moabit were huge, block-long tenements built in the nineteenth century, the square buildings running inside each other, divided by cobbled yards, until in the dark heart of the complex a small, gloomy central yard was reached. Those were the least desirable apartments, the coldest and darkest and dampest. This particular tenement had had most of its top two storeys shaved off by bombs or artillery fire, and a great deal of other damage had been done. The three policemen took some time to gain access from a gloomy, deaf old janitor, but once in they were free to make their way through the half-cleared devastation to the middle, to Heidemarie's and Anna's apartment.

The further they made their way in, the worse it got. When they came through into the last courtyard, it was dark and quite cold. The fifth and sixth floors were open to the setting sun: next to the bellpush that was labelled 'Sanders Löbke' was a wall-less void. Heidemarie's apartment was almost entirely detached from the rest of the block. It was a mystery how this had happened; perhaps fire travelling down through an air-vent had wrought this destruction before the blaze was brought under control. Kelly rang the bell but Blessed shook his head. There was as good as no chance that it would work. The sergeant banged hard on the door with his fist instead, and they waited.

From somewhere at the back a male voice shouted something in a language that wasn't German. They waited some more. Kelly banged again. This time they heard no voice. Blessed told Kelly and Weiss to keep trying, then moved off alone. He cast a quick eye over the ruined section of the building, working out which part of the surviving interior wall marked the boundary of Heidemarie-Suzy's flat. First taking his Webley service automatic from its shoulder-holster, he began to pick his way carefully towards a point in the partition wall which seemed to be a boarded-up fireplace. He could hear Kelly still knocking out the front and calling out, 'Open up! Come on, open up!' As he got closer to the wall, he could also hear a low moaning coming from the other side of the fireplace.

Blessed felt the hugeness of the building and its secrets, its gutted power, as he reached the boards, nailed without particular skill to block up a common fireplace, keeping out the cold and giving some privacy. There were gaps between the planks, and through them light was visible. He held his breath, released the Webley's safety-catch, and placed his eye at a slit.

There was a large table and a tin bath, a stove, a scattering of cheap chairs; the usual furniture of an old-fashioned, working-class kitchen where the family cooked and ate, kept warm and bathed. The light came from two candles on a shelf. On the table was the naked, writhing body of a woman, fleshy and pale-skinned, with long, dark hair that hung down the edge of the table, moving in time to her frenzied movements. The man was wearing an American army helmet, and a dog-tag around his neck, and that was all. He stood at the end of the table, feet planted apart and legs bowed to bring him to the right height for the coupling, gripping her buttocks to pull her towards him. He held her ass so tightly, pulled her so hard, that the muscles in his powerful arms bulged like a weightlifter's. Meanwhile, he thrust rhythmically in and out between her wide-spread legs, with a strange serenity that contrasted with his knotted muscles and the thrashing of her body. She was muttering something. At first Blessed thought they were words of obscene encouragement, but as he listened he realised she was forming the words in German-accented but slangy American-English, *'You come, Joe, eh? It's the cops. Cops at the fuckin' door. Come, come!'* But the GI seemed oblivious to anything she said. He just kept on thrusting and clutching, as if he had all the time in the world. As Blessed watched, he turned his head to reveal an ordinary,

183

pleasant young midwestern face. His eyes were closed. He was wearing the smile of a baby that's being tickled.

The woman's writhings were slackening a little. There was something angry and forlorn about her movements now. '*Nu komm' doch, Arschloch!*' She hissed. '*Come, Joe. Police!*'

Blessed turned away, retraced his steps. Kelly was still banging on the door when Blessed returned.

'Shall I break it down, sir?' he asked, stopping for a moment. 'I know there's someone bloody well in there.'

'You're right. There's someone in there,' Blessed said. 'But they're busy, so busy they don't want to answer the door yet.'

Kelly looked interested. 'That sounds to me like a pretty good reason for breaking it down, sir.'

'No. I think the lady will do her best to get out to us as soon as she can. Keep thumping the door just as you were doing, to show them we're still here and we're not going to go away.'

Three or four minutes later there was the sound of a bolt being drawn back, and the door pulled back a few inches onto a chain.

'Yes? What do you want?' Blessed could see that it was the dark-haired woman. She was wearing a cotton dressing gown several sizes too big for her.

'Fraulein Löbke? British Military Police, SIB.' Blessed held out his warrant card. 'We want to talk to you.'

'I have done nothing wrong,' she said, recoiling from the card.

'I didn't say you had.'

She thought about that. 'So? What do you want?'

'It's about Fräulein Sanders. Something's happened.'

'What are you talking about?'

'I think it would be better if we discussed everything inside, don't you? Can you get rid of your American friend?'

Anna Löbke cocked her head to one side, as if deciding whether she liked the look of Blessed enough to do as he said. She granted him a knowing smile, then turned away from the door, yelled in her particular brand of Berlin-American: 'Joe! You dress . . . double quick! Limey MP are here!' Her face reappeared at the gap. 'Come in. He'll be out of here in two minutes, OK?'

She disengaged the chain, let it drop and the door opened. Blessed led the advance of the three policemen into the dark, peeling hallway. Anna Löbke tossed her long dark hair and padded ahead of them along the hall. There was a wide crack running the length of one wall, a pervasive smell of damp.

184

They entered a living room of sorts, with a battered sofa and two chairs, a radio in the corner. Blessed could see the door to the kitchen. Anna Löbke had gone in there to pacify her GI and get him out of the place. She was as good as her word. Two minutes later the beefy, fair-haired young man Blessed had glimpsed in the kitchen appeared in the doorway with an embarrassed grin on his freckled, healthy face. With his clothes on, he looked younger, no more than nineteen or twenty, and fresher than anyone had a right to look after what he had been doing. He was still languidly tucking his shirt into his uniform pants with one hand. The other was holding his helmet. The strange thing was, he had worn that helmet when he had been having sex, but now he carried it shyly in his hand, like an old-fashioned gentleman caller. As he looked the three newcomers over, his expression changed.

'These ain't like no MPs I ever saw,' he said in a slow, wheat-belt drawl. 'What the hell is this?'

Blessed showed his identification again. 'Captain Blessed. British SIB. I'm in plain clothes this evening. This is my colleague, Sergeant Kelly, and this is Inspector Weiss of the Berlin Police Department,' he explained. 'All right? Please run along now, Private. We need to talk to Miss Löbke in confidence, and we don't have time to waste.'

'Joe, they are on the level,' Anna Löbke said, taking him by the elbow. She smiled apologetically at Blessed. 'He is just trying to protect me, Captain. You never know these days . . .'

For a long moment it seemed as if the boy might refuse to leave. He continued to stare at Blessed and the other two. Then he nodded slowly.

'OK,' he said. 'It's up to you, Anna. Be seein' ya.'

Anna Löbke went back into the kitchen, lifted a cigarette from one of the packs that the GI had left on the table, lit it with a silver-plated lighter and came back into the room. Blessed liked her for that. She could have waited, tried to shame a smoke out of him. Plenty of girls, English as well as German, wouldn't have thought twice about it.

'We can speak German from now on,' he said.

'All right with me,' she said, sitting down in one of the armchairs and motioning for them to relax in the remaining seats. She was a pretty, slightly overweight woman in her late twenties, with fine high cheekbones and a look of resigned sensuality that was typically German and postwar. Her way of speaking was postwar too, heavily punctuated with American words, even when she used her own language. 'So what's happened to Heide? Is that guy of hers in trouble? Or has she had an accident?'

'I'm afraid she's dead, Miss Löbke. And so's he—if it's Corporal Price you're referring to. They were both murdered.'

Anna Löbke took a long, careful pull on her cigarette, looked up at the ceiling. 'Shit,' she said then. 'Shit. She didn't deserve it. She wasn't a good girl, but she wasn't bad either.'

'When did you last see Fräulein Sanders?' Blessed asked.

'At nine am, give or take a minute, on Thursday.'

'You seem very certain.'

'She was rushing out, off to meet Ronnie—Price, you know — somewhere. He hadn't stayed the night here, which was unusual. Anyway, I was listening to the nine o'clock news on the radio—it was the first morning of the blockade, you remember, and we were all thinking it might mean war with Russia. Heide calmed down and stopped for a minute, two minutes, to listen to the latest developments. That's how I remember.'

'Then she left. And you never saw her again?'

'No . . . I . . . Usually she and Ronnie would stay here, but sometimes they would go away and stay away for two, three nights. Sometimes she would say they had been west into the Zone, or had gone partying with some pals of Ronnie's . . .' Anna Löbke stopped, wondering if she had given away too much.

'We know Price was involved in the black market. Anything you say now can't hurt him, or Fräulein Sanders, but it may help us to find out who murdered them,' Blessed said. 'And we're not interested in how you make a few cigarettes or a few dollars, either. I give you my word.'

'Don't worry, Captain. I trust you. Anyway, that's why I wasn't worried when she didn't come back Thursday night, or last night. We were always free and easy, you know? Hell, I could go places and not come back for a while. If there was a party, you know, we'd have a good time for days . . .' Her faint smile hardened into a grimace. 'I knew she shouldn't have got involved with Ronnie. He knew some funny people. I mean, not nice. He thought he could handle them—his type always does—but he was out of his depth, that stupid man, and he took Heide with him. Shit.'

'Did you ever meet any of these people you're talking about?'

She shrugged, apparently casual but guarded in her eyes. The irises were a pale wash of grey, the colour of winter skies. Now and again, in an involuntary movement, she would glance suddenly to one side or the other, just with her eyes, not moving her head. She obviously didn't even know she was doing it. It gave Anna Löbke the look of an animal emerging from its burrow.

'Well? Please tell us. It's important,' Blessed pressed her. 'Were they mostly soldiers or civilians at these parties?'

'I can't say. All kinds, I guess. Pilots. Soldiers. Even a Russian or two. Some British and German civilians. The British civilians were officials of the Military Government, so-called advisers, that kind of thing. They were pigs, I tell you, some of them. Americans can be brutal, but at heart they're simple men, easily pleased. But when you get a bad Britisher, a really perverted type . . . eck, you wouldn't want to know about that, Captain.'

'Can you remember any names?'

'They were hardly ever mentioned. It wasn't like a society party, as you can imagine. Sometimes a Christian name. Or a nickname, you know. Like one man was called "Dicey", another one "Nosher".'

'Mitchellson? Does that ring a bell?'

'I'm not sure . . .'

'A small man. Balding. Jack Mitchellson was his name. A friend of Price.'

'I think that might be this person "Dicey". That was what Ronnie always called him. Yes, "Dicey" Mitchellson sounds right. He was sweet.' Anna Löbke shrugged. 'You know, he couldn't do it, actually, but he didn't get angry. He accepted it. Do I have the right man?'

'Probably.'

'You speak very good German, Captain. Why?'

'My mother was a Berliner. I'm told you're from Poland. Is that right?'

She smiled wryly. 'Sure. *Volksdeutsch*. That's me, a glorious example of Aryan triumph in the East, born in Poland but racially German. I liked Poland. I didn't really want to come to Germany.'

'In that case, why did you leave?'

'No matter how fond you are of a place, would you sit quietly and wait to be raped, Captain? Maybe by the Russians first, then the Poles, then by any DPs who were around and happened to be feeling horny?'

'I'm sorry. It was an insensitive question.' Blessed paused. 'I'd like to get back to Price's friends. Did you know anyone called Floh? An old man?'

'No,' Anna Löbke said. 'No, I never knew anyone like that. And I would remember such a name.'

'What about Panewski? A big man in his late forties, flat-faced and muscular. A real bruiser.'

'Yes,' she said. 'I think he was at a party a couple of months ago. I didn't like him. He . . . he wanted me, but instead I went home with an English friend of Ronnie's, one of the nice ones, not a pervert.'

'This man you think may have been Panewski, how was his relationship with Price and Fräulein Sanders? Was there any sexual jealousy or rivalry?'

Anna Löbke weighed up her answer carefully. 'I'll tell you something,' she said. 'Heide flirted with all Price's clients. He encouraged her to. Maybe he thought it was good for business.'

'You're saying her flirting was a kind of ploy, that it was fake?'

'Mostly. Occasionally she'd be genuinely attracted to some guy she met through Ronnie. In the case you're talking about, though, I'd say it was very unlikely. Heide's taste wasn't what you'd call refined, but I reckon she would draw the line at a creep like that.'

'He could have mistaken her professional flirting for real attraction.'

'Sure. It would have been stupid of him, but . . . well, you know how men are . . . or maybe you don't.'

'Most important of all, do you think that this man—whoever he was—might have been capable of extreme violence?'

'You meet guys like that now and again, so you get to know the type. When they have a problem, they solve it by hitting someone, or carving them up. He was like that.'

'What about murder?'

'Maybe. A lot of people are capable of murder, Captain. Not necessarily the people you'd think. Do I have to tell you that?'

'No, you don't.' Blessed got to his feet. 'Thanks, anyway. You've been very frank and helpful. I'd like to look at Fräulein Sanders's room now.'

'Feel free. I think I'll have a drink.'

Anna Löbke went over to a cupboard by the radio, got out a bottle of Jack Daniels whisky and a glass. 'Policemen aren't supposed to drink on duty, I know that,' she said. 'And in any case, I have only one bottle, a present from a friend. I keep it for . . . difficult moments . . .'

There was a bed, a small cheap bedside cabinet, a chair. That was all. On the wall a sentimental picture of a little girl who had fallen asleep under a tree and was being watched over by angels. Blessed moved closer inside, looked around. There was also a photograph of Ronnie Price with a glass in his hand, looking happy and jokey in the countryside, presumably at a picnic. His eyes were screwed up against

188

the bright sunlight. The window to the room was open. As Blessed looked around, he noticed a general air of things having been moved. He called out to Anna Löbke. She came to the door. He noticed that she had already almost finished her glass of Jack Daniels.

'Did you open this window?' he asked.

She shook her head. 'I haven't been in here for three or four days, since well before the last time I saw Heide. She would never have left her window open, and . . .'

'What? Is there something about the room that doesn't feel right? This is important.'

Anna Löbke nodded solemnly. 'On that little shelf, by the window, she had some pictures of herself, and of herself and Ronnie, and . . . well, she had a little baby once, but she said it died. She had a picture of that. So sad.'

'A child? Was that when she was married?'

'Before that, I think. I don't really know.'

'You're sure these things have been taken?'

'I think so.'

'You didn't hear anyone break in?'

'No.' She looked thoughtful. 'Though to tell the truth, the other night—last night, actually—I thought I heard Heide coming home. If I hadn't had company, I would have come out to see if it was her.'

'It's difficult to imagine that someone would commit burglary just for some photographs. Can you see anything else missing, Fräulein Löbke?'

'I don't know if there was any money or cigarettes, or . . . you know, drugs. There sometimes were. Heide was careless. She left valuable things around. We trusted each other, there had been times when each of us had given the other all we had . . .' Anna Löbke suddenly looked vulnerable. 'We met in the spring of forty-four, you know, in Warsaw,' she said. 'We were both untrained auxiliary nurses. Looking after men, saving them from death. Would you believe it? And we stayed together until now. Price killed her,' she added bitterly. 'He didn't do it himself, nothing direct like that, but if you ask me, he was responsible for what happened to Heide.'

'How?'

'The circles he took her into. The way he showed her around. Bad people. He knew a lot of bad people.'

'But don't you worry, Fräulein Löbke? About what can happen to a woman in your world?'

Anna Löbke's face took on a closed, opaque look. She laughed unconvincingly. It was her professional, cover-all laugh.

'My GIs are all right,' she said. 'That's why I prefer them. They look after me.'

'You said she was rushing off to meet Price last Thursday. Did she mention where?'

'Somewhere in the Westend. I don't know. But I do remember she said she and Ronnie might be going to the Tabasco later. I sometimes go there . . . you can meet guys with money to spend, you know, out for a good time. They know me there. They let me sit with a glass of coloured water until a good prospect comes on the scene.'

'And did you see them there?'

'No. I went somewhere else. To the Casino, then to Bobby's, where I met a prospect. He was here when I heard those noises I told you about, and thought it was Heide back, maybe a little the worse for drink.'

'Anything else? Think hard. Every little detail may make a difference.'

'Well . . . she was in good spirits that morning, poor thing. I remember now, why she mentioned the Tabasco was that they had a big deal cooking, and if it all came off, the champagne would be on her Ronnie. Big man Ronnie, always about to pull off that last, big deal that would make his fortune. She even hinted that he might take her away from Berlin altogether if everything worked out. She always hoped that. Maybe this time she was right.'

'I see. Do you have any idea what that particular deal involved?'

'None. I knew what business Ronnie was in, but nothing more than that. Heide was very loyal. She kept his business secret, even from me. That was one of the things that came between us lately. We never had secrets before.'

'She had syphilis when she died.'

'I know. She told me about it. It was Ronnie who gave it to her.' Anna Löbke shrugged. 'In a way, she was lucky. The bastard traded in penicillin, so at least she could get herself treated.'

'What did she think of Price giving her the disease?'

'You mean, did she hate him for it, Captain?' Anna Löbke went to the window, looked out into the shadowy courtyard. 'Maybe she did, a little. But what was she supposed to do? What would most of us do? Could she walk out on Ronnie, big man Ronnie? He was the man with the *Valuta*, the Craven "A"s and the nylons. Her meal ticket, Captain, in a city where meals are not easily come by. Ronnie could screw anyone he liked.' Her lips tightened into a hard line. 'Of course,

190

Heide had to pretend it didn't matter that he'd given her the clap. I'll tell you, I prefer to do what I do, Captain. I'm not dependent on any one man. And guess what? I'm still alive.'

They walked back into the living room together. Weiss was smoking and pacing the room. Kelly seemed half-asleep but snapped awake the moment Blessed appeared, got to his feet.

'I'm going home,' Blessed said. 'There's indications of forced entry in Fräulein Sanders's bedroom. Take a look at that, please. And you can ring me at home if anything else comes up. I'd like to be kept up to date on whether Panewski's been seen about town. So far, he seems the most likely contender for the burglary. Perhaps there was something incriminating here, or perhaps he knew of valuables kept in Fräulein Sanders's room. Try to get a list from Fräulein Löbke of the items presumed stolen.'

'Do you think Panewski would have risked coming here and being caught breaking in, sir?' Kelly asked.

'If he had a pressing enough reason, yes.'

Weiss stubbed out his black German cigarette in an ashtray made from an old sardine can. 'I couldn't help overhearing your conversation in the next room,' he said. 'Fräulein Löbke mentioned a big deal Price was expecting to do. Maybe it was with Floh and Panewski. Maybe they killed him and his girlfriend, took the stuff without paying, then tried to make it look like a different kind of a murder, a crime of sexual perversity, something like that.'

'It's something we have to consider a strong possibility now. As I said, keep me informed,' Blessed said. 'It also seems, from the evidence in the other room, that whoever broke in was interested in photographs, personal stuff. Don't forget, there were no documents on Suzy's body when it was found. We thought at the time that she might have left her identity and ration cards at home, but now it seems more likely that the killer stole them.'

'But Price's paybook and money were left untouched. That's how we identified him so promptly. This is, er, extremely odd, sir.'

'It certainly is. So give the room a thorough going-over. Make sure the documents aren't still hidden around the place somewhere, will you?'

'Absolutely, sir.'

'I think we should put an extra man on watch at Floh's place, too. I'll radio that order through on the way home, and I'll also arrange for a car to pick you up from here. An hour enough for what you need to do?'

Weiss nodded. 'Have a good evening, sir,' Kelly said.

Blessed made no comment about that. He turned to Anna Löbke. 'I'm afraid we'll have to ask you to identify Fräulein Sanders's body,' he said.

She shrugged. 'I was expecting that.'

'Well, goodbye, Fräulein. And be careful.'

'Ah, yes,' Anna Löbke said with her edgy, cover-all laugh. 'Carefulness. That's a luxury item. I can't afford it, Captain, and I don't know many girls who can.'

EIGHTEEN

'YOU COULD DIE. Unless you do exactly what I say, you could die.'

He shook his head, unable to speak properly because of the six-inch, dangerously tapering cylinder of glass lodged inside the roof of his mouth.

Daphne peered at her end of the toy thermometer, flicked it. The point scraped against her father's palate. He grunted in protest: '*Hay—hee—how!*'

'The patient wants to tell me something,' she giggled, straightening her nurse's head-dress. Then she reached forward and whipped the thermometer out of Blessed's mouth. 'What does the patient want to tell Sister Blessed?'

'The patient was trying to say, "Take it out", you beastly little girl. Now try this one.' Blessed clenched his teeth and spoke as if he still had the thermometer in his mouth: '*Hiss hed pime*'.

'I give up,' Daphne said innocently. 'Say something else.'

'You know perfectly well what I said. I said, it's bedtime. I know it's the end of your birthday, but all good things have to come to an end, Daff.'

'Who says?'

Blessed grinned broadly. 'Kiss. The kisser says it.'

Daphne flung her arms around him.

'Mum said she would bring me a present back from London. Do you think I'd like to live in England?'

'I don't know. What do you think?'

'Perhaps it would be nicer. Mum says it is. She doesn't like Germany.'

'No, she doesn't.'

'Is that why she's going back to England?'

'Partly. But also because Mummy needs a rest.'

Daphne looked puzzled. 'She doesn't need a rest. Cook does the cooking, and Gisela does most of the mummying things with me . . .'

'That's not really true. Your mother plays wonderful games with you. She takes you to the club for a swim in the holidays and at weekends. She reads you stories. She talks to you like a grownup and takes you shopping . . .'

'I know, but—'

'She organised your party. You had a *marvellous* time. You told me that yourself, just a few minutes ago. Without Mum it would never have happened.'

Daphne nodded. 'But—'

Blessed stood up, tried to look stern. 'Now, take yourself off and ask Gisela to run your bath. She should have finished helping Mummy pack by now.'

'Mum gets easily bored. She told me that herself. She says it's a bad character flaw, but she can't help herself.'

'Bath!'

Daphne made a face, flounced off across the drawing room and up the stairs.

Blessed watched his daughter until she disappeared from sight along the landing. When he heard the sound of the taps running upstairs, he stood with his back to the fireplace and smoked a leisurely, thoughtful cheroot. For the first time in several days he had on a sweater and some comfortable old slacks, and he had spent some light-hearted time at home with his family. Any outside observer who had walked into that room would have put Blessed down for a contentedly domesticated man. It was unlikely they would have guessed that his wife was due to leave him in the morning. In fact, this evening Blessed felt unexpectedly calm. Of course, until the crisis with Harriet was resolved one way or the other, his feelings would probably fluctuate quite wildly. Nevertheless, in this mood he could find himself thinking that maybe it was better if Harriet went off for a few weeks. After all, he needed time to think too, about his career as well as his marriage. That was the conscious part of his reaction to her impending departure. The unconscious one was the screw that turned in his gut every time he considered the possibility that this time Harriet might never come back, this time she would leave him.

And the iron chain of the SIB rattled and clanked; every time he tried to find some room for manœuvre, it rattled and clanked. He thought of Panewski and Floh, of Anna, and of Schmidt, the pox doctor with his calculating brain. Blessed wondered with that perpetual longing and loathing what was happening out there in the darkened city, with the airlift planes roaring overhead, and he wondered whether he needed to be controlling things in person. He had sworn he wouldn't ring the office tonight of all nights.

'Right. Well and truly packed. Anything that's not in that suitcase by now isn't going on the plane.'

He looked up at the sound of Harriet's voice, saw her up on the landing, leaning over the balustrade and smiling at him in the nervous, isn't-this-ghastly-but-who-cares way that she assumed for awkward situations.

'I heard the water running. Has Gisela managed to get Daff into her bath?' Blessed asked.

'Just about. It wasn't easy. The nurse didn't want to take off her nice new uniform.'

Harriet came downstairs, headed straight for the dining room and the alcohol. Blessed stubbed his cheroot out in the ashtray on the mantelpiece.

'So. Alone at last. You and me,' Harriet said to him through the open door. She opened up the drinks cabinet. 'Drink, Jimmy?'

'All right. Whisky.'

'Good. Personally, I'm having a gin so big that if I stood it outside, the planes would crash into it, like they keep nearly doing to that bloody great brewery chimney on the way into Tempelhof Airfield.' Soon Harriet emerged with two tumblers, both filled almost to the brim. 'Cheers, anyway,' she said. 'Surely you've heard about the famous chimney?'

'No. I haven't had much time to catch the latest gossip.'

'I see you're paying as little attention to the international crisis as you are to the rest of us, Jim. Well, apparently, some Kraut brewer's got this huge thing outside his factory. A frightful hazard to air traffic, of course. But he won't have it demolished, no matter how much compensation the Yanks offer him; he says he'll go to the Supreme Court in Washington if necessary . . .'

'Harriet!' he interrupted firmly. 'I'm not interested in the bloody chimney!'

'Anyway, they're . . . what?'

'Slow down. Admit it, you're as confused and worried about the future as I am.'

Harriet looked annoyed, then she swallowed some gin, then she made a wry face, and finally she nodded. 'All right, I am. It's a big step, clearing off to England on my own. I'll miss Daff. I might even miss you. A bit.'

'Well?'

'Oh, I'm still determined to go, Jim. This may have looked like an overnight decision to you, but I assure you it wasn't. It only seems that way because you haven't been paying attention.'

'Oh yes? What about Redman? Didn't he have something to do with it?'

'Larry's an excuse,' Harriet said, with a laugh that reminded him of Anna Löbke's cover-all. 'He just happens to be your opposite. A lecherous, self-serving bastard who fiddles his official expenses and takes time off from important government business to conduct illicit love-affairs. Not very admirable, but quite attractive at certain times and in certain lights.'

'So you're saying Redman's not the reason you're leaving; all you really want to do is to get away from me. I'm not sure whether that's supposed to make me feel better or worse.'

'It's not *supposed* to do anything, Jim. Don't you see things have gone too far for that? I'm just trying to tell the truth, for what it's worth. I know I don't want to live like this any more. I need this time off to decide how I *do* want to live.'

They stood there with their drinks, several feet apart and not coming any closer, like guests at a cocktail party who've only just been introduced. Perhaps when the end of a marriage approaches, a couple return to the defensive shyness of their first meeting.

'Look,' Blessed said eventually, 'I didn't mention it at the time, but I got a summons to see Colonel Harrison yesterday. He—or rather, the powers-that-be—are planning to squeeze me out of Berlin.'

Harriet looked at him fiercely and swallowed a serious quantity of gin. 'And what, Jim, is the point of telling me that *now*, eh?'

'Food for your thoughts, I suppose. So that you know that Berlin probably won't go on forever. Almost certainly won't, in fact.'

'But the Branch will. Isn't that so?'

'It's my career.'

'Then as far as I'm concerned, nothing has changed,' Harriet said. 'I'll still be an SIB widow, whether you're stationed in Cairo or Cologne, Aden or Aldershot. I'll still go on being attracted to men like

196

Larry, who may be bastards but who at least give me the time of day. I'll still be organising birthday parties, playing jolly mummsy—always on my own, naturally.'

'I explained about Daphne's party. Twice. Once over the phone, and again when I got home. I had to go exactly there and then, or an important witness wouldn't have spoken to me—'

'You promised us. Me and Daff. Another broken promise,' Harriet said with bitter emphasis. 'The stupid thing is, I mind more than her. She was very philosophical about your not turning up this afternoon. Somehow she seems to get enough of what she wants from you . . . Well, I *don't*. Perhaps that's why you and I have both ended up feeling cheated—I got too little from this marriage, and in a way you got too much!'

'Harriet—' Blessed could feel his calm gradually but inexorably being worn away by his wife's need—not her anger, for once, but her need.

'No, Jim. I know what you're going to say. You're going to say that you hate rows. I have my doubts about them too, but let me tell you, a good row is a darned sight better than nothing!'

Blessed winced. The worst thing was that he could see real pain in her blue eyes, not just the usual icy anger. 'I can't force you to stay,' he said, in as level a tone as he could manage. 'Even supposing I could, what would be the point? If it has to be solicitors at forty paces, then so be it.'

'Very stiff-upper-lip,' Harriet said. She had finished her gin and was playing with the empty tumbler, keeping her hands occupied while she decided whether she should return to the drinks cupboard and get another. 'Strong, silent Jim, who always does the right thing. If only I could believe that was the whole story! What really makes you run?' she hissed. 'What makes you so attached to your wretched, squalid crooks and your ugly little murders? What makes you prefer all that to the good things? I—any woman—could offer you the earthly paradise, and do you know what you'd say to me? If I was really lucky, you'd say yes, perhaps, once this case is finished with, once *all* the cases are finished with . . . It never seems to end, you see. That's what I can't stand. That's the fear that makes me behave badly, do things that I hate myself for, Jim. *It never ends!*'

'Look, Harriet, I've said I *understand* why you need to go away—'

'But do you? And is it really *me* who's the deserter in this marriage? Sometimes I think you left me years ago. You just come home to visit Daphne!'

'Who's coming to visit me?' piped a voice from the landing. Daphne was standing up there, huddled in a bath-towel, watching them keenly through the bannisters and resisting all Gisela's efforts to usher her towards her bedroom. 'I want to know. Who's coming to visit me?'

Not for the first time, that old, recurrent nightmare had robbed him of his sleep. Harriet was turned firmly away from him on the far side of their bed. Blessed lay staring at the ceiling. His mind refused to give him peace; it obstinately forced him to revisit the dream in full consciousness. In the eye of his memory his small self was also lying awake in bed, and it was also the stillest, deadest time of night. The boy Blessed heard a lone motor-lorry drive past, roaring and rattling through the suburban darkness. The only other sounds were the creaks in the plumbing and his mother's Berlin-English, still exotically stilted even after ten years in London. How does a woman manage to whisper while her heart is breaking? How does a woman quietly decide the future of her marriage in the middle of the night? But quiet this desperate interrogation had to be because of little Jimmy, and in the middle of the night because then he was in bed and she and her husband could believe they were alone, that the boy would hear nothing. They were wrong. Little Jimmy Blessed had already acquired a lifetime's habit of always needing to know, to hear, to understand: a policeman's habit. That terrible night, he heard everything. Every word his parents uttered was recorded, indelibly inscribed just below the surface of conscious memory, ready to bubble up almost thirty years later in his dream; or when he lay feverishly awake, as he did now, and his mind seemed to merge with that of the small boy who heard everything, and recognised the pain of it all, but actually understood so very little.

First his mother:

'*What made you want her? What? Tell me, Alan! Tell me why you did this to me! I can't go on like this.*'

Then his father's tired, frightened voice, slightly slurred from drink:

'*Trude, Trude. I'm so sorry. Weakness. At least I told you. Give me credit. At least I told you, so that you can begin the treatment . . .*'

'*Was she prettier than me? Did she do things I will not, cannot do?*'

'*Trude. Please. Please.*'

'*But what was the fascination? Alan, what was the fascination of this . . . this unclean woman?*'

'*How could I know about the sickness? How?*'

'Because with all such women there is a risk of . . . this awful thing . . .'

A long silence. And then Blessed's father said:

'We must live apart. You must take Jimmy away. What I did was filthy, unforgivable. The fault is mine. The weakness is mine. I am a weak man. Trude. Stop crying just for a moment, please . . .'

And his father's voice petered out into a low, long, man's sob, the most desperate sound Blessed had ever heard.

Less than two weeks after that night, on a searingly cold December day, Blessed had stood beside a grave hacked from the frozen earth and watched his father's coffin being lowered out of his sight forever. He could still remember staring up at that intimidating circle of black-clad adults, gripping his mother's hand all the more tightly. After the burial, there had been the grownups' sidelong glances, the queer, knowing quality of their commiserations to him and his mother, which he had understood only many years later, when he was already an articled clerk and on his way to qualifying as a solicitor.

Blessed had been told the truth when he was twenty by his wealthy bachelor Uncle Theo—the same Uncle Theo who had subsidised his education and his year in Berlin, and who had insisted that Blessed undertake legal training in his firm. As a lawyer the old boy had made his fortune by fostering an appearance of unbending rectitude and strict discretion, monkish virtues which seemed to inspire trust and brought him many profitable clients. In private, though, he could never keep his mouth shut—especially after a few large brandies.

'Your father, being a doctor and a considerate sort of chap, knew how to make it look like "natural causes", dear boy,' Uncle Theo had told his nephew with that lugubrious alcoholic's grimace of his, which could still arouse in Blessed a mixture of awe and loathing, even now. 'That way, you see, your mother was able to bank the life insurance money and have something to live on. But actually, James, you should be warned. Alan had been straying, as certain chaps will, and had got himself and your mother into some very hot water. As a result, he was extremely "down" during those last weeks, and at one time there was the risk of a suicide verdict, which would have put the kybosh on everything.' By this time, Uncle Theo's face had been so close to Blessed's that the smell of his high-proof breath was almost overwhelming. 'So, as you embark on your adult life, let this be a warning to you to stay on the straight and narrow,' he had intoned before refilling his brandy balloon. 'A fellow should never weaken, if you follow my meaning.'

199

It hadn't taken long for Blessed to piece together the whole tragic story. His father had gone with a prostitute and had been infected with syphilis, which he had unwittingly passed on to Blessed's mother. Unable to bear the shame and the despair, he had killed himself. The newly-widowed Mrs Blessed had been ill herself for more than a year ('tummy trouble', he remembered being told). After a lengthy and painful cure, she had pulled through sufficiently to bring up her son, with the aid of the likes of Uncle Theo. But she was never the same. She had been subject to depression—and outbursts of puritanical frenzy—until the end of her life. All through his childhood and adolescence, the message was hammered so hard and so vividly into little Jimmy, until it had become divinely-ordained law for big James, *that he should never weaken*. Yea, though he be beset by all the temptations of Sodom, available if he would offer a bar of chocolate or ten cigarettes; though the whore of Babylon smile at him in piano bars and ask him for a light; though Jezebel search the Ku-Damm, downing coloured water to keep up her strength. Yea, through all these temptations Blessed would never, never weaken. No transmitter of sickness, he. No wrecker of homes, maker of sadness . . .

The first ring of the telephone jangled Blessed's consciousness but failed to make him stir. On the second he managed to reach out, and with the third he lifted the receiver. Harriet still lay motionless, apparently deeply asleep.

'Hello . . . Blessed . . .' he mumbled.

'Er, sir, we are in a very considerable bit of bother.' It was Kelly, as crisp and on-the-ball as if this were the middle of a working day. He was, however, less than usually full of himself, for reasons which were quickly apparent. 'Floh has been murdered, at his flat.'

'Oh. Dear Christ.'

'No sign of forced entry. Our boys outside didn't see the killer. They had the whole area covered, but they still didn't spot him—'

'What time is it?'

'Ah . . . a quarter past three, sir.'

'Right. How did they find him? How did they know he was dead?'

'He has a telephone in his bedroom, apparently. It started to ring and ring, and after five minutes, when Floh still hadn't answered it, our blokes thought they should investigate. In case, er, he had vacated the premises without their knowledge. They knocked on the door, there was no reply, and so they broke the door down. I know we didn't contact you first to get permission, sir, but—'

'It's all right. What appear to be the immediate circumstances?'

'Cut throat. In bed. As I said, no indication of forced entry. Of course, we'll have to look the place over properly. There's no electricity in the district at the moment, so we're having to do everything by torchlight and hurricane lamp.'

'I'll be there as soon as I can,' Blessed said, already grabbing his dressing-gown. The first thing was to wake poor Thwaite, tell him to get the car ready.

Ten minutes later, Blessed was tying his tie, mentally composing the note he would leave on the bedside table for Harriet. She was still lying with her back to him on the far side of the bed.

'Another stiff, Jim?' As usual, his wife had caught him by surprise.

'Yes. Another.' He pulled the knot tight on his tie, began to shrug himself into his jacket. 'One of the prime suspects has been murdered. Possibly by another of the prime suspects.' *So what*, he imagined her thinking.

'I see. Obviously you must get over there, then. I'd better ring first thing for transport to the airfield, hadn't I?'

'I'm afraid so. Can you tell Daff and Gisela . . .'

'Yes, yes. Go on, Jim. Run along.' *Motherly. Exhausted. Sarcastic.*

He could hear Thwaite warming up the Horch outside in the drive, gently revving the motor with all the loving familiarity of a violinist tuning his instrument before a performance.

'OK,' Blessed managed to say. 'I hope the flight's a smooth one. I'm only sorry it's ended up like this. Between us, I mean.'

There was a sigh, then silence from the bed. Blessed still couldn't see Harriet's face to interpret its expression—though God knows, the way she continued to keep her back to him conveyed a powerful enough message.

He made for the door. Thwaite was waiting for him, and there didn't seem much to be done here. He was on the threshold when he heard his wife's voice. He turned, of course, ashamed to find himself catching his breath like a character from some cheap romance.

'Jim?'

'Yes, Harriet.'

'It never ends. What did I tell you? *It never ends.*'

201

NINETEEN

FLOH HAD RENTED a roomy bachelor apartment on the second floor of a building in a pleasant part of Charlottenburg. According to the records of the police *Meldeamt*, he had lived here for more than ten years. He had been in good company. This location was close enough to the Ku-Damm and the Tiergarten to be convenient for business, but far enough away for relaxation and, when necessary, retreat. As a result, the area was much favoured by black-marketeers and entrepreneurs, all the parasitic creatures who feasted off the carcass of a once-great city. An irony was that 89 Company SIB had its headquarters in the Rüsternallee, no more than a quarter of a mile away. Blessed knew he was encroaching on the competition's territory, and had he been in a more cheerful mood to start with, he might even have enjoyed the fact.

Kelly, the three plain-clothes men who had been on watch here, and two German police were waiting at the flat, and there was also a German forensic man and a police surgeon. They had organised kerosene lamps as a temporary measure, but shortly after Blessed arrived, the electricity and gas went on for the district. German housewives would be hurrying to their stoves to bake and fry and boil, no matter that it was four in the morning. Most important of all, Blessed could see Floh properly.

The old man lay in bed in a pair of Chinese silk pyjamas. His hands and feet had been tied with wire, a bandage used as a gag. His lifeblood was on his chest and on the turquoise satin sheets. Blessed saw a phone by the bed; the German forensic man was dusting everything for fingerprints. He also saw the First Empire table on which the phone sat, and the brocade sofa, and the mahogany chairs. There was a self-portrait by Max Beckmann above the large, deep fireplace, an Otto Dix nude on the opposite wall, and elsewhere a Matisse drawing. Blessed wondered if Floh had collected those artists at the time they were working. On the other hand, maybe he had been sharp enough to buy during the Nazi period, when such pictures were officially ridiculed as 'degenerate art', and maybe also he had bought from emigrating Jews, at knockdown prices. Plenty of collections of art and antiques—not to mention whole houses, entire businesses—had passed into Aryan hands that way.

'To look at him, you'd have thought the old bastard lived in a dump. Floh did himself all right, though, didn't he, sir?' Kelly said, noticing the way Blessed was looking around the flat, appreciating the treasures. 'Not in the end, of course. Did himself rotten in the end. These types usually do, I find.'

'Black marketeers live well,' Blessed said. 'When almost everybody else has nothing, and you have something, you can live very well indeed.'

So the world went round, he thought. That table, the sofa, the chairs, were probably all theft or booty in the first place, stolen by German troops in occupied Europe—that first Empire table pinched from some château; the sofa purloined from some elegant home in Prague; these mahogany chairs bought for a pittance from some Dutch East Indiaman's widow who had fallen on hard times. And with his penicillin wealth, or his pimping pence, Floh had created this elegant little hideout. Here, however, death had finally tracked him down and had not been diverted by the decor.

The members of the surveillance team were standing by the fireplace, talking quietly, looking sheepish. Blessed beckoned over their leader, Sergeant Campbell, a balding, bespectacled figure in a German leather coat.

'Well, what do you call this?' Blessed demanded harshly. 'I call this, on the face of it, a right royal cock-up. I'll be looking through your report very, very carefully later on this morning.'

Campbell grimaced. 'I was in the Mercedes in the street. Francis and Swift took turns to patrol the entrance to the service road at the rear. And I can assure you no one went in the front, except two tenants from the block of flats. No Panewski, no other suspicious characters. Of course, there was only the three of us. But we covered all the means of access well, sir.'

'Er, no forced entry and no sign of a struggle, sir,' Kelly intervened. 'Sergeant Campbell is right. The sash windows are locked from the inside, the door from the fire-escape as well. It's a complete bloody mystery.'

'I suppose . . . I suppose it's possible that someone *might* have got up the fire-escape,' Campbell said. He blinked behind his spectacles. 'But it must have been someone he knew, or he would never have opened the door to them. Which of his acquaintances did he really trust?'

Probably very few, Blessed thought. But apparently one too many. 'The front entrance was covered all the time. What exactly is at the back?'

'A narrow service road. A fire escape, as I said, and a little bit of garden.'

'The roof?'

'There's access all right, but the janitor keeps it locked at all times except when he's doing maintenance work. He has some rich tenants, he says. Floh's not the only one who's done well on the black market. It strikes me that our janitor is well-informed. He would be worth, er, cultivating as a source of general criminal intelligence. For future operations, I mean, sir.'

'Perhaps.'

Blessed found himself curiously uninterested in 'future operations' all of a sudden. All he wanted was to find out who this killer was, which at the moment meant working out how the hell he had got in here. He realised his skin was prickly, that he was perspiring quite hard, though the room was far from warm. The need to know was like a fever. Of course, the fact that Floh had apparently opened a door to his murderer indicated someone he knew—like Panewski. Always back to Panewski.

'What's downstairs, Sergeant?' he asked.

'I don't rightly know, sir. I've had no chance to look down there yet.'

'Has anyone?'

'Better ask one of the Krauts, sir.'

'*Germans*, Sergeant Campbell. Within their hearing, anyway. Understood?'

Blessed walked over to where the two Berlin cops were standing. 'Have you investigated all means of access, including the roof and the basement?'

The senior German, a fat wachtmeister with a beery red face, nodded. 'I suppose someone could have made his way across from the neighbouring rooftops. But the only access from the roof into the building is through a trap that's bolted from the inside. Impossible. The door between the cellar and the rest of the building is usually open, apparently. First, though, you'd have to get into the cellar, and that's not exactly easy either.'

'No doors on the street?'

'Only the main entrance, which your people were watching.'

'What about service access to the building? Any hatches or doorways that my people might have failed to take note of?'

The beery sergeant shook his head. His colleague dug him in the ribs, grinned. He was wiry, nervous, with a pointed chin and an almost grotesquely wide mouth, like the great clown, Grock. 'In the basement there's this cute little hole, Captain,' he said with a chuckle, holding his hands about eighteen inches apart. 'A coal-delivery chute. That's all.'

'Take me down there,' Blessed said.

They found their way down by torchlight, because the light bulb in the basement had gone, and the janitor hadn't been able to get a replacement because of the shortages. Amazing, he grumbled: you'd think with all these black-market traders around the place, they could come up with a goddamned light bulb for the common parts of the building. I mean, d'you think they go without light bulbs in their fancy apartments?

The basement was a long, low room with a couple of sinks at the far end. Sometimes people did laundry at funny hours, the janitor said, because, you know, they *worked* funny hours, so the cellar doors were always left unlocked. The German cop had been right, though. There was no alternative access. A former service door had been taken out and the gap bricked up. There was no natural light, no skylight or grille to the street. Just that chute. The coal bunker at the bottom was empty, had been for years, the janitor told him. Access to that was through a manhole outside in the street.

'The killer'd have to have been a midget, and a skinny one at that,' the wide-mouthed German cop suggested.

'Do you know Panewski?'

'No. I'm new in the Central District. But the moment he got here Sergeant Kelly had us put out a general alert for the bastard. Big fellow, a real *Schläger*. As you English say, a "thug", eh?'

Blessed nodded. Yes, and with his height and those shoulders Panewski would probably have had trouble getting through a normal-sized doorway, let alone a coal-chute eighteen inches wide.

Upstairs again, Weiss was standing with the fat wachtmeister and looking at Floh's body. The inspector greeted Blessed in a subdued fashion. He seemed exhausted.

'Well, this scheme seems to have backfired,' he said. 'But then how did Panewski—or whoever—get in and out of here so cleanly, with your men watching outside?'

'I don't know. Gloat if you like. Tell me you'd never have risked this.'

Weiss shrugged. 'It's not my kind of stratagem. Perhaps I've served for too long in an extremely bureaucratic force, where individual initiative is not encouraged. And during the Hitler time, we were not expected to let anyone go, for any reason at all, you understand?'

'You're being too kind, Manfred. Don't bother. I made a serious mistake.'

'You—we—were outwitted by someone, James,' Weiss said. 'Someone clever and maybe very cocky. I'm intrigued by the ringing telephone. Either a coincidence, or an act of bravado on the part of the killer.'

Blessed hadn't given much thought to the ringing of the telephone, even though this had led to the discovery of Floh's body. Perhaps it had been a wrong number. Perhaps, as Weiss said, it had been some kind of macabre joke. Until now, the physical details, the evidence that could be seen and touched and tested, had seemed more immediately relevant.

At Blessed's suggestion they went outside to look around. The sun had not yet risen, and the wind was still fresh. The sturdy grey façades of the villas and apartment houses stood revealed now in that eerily seductive pre-dawn light that seems to come from nowhere. Thwaite was slumped in the driver's seat of the Horch, cat-napping, while the radio hissed and crackled on regardless, keeping vigil for messages. Blessed and Weiss made their way out into the middle of the cobbled avenue. A few brave souls were on their way towards the nearby Westend S-bahn station; a workman in overalls was struggling along on an ancient bicycle. A horse and cart plodded by. The two policemen stared up at the front of the apartment building.

Blessed pointed to a broken window in an apartment on the second floor, directly above Floh's. 'What do you think?' he said. 'Possible?'

'In theory, yes. But in practice anyone who tried to climb in there would have been seen by your surveillance people.'

Blessed nodded. 'That's a crucial question, isn't it? How could anyone have got in without being seen? Especially, of course, a man of Panewski's build.'

'What if—' Weiss began hesitantly.

'Yes?'

'What if Panewski was already hiding out in the building? Before Floh was sent home from the Knesebeckstrasse, I mean.'

'He'd have been forced to hide elsewhere—in the cellar perhaps—while my people searched Floh's flat that first evening after the Tiergarten raid. Unlikely, but not completely out of the question, I suppose.'

'Or maybe he knew one of the other tenants. Maybe he was being sheltered elsewhere in the building.'

'We'll be interviewing everyone who lives here. If that's what happened, I'm sure my boys will find out.'

They walked up the street for a hundred yards or so, as far as the next corner. There they stood in silence for a while, feeling the breeze on their faces. The forecast for Berlin was humid and showery yet again. This would probably be the most pleasant part of the day.

'Actually, the matter of the ringing telephone is interesting,' Blessed said suddenly. 'But not quite for the reasons you suggested. You see, it led us to the body in a particular way at a particular time. Just as that child guided Wachtmann Pilzinger to the first bodies. Perhaps the killer bribed that child. And perhaps he made Floh's phone keep ringing tonight, to alert our men outside and provoke them into forcing an entry. It occurs to me that he might be trying to control the timing of all these things.'

'And why should he do that?'

'I have no idea. I haven't got as far as understanding his motives.'

Weiss let out a small grunt of amusement. 'Come, James. Forgive me if I sound pompous, but I have investigated at least a score of underworld murders much like this one. My experience leads me to be very sceptical about the idea of such a subtle, not to say utterly enigmatic, master plan.'

Before Blessed could answer, a loud whistle made them turn and look back in the direction of the apartment block. Sergeant Kelly was standing on the pavement outside it, signalling frantically for them to return.

'You'd better come round the back, sir, quick,' Kelly said when Blessed reached the front door of the building, with Weiss close on his heels. 'You see, they've found a bloodstained weapon in the service lane. And the German forensic chap says it's absolutely smothered in prints.'

TWENTY

'DO YOU TRUST TOO MUCH, BENNO? Or do you not trust enough?'

Benno shrugged. 'Enough? I learn not to—'

'But do you trust the Kinder? Do we all trust each other?'

'Of course. Kinder-trust is different. Each other we trust, no one else. You beddabelieve it.'

'Yes. Bedda. Believe. Bedda. Trust,' Boss-Kind drawled.

They were sitting in the Lair. Boss-Kind lay back in his broken chair, smoking, looking down his nose at Benno and talking slow but with huge emphasis. The Wonder had curled up and gone to sleep in the corner, grabbed this chance of rest like an exhausted soldier snatching a few minutes' welcome oblivion. As for the Boss, what came to mind was some altogether higher, icier being; maybe a very tall creature looking down on the world and finding its inhabitants more and more pathetic. Although he was dressed in a shabby Sunday suit, Boss-Kind still looked every inch the arrogant young warrior-prince. The Wonder was sleeping in his best shorts and sweater, ready for the flight to Frankfurt. Riese's boys were supposed to be picking them up pretty soon.

'We have to wait a week, while I am away. The special, big business is not ready yet.' Boss-Kind ran his fingers through his hair, which was still quite wet. He and the Wonder had been out during the night—yet again, somewhere wild and secret—had arrived back and changed into their travel clothes only maybe a half-hour ago. 'The wrong things been happening,' he said. 'Bigman did some very dumb stuff, yes. His friend—the old old fart they call Floh—did even dumber. They deserve whatever they get!'

Benno had also been asleep, his first good rest in days, so he didn't feel so bad. It was six in the morning, almost light up there in the world of Hats. 'Boss-Kind, what are you talking about?' he asked gently. 'Is Bigman in trouble? Is his friend the old fart Floh in trouble?'

'Big trouble. The biggest.' And the Boss laughed again.

'How big is that?'

No answer. Am I Boss-Kind's fool, Benno thought, to be dragged out at all hours for his amusement? He had once seen a film, about a king or an emperor. This king had a fool, and the fool made him laugh so much that he got purses of real gold money to spend, and good bone-chicken and beefsteak food to eat. But the fool ended up in a dungeon, maybe even dead. See, when the king stopped thinking he was funny . . .

'And I speak to you of trust, yes, Benno,' Boss-Kind continued, as if he had never made the reference to the troubles of Panewski and Floh, 'because while me and the Wonder are away in Frankfurt, I gotta special watching-job for you, and I must *trust* you to do it. Yes?'

Benno nodded.

'Bigman-Panewski, he shoulda trusted me, taken that blade, Benno. Now he is a hunted man, Benno. Hunted by Kepten Blessed. His fault for not trusting, not taking the blade in order to protect himself. Not trusting is Bigman's weakness.'

No nod was necessary this time, Benno decided. No nod, no shaking of head, no comment. Boss-Kind was running on automatic.

'But Kepten Blessed is different,' Boss-Kind continued. 'I wanna talk to you 'bout that Kepten, 'cos you seen him, heard him . . . and you will see more of him . . .'

'You . . . you want me to keeping watching that Kepten?' Benno asked.

Boss-Kind smiled, shook his head. 'No. Just girlie.'

'*Girlie? Daff-nee?*'

'Morning. Afternoon. Schooltimes.'

'That's all?'

'That is *enough*. Enough for now. Until I return from the Hershey-Zone and I am ready.' Boss-Kind paused. 'See, if we want to save the Kinder Garden from that Kepten—*because I tell you the danger is not over, and will not be for many days*—then we gotta know his everything—his big strength, his big weakness. First his strength—you want to know what that is?'

'The Kepten, he speaks German, I heard, Boss-Kind . . .'

'No! That is true—and it also makes him dangerous—but that is not the Kepten's real strength: *His real strength is, he don' give up easy.*'

'Oh yeah? And now the weakness?'

The Wonder stirred in his sleep. He was muttering incomprehensibly; his nimble little hands were fiddling with invisible bonds, or perhaps making a cat's-cradle. Boss-Kind glanced at him before answering:

'Kepten's big weakness, yes . . . Not fear. Not that those other Tommies hate him. Not even that Mummypie shouts at him, the way you told me. None of these things. This is why, yes this is why that Hat Blessed interests me. Do you want to know what his real weakness is, Benno? *My eyes see. My ears hear. I been thinking hard. You really want to know?*'

'Sure.' Benno shrugged, drawing on his last reserves of patience. 'Sure, Boss-Kind. Tell me.'

'*It is the Kepten's girlie, Benno,*' Boss-Kind said. '*It is Daff-nee. She is his weakness. That is why you must watch her for me.*'

PART 2

THE KINDER

We will make it a city of nets
Plump little birds will be eager to enter

Berthold Brecht,
'The Rise and Fall of the City of Mahagonny'

TWENTY-ONE

DOING HIS BEST to ignore the downpour, Benno rolled himself a cigarette the singlehanded way a Siberian tank driver had once taught him, way back in the early days of the Occupation.

There was an unseasonably strong easterly that seemed to drive the rain right through to his skin, at times gusting so savagely that it all but scythed his knees from under him. Nevertheless, Benno dared not stray from this spot, though there would have been some protection from the weather in the shattered wall that lay fifty yards to his right. Skilfully cupping his hand, he lit the cigarette with one of the precious American matches Boss-Kind had given him last week before rushing off in such feverish excitement to Frankfurt with the Wonder. He sucked in nicotine, felt the burning smoke like a thrill beneath the skin, warming his bony fingers. Of course, he wished that Gurkel or the Wonder was here, but the Wonder was still in the Hershey-Zone, and Gurkel busy elsewhere in Berlin with Granit and Banana. This was Benno's sixth successive morning of waiting and watching outside the gates of the Spandau District British Primary School.

Eins—Zwoh—Drei—Vier—ahaha. Eins—Zwoh—Drei—Deutschland Awake, Eat chocolate cake. Pennsylvania six-five-thousand—six-five-oh-oh-oh . . .

Benno stamped—or splashed—his feet discreetly in time with these private, whispered tribal chants. He did not want to draw attention to himself. At least this watching, however wet, was harmless. It was better oh yes better than running packages to strange cellar hells where they looked at you with their little pinpoint eyes like you were something to eat.

215

Deutschland Awake, Eat chocolate cake.

This period of Boss-Kind's absence in Western Germany was, then, not a bad time for Benno. Three days ago there had been a rare 'orphanage' excursion organised, to visit Tempelhof Airfield courtesy of the US Airforce, which amazingly did these things through something called a Public-Relations-Department—compulsory attendance by all the Kinder, officially supervised by old out-of-his brains Doktor Barnhelm, actually led by Granit, the Boss's deputy. Naturally, this trip was just cover for corruption, some business to do with the (successful) cultivation of money-loving, customs-evading Hershey airlift pilots.

Otherwise, the only orders Boss-Kind had left were the ones for Benno to watch this school gate, morning and afternoon. A lot of Kinder-business was in suspension during this time—in fact, almost all of it, with the exception of this routine surveillance of Kepten Blessed, his girlie, and her Nannypie. There was no Mummy Blessed around any more. Mummy had gone. Benno stared at the beautiful book of matches, with its carmine-coloured advertisement for Lark cigarettes. The sight comforted him, filled his eyes and quietened his grumbling stomach. Lark meant cigarettes. For cigarettes say gold and diamonds, say rich foods from the *Schwarzmarkt*. Sweet Lark. Sing . . .

Deutschland Come Awake, Eat that chocolate cake. Penn-syl-vay-ay-ania six-five-oh-oh-oh.

Rejoice. The rain was easing off a bit. Also, the English Kepten's big, shit-coloured monster of a Horch was just nosing its way around the corner, heading for the school gates, with Blessed's fat-faced driver at the wheel. Benno whistled with delight. Here was a treat; he got bored with the girlie tripping along with Nannypie, hop-skip-jump. Today he would be able to inspect the Kepten and his car. He would watch the Kepten kiss his girlie and drive away. Then he could relax. Some days when the watching was over, Benno would go walking in the forest, or by the Havel, maybe try to touch Tommies or Hersheys for chocolate, chewing-gum, even smokes. But not today; this morning he would go back to the Bernauer Strasse, see if he could dry his clothes, then get some soup, some extra sleep. Unlike Boss-Kind, Granit wasn't interested in constantly finding jobs to keep a Kind busy.

Benno Awake! Eins-Zwoh-Drei . . .

He thumped again on the muddy ground with the heel of one outsized boot, this time like a rabbit giving warning of intruders, and made a move towards the wall-outcrop, closer to his prearranged escape route. Just in case anyone from that crappy-bappy army-of-occupation automobile got curious about what he was doing here. It was interesting to see the Kepten in his big car, but when Blessed was around, you beddabelieve life could also get justalittlebit risky.

'All right, Daff,' Blessed said, turning up the collar of his thick rubber-lined service mackintosh and trying to brush a big puddle of water from the car's wide running-board with the tip of his shoe. 'We'll take a boat out on the lakes on Sunday. *If* the weather's good. And *if* Dad doesn't have to work.'

'Dad *always* has to work.'

'No I don't. Be fair. What about our trip to the circus, to make up for my missing your birthday party?'

'You had to leave before the end. Just when the fire-eater was on and it was really interesting. I had to go home with Gisela.'

Daphne spoke so flatly and matter-of-factly, quite unlike an eight-year-old girl, it seemed to Blessed at times like this. In this mood, she was more like a manager making the best of the resources available to her. Since Harriet had left, six days ago, these had been reduced to Gisela (all the time) and her father (by no means fulltime, but a little more since the Price-Suzy murder case had reached an impasse). Beryl Watson had been to play once, but the girl had been so rude to Gisela that even Daphne had refused to have her back. Most days, Daff didn't seem to mind being left with Gisela, but today she had woken up in a demanding, slightly accusing mood. Perhaps she missed Harriet more than she liked to let on. Blessed knew that soon they would have to have a father-and-daughter chat about all that. But not now.

'I'll do my best, darling,' he said. 'Dad's got to do his job, you know. I can't just drop everything to go sailing. I have to catch bad people, and bad people don't always take Sundays off . . . Now, give me a kiss and run along, or you'll be late for school, and I'll be blamed by Miss Davenport. Just once or twice your father deigns to bring you to school, she'll say, and then he can't even get you there on time . . .'

Daphne dabbed his cold cheek with her lips. Then she poked a finger at the scar under his jawbone, where he had nicked himself shaving that morning. 'Nurse Blessed will see to that!'

'Be off with you, then,' he said. 'Gisela will pick you up from school after tea. If it's still raining, wait for her in the cloakroom. All right?'

217

'I 'spose so. 'Bye, Dad.'

'Goodbye, darling.'

And Daphne scampered off, sure-footed on the pavement's greasy skin of rainwater. Her little coat hood with its tartan lining bobbed busily as she ran through the gates and into the yard. When she had disappeared, Blessed turned, glimpsed a small boy in a threadbare coat, long ex-army shorts, and boots several sizes too large for him, standing less than fifty yards away in the shelter of a wall that was all that remained of an apartment block. The ruin had tiny alpine flowers growing from its masonry and looked strangely natural, as if it had been there for hundreds of years, instead of maybe three or four. As for the child, he was staring blankly at the school entrance and smoking a cigarette like a man. Berlin-become-Calcutta, as someone had said at the Officers' Club the other night. This one couldn't be more than eleven, maybe a stunted twelve or thirteen. It was often impossible to tell unless the child was closely questioned or—because they rarely told the truth—medically examined. That went especially for the girls—and boys—who lived and worked on the streets as under-age prostitutes.

Then Blessed remembered the child who had seemed to be observing him from the service entrance of the Rio Rita a week or more previously. Of course, he couldn't be absolutely sure, but . . . Without even making a conscious decision, he found himself squelching purposefully towards the edge of the ruins, shouting in German, 'You! Come here, kid! I want a word!'

When Blessed got within thirty yards, the boy calmly tossed away his half-smoked cigarette, turned on his heel, and bolted for the cover of the ruins. Despite his huge boots, he ran very quickly and nimbly across the slippery, compacted rubble, swinging his skinny legs and arms like a sprint-skater to keep his balance. Blessed reached the point where he had been, saw him duck through an archway, followed. Fifty yards further on, his feet soaked and with his eyes smarting from the driving rain, Blessed found himself in a cemetery. He had never been here before. In the past when he had dropped Daphne off in the morning, he had watched her run into the playground and driven on. Now he saw the real world that surrounded the school, and it was full of dead people. Not far from him stood a gravedigger's hut. He headed for it.

The little brick building was firmly locked. Blessed searched around every corner, checked in every direction, but nothing was visible and during the couple of minutes that he prowled the area, nothing stirred. It would be impossible to search every hiding-place, look behind every bush and tree and headstone. In any case, he couldn't hang around here—apart from the risk of catching double pneumonia, in precisely twenty-three minutes he was due at 248 Company for a meeting with Colonel Harrison and the Public Safety Officer, a certain Major Pilsbury, to discuss the Price-Suzy mess and what to do next. It would do his cause no good to be late. Pilsbury was notorious for being punctual, and now there was a risk that even Thwaite wouldn't be able to get him there on time.

'I recognise you,' Blessed muttered. 'But who are you, you cunning little bastard? And what the hell are you bloody well up to?'

Through the curtain of rain Blessed could see the outline of a cloaked figure moving about between himself and the car. He soon realised that it was Thwaite, dressed in the waterproof cape he kept stowed in the boot of the car in case he had to change a wheel in bad weather. His driver was wandering the rubble of the apartment block in the downpour, looking for him.

'Ah, there you are, sir. What happened?' Thwaite said, with a hint of reproach. 'You got out wi' Daphne, then suddenly you disappeared, just like that. The windows were steamed up, so I couldn't see what you were doing . . .'

'I made a fool of myself,' Blessed explained simply.

'I beg your pardon, sir?'

'There was a kid I thought I recognised. A German street-kid. I tried to talk to him. He ran away. Let's get back in the car.'

Clucking like a mother, Thwaite ushered Blessed towards the car and out of the rain. He forced him to discard his wet coat, which he consigned to the boot of the Horch, along with his own dripping cape, before eventually returning to his position at the wheel. He made to start the engine. Then he hesitated, turned towards the back seat and looked intently at Blessed.

'You all right, sir?'

'Yes.' Blessed was still slightly out of breath from the short but intense chase. 'I'm fine.'

'You don't look it to me, sir, if you'll excuse me saying so. You look as though you've seen a ghost.'

'No. The child was real enough.'

Surprisingly, what Blessed felt at that moment was not so much anger as guilt, as if in some way he had let that kid down by giving up the hunt so easily, bowing to the pressure of the meeting with the colonel and Pilsbury. Berlin-Calcutta again. The Sahib sees, the Sahib's heart bleeds, but in the end the Sahib does nothing because he doesn't want to upset his plans for the day.

'They get sent to places like this, you know, sir,' Thwaite said.

'What?'

'To places where Brits and Yanks and the like are to be found. Them kids get sent to beg—and steal, for that matter—from members of the Allied forces of occupation and their families.'

Blessed nodded. 'You're right, of course.' He told himself he would talk to Weiss about this, ask his advice. He was glad he had asked the inspector to report to the Knesebeckstrasse and make himself available for the meeting; there might even be time to discuss the worrying business of this child with him before it started. 'Now start the car,' he told Thwaite. 'And put your foot down. Let's see if we can get to 248 Company with a few minutes to spare, rain or no rain.'

The rain still hadn't stopped when Benno arrived back at the Kinder Garden. The place was quieter than the cemetery. Even the guardroom was empty, though he had heard the voices of Kinder upstairs in the old orphanage building, maybe in Doktor Barnhelm's apartment, so he knew the place was not completely unprotected. He was beginning to feel slightly let-down, depressed, because by the time he got here he had been looking forward to some company, when he noticed Gurkel dozing in the corner of the dormitory-room beside the cold army stove. Grinning in anticipation, Benno crept over to his friend, took aim, and woke him up with a playful but painfully well-placed prod in the ribs. Still clumsy with sleep, Gurkel chased him round the cellar. As they ran and struggled in loose wrestling holds, Benno's wet clothes clung to his skinny body, his sweat turned to steam, misting the enclosed space.

Finally the two of them collapsed laughing in a heap near the stove and shared a smoke.

Gurkel blew his nose on the sleeve of his filthy old green sweater. He had a summer cold, was always snotty or coughing these past few days. It made his face puffy, like a badly-cooked pudding, his sore nose a squashed cherry in the centre. 'You been watching this Kepten and his girlie all this time?' he asked.

'You beddabelieve, Gurkel.'

Benno suddenly decided not to mention being chased by the Kepten round the cemetery in Spandau. He wanted the thrill of describing how he squeezed through the crack into the ruined mausoleum, waited and watched, felt death's icy presence there beside him. *Oi jeh!* But he couldn't. Dangerous to admit the Kepten found him out. Boss-Kind was in Frankfurt, but he never missed a thing. And he got angry—these days angrier than ever before. He took a drag on the shared cigarette, passed it over to Gurkel.

'You know Boss-Kind is back,' Gurkel said suddenly.

Benno's good humour evaporated instantly. His heart hit his boots. But for Gurkel's benefit he nodded, smiled.

'Boss-Kind is back, here in the Kinder Garden?'

'Oh no. He and the Wonder arrived, collected Granit and some others. Then they went off to the Russkie-Sector, to the Lake. Big business there, I think with Riese, plus Fatski and Thinski.'

Fatski and Thinski were two of Riese's strong-arm boys. 'You see the Wonder, then? He tell you about the Hershey-Zone?' Benno asked.

Gurkel shook his head. 'I was out. When I got back, the Garden was empty 'cept for those guards upstairs, checking on Doktor Barnhelm, making sure he got his mor-phine for breakfast, to keep him happy.' Gurkel was smiling. Suddenly his smile turned a little sly. 'I heard Boss-Kind wants to see you by the lake, Benno, the moment you get back from Spandau.'

'Eck. Nix Lake, Russkie-Sector,' Benno groaned, lapsing into his own brand of comic Russkie-Deutsch, acting stupid-Soviet, the way he often did to hide his feelings when he felt angry or confused. 'Ex-haus-ted. Sleep. All morning standing outside girlie's school in the rain. Nix, nix, nix . . .'

'You better go to the Lake,' Gurkel insisted nervously. 'Boss-Kind, he says he wants to see you, that's what's wanted.'

'Nix sense. Nix sense, this "Lake". Benno no understand.' Still the playful joke-Russkie.

'Benno, *Boss-Kind* knows what makes sense. He led the Kinder through all those troubles, from Point Null with Nazi Black-Hats playing deadly heroes, and Russkies yowling for blood . . . How else did we manage to stay so good, so strong all this time since? You tell me, Benno!'

Benno let him finish. Maybe at that time, tight unity had been essential for the Kinder to survive and live safe, and maybe Boss-Kind above all had made that possible, by turning Doktor Barnhelm into the Kinder's instrument and slave. But it hadn't been only Boss-Kind

221

who had given the Kinder what little they had since Point Null. And you know, Boss-Kind didn't always get things right. In fact, he was getting more and more wild, up-and-down crazy lately . . . Ah, but Benno sensed the same strong reluctance he had felt when it came to confessing to Gurkel about the English Kepten's recognition of him at the Spandau school. Something told him it wasn't wise to share these potentially perilous secrets around in this company, even though Gurkel and The Wonder were his own best, special, best friends, closer to him than anyone else in the world.

'Will you come to the Lake with me, Gurkel?' he said instead. 'We can talk on the way.'

'Nah. Gotta stay here, someone gotta stay, says Boss-Kind. You go solo.'

'So when did Boss-Kind go? When did he issue these Führer-orders, eh?' Benno asked with cold aggression, to hide his disappointment. It was a long trip to make alone. Especially if there were no trains beyond Karlshorst.

'He went two hours ago maybe. He left those . . . orders with the guards.'

Benno got to his feet. 'You know I need soup before I go,' he said, looking hungrily towards the kitchen cellar, where there was usually a pot simmering on the stove.

'Forget soup,' Gurkel said sternly. 'Boss-Kind, he says this Russkie-blockade means we gotta save food. Belt-tighten, belly in. So we all pull through together, yes.' He was imitating Boss-Kind's special way of talking, but the mimicry seemed quite unconscious, without humour or irony.

Benno couldn't suppress a barbed retort. 'Gurkel, I am not so young I can't remember that stuff on the ol' Nazi Death's-Head Greater-German Radio, when things began to go wrong before Point Null! Remember that Hanns kissmyass Fritzsche at the microphone? Pull-Together-Blah is only that same lame-tame Nazi-Blah.'

'Careful how you mock the Boss,' Gurkel said, his broad face creased in a frown that was part disapproval, part fear. He was checking there was no one lurking among the shadows, listening in to their conversation. 'Boss-Kind is fair,' he added quickly. 'You march lakewards, you get food, maybe even Mecklenburg sausage, they tol' me. When you have *earned* it.'

'You are saying that only Boss-Kind decides who has earned food?' Benno interrupted sharply. 'I tell you, for saying that you can kiss my ass, Gurkel! Is this talk between equal Kinderwaifs, or what?'

222

But Gurkel only frowned. 'You . . . you get you and me both into trouble, Benno,' he said. He pinched the nostrils of his sore, suffering nose to preempt a sneeze. 'Sometimes *ach scheiss* sometimes you tell me the wrong, wrong things. Boss-Kind don't forget that. He hears, he sees, and you beddabelieve he remembers *every*, yes, *everylittlething*.'

TWENTY-TWO

'DESPITE ALL THE EVIDENCE you appear to have at your disposal, it will be extremely difficult for you to bring this investigation to a successful conclusion,' Major Pilsbury suggested in his clipped, unemphatic but infuriatingly unstoppable way. 'Almost impossible, in fact,' he added, and made a dignified stabbing-motion with his filled but as yet still unlit briar pipe. '*If* this Panewski individual, whose fingerprints from Kripo files match those on the murder weapon, has indeed taken refuge in Russian-administered territory. And *especially* if, as seems probable, he is no longer to be found within the territory of Greater Berlin.'

The Public Safety Officer for Berlin-Centre returned the briar to his mouth, and folded his arms as if to say, 'I rest my case.'

'Well, James?' Colonel Harrison asked, turning to Blessed. 'Before you answer, I can confirm the truth of what the major says. Even before the blockade, it was difficult to trace criminals when they went East, but now it's damned near impossible. The Russians and their German friends are being bloody awkward, even on routine policing questions.'

'I'm aware of that, sir,' Blessed said. 'If I thought Panewski had got clean away from Berlin, I might begin to share Major Pilsbury's pessimism. As it is, there are at least two good reasons why I don't.'

'Oh yes. Explain, please,' Pilsbury said. His square, pasty face was immobile. He had lit the pipe by now, though, and it was puffing away like a pump-engine, more alive at the moment than its owner.

'First, Panewski is a Berliner. He only feels safe in this city. He would be like a fish out of water if he went to the countryside—or even to another German city. Criminals are parochial, they stick to the streets they know. It's no different in London. Cockney villains won't stray from Stepney or Bow, even if they're far more likely to be arrested there. They may vow to disappear, but they rarely stay away for long. Sooner or later they come back. Sooner, in my experience.'

Pilsbury nodded in a way that could have meant anything from, 'You're right' to 'What did I tell you? This man Blessed is a complete fool'. He was a veteran London CID man who had been co-opted into the Military Police at the outbreak of war and was now coming up for retirement. He was a hardworking careerist, and a stickler for procedure, which in most respects made him perfect for the job of liaising with the German police. Unfortunately, he had realised early on in his career that the men who showed initiative and took risks were not necessarily the men who gained promotion. Over the years, this reluctance to go out on a limb had petrified into a stubborn aversion to making any meaningful decisions at all, and with the prospect of a gratuity and a comfortable pension drawing near, Pilsbury was not about to change the habits of a lifetime just in order to help out James Blessed.

'That's an interesting supposition,' Pilsbury said eventually. 'You said there were two reasons. What would the second be?'

'I'm being watched, I think. I have reason to believe this may be connected with my investigations into these murders. Extra reason for concern, and also extra reason to believe that Panewski may be in Berlin, or at least closely in touch with certain individuals here.'

'And who is watching you, Captain?'

'A child.'

'A child?'

'Yes, sir. At least one.'

'I see.' Pilsbury's briar was sending up wild smoke-signals of disbelief.

'I understand why you'd like to stick this one out, James,' Harrison said smoothly, ever the diplomat. 'But I think Major Pilsbury was trying to say that you—we—may have to admit that we've reached an impasse in this case. The fingerprints found on the knife used to kill Floh are undoubtedly Panewski's. Panewski had a record of violent crime; he had the motive and the means. He has fled from the British Sector, probably to Russian-controlled territory. We have informed the Russians that he's wanted on suspicion of murdering a British serviceman, requested that the Soviet authorities find him and hand him over. What more can we do?'

'Listen, Captain,' Pilsbury chipped in with a frown of irritation. 'The fact is, we're snowed under at the moment, all of us. Both Colonel Harrison and myself are under intense pressure to provide security personnel to cope with the effects of the Russian blockade and the consequent airlift operation. We're very short of men. And, of course, we are experiencing . . .' With Weiss in the room, he was careful not to offend German sensibilities '. . . certain difficulties in our dealings with the Police President's office.'

'We're well aware of them, sir,' Blessed said. 'And so, more than any of us, is Inspector Weiss. I can personally vouch for his reliability in that respect. He is a hardworking, straightforward policeman, without political bias, of the kind we need to encourage in Germany.'

'Nothing personal, but these days one has to beware. Markgraf is sacking non-communist police by the dozen,' Pilsbury said. 'I'd like Inspector Weiss to explain why he's been exempted.'

Weiss did not turn a hair. 'I have no idea,' he said after a short pause. 'Perhaps he does not want to attract attention by mistreating an officer who is working closely with the British. In any case, he cannot dismiss every non-communist policeman, or he will have no experienced officers left.'

Pilsbury nodded again, jotted something down in his notebook. 'This doesn't change the fact that we're very short of resources,' he said.

'It also doesn't change the fact that we're faced with three unsolved murders!' Blessed flung back at him. 'One perpetrated on a British soldier, and all exceptionally nasty—even by the exacting standards of postwar Berlin,' he continued. 'This continuing carnage is connected with large-scale illegal trading in drugs—precisely my area of responsibility. An area in which not only I, but our entire military administration here, urgently need to notch up some conspicuous successes if we are to restore respect for the law among civilians and servicemen alike. Especially at a time of extreme shortages such as this.' Blessed's voice was heavy with sarcasm. 'Or, gentlemen, have I got it wrong? Are we actually supposed to *forget* the entire brutal business just because the Russians have shut down the land corridors into Berlin and we're running low on soap and baking powder?'

Pilsbury let his rhetorical question hang, exchanged po-faced glances with Harrison.

'Of course not,' he said. 'But we need to apportion our resources with the utmost circumspection. It's a question of correct priorities.

226

And let's be frank, Blessed: this Price chap who got himself murdered was a bad egg. A very bad egg. Of course, we shall do our best to make an arrest. However, we must also remember that Price was without doubt involved in criminal activities. This was hardly an unprovoked attack on an innocent serviceman—'

'Are you suggesting that he deserved what he got, and so good riddance?' Blessed asked incredulously. 'And are you ignoring the other two deaths? And are you totally incapable of seeing that the murderer could kill again?'

'Oh no, Captain. These are extremely serious capital crimes.' Pilsbury said silkily. 'No, dear chap, I am merely questioning how much effort and how many resources we can spare for the investigation during the current crisis. I am asking us to weigh up the pros and cons.' He took his briar from his mouth and exhaled smoke long and slow, like a locomotive coming to rest at the end of the line. 'Of course, I'm here purely in a consultative capacity. I can only make recommendations.'

This game of bureaucratic hide-and-seek could go on all morning, Blessed decided. He could feel his frustration throbbing inside him like an electric pulse, but he knew that against a bureaucrat like Pilsbury angry or insulting words would have no effect. Instinct told Blessed that only a procedural challenge, watertight and well-aimed, would defeat him.

'So are you and the colonel telling me to drop this case, sir?' he asked Pilsbury with icy deliberation. 'If so, I must enter a formal protest. I shall also send written reports to the city commandant and the Military Governor outlining the situation and expressing my intense disquiet. As you know, the Military Governor himself has recently deplored the widespread complacency among the occupation forces regarding corruption and black-market dealings.'

Blessed saw that his gambit, a piece of hypocrisy so exquisite that he wasn't sure whether to be proud of it or ashamed, had caught Pilsbury in an exposed position. The fact was, as both he and Blessed knew, that whatever pious sentiments the Governor, General Sir Brian Robertson, expressed, they were for public consumption only. Though Robertson himself was honest, he shared the general feeling of cynical helplessness, the sense that corruption had become so widespread and had extended so high into the military government that a root-and-branch drive against it would totally paralyse and discredit the entire British Zone administration. 'The revelation of these affairs,' he had said recently in a private conversation that had quickly been leaked to other senior officers, 'would start a whole avalanche which could not then be stopped.' Nevertheless, there was a limit to what Pilsbury could say in reply, especially in front of a German police officer. For the moment, Blessed had him where he wanted him.

'Neither Colonel Harrison nor myself intend any such thing,' Pilsbury said mildly. 'Of course not. We all share the Military Governor's determination to eradicate corruption, violent crime and theft.' The Public Safety Officer methodically tapped his ash out into a large glass ashtray. 'Which reminds me . . . I . . . ah . . . gather you haven't replied to Colonel Harrison's memorandum regarding security measures at RAF Gatow.'

Pilsbury was a slow player, but no less formidable for that, Blessed thought ruefully. A gambit like this was crude but also effective, especially if the major had Harrison on his side, which it looked as though he did. Also, now that he was forced to recall it, the original note about security at Gatow had come straight from the British commandant's office. If he tried to complain to the commandant about Pilsbury, the major could point out that Blessed was the kind of irresponsible adventurer who ignored urgent requests, even when they came from the highest quarter. Pilsbury probably knew about the Jamail fiasco in the Lebanon too, and knowing him he would find a way of mentioning that in the most damaging way possible.

'No, I haven't, sir,' Blessed said. 'Pressure of work, I'm afraid.'

Pilsbury nodded, checked his watch. 'Speaking of which,' he said, 'I have to be somewhere else. In fact, I should have been there five minutes ago.' He got to his feet. 'Thank you for your frank expression of views. It has been most helpful. I think we all know where we stand. Good morning, Captain Blessed. Inspector Weiss.'

As Blessed was about to leave too, Harrison called him back. 'We'll have a chin-wag later, shall we, James? About the new priorities.' He smiled cosily. 'When we've got more time.'

When they reached the Ku-Damm, Blessed steered Weiss into the terrace of a pavement cafe and ordered two big, bowl-like glasses of Berliner Weisser—the thirst-quenching summer drink made with light beer and a dash of cherry syrup. The sight of British currency ensured that they would get real beer, brewed from hops, and not the synthetic variety known as *Hefesud*.

'I think we're in trouble,' Blessed said. 'Pilsbury's obviously got it in for me, and it looks like Harrison's not prepared to back my view of things. In fact, I'd guess that by the time we have that chin-wag he'll have a plan ready—one that I won't like but I'll have to go along with.'

Weiss sipped his beer, smacked his lips appreciatively. 'Pilsbury, I thought, had no power over BlessForce. As I understand it, you report to the Acting Provost-Marshal—Colonel Harrison, that is—or even, under certain circumstances, directly to the British city commandant.'

'Right. Pilsbury can't order me around. But he does have a lot of power. As Public Safety Officer he is ultimately responsible for keeping order in this part of the British sector. This ensures him privileged access to the sector commandant. Harrison doesn't want to get on the wrong side of him. The colonel likes an easy life.'

'So you are saying, the commandant kicks Pilsbury, Pilsbury kicks Colonel Harrison, and Colonel Harrison kicks you?'

'That's just about it. And given the kind of man Pilsbury is, I'd say Harrison is probably getting a very sore behind.'

'Then by the sound of it, there is not much hope for us, James,' Weiss said flatly. 'There is a big crisis on. The survival of an entire city is at stake. Our little murder case will be forgotten. It is just as I suspected when we first spoke together.' He shrugged. 'So you will be chasing flour-thieves in the unloading bays at Gatow, and I shall be back to clearing up the mess after yet another falling-out in some black-market dive.'

'Not if I can help it. It's possible that if we made dramatic progress in the Price-Suzy case, Harrison would be forced to change sides and back me.'

'But—forgive me—Pilsbury does have some justification for his attitude. All the evidence points to Panewski. He has disappeared, the rumours in the bars say he has fled to the East. Progress? So how do we progress? Ask your Russian so-called allies for their cooperation? The Soviet Zone is fast becoming a hostile foreign country . . .'

'Then we'll take another direction completely,' Blessed said, finishing his beer. 'We'll see if we can find a link between these kids who keep cropping up—the one who led Wachtmann Pilzinger to Price's and Suzy's bodies, the one who's been following me around until this morning—and Panewski. The first thing I want to do is to talk to Pilzinger again. There may be something we missed the first time round.'

'You don't give up easily. I can see why you are not a popular man in certain circles.'

'Just get him for me, Manfred.'

'James, I remain unconvinced about the children, as you know, but of course I'll have Pilzinger report to you. Also, I shall make informal enquiries about Panewski's whereabouts from colleagues in the East. I may get results where men such as Pilsbury and Colonel Harrison, who must go through the official channels, cannot.'

'Thanks.' Blessed put money on the table, rose and pushed back his chair. 'There's something else, actually. You know, despite the fact that Panewski's fingerprints were all over the murder weapon used on Floh, I still can't work out how he could have got into all those places and then got away without being noticed. Then there's the burglary at Anna Löbke's and Suzy's flat. There are more people involved than just Panewski, I'm convinced of it.'

'Maybe.' Weiss gestured to indicate that he would be a little while before he finished his Weisser. 'What time do you want to interview Pilzinger?'

Blessed looked at his watch. 'Say, one-thirty. I'm going home. There's someone else I'd like to talk to first.'

At first sight, there was no one about at the Villa Hellman. Blessed walked in the front door, hung his hat, went into the kitchen, then through into the living room, calling out Gisela's name.

In the conservatory there were fresh flowers in tall vases, but no sign of a human being. He started to walk back along the long hall, then saw Gisela coming down the stairs towards him. She wore a red dress and no shoes.

'Gisela, there you are.'

'Yes. And you are there too, home in the middle of the day. This is unusual.'

She looked at him, he thought, as if she were a nurse and he a patient. Or she the nanny and he the child.

'I want to talk to you about something,' he said. 'Over a cup of coffee. This is sort of official.'

'Excuse me. I have no shoes on. I was doing housework, you know. It was warm. I will—'

'Don't worry.' He still couldn't help staring at her bare feet. They were, in fact, beautiful, smooth and brown as her legs, the nails perfectly clipped. 'This is also informal.'

'Official and informal? Captain Blessed, you are talking to a German? How can you mix those things?'

'Easily.' He led the way through into the kitchen. She automatically went through to the kettle and put it on the gas stove, ready to make the coffee.

They said nothing much else while she made the coffee. Blessed sat at the table, thinking how long it was since he had been in this house in the daytime with no one else there—except Gisela, that was. She padded over with the cups, his black and hers with cream, sat down opposite him.

'So? How can I help your "informal-official" quest, Captain?'

'I want to know exactly what the boy was like, the one who followed you and Daff back from school last week.'

'The night before Daphne's birthday?'

'That's right.'

Gisela sipped her coffee thoughtfully. 'Oh . . . he was about eleven, grubby, shorts . . . a grown man's boots, he wore, into which he must have stuffed newspaper so that they would fit him. This is quite common with such children.'

'Thin?'

'Quite thin, yes.'

The shorts and boots appeared to match with those worn by the boy this morning, Blessed established. Then he asked: 'Did he smoke?'

'Yes. He smoked. They all do. By the time peace came, those boys were the only men left in Berlin. It is no wonder that they behave accordingly.'

'You sound bitter.'

Gisela frowned. 'I'm sorry. I didn't mean to.'

'Is it because of your parents?'

She shook her head.

'Someone . . . else?'

'Very well, I will tell you. Why not? There was a boy,' Gisela explained. 'He was nineteen, and so was I. He went off to the war in Russia and never came back. Missing. For four years he has been missing. His name was Thomas, and he played the piano beautifully. Ironically, his favourite composers were Russians: Tchaikovsky, Rachmaninov.'

'I'm sorry.'

'It is no longer important. For a while it was. Now, no longer.' She looked straight at Blessed, smiled. 'Shall we get back to your street-urchin?'

'All right. Have you seen the kid again since?'

'No.'

'What about other German children?'

'There have been one or two other occasions when German children have watched us, yes.' She sighed. 'Not only lately. It has always been so. It is so. It will be so until our children—German children I mean—have some kind of normal life, with school, and enough to eat, and so on. English children represent something unattainable. They want to watch them, make contact with them . . .'

'Tell me, do the German kids hate them?'

'That's an unfair question, Captain.'

'It's a necessary one. Please answer.'

'The feeling is hate, envy, curiosity, all mixed up.'

'Thank you,' said Blessed. 'And how do you feel about the English, Gisela?' he found himself asking.

'Please . . . I am . . . very fond of Daphne. She is a wonderful little girl, whether she would be English or German or the little child in the moon,' she answered, with a defiant edge. 'And she also has a difficult life, you know.'

'Oh yes?'

Gisela nodded firmly. 'Oh yes. Mrs Blessed is not an easy person in some ways. She means well, but staying home with a child does not come naturally to her. She is . . . affectionate but not very consistent. And, of course, you are not here most of the time. That's the way it is, and maybe in the long term it doesn't matter, but life is not straightforward for Daphne. She copes very well, actually, if you consider the problems she faces.'

'You're right,' Blessed said, automatically reaching into his pocket for the packet of cheroots.

He had to admit that during the past few days he had tried to suppress those truths, to convince himself that everything was really all right, that life would sort itself out if only they could take a holiday, relax together. Harriet had phoned twice during the day and talked to Daphne, once at night and talked to him. Neither of them had had an interest in going deeper than the usual polite banalities. Everything had been factual, superficial; there was a kind of tacit agreement that until Harriet returned—or until the tension became unbearable for one or other of them—they would be terribly English about it, content to maintain a 'holding action'.

'So you're fond of Daphne. But do you hate the British?' he said then. 'I'm sorry. I have to keep asking this until I'm really clear about it.' He paused. 'Do you, for example, hate me?' The truth was, he

232

felt a dangerous excitement the more he pressed Gisela about her personal feelings.

'No. I don't hate you at all. The opposite. But I don't like what becomes of you at certain times.'

Blessed was so astonished by the honesty of her answer that for a moment he was struck speechless. Then he said, 'What times are you referring to?'

'Times such as now. I think you are like an unhappy boy who wants to know everything bad about grownups. When he knows it, it doesn't make him happier—but he cannot stop himself, he must confirm how wicked adults are over and over again. And—' Gisela reddened, suddenly aware of how bold she had been.

There was a silence. After a while, Blessed opened the packet, took out a cheroot and lit it. Then he asked, 'What were you going to say before you stopped yourself?'

'I . . .' Gisela swallowed hard, began again. 'You know, when you are with Mrs Blessed, you put up with things that you should not put up with. You have some difficulties within your own personality, as I already said, but you are a good man, who cares about truth. Why do you allow your wife to get away with treating you this way? I am sorry to say this. Perhaps you will throw me out onto the street, but you asked me and I have to tell you, Captain.'

'So you don't hate me?'

She shook her head vigorously but said nothing. She was blushing, Blessed realised. He liked the way she blushed. It was not girlish or immature, but the act of a human being who was capable of feeling doubt and shame.

'I'm glad of that,' he said, because it was true. 'And I won't throw you out. You're right, anyway. I let Harriet get away with a lot, because I feel I'm responsible, and because I don't want to break up the marriage.'

'It holds you both prisoner—you, and Harriet—this marriage of yours,' Gisela said. 'But it is up to you. I know it is difficult, because you have Daphne, but I think the fact is, you will stay hurting each other for a long time unless you release each other. Although she has left, Harriet is as guilty as you are of this.' She got to her feet, smoothed down her skirt. 'Is there anything else you need to know, Captain Blessed?' she asked.

'I think that'll do for now.' He smiled. 'This is about as much as I can take.' He looked at her and wanted her, her slim, brown body, her smile, her calm strength, her intelligence, her goodness. There

233

was fleeting shame, the old learned instinct that said, *You're just like your father. You can't stick with one woman. Weak* . . . in his mother's German accent, but it somehow didn't last. This desire felt clean, as if only good could come of it. 'As far as the child goes, I've found out all I wanted to know,' he said, pulling himself together. 'I'm grateful for your co-operation.'

'It's all right. Do you think the child was a thief, is this what you're wondering?'

'Something like that. I think he may have been working for a criminal, keeping watch on me. Perhaps that's over now and we'll never see him again.'

'They have become capable of terrible things, our children,' Gisela said. 'And why not? They have seen only too clearly what adults are capable of. They have witnessed such cruelty, undergone such deprivation. I don't think the sense of safety will ever really come back for them. Or for us,' she added with a shrug. 'And now I must finish the housework. At two-thirty I pick up Daphne from school. I will be careful from now on, always make sure I meet her at the gate and that she does not go wandering around the street.'

'I told her the same thing this morning,' Blessed said. 'I'll try to take her to school myself whenever it's possible. Otherwise I'll have Thwaite run you both to the school gate. I'm sure it's me they're after, though, if they're after anyone.'

Gisela nodded. 'It ought to be true, what you say, but who knows? Who can be sure of anything?'

Blessed took the stairs up to BlessForce two at a time. It was twenty-five past one. Kelly was lurking in the anteroom to his office.

'Afternoon, sir. You seem to have a spring in your step.'

'Afternoon, Kelly. Where's Weiss? He was supposed to be bringing that German policeman, Pilzinger, in for another once-over.'

'Ah, Inspector Weiss phoned about half an hour ago from the Alexanderplatz,' Kelly said after consulting his desk-pad. 'He has had some problems, apparently. He couldn't say what they were—you know how it is, phoning from over in the Russian Sector, you never know who's listening in. But he said he'll get here as close to two o'clock as he can, at which time all will be explained.'

'He was sure of that, at least, was he?'

'Yes. He was very cagey about everything else, though. He sounded scared. I reckon he'll be glad to get back into our sector. The situation

234

over there's starting to turn nasty. Doesn't make our job any easier either, does it?'

'No. It damned well doesn't.'

Blessed sat down heavily in his chair, looked out of the window. There was a British Dakota in the sky over the city to the west, coming gingerly in to land. It was an ungainly machine, but still a beautiful sight, a reminder that the Berliners had not been deserted by their friends. The blockade affected everything, from the fruit and vegetable supply to the balance of power inside the Berlin Criminal Police. Ruefully he remembered Weiss's warning to him right at the beginning, at the site of the Price-Suzy murder. *My friend, in Berlin at this time, especially so far as the Russians are concerned, everything is political.* Weiss was a wise bird, Blessed thought. A little over-cautious at times, but a good man to have on your side.

On his desk was a note from Harrison asking him if he would like to drop over to his office as soon as convenient, plus a message that Anna Löbke had telephoned at a few minutes after midday and would be ringing back later.

'Who took the phone message from Anna Löbke?' Blessed asked Kelly.

'I did, sir.'

'Any idea what she wanted?'

'Something had come up that she thought would be helpful regarding the thefts of personal items from Price's girlfriend's flat last week. She wasn't sure, but she felt she should ring.'

'If she felt she should, I'll talk to her,' Blessed said crisply. He lit a cheroot. 'Make sure she's put straight through when she rings back. At this particular moment we need all the bloody help with this case that we can get.'

Anna Löbke rang from a bar. She had been drinking a little, he thought, but her voice was factual and calm. Someone was talking English in the background. A 'prospect'.

'Captain,' she said, 'I must be quick. I just wanted to let you know, I met an acquaintance this morning who lives in the block next door. I told her about how Heide's things had been stolen, that we didn't know who did it . . . and she said she had seen a couple of strange boys in her block one afternoon, carrying stuff. The point is, they were coming out of a basement, which—I didn't know this or I would have told you about it last week—actually connects through to my building. She yelled for the caretaker to come. They ran off.'

235

'How old were these boys?'

'One very young, the other in his teens. The older was wild-looking, with long hair and wearing a funny army coat. She said he looked at her like he could kill her. Of course, I don't know if this will help in catching the man everyone thinks killed Heide, but—'

'That's fine, Fräulein Löbke,' Blessed said. 'You were right to ring.'

'I hope this is of some help for you in catching this man, this . . .'

'Panewski. Yes. Could your friend, the one who saw the boys, come here?'

'It's difficult.'

The English voice was getting louder. 'Come on, you cow,' it was saying. 'You want it, let's go. I'm not standing 'ere all fookin' day.'

'It's important,' Blessed insisted.

'I'll try later this afternoon. But I don't know whether I can find her again today. She . . . she's not always around, you know how it is, Captain.'

'Did anyone else see the boys?'

'Yes. The caretaker of her building. He chased them out and then down the street, I think.'

'Ah. Thank you. Telephone again if you contact your friend, can you? If I'm not here, just leave a message again.'

'C'mon for fook's sake . . . bloody tart. Jesus, there's plenty of other fookin' frawlines around, y'know . . .'

'Goodbye, Captain. I must go.'

The line went dead. It was now almost a quarter to two. Blessed replaced the receiver, explained to Kelly what Anna had told him about the two boys.

'I need a cup of tea,' he said to the sergeant then. 'I'll give Weiss twenty minutes or so to get here. After that, we go down to Moabit again to get a description of those kids. I've been waiting for something like this, by Christ I have.'

Kelly shot him a sceptical look. 'I'll organise the tea, sir. Will you be seeing the colonel? He really did sound very insistent . . .'

'Afterwards.'

Weiss came hurrying into the office just before Blessed's deadline expired. He looked tired, anxious.

236

'I'm so sorry, James,' he said. 'Pilzinger has disappeared.' He shook his head gloomily. 'No one in the Police President's office will confirm it, or explain why, but everyone knows it's something to do with the SMA and Markgraf. The whisper at Alexanderplatz headquarters is, Pilzinger has been arrested on suspicion of anti-Soviet activities.'

Blessed sipped at what was left of his tea, pondering the implications. 'Unlikely,' he said laconically.

'Impossible, I would say! He is just not the type.'

'So who is responsible for these political purges, Manfred? Who can our side talk to about this?'

Weiss shrugged helplessly. 'I don't know. You see, it's the old story. Nothing has happened officially,' he explained. 'Officially Pilzinger has merely been listed absent from his job and his home, and that is the end of it. I managed to speak to his wife, by the way. She said he went off to work three days ago as usual, but did not return. She was very frightened.'

Blessed nodded. He understood how these things worked over there. If the British approached the Soviets, the Soviets would state that this was an internal matter for the German civil police and politely refer them to Police President Markgraf's office; at Markgraf's office they would shrug their shoulders and say they had so many missing persons on their books already, perhaps the Soviet authorities could help find him. Everyone would deny everything. It was the same when anti-communists were kidnapped from the streets of West Berlin and never seen again. Everyone denied everything. He and Weiss were up against a wall of silence that had been built by experts.

'Does Panewski have friends over there in the Russian sector?' he asked.

'Maybe. Smugglers. Old Friedrichstrasse cronies from before the war.'

'And what about contacts in the police department? Could someone have been bribed?'

'One can never tell. But you know how it goes. In a moment of weakness, Policeman X takes some money or food to overlook a misdemeanour. Or he lets a criminal off in exchange for some information—which is not strictly within the rules, but enables him to make an arrest. Before you know it, the underworld has a hold over him . . . I'm sure it's the same in London.'

'Well, there's got to be something going on. It's too much of a coincidence that they have arrested Pilzinger now, of all times.'

'Yes, but remember that officials are being dismissed, purged, arrested all the time at the moment,' Weiss said. 'The Soviets and their German allies are making a bid for control of Berlin, and they are determined to eliminate all opposition. Dozens of officials have been sacked in the past week, as your Major Pilsbury was only to glad to point out this morning.'

Blessed got up and stood at the window, once more enjoyed the spectacle of an aircraft approaching Tempelhof. They were landing every six minutes now. Huge gangs of German labourers were working at resurfacing the cracked concrete-slab runway. Several thousand tons of fuel and provisions every day. A massive, heroic defence of human freedom.

'Perhaps Harrison and Pilsbury are right,' he said. 'History's being made here. Maybe you and I should become part of the great and noble defence of Berlin, instead of worrying about this grubby dead-end case, these worthless people . . .'

But even as he spoke, Blessed thought of Panewski's cruel, flat-featured face, and of the urchin boy outside the school, and of the courageous Anna Löbke, who was still doing all she could to help bring the killer of her friend Heidemarie to justice. Someone out there in the city butchered without compunction, with an ingenuity and bloody efficiency that could be unleashed on anyone at any time. If it was Panewski, Blessed had a duty to catch him. If not, then he had to find another murderer. After all, could anyone say for sure that the roll-call of killings would stop with Floh, Taffy Price and Heidemarie Sanders, *alias* Suzy? Damn Harrison. Damn Pilsbury. Damn the lot of them and their 'priorities'.

'It's your choice, James,' Weiss murmured. 'I'm a Berliner. I pray for the success of the airlift, day and night.'

'Glorious defences of freedom are all very well,' Blessed said finally, turning away from the window. 'But at times like this I ask myself, what can be more dictatorial and cruel than murder, which is the violent suppression of that most important of freedoms, the right to life itself? And I tell myself, there are thousands of men and women out there who can make the airlift work. But who's going to catch the man who killed Price and Suzy and that old villain Floh, if we don't?'

The phone rang. At a nod from Blessed, Kelly picked it up. The sergeant listened, then put his hand over the mouthpiece and said in a stage-whisper, 'It's Colonel Harrison, sir. He says he absolutely must see you now. It's urgent.'

238

'He's unlucky, Kelly,' Blessed said. Suddenly the decision felt easy. 'I'm afraid I've just gone out, and I'm not sure when I'll be back. I have an even more urgent interview. With a witness.'

TWENTY-THREE

THE CARETAKER OF THE BLOCK of flats had once been a part-time jailer at the Moabit Prison in the Lehrterstrasse. But he was quick to tell Blessed that, though he had served there all through the twelve Nazi years, he had never dealt with the political or military prisoners. He had worked in the criminal wing with the burglars, the embezzlers, and the rapists and the murderers, so avoiding the more obvious moral dilemmas. They were sitting in his tidy, sparsely-furnished apartment, set like a gatekeeper's lodge just inside the gate that gave access to the tenement building from the street. It would be almost impossible for anyone to come or go without the caretaker's seeing them.

'Moabit Jail!' he boasted. 'In that *Knast* there, I got to know all sorts. Cold-eyed killers, clever fraudsters, hot-headed strong-arm men, the lot.'

The caretaker had introduced himself as Willi Jauch. He was a stocky, ugly man in his mid-fifties with a flat, shaved cranium. His accent told Blessed he was dealing with a Berliner born and bred.

Blessed offered him a cigarette. The caretaker grabbed it and stuck it in his shirt pocket quite shamelessly.

'All right. I'd like a description of these boys, please,' Blessed said. He nodded to Weiss, and the inspector took out his notebook.

'Very well. Here goes. The elder one was crazy-looking, long hair and a long coat and a bandanna around his neck, about seventeen, eighteen. He carried something like a rucksack—for the loot, I would say. His friend was much younger. Very skinny. Small. I don't know, maybe he was as young as eight or nine. It's so hard to tell these kids'

240

ages these days, and they're all trained thieves, even the teeniest ones, I tell you that, honoured sirs . . .'

'The older one. Colour of hair and other salient aspects, please. Be precise. Take your time.'

'About one metre seventy-five, one metre eighty, that boy. Hair dark blond. Sharp features, could've been goodlooking, you know, 'cept for the crazy eyes, which were bright as a cat's. You follow me? I'm talking about the way a cat looks at a mouse, and it wasn't nice. He had long legs and arms.'

'His clothes?'

'A long greatcoat, even though it was warm, and underneath it a plain, open-necked shirt and this bandanna which was red with white spots.'

'The other boy. Take your time, as I said, Herr Jauch.'

'Ach, what can I say? He was in shorts, a nondescript old shirt, brown I think. Black shoes.'

'Boots? Much too big for him?'

'No, sir. These were cheap kid's shoes, almost like gymnastics pumps. The boy was very, very small for his age, I think. Not quite a midget, but—'

'How old do you really think?' Blessed asked, disappointed. It wasn't the boy he had seen in the Ku-Damm, and later outside Daphne's school.

'He was probably a lot older than he looked,' Jauch said after some thought. 'Maybe twelve, thirteen. His face was older than the rest of him, you follow? Y'know, he was like a kind of a pet to the other lad, like a terrier or a whippet. He kept close to heel and obeyed on command . . .'

'What made you think they had come from the neighbouring apartment block, these two boys?'

'Downstairs where they had come from was only the boiler, which doesn't work, and the hole that leads through into the cellar next door. When I checked afterwards, there was clear evidence that they had found their way through, or at least the little one had.'

Blessed looked at Weiss, got to his feet. 'Show us, please, Herr Jauch,' he said. 'Take us down there.'

They walked diagonally across a courtyard and along an alleyway until they got to a door. It opened to reveal the top of some steps. Jauch lit a hurricane-lamp, led the way down into a long, vaulted room that was cold and damp even at midsummer. Parts of it had been roughly

241

repaired, the ceiling had been propped up, and there were piles of broken bricks by the back wall. It looked dangerous. They stepped gingerly over the uneven floor.

'This was the air-raid shelter for our block, you see,' Jauch said when they had reached the middle of the vault. He held the lamp high so they could just see the room's full extent, about fifty feet. 'And the boiler-room for next door, which would be Fräulein Löbke's apartment block, adjoins us at that far end. Now come with me, honoured sirs.'

Up close they could see, at about waist height from the ground, a hole some two feet square that seemed to have been cut from the wall. On the ground in front of it lay rusty corrugated iron the size and shape of the hole.

'There's a fascinating story connected with this place,' Jauch offered. 'See, when next door was hit, there were a couple of hundred souls in there. As it happened, the bomb buried the shelter entrance, leaving them trapped inside, with no fresh air coming in. Within a few hours, the poor folk would have suffocated, eh? Now, I don't know exactly, because I was on duty at the Lehrter Strasse prison that night, but they told me later what happened. Because it would have taken too long to dig their way down through the other block's entrance, they came in here and got a drill and pickaxes and banged this hole, to let in air. They succeeded! The lives of most of those two hundred people next door were saved. They had air, they had water and food being passed through to them until the teams could dig down from the other side and mount a proper rescue. That's why the hole's so small.'

'But sufficient for a child,' Blessed concluded.

Jauch nodded. 'Correct, sir! It's easy to tell that you are a real professional detective, eh?' he said with a laugh. 'They sent some little nippers through from the Hitler Youth, I heard. *Jungvolk*, only nine or ten years old. The kids took through soup, bread, things like that, helped calm everyone until the grownup rescuers could get through. Quite a tale, eh? Anyway, we never had a chance to do more than just cover up the hole with the bit of old iron, didn't bother much with it, to be honest. Repairing the rest of the building seemed a much more urgent priority.'

'What's on the other side?'

'As I said, another cellar. The steps have been repaired well enough. I mean, I wouldn't go leaping around in there for fun, but if you wanted to get through, and were careful, you could.'

'Where would you come out if you found your way through next-door's cellar and onto the surface, Herr Jauch?'

'I'm not sure exactly. Somewhere towards the middle—that's where Fräulein Löbke lives, isn't it?'

Blessed turned to Weiss. 'I think we'll need to go back next door.'

'If you say so. I suppose we have to cover everything.'

Back outside in the courtyard, Herr Jauch took a deep breath. 'Imagine. This is what it must have felt like for those poor people who were almost buried alive,' he said. 'To get some fresh, clean air in your lungs once more. And I shall see if I can find some sand and cement from God knows where, and block that hole in the wall. You gentlemen will write a report, perhaps, and support me requisitioning some for security reasons . . .'

'Later, perhaps. Meanwhile, thank you for your help.'

Herr Jauch was not easily fobbed off. He saw his chance, and he was determined to press it home. 'Not too much later, I hope, gentlemen. These thieving children are everywhere. We must be vigilant. Those are the only two boys I caught escaping with loot, but I tell you there have been others.'

Blessed had turned to go. He stopped in his tracks. 'Others? When?'

'During the few days before. It reminded me, when you mentioned the big boots, that there was another kid, eleven or so, wearing these huge clodhoppers. He was poking around, might have been down in the cellar, ran away when I shouted at him. He was damned fast too, boots or no damned boots.'

'Old adult-sized army shorts too? And an old blue sweater?'

'There you have it, sirs. You must know him. He was on his own, though. The next day I shooed another kid away, didn't even get much of a look at him, because it was dusk . . . let me see, that would have been Wednesday, and then three days later I saw the big, crazy-looking lad and his little friend sneaking out of the cellar entrance with their swag from next door.'

'Well? Still sceptical?' Blessed asked Weiss as they drove back from Moabit. 'There have been times when even I wasn't certain about the connection with the children, but how can we possibly doubt it now?'

Weiss raised his hands in mock-surrender. 'All right. It sounds possible that Panewski has been using youngsters as messengers, spies,

243

even as burglars. This is not unknown. Even before the war, gangsters employed children.'

'Drug-dealers everywhere use them a lot. Smugglers too. If the kid gets caught, the judge may go easy, because he will say that grownups corrupted him, because he lives in a slum, because his family has no food, et cetera et cetera.' Blessed was happier than Weiss had seen him for days. 'This could be a network. This could be the link we've been looking for.'

'But a link with what, James?'

'Don't you see?' Blessed exclaimed. 'If the kid could get through into the cellar through that tiny hole, he could have got into the coal chute at Floh's flat. And what about the older one? There was talk of an older boy outside Dr Schmidt's surgery, having a furious argument with Price and Suzy.' He gazed out of the window at the glistening-wet streets, and he smiled. 'If we can't lay our hands on Panewski, we'll just have to trace these children instead!'

'The communists seem to have started kidnapping my key witnesses,' Blessed said. 'Are you trying to tell me that you don't care?'

Colonel Harrison drummed his fingers on the desk-top. 'No. I'm just trying to keep track of your latest theory,' he said with uncharacteristic sarcasm. 'I gather it's now all a communist plot.'

'I didn't say that. But we have to consider the possibility that there's a political motive for all this. It also puts the fact that Panewski probably fled to the East in rather a different light, doesn't it?'

Harrison smiled. 'Jim. The Soviets are like naughty children. They have an uncanny knack of always doing precisely what you don't want them to do. Perhaps when they found out that Wachtmann Whatsisname had been here to talk to you, they decided he was a "spy". Perhaps when they really thought about it, they just didn't like his face . . .'

'They could also be protecting Panewski.'

'I suppose they could. I'll make the usual enquiries, lodge a protest if you insist, but the fact is, we can't make the Soviets do anything they don't want to.'

'The children—'

'Them again, Jim? Do you really think interrogating some snotty little Oliver Twist character will get you anywhere so long as Panewski's over in the East? Listen,' Harrison said, leaning forward on his elbows and fixing Blessed with a fatherly, confiding gaze. 'I need to know. The commandant's office needs to know. How much progress are you

244

making on the smuggling business that you were originally interested in? Let's put the murders on one side for the moment, eh?'

Blessed shrugged. 'We pulled in three others apart from Floh. We're pretty sure they have no connection with the Price-Suzy case, though we may get a conviction on another matter entirely.'

'Bravo! Is the smuggling still going on, do you think, or has the death of Price and the arrest of Mitchellson put a stop to it?'

'Probably. In any case, since the blockade, the land-route we were investigating—importing the stolen drugs to Berlin in British Army trucks along the transit-autobahns—has obviously become inoperative.'

'Then what about the air, Jim?' Harrison said with sudden enthusiasm. 'There's a transport landing every few minutes these days. Hard to check every one. And you know how easy it is to bribe ground-staff, or even crew . . .'

Blessed looked doubtful. 'I'd have thought it would have taken longer than ten days to set up such a route.'

'It's not impossible, though, is it?'

'No. I have to admit it's not impossible.'

'Yes. Well, Jim, you have your chance to find out.' Harrison looked at Blessed carefully. 'As you know, the commandant's office, and the RAF, have made a few requests for your services as a security adviser . . . I know how busy you've been, so I haven't been surprised you haven't responded . . . and now they're pressing extremely hard. What with the impasse regarding Price's murder, and the difficulties you're having in pursuing the drug-smuggling business under the changed circumstances, it's all quite convenient. You can have a look at how things are organised at Gatow, and while you're at it you may pick up some new leads . . .'

Blessed felt his gut tighten. The old hypocrite had him exactly where he wanted him, which was shunted over to Gatow airfield as an adviser. At one stroke, Harrison would keep the commandant's office happy and Pilsbury happy. The messy, time-consuming business of the murders would be swept neatly under the official carpet. The beauty of it was, the captain would not have been taken off the case—at least not technically—merely given extra duties because of the political crisis. All Blessed's instincts told him there was nothing he could do to prevent this.

'Is this an order?' he asked.

'Come, Jim—'

'I'm sorry, sir. I need to know. Is this an order?'

'I suppose it is, yes. I've spent a lot of time fending off these people on your behalf, and I can't do it any more. Surely you can see that the international crisis, and the blockade, have to take precedence?'

'So I'm being told to drop the case.'

'Drop it? Of course not,' Harrison said blandly. 'What a suggestion! I'm only sorry I have to burden you with other duties.'

'You all right, sir?' Kelly asked when Blessed got back into the office.

Blessed shook his head. 'We're minding the RAF's luggage from tomorrow. We're going to have to work our arses off to keep up with our other investigations. I just heard the news from Colonel Harrison.'

'This would be the Gatow assignment, would it?'

'The very same. Is Inspector Weiss in?'

'He went out for a while, but I think he just got back, sir.'

'If he's about, send him in to see me.'

Blessed had been closeted in his office for a couple of minutes, smoking ferociously, when Weiss knocked on the door. He sat the inspector down, frankly described the meeting at the Knesebeck-strasse, explained Harrison's orders. Although he was talking to a German, Blessed threw occupation etiquette to the winds, making no attempt to diguise the fact that he was incensed at the way his superior had forced his hand.

'Well, well. So how does this affect me and the other Kripo men who have been assigned to the investigation?' Weiss asked.

'No one has officially told me to take you off the case,' Blessed said. 'That's the one bright spot. Listen, there's nothing to stop you from quietly carrying on with your work here—just don't attract undue attention or show your face in the Knesebeckstrasse, in case Harrison or Pilsbury or one of their minions sees you. I'll still be involved, as much as I can. But for the moment I'll be relying on you to do most of the donkey-work. It'll mean a big increase in your workload. How do you feel about that?'

'I don't mind. I tell you, anything's better than being back at Kripo Headquarters, constantly trying to keep out of the political firing-line.' Weiss dressed himself in one of his grins. 'The food is better if I work with you. Also, I am becoming very fond of those black cheroots . . .'

Blessed laughed, tossed him one. 'I have to be at Gatow first thing in the morning, for an interview with the officer commanding and his security man. We should be finished by lunchtime. I'll meet you somewhere and we'll discuss progress. Is there anything you need to talk to me about now?'

'Not really, James. First I have been asking colleagues about child gangs, making up a list we can discuss tomorrow. Especially, I am concentrating on children who are known to be experienced drug-couriers.'

'Very good. In light of what the janitor of the other block of flats told us this afternoon, I think we should also do all we can to find out about teams of child burglars known to be operating in the central area of the city. With any luck, there might be a team that fits the janitor's description—a long-haired, late-teenage boy with an extremely undersized child assistant. You check your records, and I'll do the same here.'

'Very well, James. Where will you be this evening if I need to get in touch with you?'

'In Spandau. I promised my daughter I'd get home before her bedtime just for once. You know how it is.'

Blessed wished he hadn't made that last, careless remark. When did Weiss see his children, even the sick one? He always seemed to be at his office, or at BlessForce, or tramping the streets looking for witnesses, evidence. Weiss, he thought guiltily, was a slave. True, Weiss benefited from his servitude, and he was treated with respect—by Blessed, at least—but nothing changed that fact. The inspector could not give himself the luxury of signing off duty early for the sake of his children or anything else without endangering his job and his all-important special rations.

'How are yours, by the way, Manfred?' he said, hoping he didn't sound too condescending.

'My children?' Weiss's expression was oddly neutral. He seemed neither embarrassed nor pleased by Blessed's enquiry. 'They are not so bad. My eldest, Rudi, takes his *Mittlerere Reife* examination this year. He is studying hard, but things are not easy with the electricity shortages . . .'

'And your youngest? Peter, is it? The one who was ill.'

'He's better, thank you. Still delicate, but—' Weiss shrugged. 'He's alive. And you are right. To have life is the most important freedom of all.'

Gisela and Daphne had set up a ping-pong table in the garden and were hard at it when Blessed found them. Gisela was, of course, taller, stronger, and more skilled, but Daphne was responding well to her coaching. Blessed watched them for a while, admiring their best shots, and watching his daughter go down bravely by a wide margin.

'Dad, you play!' Daphne demanded when the game was over.

Blessed shrugged, made to take Gisela's bat, but Daphne said, 'No, you play with Gisela. She's very good, isn't she? She'd be some competition for you. I want to rest and have some lemonade and just watch.' She plonked herself down in a chair, reached for her lemonade glass. 'Go on. Please.'

'You're a good player,' Blessed said to Gisela. 'Did you learn at school?'

She shook her head. 'At the beginning, at home. Then there was a year when I was drafted into the air defence. We would relax by playing table tennis, work off our aggressions, as they say. So I became not bad. And I do not let anyone win . . . not even Daphne.'

'I wouldn't want you to,' Daphne said firmly. 'Now come on, you beat Dad too. It would serve him right.'

'Serve me right for what?' Blessed asked.

'Oh . . . for spending all your time at the office, and for not giving me enough pocket-money, and . . . for being a *fat pig*!'

'Daphne! Don't talk to your father like that!' Gisela scolded.

Daphne giggled. 'He knows I don't really think he's fat. Don't you, Dad?'

'I suppose so.'

'Get on with it, then!'

So they did, and it was very tight. Blessed had the stronger serve, and a very good smash, but Gisela was mobile, fast and cunning, often placing the ball right in the corner of the table so that he either couldn't reach it or had already let it go. She generally served with a subtle top-spin, usually just on the right side of the line. Daphne watched and applauded them both.

At nineteen-all, Blessed served. He hit the ball hard, straight at the left-hand corner, where he had rarely served before—this was one he had been saving up—and it seemed that Gisela would never get to it. But she did. A flick of her wrist and he was surprised to see it come back, though not at any special speed. He played it just across the top of the net and she managed to scoop it, lob it up so that it dropped on the edge. He still got to it and scudded it back for a winner.

'Good old Dad! Just because he's a fat pig, it doesn't mean he can't play table tennis!' Daphne was still spluttering with barely-suppressed excitement when Blessed served for the match.

He didn't serve well. It was not hard enough, or devious enough, though it went into her quarter cleanly and at good speed. Nevertheless, Gisela had enough time to be clever with it, and cleverness was her strength. She spun it into the left corner, quick and nasty, almost wrong-footing Blessed. By now, though, he had begun to read her game in advance, and he was already half-prepared for that tactic. As the ball came over the net he was swapping the bat from his right to his left hand, gliding to meet it. He just reached the ball as it bounced, but didn't quite manage the sureness of touch that would have sent it back at the same height. The ball lifted without enough control and sailed over to Gisela's side. The German girl moved towards it, preparing for a big smash return.

'Out! Out!' Daphne yelled, leaping to her feet.

Gisela had been going for the ball; now she hesitated, her concentration broken for just long enough to let the ball go too far. When she did decide to go for it after all, it was a wild swipe that sent the ball way over the top of Blessed's head to lose her the point and the match.

'Christ, sorry,' Blessed said, and looked angrily at Daphne. 'Why did you do that? That ruined the shot for Gisela. She would have got it back.' He turned to Gisela. 'We'll take that again,' he said. 'It's not fair for you to lose because of Daphne.'

'I should have ignored her. That is the first rule of any game. You never pay any attention to what the spectators shout.' Gisela smiled, deliberately placed her bat on the table.

He looked at her. There seemed to be no guile or hidden anger in her eyes. She really didn't seem to mind.

'That was naughty, though,' he said to Daphne. 'Why did you do it?'

'I thought it was out,' she said not very convincingly. 'Really I did.'

Blessed put his own bat on the table and walked back through the French windows. He was already in the dining room pouring himself a whisky when the other two came back into the house. Gisela told Daphne to go up and start to get ready for her bath. She would be up in a moment, she said.

'There is some cold ham in the refrigerator for you, Captain,' Gisela told Blessed as Daphne ran upstairs. 'You must eat, not just drink.'

Blessed smiled wryly but said nothing. First Daphne cheats on his behalf, then the nanny warns him about drinking on an empty stomach. The Sahib may strut around Berlin putting it to rights, he thought, but at home he's less than all-powerful. To be honest with himself, he found all this shamefully comforting.

'A hard day?' Gisela continued, obviously reluctant to leave. He could hear Daphne whistling shrilly in her room.

He nodded. 'Extra work in future because of the blockade. God knows, I get home little enough anyway. Well, it will probably get worse over the next days and weeks.'

'I know you are bound to be very busy at a time like this. But can you not delegate some of your work, Captain?'

'Not the bits that matter to me, unfortunately, no.'

Gisela thought about that. She was wearing a white blouse and white shorts, and her skin was becoming brown from the sun. Then she smiled, and her teeth were white too, white against brown.

'I'm sorry Daphne was rude about your work. Also about your figure. You are by no means fat, Captain Blessed. I think you worry too much to get fat.'

Before he could answer, she had turned and was making her way up towards the bathroom to turn on the taps for Daphne. Blessed took his drink through into the living room, where there were copies of the American-licensed *Tagesspiegel* and the pro-Soviet *Berliner Zeitung*. He stared at the front pages of the *Tagesspiegel*, which were packed with lists of figures, totals of tonnage landed at Gatow and Tempelhof—over a thousand tons for the first time yesterday. The news was encouraging. There was now a probability, no longer just a possibility, that Berlin could be supplied entirely by air, enabling the city to last out the Soviet siege. If that was so, then, short of a shooting war, these two million people would stay within the western bloc. Blessed glanced at the entertainment pages. Most of the films being shown at the cinemas were American or British. Some pre-war German films, especially undemanding Hans Albers comedies about jolly, skirt-chasing Hamburg seafarers, were doing well. Postwar German film production was still a little tentative, nervous, concerned with 'national re-education'. And, of course, the cinemas were affected by the power shortages just like everything else. They were showing films at midnight or later—though apparently this didn't stop theatres being well-filled with distraction-hungry Berliners.

The paper brought Blessed back to the larger world of politics and principles, of war and peace, away from his obsessions of the past few days. It looked as if he would become part of all this airlift business, whether he liked it or not, and so he might as well relax. Blessed sipped his whisky, idly turned the pages of the *Tagesspiegel*, stopping at a photographic feature on the airlift. Here, at Gatow, smiling German workers and British troops co-operated in unloading plump bags of flour and cartons of dried potato from an RAF York. There, another picture showed American pilots handing out chocolate bars to happy kids on the tarmac. The caption said: *At Tempelhof Airfield, heroes of the Airlift make friends with German orphans who have come to watch the 'Bridge to Freedom' in proud operation!*

He was turned slightly away from the camera, as if shying from it, the child who had just received his gift from a handsome grinning giant in USAF uniform. No matter. That face, that haircut, the baggy, threadbare shorts and outsize boots were so indelibly etched in Blessed's memory that he would have recognised their owner anywhere. The child's identity was unmistakable, despite the poor quality of the reproduction. He'd need the original print of that photograph, though, as well as all the rest of the information the newspaper photographer and the reporter would be able to supply him with.

I damned well knew it. This case really is different. There's simply no escape from it, not this side of the grave, Blessed told himself as he made a lunge towards the phone, almost spilling his drink in his haste. *You tried, but there's no escape. Your mother, Lord help and save her, would have said this was a sign from God.*

TWENTY-FOUR

BOSS-KIND GREETED HIM with a relentless assault of words, as Benno had known he would.

'Oh yes—all right for you, Benno–Liebchen! You can still go wherever you like, no trouble! Those Russkies love you, weep fat vodka-tears when they think 'bout you, in-no-cent little child! But you know these days it's getting harder for me and the other tallboys when we get stopped by commie patrols—and I tell you, I nearly get *echt* big trouble today, I mean *hot*!' A moment's silence. Then more slowly: 'Soon I gotta stop coming to the Lake. . . . *Ach scheiss* this time you know they ask if I—the Boss!—wanna join their crappy-commie FDJ Red-Youth, those Stalin-sucking shit-kids, and if-not-why-not . . . I tell you, this Russkie-sector of old Berlin is getting *dangerous* for a free Kind!'

After that final crescendo, Boss-Kind's voice died away. He sighed like an old man who has forgotten what he was going to say but decides it doesn't matter anyway. Then he reached for a cigarette and lit up. All at once his face took on a tired, drained look. He had flown high these past days, and now his mood had plunged into the depths again. It was the Boss's pattern. But the tirade had been bearable. From Benno's point of view, so far, so good.

As often happened lately, once Benno finally arrived at the Lake house he had been kept waiting for his audience with the Boss. Nine hours had gone by before he had been shown in here to face that crazed greeting.

Benno estimated that it was now midnight, maybe one in the morning. The atmosphere here, among the élite of the Kinder, was intimate and yet somehow inexplicably chill. Riese had been, and he had gone, but his muscle, the notorious Fatski and Thinski, were still around somewhere close at hand, Benno had heard. The rumours even said they would be guarding Boss-Kind permanently, because of the deal with Riese and the 'security' problems involved.

So, it looked like something strange was brewing, but no one knew what it was. Not even the Wonder. Benno and his friend had managed a whispered conversation while they were alone for a few short minutes earlier in the evening. Benno hadn't seen Wonder for a week, and it was longer still since they had talked Kind-to-Kind. Since the Boss had started to use Wonder for those unexplained burglary-jobs, because Wonder was so small and so nimble, Boss-Kind had kept him close at hand, even taking him to Frankfurt. Tonight, when he had been free to talk, Wonder had seemed shy and nervous, as if he were troubled but dared not share his burden with Benno. Bad things were behind Wonder's reluctance, no doubt.

Benno was still confused. Had he been forced to come all this way just to listen to the Boss's gripes about the increased vigilance of Russian and German-communist patrols? Maybe Boss-Kind himself had forgotten the reason, he was beginning to think. Meanwhile, it was getting oh-so-late . . .

Without any warning, Boss-Kind lunged forward, grabbed Benno's shirt front. '*But* what you been doing being *seen* by Kepten Blessed, eh?' he snarled, fully alive again and unfortunately also fully crazy.

Benno was dumbstruck.

'*My eyes see* the Kepten chase you!' Boss-Kind hissed. 'And after you escape, you tell nobody—but specially not *me*—that Blessed seen you and chased you outside the sweet little Spandau school. *Ach scheiss*, what spiel are you spieling, Benno-boy? First you lose Bigman-Panewski! Then the Kepten sees you! Can this just be chance yes *Zufall*? Or do I smell a *traitor*? Benno, you better tell me or there will be Kinder-trouble for you just beyond *belief*!'

Boss-Kind released his grip on Benno's shirt, but he continued to stand so close that his looming figure shut out the whole world. He was seething, consumed by his anger and his excitement, at his most unpredictable.

'Who tol' you? Who says this?' Benno muttered, playing for time.

'*My eyes see. My ears hear*,' Boss-Kind spat. 'You . . . just . . . explain, *Liebchen-Lämmchen*, because I am wait-ing . . .'

Benno swallowed hard. 'The Kepten, you know he *hates* beggar boys, I notice that,' he began, trying to sound professional, matter-

253

of-fact. 'So, outside that Spandau school he sees me and thinks I am
a beggar boy, maybe bother those English girlies, specially Daff-nee.
So . . . he run to *arrest* Benno, vagrancy or some dumb charge, any
charge, I don' know what.'

Benno knew a lot depended on how he turned this interview. He
had let himself be disarmed by Boss-Kind's apparent vagueness. In
fact, it had seemed like maybe Boss-Kind been tasting dope, not just
selling it. Well, now Benno was paying the painful price for dropping
his guard.

'Boss, you really think Kepten Blessed got any idea why I was
watching? Good-gadawlmighdy, for a week now he been busy hunting
Bigman-Panewski and only Bigman-Panewski!' Benno continued,
braving the ominous silence. Above all, he knew he must not show
fear, because Boss-Kind could smell it in the air, as a shark is drawn
to blood in the water. Instead Benno must be brazen, wait and find out
what the Boss was really hunting for with his questions. 'That Kepten,
he was chasing a beggar boy!'

Having said his piece, Benno shrugged to show his indifference.
Then with dignified assurance he pulled out the saved remnant of a
handrolled cigarette from his pocket, made to light it from his beloved
book of *Lark* matches.

Boss-Kind reached out and knocked aside Benno's match and
cigarette with the flat of his hand, sent them both flying. His voice
was low, insistent. 'Ach I'm still waiting for the whole story, Benno-
boy. Now you better tell me the Kinder-truth on your gadawlmighdy
Kinder-life!'

And now the Boss's blade appeared, apparently from nowhere. The
brass knuckleduster gleamed on the back of his hand like a part of
his body. From it protruded the open blade, a lethal outgrowth with
its point at Benno's Adam's apple, almost piercing the taut flesh.
This is serious business, this questioning, the blade said. *It can kill.*
The still-burning cigarette in Boss-Kind's other hand hovered no
more than half an inch from Benno's cheek, so he could feel the
concentrated heat on his skin, smell the acrid black tobacco, hear its
soft but ominous fizzing and crackle.

Now this was not the first time Benno had witnessed Boss-Kind
behaving like a Gestapo-killer with that knife—it was Boss-Kind's
way from time to time in jest, with girlies or with some of the dumber
kids, and with Hats famously and not so jestingly. But never before
with Benno. Benno was one of the special Kinder who had all been
together since before Point Null, when Doktor Barnhelm had been a

254

real orphanage director, and all the Kinder had been his slaves—*even Boss-Kind*, let that never be forgotten! Benno was Boss-Kind's *equal*. If only the Boss wasn't so big these days, and so angry, and if only he didn't know so amazingly and terrifyingly much . . .

Meanwhile, the Boss continued remorselessly, 'Benno, I tell you *my eyes see* you run, see Kepten Blessed search. *My ears hear* Kepten say, "this boy there I know I seen him before, and he is no good". *My ears hear* Hauptmann Kepten Blessed say, "*I w-i-l-l f-i-n-d t-h-a-t G-e-r-m-a-n b-o-y* . . ." ' Boss-Kind smiled. 'By *that boy* he mean you, Benno-boy, he mean only only only you . . .'

Oh the gleaming, vicious blade. Oh that glowing, merciless cigarette. Oh this bright and savage moment when all is lost or won. You weaken justalittlebit, Benno thought, then you *ach scheiss* you are lost and you beddabelieve it.

'You send a different watcher tomorrow, Boss,' he said coolly, although his heart was beating wild, undisciplined, and his bowels were screaming to be given the freedom to open . . . 'You think I care? You find a better watcher! You send *him* to watch the Kepten, watch girlie, watch Nannypie. I have had a real nose-full of watching allthetime watching! And that is no less than the Kinder-gottverdammt Kinder-gadawlmighdy Kinder-truth!'

There was what to Benno felt like an agonisingly long sequence of seconds, anywhere between six and sixty. Then Boss-Kind lowered both the blade-point and the burning cigarette. He let his hands slide and collapsed abruptly into the battered cane chair that was the only furniture in the room. In that position he laughed loud and long, head back and throat wide like a wolf separated from the pack. When his outburst was over, he took a drag on his neglected cigarette, ran a hand through his long, lank hair.

'*Heil Benno!*' Boss-Kind chuckled, raising his right arm in a satirical Nazi salute. 'You have passed the great test! This Kind Benno here is *not* to be duped, this Kind Benno here will de-fin-itely *not* be te-rr-or-ised . . .'

Then, without moving from the chair, he began to recite one of his improvised doggerels, in a kind of sing-song chant, swaying slightly from the waist and tapping his foot to the rhythm as he felt his way into his story:

> Ach Kepten Blessed he think he fool
> Us Kinder when he visit School—
> No Mummydear, no Nannypie
> Just Watch-Kind Benno, and Boss-Kind's eye.

The Kepten think he frighten us
That noise that chase that cuss that fuss
But Boss-Kind see and Boss-Kind hear
With his all-see-eye and his all-hear-ear.

Now Kepten look 'bout everywhere
Panewski flown, it *just* ain't fair
He think Panewski hiding in the East
Because Panewski a *murdering beast*.

I tell the Kepten, I show him clues
I send him Benno, I give him news
Seems he got no sense, he got no power
But Boss-Kind gets stronger by the hour.

The Kepten fright the Kepten funk
The Kepten got that whisky drunk
But oh no Kinder, we get that man
Boss-Kind he make a *change of plan*!

Boss-Kind uncoiled his lanky body and rose to his feet, padded over to the window, looked for a short while at the risen moon suspended over the indigo surface of the Grosser Müggelsee, lighting the way right across to the East Berlin suburb of Friedrichshagen.

This old timber-framed boathouse was Boss-Kind's retreat, his extra-secret place. He held its tenancy because of the morphine he supplied to its owner, a once-famous left-wing film actor who after years of being blacklisted by the Nazis had found favour with the new Soviet masters in 'Democratic' Berlin and was being given plum parts in propaganda films these days.

'*Ach scheiss* the dumb old Hat who owns this place, you know that ac-tor?' Boss-Kind said conversationally, turning back into the room. 'You know he *bleeds* for youth, and po-ver-ty, and all that gadawlmighdy *Romantik*—not forgetting the *dope*!' he added with a high-pitched, barking laugh. 'Anyway, this Hat is *so* dumb he maybe thinks the Kinder play cowboy-indian games here, or something. Who cares what he believes? So long as the actor believes in *dope*, the tenancy is assured, eh?'

'You bet, Boss-Kind.' Benno was smoking with apparent content-ment, enjoying the dog-end he had retrieved from the wooden floor, but behind his nicotine-screen he remained totally watchful. The Boss was building up to some revelation. Why else bother with this irrelevant story about the actor who owned the house?

'Ach, but soon it must come to an end anyway, the lake house here in the Russkie-sector, and the travels across and between and under the perilous sector borders . . . Benno, the sweet Kinder-time of chaos is *over*,' Boss-Kind said. 'This is true?'

Benno nodded. It was true.

'Three years now since Point Null,' the Boss continued. 'Blockade or no blockade, the no-name, no-law Berlin will soon become just anywhere/anytown/anytime . . . I *mean* this city will become once more a city of *Hats* . . .' He waited for Benno's response.

'Then we got trouble, Boss-Kind,' Benno said boldly. 'True, Hats will soon be everywhere, meaning no ruins no cellars no safety for Kinder . . . And what will the Kinder do when those Hats want to turn us back into slaves?'

'I can deal with the Kepten and Panewski, so don' you worry, Benno,' Boss-Kind said. 'Like I already dealt with everylittle other problem . . . Ah, see, I have this plan . . .' He was standing facing the younger boy now. His hands were clasped together in front of him with the long fingers contorted, as if he were wrestling silently with himself.

'Plan? What plan, Boss-Kind?' Benno urged him on.

'This plan! I tell you!' Boss-Kind said. 'You know we already have Hersheys flying our cuteboy package-takers Hershey-Zonewards, to Frankfurt, then turnaround back to old Berlin—Gad-Bless-the-Airlift because they got cargo space for Kinder. You remember I sent you all to Tempelhof while I was away in the Hershey-Zone, Benno? Yes you was there, you saw how our little orphans get anylittlething from those dumb Hersheys for a smile and a melody!' Boss-Kind giggled suddenly with the pleasure of that deception. 'Soon the Kepten will be beaten!' he exclaimed. 'Soon that shit Hat Bigman will get his just des-erts! And because of Riese there will be sweet dollars *ach scheiss* so many dollars.' Now Boss-Kind grabbed a deep breath and moved on to his climax: 'Plan is we all fly Hershey Zonewards, Benno, and stay. *Stay for ever and ever!*'

There was a silence, except for the lapping of the water and the murmur of conversation in the main room of the lake house, where older boys were playing dice. No surprise that Wonder was so disturbed, so silent and closed-mouthed these days, Benno thought. No surprise at all, if his friend was forced to listen to this maniacal shit all day and night.

'Real plan you got there, Boss-Kind,' Benno said non-committally.

'Not just real plan but *good* plan, *stimmt?*' Boss-Kind demanded

257

almost plaintively. 'You see, Benno? There in the West, a new Kinder Garden! No Russkies also no Kepten Blessed! You see, no Hat will know us. You see, no names . . .'

It was the first time Boss-Kind had revealed his plan to move the Kinder out of Berlin, found a new Garden in the American Zone, hundreds of kilometres to the west. Benno didn't much like the sound of it. And what was this wild talk about 'dealing with' the Kepten and Bigman? Was this to do with Riese? Benno felt in his guts that there must be some important details that Boss-Kind wasn't sharing with him and the others.

But Benno had learned not to argue with Boss-Kind, because that *always* ended in tears. Nowadays he just agreed with him and waited for the storm to blow over. And tonight there was more reason than ever to tread warily. So he smiled in seeming approval for Boss-Kind's plan. But the fact was that tonight—what with the blade and the mad talk and the new plan—some little but vital thing in Benno had snapped. For weeks and months he had been having his quiet doubts. Now he *knew*. His finely-tuned watcher's instincts told him that Boss-Kind had finally gone over the edge. *Yes, for some shit reason the Boss had gone completely crazy . . .*

Boss-Kind nevertheless seemed satisfied with Benno's answer. His eyes locked on Benno's face, searching for some unknown, perhaps unknowable thing, and then drifted away. He gradually began to sway, first mouthing words silently and only when he was sure of himself crooning in a limpid, almost childlike voice that suited his changed mood:

> In gadawlmighdy Hersheyland
> Happy live the Kinderband
> In Hersheyland is tree and field
> Forest be the Kinder's shield.
>
> No sector checkpoint sector border
> No sector papers sector order
> By Frankfurt, Mainz, and old Wiesbaden
> We build a brand-new Kinder Garden.

'Soon enough. Soon you will all find it, the new Kinder Garden,' Boss-Kind said with a hint of sadness, his short new poem done and gone, consigned to the lake waters, and the ether beyond. 'But for now you must sleep, Benno. Tomorrow you will be busy busy—but no more watching, because I find new watch-Kinder for Kepten and Daff-nee and Nannypie to help *my eyes see.* Tomorrow, Benno, you will go on a special mission for me. Maybe to Riese. You know there are so many things to be done . . .

Boss-Kind was starting into one of his famous dreamings. He would probably not sleep at all tonight; just sit staring out of the window and dreaming. All the Kinder knew the signs. He touched Benno on the shoulder, palmed him an American cigarette as a parting gift, pushed him gently out of the door and back into the big room to join Wonder and the other élite Kinder.

'*Ach scheiss*, Benno, much to be done,' Boss-Kind repeated before the door closed between them. 'Things beyond belief. So many things.'

TWENTY-FIVE

EGON HAFFNER WAS ABOUT THIRTY. He wore a little dark beard and an ancient black beret. He did not take the beret off when he was marched into Blessed's office by Kelly. The captain, having hurried here from Spandau, was still in his own trenchcoat and cap.

'I'm very grateful you could come,' Blessed said pleasantly. He liked the look of Haffner. This was the kind of drily humorous, don't-give-a-damn Berlin Bohemian type he had got drunk and talked nonsense with into the small hours as a student nearly twenty years before.

'Say what you like about the British, but on the whole they have very good manners,' Haffner said. The photographer spoke softly but fluently, and his wry, observer's smile seemed a permanent fixture. 'It may be past eleven o'clock at night, the two insistent gentlemen you sent to fetch me may have ruined my chances with a beautiful, willing young woman, and I may be slightly drunk—all these things are true. Nevertheless, like any good German of the new, reformed, democratic kind, I am always willing to co-operate with the Allied military authorities, no matter what trouble it costs me.'

'Sergeant Kelly lacks a certain refinement, it's true, but I confess he was doing as he had been told. You see, I couldn't wait. I had to talk to you here and now. Can I at least offer you a smoke?'

Haffner took a cheroot with an appreciative smile, but he didn't drop his guard. 'They said you wanted to talk to me but wouldn't say what about. This reminds me—unfairly, I'm sure—of the bad old days, when the men in leather coats came knocking and you didn't know whether it was for a cosy chat or to haul you off to Buchenwald.' He

260

looked at Blessed and his brown eyes took on a surprisingly hard sheen. 'So I'm asking, which is it now, Captain?'

'Relax, Herr Haffner. Nothing so dramatic. It's just about some nice, uncontroversial pictures you took for the *Tagesspiegel* at Tempelhof Airfield a few days ago.'

The eyes, though still wary, softened. Blessed showed Haffner the photograph of the 'orphans' at Tempelhof, pointed to the particular boy he was interested in. He had privately christened the urchin 'Buster'.

'I want to know about these children,' he said. 'And especially who that boy was. That's all.'

Haffner puffed gratefully on the cheroot as he squinted at the fuzzy half-tone of the group. 'I didn't take those shots yesterday. They're three or four days old,' he said. 'I can look through my notes to check, but as far as I recall, I never knew where those damned kids were from. As for asking me to identify that individual boy . . . no chance.'

Blessed was staring hard at the picture too. 'Who's this German civilian on the left, wearing the dark glasses and fighting shy of the camera?' All he could tell from the photograph was that the man was quite elderly, with a widow's peak. He was holding a hand up over his eyes as if to protect them, effectively casting his face into shadow.

'I think he was the orphanage director. He seemed in charge in an ineffectual sort of a way,' Haffner said. 'But I didn't ask him. I just saw the thing going on, I knew the paper was looking for heartwarming airlift material, and, hell, I knew it was a good shot that I might even be able to sell to the Anglo-American press for hard currency. For Christ's sake, I don't even know whether the little bastards actually were orphans.'

'The caption seems pretty specific. What about your reporter? Didn't he interview anyone, take any names?'

'I don't work with a reporter. Didn't the paper tell you that when you rang them? I'm a freelance photographer, Captain. I just prowl the likely spots and take pictures that I hope I can sell. I supplied the picture, they captioned it.' Haffner shrugged. 'The fellow *looked* like an orphanage director. The kids *looked* like goddamned orphans. What more do you want?'

'You mean, what more do *you* want?' Blessed thought for a moment, weighing up the possibilities. Then he asked casually, 'How long do you think that young woman will wait for you, Herr Haffner?'

'An hour or two. My flat's pretty comfortable. She might even have decided to take a nap and see if I actually come back. I promised her I would return in no time. But then I would, wouldn't I?'

'You would. Where are the originals of these Tempelhof photographs?'

'They're at my flat.' The easy atmosphere suddenly evaporated. Haffner looked at Blessed with suspicion. It was obvious that he regretted his admission almost as soon as he made it.

'Negatives? Prints?'

Haffner seemed to realise there was no point in pursuing an unequal struggle. 'Both,' he said heavily. 'I got the contacts back from the *Tagesspiegel* because I wanted to see if I could sell something to *Stars and Stripes*, or even one of the American papers' bureaux over here.'

Blessed nodded. 'Then we'll make an arrangement,' he said. 'I'll let you go home to resume whatever you were doing with your girlfriend. In return, you give Sergeant Kelly your contacts and your negatives when he drops you off at your flat.'

'Jesus. Do you know how . . .'

'Yes. I do know how valuable they are. They'll be delivered back to you within forty-eight hours, probably less. We have our own processing laboratory.' Blessed paused. 'Listen, Herr Haffner: I don't have to let you go. I could keep you here, take out a warrant, have your flat searched—girl or no girl—and have all the relevant negatives and prints impounded as evidence, without any guarantee of their early return. The choice is yours.'

Haffner gave Blessed a round of mute, sarcastic mock-applause. 'And may I ask why you want these prints?'

'You can ask. I'm not at liberty to answer you, though.'

'Now that's what I call negotiation,' Haffner said bitterly. 'Heads I win, tails you lose, is, I believe, the formula for success in that field. Herr Hitler operated in that way all the time.'

Blessed looked at him with sympathy, but he also felt his heart harden. He liked this man, at any other time he would have loved to sit down with him and drink schnapps, discuss the world and its shortcomings, but at the moment what he really wanted were those pictures, and he wanted them fast.

'Perhaps he did,' he agreed. 'But those remain your options, Herr Haffner. I'm sorry.'

'So sorry,' Haffner mimicked grumpily. 'How English of you.'

'I suppose it is, yes. We're not Gestapo, Herr Haffner. But we are policemen, and we are trying to solve a crime. We're different from civilians in that respect. I'll even apologise again if it makes you feel better. Here it comes: Sorry.'

Sergeant Kelly arrived back with the photographs at a quarter to one, put them down on Blessed's desk with a deferential yet satisfied cough.

'There you go, sir.'

'Thanks, Kelly.'

The prints showed the plane, then the pilot trying to comply with Haffner's instructions as the photographer browbeat him into the best pose with his candy bars. There were a dozen or so shots of the candy-distribution, which clearly showed Buster, the boy Blessed had seen in the Ku-Damm and outside Daphne's school. He had a solemn, bony face, a shock of light brown hair, and, of course, those terrible shorts and boots. There was absolutely no mistaking him. So they had Buster: the only trouble was, the 'orphanage director' had managed to avoid Haffner's lens altogether in the rest of the shots, and the one photograph of him they had was virtually useless for identification purposes.

'Kelly,' Blessed said to the sergeant, who was still hovering in the room, 'Ring Tempelhof. Talk to someone in Public Relations there. We have to find out the identity of the civilian who escorted this group of orphans when they visited the airfield last week. OK?'

'It's a bit late, sir.'

'If there's no one about, then just get me a name from the night staff. If we've got a name and a phone number we can contact him first thing, before I keep that appointment at RAF Gatow.'

While Kelly busied himself with calling Tempelhof, Blessed sat very quietly and thought about the implications of the evening's information. Then he unclipped his pen from his pocket, flipped open a pad, and wrote: *'(1) If this adult was in charge of Buster and his friends, we are really getting somewhere. We couldn't find Buster but we should be able to find him.'* Pause. *'Contact Magistrature's department for orphans' welfare and show them the shot of the adult. Just on the off-chance.'* A much longer pause. Then Blessed wrote, *'(2) How do we flush Panewski out? If he's still around his old haunts, we have to provoke him, get him to make a move and so betray himself. If he's not around his old haunts, it won't work. But if he isn't, why is he sending these children after me?'*

He read through his scribbled notes. The existence of the adult in the

263

Tempelhof party was a breakthrough. Until now, Blessed had assumed that the urchins who had been following him were living unofficially in some cellar somewhere, completely outside normal society, and that tracing them would mean undertaking a major trawl through the entire Berlin underworld—a task for which he had neither the resources nor, if he was honest with himself, the justification. Well, there was now the possibility that the children could be traced more easily, through official records.

As for the memo he had jotted down about Panewski, he was initially less clear. It had just come out onto the page that way. He was making two assumptions—the first, that Panewski and these children were in some way connected; the second, that Panewski could be got at through the children. Both the assumptions were reasonable. The first he had always felt to be true, and the second had only occurred to him a few minutes ago. Now, what action?

'A Yank airforce major by the name of O'Hara was in charge of the press office that day, sir,' Kelly said, putting down the phone. 'The chap I just spoke to knew the photo; they were very pleased with it. The bad news is that O'Hara's in Frankfurt and won't be back before tomorrow afternoon.'

Blessed nodded. Maybe he didn't necessarily have to talk to O'Hara personally. He certainly couldn't wait until he get back from Frankfurt. As for the other problem—Panewski's connection with the kids—he could do something about that immediately.

'Kelly,' he said, 'I want you to get back on the phone to Tempelhof and ask your man there to look at the register for conducted tours—they must have some kind of record—and give us a list of all the parties admitted to the airfield over the past few days. Especially, we're interested in parties of orphans or schoolchildren, and the names of the adults who accompanied them. Meanwhile, I think I'll give the *Tagesspiegel* another ring.'

The newspaper's night editor was helpful, but obviously under a great deal of pressure. Blessed identified himself as an officer of the Military Police, gave the address of the main CMP station down the street, and told the editor he wanted to insert a small advertisement in the personal column of their next edition. No, he couldn't wait until tomorrow. So they had just finished printing their early edition? Fine. It could go in the midmorning one. If they refused, they would find themselves in big trouble with the British commandant's office. Yes, and if the Herr Editor felt like calling the Villa Lem and waking up the commandant now, he was perfectly free to do so. Blessed would even give them the correct number to ring. The commandant would confirm that Captain Blessed was who he claimed to be, and the commandant would doubtless also be very annoyed. Oh, the Herr Editor would take his word for it? Thank you so much, Herr Editor. The message he wanted the *Tagesspiegel* to run in its very next edition was precisely as follows:

> *Herr Panewski. Since we saw you in the Tiergarten we have found your children. We are aware of all your problems. Why not ring our number and give up worrying?*

It should be on the streets about eleven that morning. They would even put a box around it so that it was noticed. He would not forget this favour, Blessed told the editor. If they ever needed any help from now on, the *Tagesspiegel* had only to ring him.

'Any luck?' Blessed asked Kelly when he had finished with the paper.

'They're looking. He thinks O'Hara may have put the book in his safe, or even taken it with him. Sounds as if O'Hara is not all that well liked. Anyway, my man's looking and he'll phone back in half an hour. You look tired, sir.'

Blessed extinguished his cheroot in the ashtray, nodded. 'How do you keep going, Kelly?'

'It's a question of my constitution, sir. And I don't have an awful lot on my mind apart from my job, of course. That helps.'

'If you're all right, then I think I'll go home now and get a few hours' sleep.'

Thwaite was snoring in a chair in one of the other offices. Blessed woke him gently. 'Home,' he said simply. 'Take me home, Thwaite.'

They didn't speak until they were about halfway back to Spandau, not too far from Floh's apartment in Charlottenburg. Then Blessed leaned forward and asked his driver a question.

'What do people think of me?' he said, 'In the Branch, and at 248 Company?'

'*Think* of you? What d'you mean by that, sir?' Thwaite answered cautiously, in much the same way a priest would speak if you asked him a loaded question about the Church's attitude towards God.

'I mean, what's the gossip? I know you talk a lot, keep your ear to the ground. Tell me, do they say I'm mad?'

Thwaite took his time to reply. 'They consider you a very zealous officer, sir,' he said eventually. He cleared his throat. 'I must admit, there are fellows who think you're a wee bit over-zealous.'

'Tell me more. It's important for me to know. What about the Price case? What do people think of the way I've been handling the Price case?'

'Well . . .' Thwaite sighed deeply, then decided to take the plunge and tell the truth. 'They think you're the only person in the 'ole of Berlin as can be bothered with it, sir. There's no bugger's got the smallest bit of sympathy for Price or his tart, or that horrible little sod Floh, and they wonder what's eating you about the business that you keep worrying at it.'

'Does "they" include you?'

'Sir! That's like askin' a wife to testify against her husband, in't it? You can't ask a bloke in my position a question like that. To be honest, I don't understand the fascination of this Price business, but . . .'

Thwaite let the sentence drop, shrugged expressively and made hard work of turning off the Brunsbütteler Damm to pass under the S-bahn bridge and head up the next-to-final stretch along Zeppeliner Strasse.

'But what?' Blessed asked.

'You're the boss. You've been in the business all these years, sir. You have to follow your instincts, don't you? You got to have the courage to swim against the tide. Er, wi'out bein' foolhardy, like.'

'Thanks for the information, Thwaite. It's pretty much as I expected,' Blessed said. 'I just wanted to know what attitudes I was up against. I seem to have been so busy lately. One gets out of touch.'

Thwaite stole a glance at him in the rear-view mirror. 'Aye,' he agreed. 'It can get so's you don't notice the way things've changed.'

Blessed didn't answer. He wound down his window and looked out at the sky, enjoyed the warm, refreshing night air on his face. There were aeroplane lights up there, and the now-familiar, friendly drone of engines. Thwaite's words applied to this situation too. How strange it must be for the Berliners. A little more than three years previously, they would have fled to their cellars in terror at the sound and sight of fat, heavy-laden American and British planes in the sky above their city. Now they welcomed them, loved them, could not live without them. The aircraft had changed from life-takers to life-givers. If only the change were as simple for human beings.

TWENTY-SIX

THE ROAR OF THE DAKOTA'S powerful 1200-horsepower Pratt and
Whitney engines rose briefly to a throbbing scream as the transport
aircraft gained speed, striving frantically to lift itself from the crowded
Gatow tarmac. There seemed, at that critical moment, no possibility
that it could avoid crashing into one of the tight lines of planes still
being unloaded nearby. The Dakota had arrived from Wunstorf two
hours previously, packed with a little more than two tons of coal for
Berlin; it was returning to the West with electrical goods from the
Siemens factory. Apart from supplying the city with the necessities
vital to life, the airlift also allowed some semblance of export industry
to continue, so that Berlin could pay some of its way and keep at least
some of its highly-skilled workers in jobs. The machine's frustration
mirrored Blessed's as he watched it from a windy observation platform
next to the control tower.

'We've got some Yorks coming in now,' a squadron leader from
Transport Command with a red moustache was telling him. 'More
cargo capacity. That should step things up. I mean, we call it an
airlift, but actually—whisper it not in Gath . . . or Gatow for that
matter—we have some way to go before we can even remotely fulfil
this city's needs.'

'Which are?'

'Now let me see . . . That would be 641 tons of flour, 105 of cereals,
106 of meat and fish, 900 of potatoes, 51 of sugar, 10 of coffee, 20 milk,
32 of fats . . . oh, and three tons of yeast. And that's just the food. We
also need 1000 tons of hard coal a day just to keep the gasworks going
at the present, rationed rate. Also, have you thought about the other
things? Do you realise that during the next month this city is going
to need 20,000 square metres of X-ray film and 20 tons of plaster of
Paris for its hospitals?'

'You've done your homework.'

'Oh, we had to, old boy. When the Russians told us—back in
forty-five—that we'd be completely responsible for feeding our own
sectors of Berlin, we promptly got in the chaps with the bowlers and the

briefcases from the Ministry of Food and the Ministry of Power, had them do the appropriate calculations. I learned them off by heart just so's to dazzle outsiders.'

Blessed nodded. 'And how much have you . . . I mean we . . . managed to fly in these past two weeks?'

'Well, I'll be frank. The first week, it was only twelve hundred tons all together, and never mind the propaganda. We're stepping it up, though. You just wait,' the squadron leader said with a boyish grin. 'Do or die, old chap; do or die!'

The Dakota had managed to stagger into the air. Another cargo plane was coming in to land from the west. Gatow, a former German Luftwaffe base, was, in fact, technically not part of Berlin at all. In 1945 the British, who lacked an airfield on their territory, had done a deal with the Russians, swapping a bit of their assigned sector for this patch of ground just across the Havel river and outside the old limits of Greater Berlin. This put the RAF in a highly exposed position on the very western extremity of the city; bizarrely enough, even their electricity supply came from a generator inside the Russian Zone. Any false moves or major 'incidents' and there could be really serious trouble. The fact that the Soviets hadn't tried any tricks with the power probably proved that they wanted to avoid armed confrontation. That was the optimists' view, enthusiastically proposed by the squadron leader.

Blessed watched, his interest alloyed with apprehension, as the dumpy, twin-engined beast of burden bumped noisily to land, seemed to bounce gently, making a soft crunching noise, and then began to grind along the runway towards them. The plane finally slowed down sufficiently to begin taxiing towards the part of the apron reserved for arrivals. Disciplined teams of Germans in drab overalls were heading towards her, eager to begin stripping her holds, picking her clean ready for the outward-bound load.

'A quick break now for the poor bloody aircrew,' the squadron leader commented. 'Off to the Malcolm Club for a cup of tea and a bun while our Kraut coolies do their work. Then it's back into the air, of course . . .'

'Those German labourers out there are putting in some very hard work too, Squadron Leader. They must have a powerful motivation.'

The squadron leader looked momentarily astonished, then said: 'Where have you been lately, old boy? Don't you read the newspapers? We're reckoning on another 100,000 unemployed in Berlin by the end of this month if the blockade continues. The people we've taken on this past week get a Number One Heavy Workers' ration card plus a hot midday meal. It's not a bad offer if the alternative is gnawing on an oily rag. We've had big-shot intellectuals and aristocrats in here, I'll tell you straight. Begging to be allowed to hump sacks of potatoes.' He nodded sagely. 'And that's also why you've got thousands of Krauts swarming over to the French sector to Tegel, humping rocks the size of car tyres all day long, building a proper airfield on Göring's old flak gunner's training ground. All for a Mark twenty a day, a pot of watery vegetable stew, and a hunk of bread that looks and tastes like steel wool.'

'OK. But would you say there's an element of anti-communist fervour in the workers' attitude? On the whole, you see, idealists don't steal from their own side.'

'Oh, naturally there's a political angle for the Germans. The fact is, they're up shit creek here if we don't make the airlift work. *Kaputt.* Berlin under the Russian heel forever. And they know it.'

'So, how does all this tie in with the thieving I've heard so much about, Squadron Leader?' Blessed said, deciding it was time to cut the chit-chat and knuckle down to the security question. He didn't want to stay here for any longer than he had to. 'What percentage of the cargo would you estimate has been disappearing?'

'You want to know what *percentage*?' The squadron leader chuckled fruitily. 'Oh, I don't think we need to look at it in quite that way.'

'If you've got a major problem, surely you can give me an estimate?'

The squadron leader seemed genuinely puzzled. 'But we haven't got a major problem, old boy. Actually,' he said, 'there's been remarkably little in the way of naughty goings-on. The loading and unloading happen too quickly, and anyway there's too many of our people about for them to make off with more than tiny amounts of stuff. I can tell you some rather funny stories about the bits of petty pilfering we've dealt with—'

'Just a moment. The commandant's office seemed very concerned. I was told that you were crying out for expert help against these thieves.'

'Oh really, old chap? That's a new one on me. The high-ups had their own good reasons, I daresay.' The squadron leader shrugged and laughed again. His apparently limitless capacity for innocent amusement under unamusing circumstances was beginning to grate on Blessed's sleep-starved nerves.

'Are you saying you made no such request?'

'We're frightfully busy, but we'll give you all the help we can, of course . . .'

'Answer my question please, Squadron Leader. Did you request my presence here, or did you not?'

The squadron leader gave him a look of aggrieved surprise, like a child who has just been rebuked for doing something that had always garnered praise in the past. Then his jaw tightened and though the smile returned, the tone was altogether more acid.

'Request? No. What actually happened was, one of your officers rang *us* and asked *us* if we wanted your help, Captain,' he said. 'My superiors were far too polite to say no. No offence to the Branch, but personally I reckon a couple of sharp-eyed aircraftmen set to patrolling the tarmac suffices to nip nefarious activities in the bud. Oh, there's thievery afoot, I'm sure, but I suggest you look elsewhere—namely at the distribution and storage—if you and the high-ups are really interested in bringing the light-fingered brethren to book.'

'Well,' Blessed said when his host had finished, 'that's very interesting. You seem to have the situation under control without my help. The only trouble is, I'm still stuck with my orders. According to them, I'm supposed to be having a good poke around here, and then turning in some kind of a report. You know, something to keep the commandant's office happy . . .'

'Yes. I can see your problem.' The squadron leader relaxed, realising that Blessed was not going to make trouble for him. 'Well, you've had the tour, haven't you?' he said, and winked. 'Any other information you need to, er, pad things out, all you have to do is ask.'

'I'll keep out of your way as much as I can. In fact, I'll follow your advice and broaden the frame of reference of my enquiries. Shift the emphasis away from the actual airfield. Do you understand my meaning, Squadron Leader?'

'Oh, I think we understand each other perfectly, Captain.'

Thwaite was drinking tea up in the observation tower, fascinated by the air controller's art.

'That was quick, sir. I thought we were goin' to be here all day,' he said, pulling a disappointed face. 'In fact, I was rather enjoying the prospect. Did you know that they've got this brand-new gadget called "GCA"—that's Ground Control Approach—so you get a sort of a radar picture of the plane even when it's twenty miles off. One of the controller blokes was telling me they reckon that with a bit more practice they'll soon be able to land a plane every five minutes! How about that, sir?'

'Extraordinary. I've seen everything I need to see for the moment, though,' Blessed said. 'I'm afraid I have other plans.'

As they left, Blessed noticed the solitary figure of a Soviet air force major standing sadly but watchfully in a corner, observing everything that was going on in the control tower. This was the Russian liaison officer, a leftover from four-power co-operation, now cold-shouldered by his former colleagues but grimly sticking to his post. Blessed knew how he felt.

'Take me to Tempelhof Airfield, Thwaite,' he ordered, relaxing into the leather upholstery of the Horch and fishing out a cheroot from his coat pocket. 'We're going to talk to the Americans about aeroplanes, and one or two other things besides.'

'Right-oh, sir. It's good to get out and about again.'

Thwaite's unspoken implication was that it was good to be no longer stuck with the Price case. Little did he know, thought Blessed. Little did any of them know.

In the thirties, Berlin's most central airport at Tempelhof had been the show-piece of the German aeronautics industry. Its grandiose specifications had included huge plate-glass observation windows behind which hundreds of spectators could sit, drinks in hand, and marvel at the air displays put on to the greater glory of the Reich. What Tempelhof had not been was a serious airfield, of the kind that could take heavy civilian or military traffic. Since it was the only airfield in their sector, the Americans had done their inventive best, but the place still looked like a splendid sham, an impractical sports-stadium of the air. It was also surrounded by high buildings, including the famously tall brewery chimney that Harriet had joked about. Nevertheless, the activity on the tarmac was very impressive. Blessed went to the reception desk and asked for Major O'Hara's office.

'Major O'Hara is over at Rhine-Main at the moment, meeting with their people on airlift business,' a tall, dark captain of Mediterranean appearance told him cheerfully. 'I'm his stand-in. Ed Dracoulis is the name. Can I be of help to you, Captain . . . ah . . . ?'

'Blessed. James. SIB. We're like your own CID.'

Instead of showing surprise or alarm, the friendly captain smiled even more broadly. 'The *police*?'

'I'm afraid so. It concerns a group of orphans—or supposed orphans—who toured the airfield the other day. On Tuesday in the afternoon, to be precise,' he added.

'Sit down, Jim. Frank Burbage said something about that this morning before he went off duty. I'll get you some coffee and we'll see what we can find.'

On the whole Blessed liked Americans very much. It was just that he didn't really understand them, finding their ever-friendly approach as alien in its way as Japanese politeness or Levantine flattery. He guessed that to most Americans he must appear morose to the point of outright hostility, but there wasn't much he could do about that.

The coffee, dark and strong as the best at Kranzler's or the Romanischer Café in the old days, came straightaway. Ed Dracoulis returned after about five minutes with a fat book bound in dark-green leather.

'The visitors' book. Seems we had four parties that afternoon. One orphanage.' A lopsided grin. 'But here's something that may be significant, Jim. We promised to send that fellow from the orphanage the prints of his kids and the pilot—we had a bunch of quick copies made for our own PR purposes, you know?—and, well, we mailed them—and today we got them back, not known at this address. The address he wrote in the book is just a vacant lot.'

'Where?'

'Ah . . . Dessauer Strasse. That's a couple hundred yards from the Potsdamer Platz, just inside our sector. You know . . .'

'I know where the Dessauer Strasse is, thanks,' Blessed said, more sharply than he meant to. 'Are you sure you didn't misread his handwriting? Perhaps he wrote in German script and you got the house-number wrong.'

'That's what we thought. So we called the Reich Post people. They said there's definitely no orphanage or school or anything of that nature anywhere in the Dessauer Strasse. Anyway, you go ahead and take a look for yourself.'

Blessed checked. The writing was spidery and old-fashioned, but the address was clear. There had been no mistake. The orphanage director had signed himself 'Dr Kannowitz', but had given no name for the institution he supposedly directed.

'Well, we seem to have reached an impasse, Capt . . . I mean, Ed. Unless this gentleman who calls himself "Dr Kannowitz" shows himself here again. In which case, please hang onto him and inform me immediately.'

'Anything you say,' Dracoulis assured him. 'So what's the story?'

'One of the orphans may have something to do with a murder.'

Dracoulis nodded, frowned. 'The experienced guys tell you about these things. I've only been in Germany three months. I heard life was even tougher for the Krauts a couple years ago. But you know, kids of

273

eight, ten, stealing and robbing and even killing. Can you imagine that happening in *America*?'

'They're desperate, Ed. They're lost. And they've witnessed terrible things. They're hardly children at all as we would understand the word.'

'So did this kid *kill* somebody?' Dracoulis asked incredulously.

'No. Not the one I showed you the picture of. Or at least I don't believe so. But I think he may be involved in some way. Anyway, I'd give my eye teeth to talk to him.'

'Right. Well, I'm sorry we can't help you any more at the moment, Jim. Do you want to talk to Major O'Hara when he gets back this afternoon?'

'I'll speak to him on the telephone.' Blessed looked at his watch. It was just after half-past eleven. The late edition of the *Tagesspiegel* would be out now. He needed to be back at BlessForce, waiting by the telephone for any response from Panewski, using the time while Harrison/Pilsbury still thought he was wasting hours with the laughing squadron leader at Gatow.

'Fine. I should still be here when he lands. I'll make sure he gets the message personally.'

Blessed got to his feet, picked up his cap. Then, as if it were an afterthought, he said, 'Do me a favour will you, Ed? Talk to the ground crew and any other staff who were around when the German photographer was taking his pictures. Anyone who came into contact with those kids in any way. Make me a list, and if it seems worthwhile, I'll send over one of my sergeants to talk to them. All right?'

'I'll do my best. We're kind of busy, but . . . OK. Between now and tomorrow, I'll check out those guys.'

'Thanks.'

'You know, I feel kind of sorry for these Germans, Jim. The kids and all . . .' Dracoulis sighed and shook his handsome, innocent head.

They shook hands and Blessed walked out of the building. On the way he saw GIs and girls sitting in the café seats so thoughtfully provided by Hitler's designers in the observation lounge, watching the landings, the cargo-handling procedures and take-offs on the airfield itself. The scene was much as it had been at Gatow; even the planes were the same—the aircraft that the British had christened 'Dakota' was known to the Americans, more prosaically, as a Douglas C-47. The difference was in the atmosphere. One conspicuous little group in the lounge was laying big-money bets on which planes would manage to 'turn around' most quickly. The men were cheering on 'their' aircraft

274

and unloading-crews as if they were on a day out at the track, and what was going on out there was a horse-race, not a world crisis. In fact, the high picture-windows resembled a cinema screen showing a teeming, three-dimensional film show round the clock. There was even a sound track. Booming over the PA system at the moment was a big hit from a year or two ago. It was an old drinking-song, rollicking and suggestive, jazzed up for the modern age of PR, where you mixed hemlines and frontlines, face-lifts and airlifts.

Roll me over
In the clover
Roll me over, lay me down and do it again . . .

The Americans, Blessed thought on his way to the car, were on their way to inventing something revolutionary and slightly frightening: wars that came complete with their own musical accompaniment.

TWENTY-SEVEN

NOTHING HAPPENED UNTIL three-fifteen in the afternoon. Blessed smoked, talked to Kelly in the next room. Weiss, out on the streets with his Kripo boys and still having no luck, phoned in at lunchtime to see if there had been any response to the *Tagesspiegel* advertisement. Blessed summarised the meagre results of his visit to Tempelhof. They promised each other they would try to meet before the end of the day to bring each other up to date.

In the meantime, the captain began to draft a report that drastically inflated his dealings with the laughing squadron leader. Out of one tiny story the squadron leader had told about a German labourer who had tied bags of airlift coffee to his legs, hiding it all under his baggy trousers, he created the saga of a possible black market ring. According to information from anonymous but usually reliable sources known to Blessed, thousands of pounds' worth of goods could soon, he warned, be walking out of airfields, inside hundreds of worn pairs of Oxford bags. To counter this threat, he and his team would be flitting between the various airfields, sometimes operating under cover, interviewing military and civilian personnel. Owing to the peripatetic nature of the task at hand, he himself would be contactable only through messages left with his office.

'Kelly!' he called through. 'If anyone from Knesebeckstrasse rings, tell them you're not sure if I'm in the office, and then inform me. Understood?'

'Whatever you say, sir.' Kelly's reply was unenthusiastic. He was concerned about Blessed's increasingly erratic-seeming behaviour, worried that if it came to a battle between the captain and his superiors,

276

his own promotion prospects could be an incidental casualty. 'What if anyone else phones?' he asked plaintively. 'What shall I tell them?'

'If it's not Weiss or Panewski, check with me first.'

Blessed got back to polishing his report. He had hardly re-read more than a few sentences when there was a bellow from the corridor, unmistakably that of a man in pain. He got to his feet, heard a scrabbling sound and the rap of boots, doors being opened and men running towards the commotion.

At the end of the corridor, just by the stairs, was a sort of a scrum of men, some in uniform, some in plain clothes. Blessed made for it. Kelly had just emerged.

'There's a kid here,' Kelly panted. As he spoke, the crowd opened up. Soon all that remained was a single, red-faced man, Sergeant Guyler, waggling one meaty hand, which was oozing blood, but with the other arm firmly locked round a German child dressed in shorts and a greasy dun-coloured windbreaker.

'What's this?' Blessed demanded. 'What happened?'

'The little bugger bit me, sir,' Guyler said, unnecessarily extending his damaged hand for Blessed's inspection. 'He bloody well bit me.'

'Wait a minute. Are you saying that you arrested this boy because he bit you?'

'Christ, no, sir. See, I found him creeping around on the stairs when I came in off the street. I asked him what he was doing there, he tried to duck past me and escape. Naturally I grabbed hold of him to prevent him from doing so, and that's when he bit me.'

'I see. Bring him to my office.'

Guyler dragged the boy along the corridor to Blessed's office, then went off to get his hand bandaged. Kelly prowled the room, hands thrust deep in his pockets, watching so that the boy didn't try to make another run for it.

'So? What's this about, kid?' Blessed asked in his best Berlin German.

The boy said nothing. He was about ten, pale and undernourished, with blue eyes and hair that, if it had been washed at any time during the past month, would have been golden. An attractive child in the classic German way. In his decayed brown tunic and ragged shorts, his gaze cunning and defiant as an old lag's, he looked like a Hitler Youth poster turned into a nightmare.

Blessed shrugged, wordlessly opened his drawer, pulled out a packet of Senior Service, tossed one across to the boy.

'Take it easy. Have a smoke, man.'

277

The boy's hand snatched up the cigarette. Blessed lit it for him.

They sat in silence while the boy puffed greedily. Then Blessed said, 'OK. What were you doing here? I'm not going to have you arrested unless you actually stole something.'

The boy's eyes narrowed. Still he refused to speak.

'Got any papers?' Blessed asked. 'Ration card? Identity card?'

The boy shrugged.

Blessed leaned forward. 'I'm interested in you,' he said softly. 'I'm not going to let you go until I'm sure who you are and why you are here. You may not realise it, but you have strayed into a place that you really shouldn't have. This is not an ordinary barracks or some Military Government office where they'll just tan your behind and send you off with a flea in your ear. I'm a policeman. I can have you put into youth custody, or if you can't prove you're being looked after, a closed orphanage.'

The boy thought it over, staring at Blessed through a protective barrage of cigarette smoke.

'This bloke comes up to me in the Ku-Damm,' he said at last. His accent was heavy Berlin working-class, Wedding or Kreuzberg. 'Big sod. Ugly as a warthog's arsehole. He offers me a packet of fags if I'll nip up them stairs and leave an envelope where you Tommies can see it.' The boy grimaced. 'He said there was never anyone about here. He said it would be easy. Yeah, well I'm just on me way out when that fat shit-head comes clomping up the stairs.'

'Where's this envelope you mentioned, then?'

'Propped up on the landing, along with the empty bottles you leave there for the milk man,' the boy said promptly. 'Your blokes are so bloody stupid, they never noticed it. They wouldn't last five minutes out there on the streets, I'll tell you that for nothing.'

Blessed nodded to Kelly to go and look. When the sergeant had left the room, he delved back in his drawer and pulled out his folder of photographs. Strike while the iron's hot, he thought. The first one Blessed handed the boy was one of the children at Tempelhof, with Buster ringed in red.

'Do you know any of these kids?' he asked.

The boy stared at the picture, then shook his head.

'You're not an orphan, are you?'

'Lost my dad in Russia. The Ivans did for him. My mum goes with Yanks. I please meself.'

Blessed next showed him a police photograph of Panewski that had been taken at the time of his last criminal conviction, in 1932. 'He's quite a bit older now. He'd be about fifty.'

The boy sucked in his wan cheeks. 'I didn't do nothing,' he said. 'I didn't know I was breakin' the law.' His knowing eyes fixed Blessed's. 'You don't have to arrest me, do you?'

Blessed shook his head. 'All I want to know is, was that the man who accosted you on the Ku-Damm?'

Before the boy answered, there was a knock on the door. Kelly walked in, laid a cheap, buff-coloured envelope on the desk. It was addressed to 'The Commandant, British Military Police *Kriminalpolizei*'. The handwriting of the address was careful, slightly childish. Blessed opened the envelope with a paper-knife and pulled out the letter inside. It began formally with *Highly-respected Herr Commandant* and continued in the same vein of laboured sycophancy mixed with criminal bravado:

Well I saw your advertisement in the paper and was suitably amazed at the progress you have made in your investigations. I will be frank about it I was surprised. But you still don't know the half of it, you don't know what's really going on. I'll tell if you protect me. Yes protect me. (this was underlined heavily) *You see I am the one who needs to be saved because I was set up, I did NOT kill anybody. Maybe with what you know so far you can start to believe me. If you will agree to protect me, I will tell you what really happened with Price, Frl. Sanders and my old friend Floh. It is not what you think. Commandant we must meet privately* (more heavy underlining) *under a white flag so to speak. If you agree then put another advertisement in the first edition of the Tagesspiegel and say, ANTON, COME HOME. IT IS SAFE NOW. COME HOME. YOUR LOVING FATHER. If you do not agree, then I must stay where I am, which is a safe place. I cannot risk being persecuted for crimes I did not commit and don't forget I never deal directly, even this letter will be coming by a messenger who knows neither you nor me. Lucky that I still have friends! I WILL NOT TOLERATE TREACHERY. If we can agree I will tell you of the Kinder and of Boss-Kind and about murder. You never thought Berlin was a Kinder Garden! Or perhaps you and you only, highly regarded commandant, will understand what I am trying to say.*

I remain yours most respectfully,
Karl-Heinz Panewski.

Blessed looked up. 'You didn't say if that was the man who approached you,' he said to the boy. 'Well, was it?'

The boy eyed him searchingly, decided there was no point in holding out for a bribe, and said, 'Yeah. That was him. He hasn't got prettier in all them years, has he?'

'No, he certainly hasn't. What exactly did he say to you?'

'He told me to bring the envelope here. He just gave me the address. He didn't say it would be full of Tommy *cops*!'

'Was he tough, aggressive? Did he threaten you in any way?'

'Nah. It was like some old cripple whinging for you to help 'em cross the road. He was scared, if you ask me. Kept looking about. Looked as though he couldn't wait to find a nice dark hole to duck into.'

'Right. Now tell me your name and address, please. We'll have to keep you here until we've made sure those details are correct. I'd like to let you go immediately, but I can't. I need to know where I can find you if we need you as a witness.'

Blessed realised that it never occurred to him to talk to this child as if he were just that, a child. He instinctively spoke to him as if he were a Floh or a Panewski, or at least an adult in trouble.

'My name is Josef Streit,' the boy muttered grudgingly. 'My address is Hausotter Strasse 57, basement, bei Wollweber.'

Blessed made a note of it. 'In the heart of Wedding. Fine. Which school are you enrolled at?'

'Amende Strasse.' A knowing smirk. 'But I never go there. School is for suckers.'

Blessed wrote down the school address anyway, turned to Kelly. 'Have all this checked,' he said, tearing the sheet from his desk-pad and handing it to the sergeant. 'Meanwhile, I'm afraid young Herr Streit will have to cool his heels in the interview room. No one's to treat him like a criminal, because he isn't one, all right? Just make him as comfortable as you can and give him something decent to eat.'

'What about a cigarette?' the boy protested.

'You're too young to smoke, Josef. Didn't anyone ever tell you that?'

'But you gave me one just now, you old bastard!'

Blessed smiled paternally. 'Remember this, Josef: So long as you have something people need, they'll give you anything in order to ensure they get it,' he told the boy. 'When you don't any more have what they want, or when they have successfully obtained it, they often start finding all kinds of moral reasons why you shouldn't have what they freely gave you before. This is a very important lesson in life. When you get older, you'll have to pay for such lessons. I give you this one free of charge, because you've helped me.'

Josef Streit looked like thunder as Kelly led him out to the cells, but at least he didn't bite.

Blessed studied the letter again, considered the problems it presented. Firstly, apart from the boy's claim to have been commissioned to deliver it by Panewski—which could conceivably have been a lie to get Blessed off his back—was the evidence of authorship convincing? Weiss would probably be able to get an example of Panewski's signature from Kripo files. Even without that confirmation, though, Blessed felt that the writing fitted an ill-educated adult rather than a cunning child, its tone everything he would have expected from a vain smalltime crook like Panewski. Secondly, what about the letter's contents? Was what Panewski wrote the truth? Was he really innocent, at least of the murders? No matter, Blessed thought, in one sense. At least Panewski had been lured from his hiding place. Vanity, or fear, or even a desire for justice, had coaxed the man out into the open.

Blessed's thoughts were interupted by the return of Sergeant Kelly.

'So that's the boy, little Joe Streit, tucked away in his dungeon. I've told one of the lads to confirm his details are correct,' Kelly said. 'Joe's not very pleased. In fact, he's bloody furious. He was reckoning on your letting him go straightaway once he'd identified Panewski.'

'I need to feel sure he's not going to just disappear. Once we know he's got at least one parent and some kind of permanent address, I'm prepared to let him go.'

'You don't think he's one of these kids we've been looking for?'

'No, though that's an additional good reason for checking up on the name and address he gave us,' Blessed said. 'Panewski may be stupid in some ways, but I can't believe he'd send someone we could use to trace those other kids. Our ignorance of their whereabouts is his trump card.' Blessed shrugged his shoulders dismissively. 'I'm pretty sure Panewski just chose young Josef at random from the street boys on the Ku-Damm, offered him the cigarettes to bring the letter here. He didn't know the kid would get caught, but he must have taken that possibility into account.'

'He might even have intended it, sir. Perhaps he wanted to confuse us, make us waste time and manpower trying to find out about the kid's background, whether he knew anything about the murders, things like that.'

'You may be right,' Blessed conceded. He picked up the letter from Panewski, passed it over to Kelly. 'Now read this,' he said. 'After you've finished I want to ask you a very simple question, to which I want a simple answer.'

'Very well, sir.' Kelly somehow managed to pack a lot of implied disapproval into that crisp, deliberately formal response.

'Take your time.'

While Kelly read slowly and thoroughly in his usual way, frowning at the German words he found most difficult, Blessed turned to look out of the office window. At first he was intent simply on watching the thick, honey-coloured beams of the afternoon sun play on the scarred brickwork of the apartment building opposite. Then he noticed that two German civilians were gossiping quietly and smoking in the yard behind the shop downstairs. One of them must have been sixty or so, with his hair almost white and his lugubrious face ruddy and wrinkled as an old tomato left too long on the kitchen shelf. He was acting out the sequence of events of a plane crash, giving his personal commentary as he did so. It seemed that a cargo plane, American or English, had come down near Tempelhof, and several people had been killed. But *Gott sei dank* for the airlift nevertheless, the other man was saying. He had never thought he would have cause to praise the Anglo-Americans, but now he was doing it, let his friend be his witness before the Almighty.

Blessed heard a diplomatic cough. He realised that Kelly was standing just behind him, waiting, having finished reading the letter. Blessed sighed and turned back into the room.

'Well?' he asked. 'Do you think Panewski is telling the truth?'

'It makes sense to suppose so, sir. Why else would he write the letter?' Kelly paused uneasily. 'Unless, on the other hand, he's some kind of real homicidal lunatic and wants to get a crack at you too. And, mind you, there's the matter of his prints being found on the Floh murder weapon. I mean—'

'I said a simple answer. What's your instinctive feeling, Kelly? True or false? Yes or no?'

'They all say they're innocent, don't they, sir?' Kelly said. 'I just don't know. Mind you, the prints on the knife are the only hard evidence we have, and they could have been a set-up, as Panewski claims.'

Blessed looked at the sergeant for a moment, then nodded. 'The

282

letter impressed me too in its peculiar way,' he said. 'Which in most respects is not good news. If Panewski's claim is justified, and he didn't commit the murders, then it upsets everything. We have to look for a new killer. And I have to turn up to this "white flag" meeting with Panewski—probably on his terms, unless I want to risk frightening him away for good. Neither of those things do I look forward to, Kelly. Neither of these prospects fills me with joy.'

He picked up the telephone and asked to be put through to the *Tagesspiegel*'s office. Slowly he dictated the advertisement to the day editor. He had to explain things very exactly and forcefully, just as he had to the man's colleague on the night desk.

Eventually a fictional, but nevertheless much-missed son went into the early edition of the paper, set in bold type, with his own neat little box:

> ANTON: COME HOME.
> IT IS SAFE NOW
> —Your Loving Father

TWENTY-EIGHT

BOSS-KIND HAD STILL been at the Lake when, after his promised sleep, Benno left for his return-trip to the Kinder Garden, but Boss-Kind had already got back when Benno arrived there. There was only one explanation: the Boss had been given a ride in a car or a truck, had been whisked through the Russkie-Sector on motorised wheels for an urgent and secret deadline. This and other realisations would not have been important except in the light of the things Benno understood quite a lot later, when events came to a head. Then, every remembered detail, every unsignposted stop on the zig-zagging path to disaster, became not just important but vital.

The summons to Boss-Kind's Lair came in the late afternoon. Maybe after the experience with Panewski he shouldn't have been, but Benno was nevertheless surprised to find the small, spartan room crammed not just with the Boss but also with Riese's boys, Fatski and Thinski.

'You know, Benno, this is Karl and Erich.' Boss-Kind introduced them more for their benefit than for Benno's. After all, every Kind knew these Hats. Every Kind hated and, more importantly, feared them.

'Sure, Boss-Kind. I know that,' Benno said. 'They got something for us from Riese?'

Meanwhile, he was also studying the two hoods. Karl was Fatski. He was wearing a very old chalk-striped suit, double-breasted and straining at all its buttons. How did such a Hat manage to stay fat all through the hard, foodless times since Point Null? Maybe that was why he had turned to crime, to keep on eating. Erich/Thinski was a total contrast, like a character from an old film about vampires, with white

284

face, greasy-grey, unkempt nest of hair, and long, sinuous fingers. He wore a leather jerkin and baggy slacks that flapped around his skinny legs.

'Hi, kid,' Thinski said. He grinned.

Against common expectation, it was he, the skinny one, who liked to appear jolly. Fatski, on the other hand, seemed to have only two ways of dealing with the world: either with a scowl or a wordless snarl. But it was in Thinski's pocket that a bulge indicated the likely presence of a gun.

'You're a good choice for this job with us,' Thinski added when Benno didn't reply to his greeting. 'I can tell.'

'Choice? And what job with *you*, anyway?'

Thinski slipped a glance at Boss-Kind, shrugged.

'Package-collection, Benno. From Riese's place,' Boss-Kind explained. 'Erich and Karl here, they will take you into the Ku-Damm in their *car* to collect it.'

Benno knew that Riese had several 'places', including one near the Ku-Damm, which he used as his office. It was a room behind a drinking-club-cum-pickup-joint he owned called the Tahiti, in the Augsburger Strasse. Benno had delivered something there a few months back; other Kinder had been there more often. Anyway, the Tahiti would be the place Boss-Kind was referring to.

'You are, yes you are the Boss.' Benno folded his arms and waited.

Boss-Kind nodded. 'I tell you something else, too,' he said softly. 'I tell you too, that tonight, some time but not long after you come back, we are leaving the Kinder Garden, Benno. The time I talked about has come!'

Now that Benno thought about it, there was something nervous in the Boss's manner. This news would explain that only too well. Then the realisation hit home: *Boss-Kind just said something astounding, something momentous. He said they were leaving their Kinder Garden for good* . . . Of course, the Boss had told him about this last night, but somehow Benno had assumed then that the move lay somewhat in the future—or even that it was merely another of Boss-Kind's fantasies.

'*Tonight?*' Benno said finally. 'You are saying, maybe sometime soon, but so much to do first—'

'*My eyes see* . . .' Boss-Kind murmured. '*My eyes see* we gotta hide. Riese has found us a place. Until we leave for the new Kinder Garden. New names, new places . . .'

Thinski, meanwhile, was starting to get restless. Fatski was sneering into the middle distance, sweating in the unconscious way of the seriously overweight. There was tension in him too, though; one great ham of a hand, with its sausages for fingers, was gripping the arm of the wrecked chair, and it seemed that only self-discipline was stopping him from snapping it off.

'Tonight,' Benno repeated dully.

'I tell the other Kinder soon. I only tell you now, Benno, because you will not be here when I address that Kinder-meeting. You will still be package-bringing. Think—we will soon have *no names, no pasts*, and *nothing will touch us . . .*'

Except a little bit of desperation, thought Benno, studying the quivering of Boss-Kind's lips.

Fatski and Thinski were on their feet.

'Come on, kid,' Thinski said in his deceptively cosy way. 'Everyone's in a hurry. We have to go and do some business, eh?'

Fatski let out a loud, offensive *hurrumph* sound, put on a dark-grey homburg, walked straight out of the door. That left Thinski to usher Benno into the cellar and up the stairs to the street. The door to Doktor Barnhelm's apartment was wide open. Barnhelm's own hat, an antique derby, had tumbled from its usual hook just inside the door and was lying forlornly in the corridor outside. From where he and Thinski had arrived, at the top of the cellar stairs, Benno saw Fatski take a deliberate step to the right and stomp on the hat before opening the door and proceeding out into the street.

Boss-Kind had been right, they did have a car, of a sort: a German Ford van from pre-war, even pre-Hitler days. There were frames of rust round the cab doors, and the back loading-doors—through which Benno was cordially invited to hop—were held together by a loop of twine hooked around the battered handles.

It was dark in the back when they set off, with Fatski driving. There were filthy little quarter-moon windows in the loading-doors. Benno, alone on a bed of rancid sacks, wondered fleetingly how this pair came to be driving such a vehicle around this rationed, threatened city, then decided not to waste his energy on such speculations. Riese had money, power and connections. For all Benno knew, this van was registered as a charity vehicle, and Fatski and Thinski had surefire, stamped and signed papers, bought and paid for, that identified them as noble volunteers on an errand of mercy for the Jewish Community or UNRRA. So long as nobody checked Thinski for concealed weapons.

286

So, on they rattled, through the badly-repaired streets of Wedding. By careful monitoring of the changes in their surroundings and in the position of the sun, Benno worked out that they had begun by driving north, and were now heading west. This was not the shortest route to the Kurfürstendamm from the Kinder Garden; the most direct way lay straight south through the narrowest part of the Russkie-sector, the bulge of territory containing Berlin's historic centre, which on the map jutted into the western-ruled half of the city like a little snout. He wondered if Riese's boys were deliberately trying to confuse him, or whether there was some other reason for this detour.

'Nervous, kid? Wondering what the score is?' When they had been driving for ten minutes or so, Thinski turned round and smiled into the darkness of the rear cargo space. Benno was crouched in the far corner with his knees drawn up to his chin. He shook his head and said nothing.

'*What*, kid?' There was a stagey hint of menace in Thinski's voice. 'Don't they teach you manners in that orphanage? Don't they teach you to be polite to grownups?' he said. Then he let out a loud guffaw. Fatski hurrumphed in support of his friend's mockery, but kept on driving.

'You beddabelieve, I am not frightened,' Benno said. 'I am doing my job for the Kinder Garden.'

'Sure.' Thinski laughed again. 'Sure.'

After that, Thinski started whistling, a weird *mélange* of tunes, only some of which Benno recognised. Another five minutes passed, at the end of which Benno, to his alarm, realised that they were not in the Ku-Damm area, which they should have been approaching by now, but on the Spandauer Damm, still heading into the sunset, which meant westwards.

Benno took a deep breath. He was wondering if the doors could be kicked open from the inside. Then he said: 'Erich, you know Boss-Kind told me we were going to the Ku-Damm. But we are on the Spandauer Damm heading west . . .'

Just as he finished speaking, Fatski swung the wheel and they abruptly turned left down a sidestreet. Benno was thrown against the doors, which gave slightly but did not burst open. He hit the side of his head and could not help but let out a breathy yelp. Hurrumph, went Fatski, and then hurrumph again. Benno realised dimly, through his pain, that this might be Fatski's way of expressing amusement, the nearest he ever got to a laugh.

'Don't worry, kid,' Thinski chuckled. 'We got another . . . errand . . . before we head back to the place. Trust us, eh? In two minutes we'll be there. Another ten minutes after that, we'll be on our way again.'

A warning hurrumph from the driver's seat.

'All right. Maybe fifteen minutes. To please my old friend Karl.'

In fact, the van did stop very soon. The two Hats got out, and there was a whispered conversation between them on the pavement, after which the back doorhandles were untied and there stood Fatski, beckoning Benno out. When Benno was too slow, Fatski picked him up as if he were a puppy, by the scruff of his neck, and swung him out. For a moment Benno was terrified that this creature, with all the strength he had hidden under those layers of fat, would choose to simply smash him against a wall, dash his brains out like they said the vodka-maddened Russkies did with German babies.

They had parked outside a nondescript tenement, one of several in a shabby, ordinary street. Holding Benno by the arm, Fatski led him to a stout door set just back from the street. Big, boarded-up windows to the left of the door indicated that this might have been a shop in better days. Thinski was already knocking. A few moments later, a spyhole opened, there was a whispered exchange. A high-pitched snort from inside the building, more whispers, then the door swung open and Benno found himself inside.

They were standing in a lobby that smelled strongly of dry rot and urine. It had been lined, in an attempt to make it glamorous, with several different kinds of fake-flock wallpaper. There was a print of Rubens's 'The Judgment of Paris' hanging at a slight angle on the wall. Benno didn't know the painting or the artist, of course; all he saw was a confusion of rounded, creamy buttocks, bellies and backs, hard to tell which was male and which female until you worked out who had the beards and who had the breasts. There were two chairs against that wall, and in the corner, having just resumed her seat, was stationed a grey-haired crone of indeterminate age. This was the woman who had answered the door.

'It's the girls' break-time, as you know full well. They won't be pleased,' she said. Then she half-turned, shouted into the room beyond: 'I told them you won't be pleased!'

A sleepy, irritated voice answered, but Benno didn't catch what it said. Fatski had let go of him. He shifted position a little, saw through the half-open door that led into the backroom. There were curtains hanging to one side. At the far end was a mirror in which, as he watched, a curtain was pulled back and a flash of pale leg became visible. He realised that the backroom was divided up by the curtains into several cubicles. If the one he could see was anything to go by, then each contained a mattress.

'Better *they're* not pleased than *Riese's* not pleased, eh?' hit back Thinski.

The crone shrugged. 'I want to know, what's the boy got to do with this?' she asked sharply. She wore a pinafore over a shapeless dress that bore a suspicious resemblance to the curtains. A bundle of knitting was lying on the boards beside her.

'Him?' Thinski glanced at Benno, smiled and rolled his eyes. 'He's along for the ride.'

'You're disgusting,' the crone retorted matter-of-factly. She picked up her knitting. Her needles began to clack busily, like distant small-arms fire.

A girl no older than sixteen appeared half a minute or so later at the doorway to the backroom. She wore only a crumpled chemise, and treated Thinski and Fatski as if they were old acquaintances, not necessarily welcome ones.

'It's you,' she said. She would have been pretty if it hadn't been for the gauntness of her features and the scar running across the right side of her face. 'Erich the funny-man.' She looked at Fatski. 'And your friend the man-mountain.'

'Yes, Monika. Aren't you lucky? We've come especially to see you and little Jutta. We're going away soon, you see. We didn't want to go without a celebration,' Thinski said.

'Shit, don't you know we rest at this hour?'

'This is the only time we could make it. We're so pushed, kept so occupied on *Riese's* business. We got just a few minutes. Understand?'

'I hope the kid's not included,' the girl said drily, pointing at Benno. 'We don't do that kind of stuff, not even for Riese's boys.'

Thinski laughed, a staccato ha-ha-ha. 'Don't worry, Monika. Even I can see he's a bit young. He's not ready for man's work yet. Isn't that so, kid?'

Benno stared straight back at Thinski and said nothing. The girl nodded, and she may even have smiled in Benno's direction, so fleetingly that only he could notice. Then, with a resigned shrug, she turned and went back into the far room. Benno heard her whisper scoldingly: 'Jutta! Jutta! Wake up!'

And so the two men disappeared through the door, Thinski first, already taking off his jacket, and Fatski lumbering after him like a tame bear, clumsy with lustful anticipation.

Benno quickly got bored. And curious. He had heard plenty lately, from Granit and Banana and some of the older Kinder, who talked of girls their own age who would do it, do anything, for a cigarette or a slab of chocolate, or even sometimes for no reason at all except they wanted to. Only Boss-Kind never talked about it. The Boss left his lieutenants to their whims, but he allowed no girls in the Kinder Garden. What Benno wanted to find out was how that gargantuan lump Fatski could lie on top of such a little girl without killing her; in other words, he was interested in the engineering.

Click-clack, click-click-clack, went the crone's needles. Soon, Benno heard a rhythmic crump from the far room. He shuffled to the right, craned, took a half-step back, and finally caught sight of a reflection in the mirror. Eck, but *of course*: she was balanced on top of Fatski's huge, hairy, white body. Benno could see her little dirty heels pushing back as she laboured. The chemise was all rucked up, so that Fatski's eager sausage-fingers could knead at her bare flesh. Eck, he thought, but that was hard work she had here, and with bad people. At that moment he felt lucky, despite everything, that he was a boy and a Kind, able to work and eat and still keep a little freedom, a remnant of pride.

'*Tut!*'

The crone was suddenly on her feet, pulling the door closed so that Benno could no longer satisfy his curiosity. He moved away, expecting a tongue-lashing, but, her correction done, she settled back and began to knit again in silence, unperturbed by the crump of the mattresses and at least one tiny scream from next door. Benno noticed that she looked as though she was knitting a sweater for a baby, in blue and orange. He didn't have the energy to ask her, and the crone never said another word to him.

Fifteen minutes later, he was back cowering in the belly of the van and heading east towards the Ku-Damm. Upfront, Thinski was smoking in a relaxed way. Fatski was once more a dark, rocklike shape behind the wheel. Everything was as before, as if the sights, the smells, the sounds of that place where the girlies plied their hard, uncomfortable trade had all been a daydream.

Again Thinski directed his attention to Benno. He took a last drag on his cigarette, tossed the dog-end out of the open window, smiled encouragingly.

290

'Hey, what do you think about being an orphan?' he asked. 'Do you like it?'

Benno shrugged slowly, in a way that he meant to show he was indifferent to such considerations.

'Really? You don't mind? Say it. Go on, say it! Let me hear you say you don't mind . . .'

'I . . . don't . . . mind . . .' Benno said slowly and clearly.

'See?' Thinski jabbed Fatski in the expanse under which, somewhere, lay his ribs. 'What did I tell you? See how shrewd the kid is?' He turned back to Benno. 'Yes, you're right when you say that, because the way your life has turned out, you haven't missed a damned thing. For instance, do you know who that old bag was with the knitting, who let us in to see Jutta and Monika?'

Benno shook his head silently.

'Well, you better know this, kid—she's their mother. How about that! Would you wish you had a mother just like that one?'

Ha-ha-ha, Thinski cackled. Hurrumph, went Fatski. Hurrumph, hurrumph, hurrumph . . .

In contrast with Monika's and Jutta's depressed little shop of pleasure, all was activity in the familiar surroundings of the Tahiti on Augusburger Strasse, Riese's headquarters and the jewel in his crown. Benno glimpsed passing faces as the van slowed down, heard a snatch of loud music from somewhere close by.

Soon, though, the van turned off the street, and ducked round the rear of the building, away from the attentions of the customers and the passersby. At first, the two Hats got out, locking the doors behind them, and left Benno alone in the back. Two or three minutes passed, and he began to feel his heart thumping, his gullet becoming tight with fear. Then the loading-doors were untied and flung open, and there was Fatski. The huge Hat plucked Benno out into the light as he had at Monika's, carried him for a few metres, then all but threw him down a shallow flight of stairs that led down to the basement.

'*Na*, Detlev! Com here!' he ordered in a strong Bavarian accent. It was the first time Benno had heard him speak. Fatski's voice turned out to be as wheezy as an asthmatic's, with an incongruous tendency to squeak. No wonder he kept up that silence most of the time, Benno thought; anyone would do the same if they sounded like that.

A young man of eighteen or so emerged from the shelter of the basement doorway. He had long, slicked-back hair, so blond it was almost white, a sallow-complexioned face, and he wore a short-sleeved shirt, rolled up to show off his biceps. A typical would-be hood, hanging around the underworld veterans and hoping to be admitted to the inner councils of crime if he made himself useful enough, often enough. 'What, Karly?' he said, attempting to growl like a real gangster.

'This here brat, take him inside and keep him out of the way until he's needed. The Chief has a parcel for him. I'm going to be busy, eh?'

'You and Erich, you're—'

'Detlev, shuddup. You'll get yourself into big trouble with that mouth of yours.'

A final angry hurrumph and Fatski was gone.

There was nothing to do but follow this Detlev *Drecksack* into the cellar. Benno could hear sounds of activity upstairs. More music. The room here was for stores, such as they were. A few cases of beer, some bottles that claimed to be champagne. The dregs of the black market, lying here ready to be sold at scandalously inflated prices to the hard-currency aristocracy upstairs. Benno understood immediately that Detlev was no more than casual help, a menial, no matter what grand, tough-guy airs he tried to give himself.

'You keep those light little fingers off this stuff, got that?' Detlev said roughly. 'The Chief's been known to slice 'em off if they stray among these goodies.'

Benno shrugged. If Detlev really thought a Kind would be so dumb as to risk stealing from a gangster like Riese, then there was no helping him.

'You . . . you one of those brats from the Bernauer Strasse, eh?' Detlev said, sitting down on an upturned beer crate.

'You beddabelieve.'

'Parcel . . . Tempelhof . . .' Detlev grinned. Made the motion of a plane coming in to land. 'The Chief's most valuable stuff. OK, he must trust you. All the way to Rhine-Main . . . He got you *scared*, though, isn't that right?'

'Scared?' Benno eased a thin half-cigarette from his pocket. '*Kinder? Scared?*' He laughed, shook his head in tolerant disbelief.

'Yeah.' Detlev clearly didn't intend to give up. He seemed like a natural taunter. Taunting was what Detlev fell back on when things got slow and a likely victim could be coaxed into his sights. 'And you know what they say? You know, they say those Yank pilots got a thing for little boys, and that's how you get them to take you. They say you little boys from the Bernauer

Strasse do anything for those Yanks. Know what I mean? You got that?'

Benno lit his cigarette. This was all quite normal. You just let it slide off you. You developed a hide of pure, inch-thick panzer-steel.

'Well? Is it true?'

It wasn't. It was almost exclusively business. In the very early days, they had done trial runs out with Hershey aircrew who were so dumb-sentimental that they could be talked into taking unscheduled cargo by heartrending tales of dying mothers and such, but now the fliers—ones known to be corrupt—had their palms greased by Riese's agents, along with essential ground-staff. The only real deceit was having the package-takers met at Rhine-Main by the necessary adult 'relatives', again hired agents of Riese's. Benno had never been sent on a package-taking trip to the West, but he knew all these details from the likes of Flix, who had.

'C'mon. Is it true? And what are you doing, keeping that smoke to yourself?'

Benno took a long pull on his cigarette, almost burning it down to nothing, it was so thin and tenuous, and said coldly: 'You heard of Boss-Kind? You met him?'

Detlev nodded.

'I tell him, Detlev. You don' shuddup, you know I will tell Boss-Kind how you go on here.' Benno spread his fingers as if opening them to fit a knuckle-duster, then bunched his fist, made an abrupt, arcing little cutting-motion. He smiled. 'Boss-Kind is crazy, Detlev. That's the trouble,' he said. 'One thing he can't stand, it's hearing the Kinder been insulted. Yes, then he loses his *mind*. *Got that?*' he added in mocking imitation.

Detlev had taken a couple of steps, and maybe he would have come further, and maybe not, but in any case there was a shout from upstairs, someone calling his name in a way that made it clear he was expected to jump to it.

'You better go, Detlev,' Benno said. 'Someone calling. They want the kitchen-boy.'

After Detlev had disappeared up the stairs, uttering a string of implausible threats, Benno took one more drag on the cigarette. Then the miniscule remains were dropped to the ground and stepped on. He folded his arms, looked around. The music upstairs had changed to a sugary German hit he hated: 'The Fisherman of Capri'. He hoped this wasn't going to be a long wait. And he hoped he hadn't pushed Detlev too far. Suddenly Benno felt an almost overwhelming urge to run, to run anywhere, get away from these people, these places, to escape the constant necessity of being so gadawlmighdy *brave*, allthetime so cou-rage-ous. Ah but that would mean unthinkable disgrace. In the eyes of Boss-Kind and the rest of the Kinder he would become an outcast. And if Benno couldn't return to face his tribe, his only friends, then *where* could he go? And *who* with? And *how* would he live??

In the crowded silence of those thoughts he heard interesting sounds in the yard. The door leading to the stairs was slightly ajar, so he ran to it and pushed it open a little more. The only voice at first was Thinski's, and he was cursing like a carter: 'Come on, you bastard! Move!' It was impossible to resist the temptation that this presented. Benno glanced behind himself to ensure that Detlev was still occupied upstairs. Then he edged his way outside and up a couple of steps so that he could just about see into the yard, facing the spot where the van had been parked. Further he could not go without risking being seen, and his instincts told him that in this place, of all places, idle curiosity was not looked upon with favour.

'Come on! Move! We've got an appointment!'

A grunt of pain. And coming round the corner of the building, heading for the van, two figures Benno recognised. No. Three . . .

First there was Thinski, no longer even pretending to laugh, instead gesticulating threateningly with his gun. Then there was Fatski, dragging at a pair of handcuffs as if he were dragging a bull from its stall, and swinging back his fist as if eager to land another blow before the fettered man between them could climb—or rather, fall—into the back of the waiting van. Finally there was their prisoner, tall and hulking, his hands in steel cuffs and his feet hobbled with rope, his features bruised and bleeding but still instantly recognisable to the boy watching from the steps.

Even after such a confusing, disturbing, and eventful week, how could Benno forget the flat, ugly face of Bigman Panewski?

TWENTY-NINE

BLESSED COULD SEE the plump midsummer moon from his study window at the Villa Hellman. Tonight, at its fullest power, it lit the streets almost as well as the streetlights that the Russian blockade had extinguished since the end of June. It was past midnight, but he was still feverishly awake. Weiss's men were pressing on with the hunt for the 'orphans' and the 'Orphanage Director'; Captain Dracoulis at Tempelhof would be reporting in the morning on the search for witnesses there; and at any moment Panewski would be reading the message to 'Anton' in the *Tagesspiegel*. How could Blessed let himself sleep, even though his body was weary to the marrow?

It occurred to him to look in on Daphne again, but then he remembered that he had already done that twice in the past hour. He had got home in time to read her a story and tuck her into bed. Apparently Harriet had phoned from London at teatime and had a harmless chat with her. So their insulated little world in Spandau, though far from perfectly calm, went on from day to day without any decisive upsets, perhaps even happily. The crunch would come when Harriet decided one way or the other, to go or stay . . .

The telephone rang, rousing him from a half-doze. He picked up the receiver.

'*Ja? Hier Blessed. Wer ist das?*' he asked in German. Then he repeated, realising the caller might be a non-German-speaking soldier from the night watch, 'Blessed here. Who am I speaking to?'

'Me, of course.' A brittle, well-prepared laugh. 'For a moment I thought you'd decided to change nationality at last, Jimmy.'

'Harriet. Well, hello.' It didn't surprise Blessed that his wife had rung, or that it was well after midnight. What surprised—and shocked—him was the fact that it had taken him several seconds to recognise her voice, and a fraction longer still to accommodate himself to a world where Harriet Blessed née Fiske existed. 'You sound pretty drunk to me,' he commented.

'My God, what's life in grey old Fortress Berlin done to you? We've turned puritan suddenly, have we?'

'OK, OK. I'm sorry. How are you?'

'You were right the first time, actually. How I am is, I am a touch under the influence. Aren't you?'

'No. Not tonight.'

'Oh, tough luck on you, Jim!' Harriet underwent one of her sharp, unexplained changes of mood and giggled girlishly. 'Anyway, I'm ringing from Daddy's flat in London. You remember the flat, don't you? It's still the same, except the damp in the bathroom's got worse, and the new porter's Spanish, or Portuguese, or something equally exotic . . .'

'You rang Daff this afternoon.'

'That's right. Your intelligence is correct, Captain. I missed her. We had a lovely talk. It was easy to get through then. But do you know, it took me almost three hours to get a line to Berlin tonight—even after screaming blue bloody murder and pulling every bloody string, dropping every bloody name I could think of? Three hours!'

'All right, Harriet,' Blessed said. 'I think I understand the situation. Is Sir Hugh with you?'

'No. But his drinks cabinet is here, large as life and twice as full . . .' Suddenly he caught a crack in her voice and realised that she was close to tears. 'I couldn't stand it down there at Trevallier. I had to come to London to *breathe* a bit.'

Blessed suspected he knew what was coming; he felt anger burning inside him. There was the usual drag of guilt too, but the anger was stronger. 'So now you're breathing,' he said. 'How does it feel?'

A silence, then Harriet continued in a smaller voice: 'When I spoke to Daff this afternoon, she said she was very well. She sounded a bit peaky to me, but perhaps I'm reading more into the situation than I should. Of course, she's on her own a lot at the moment. I'm sure you're still very busy . . .'

Blessed guessed that he was supposed to involve himself in some ritual of mutual forgiveness at this point. He knew the pattern, and he knew that the booze wasn't the main arbiter of his wife's behaviour.

Harriet was not a habitual drinker. As a rule she used alcohol pre-emptively, to blunt the edge of her anxiety when she was flying too high and knew she could soon fall to earth. Or she would exploit it as a prop to her 'scenes'. There was always a feeling Harriet wanted to feel, an impression she wanted to create, or a reaction she wanted to goad into life. Blessed wondered what had happened between her and Laurence Redman, MP, but he was damned if he was going to ask.

'Daff's got Gisela for company,' Blessed said, refusing to be drawn. 'I try to get home before she goes to bed, and to see her in the mornings before I leave. I don't always succeed. You know how it is.'

'No. I don't know how it is. But I know how it was.'

There came the sound of her drinking. Then of ice-cubes against glass. Followed by a silence, which Blessed was unwilling to break. He could hear her watery breathing. Or was she crying softly? Suddenly he wished this woman would shut up for good, stop making claims on him, do this thing cleanly. His anger had subsided for the moment, leaving behind little more than a numb desire for solitude. He knew, though, that Harriet would work relentlessly to regain his allegiance, just as she had mercilessly pushed him away when escaping to England. Things would be much easier if they had never had Daphne—or if he cared about his daughter less. Daff was Harriet's hostage in his heart.

'Have they got you on airlift duties, then, Jim?'

'I was at Gatow today,' Blessed said cautiously. 'And Tempelhof. Looking for thieves. Doing my bit for the Free World, as they say.'

'Look. Can't you and Daff come over here?' Harriet said with a sudden, brittle enthusiasm. 'If only for Dad's sake. She is his only grandchild, after all. You know you're almost finished with Berlin, anyway. You told me, Harrison said they're getting rid of you soon. You could even—'

'Where's Redman?' At last he gave in and asked the crucial question.

A long sigh. 'He's in Washington for a few days. But . . . I've had a chance to think, and that's the point, don't you see . . .'

Blessed saw very clearly, but not quite as Harriet had wanted him to. He saw her sitting on the old tasselled sofa in her father's flat in Eaton Square, staring at the standard-issue horsey oil-painting above the fireplace ('School of Stubbs, failed his final exams, I suspect,' as Harriet had once said of the obscure painter's work), with no one to talk to or go to bed with, or otherwise get some kind of reaction from. Redman, by accident or design, had removed himself several thousand miles from her vicinity, her father was in Cornwall, which left only Blessed's distant shoulder for her to cry on.

'No, Harriet,' Blessed said. 'Daff and I are not going anywhere, and least of all to London. I'm still hard at work on the Price murders. I can't just drop the whole thing. We can take a holiday later in the summer.' He didn't know why he had said the last bit, about the holiday. That was the old Jimmy-boy, the patcher-up, who always came running in the end.

'Jam tomorrow. Always jam tomorrow! Well, you can't fool me. Admit it, you're fucking Gisela. Well, aren't you, Jim?'

Blessed was surprised by his own hesitation. Why so tongue-tied when the accusation was untrue, when he knew she was just lashing out wildly. Drunk or sober, up or down, Harriet knew precisely where to plant her barbs, he thought bitterly.

'No,' he said.

'Is that all you've got to say: "No"?'

'Yes.' Blessed laughed harshly, a humourless release of tension. This was like one of those cruel, futile games drunks played at failed house parties. Oh God, let it just stop. He had to make it stop.

'Don't you bloody well laugh at me!' Harriet hissed. 'You and your tight-lipped bloody mono . . . mono . . . mo-no-syll-ables . . . They just hide everything. You always hide everything . . .'

'There's no point to this, Harriet,' Blessed cut in. 'I'm here if you want to come back and talk things over. But I'm not coming to London, with or without Daff. I'm sorry. Listen, why don't you ring back when you're sober?'

There was a sharp intake of breath at the other end of the line. 'Bastard!' she said and slammed down the phone.

Now there was not a sound in the house. He could see Harriet in his mind's eye, striding across that over-furnished room in London to refill her glass. She would be shaking with anger. At first she would congratulate herself on having shown Jimmy-boy what was what by putting the phone down on him. She had made something happen, all right. But then, Blessed knew, she would calm down. Her problem would become clear. After all, if there was no actual contact with anyone, it was impossible to make anything *more* happen.

Perhaps Harriet would try to reach Larry Redman in Washington first. But the next call to Blessed, whether remorseful or angry, could come at any time. Sooner or later—she probably wouldn't hold out for as much as a day, since there were no other distractions physically to hand—Harriet would pick up Daddy's telephone again and then charm and wheedle and threaten until some overworked wretch of an operator succumbed and put her through to Berlin. Perhaps, after refuelling with pink gin, she was already dialling the international exchange. She would probably claim to the operator that she had been cut off during a conversation essential to national security, or a call involving a life-or-death medical matter. How she loved the excitement of the imagined emergency, the beauty of a newly-minted lie, and how quickly she persuaded herself that, in a *deeper* sense, what she said was *true*. Everything that had happened tonight had happened before—including the way he had finally seen her off, brutally and hurtfully. God, despite all the provocation, he still hated himself for that.

The telephone rang. Blessed frowned. The phone kept on ringing, like a wilful infant that's woken in the night. He stared at it balefully, began to count slowly under his breath. If it was still ringing on the count of twenty, perhaps he would pick it up. Twelve . . . thirteen . . . fourteen . . . fifteen and sixteen and seventeen and eighteen and nineteen . . .

'Hello. Blessed speaking,' he said, cursing himself for surrendering yet again to his guilt. 'No change of nationality this time. Satisfied?'

'*Wie bitte?*'

'*Hier spricht Blessed.*'

'*Ach.* The Herr Commandant? I am speaking to the Herr Commandant?'

'*Ja, ja* . . . Who is that?'

'I am Karl-Heinz Panewski.'

'Ah.' Blessed's world tipped wildly. He struggled to regain equilibrium, finally managed to say: 'Yes? Where are you?'

'In a place not so far away.' The voice was rough-edged, a voice of the Berlin streets and dives, but its tone was surprisingly measured, rational.

'And what do you want, Herr Panewski? Are you willing to give yourself up?' Blessed asked. He was always meticulously polite with criminals when negotiating. In his experience, even the toughest gangster tended to respond a little better when treated like a gent.

'Perhaps.' The voice was equally respectful and guarded. 'I don't want to spend the rest of my life on the run for crimes I did not commit. First we must meet, just you and me. I saw the advertisement you put in the *Tagesspiegel*, Herr Commandant. That meant you agreed to such a meeting.'

'I'm prepared to consider it. Listen, how did you get my home telephone number?'

A snort of amusement. 'I'm a professional. I have contacts. Please: the important thing is that we meet quickly. You know the old gasworks, part of the industrial area beyond the Eiswerder bridge, east of the Neuendorfer Strasse?'

'Isn't that a restricted area? There may be security patrols.'

'At the old gasworks itself, yes. But if you drive some way further down the Schützenstrasse towards the water, you'll see a bombed-out warehouse to your right with the name A.E. BERNBACH & Co. painted on the front.'

'Just a moment,' Blessed said. 'If I come alone, how do I know you'll do the same? Who are these Kinder you wrote about in your letter? And this person called "Riese"?'

'I'll explain everything when we meet. You must trust me.'

'Why should I?'

'Because, after all, I have to trust you also.'

'This is risky for both of us. Why don't you come straight to the British military police station? You know where it is. Or we can pick you up from wherever you choose. The sooner we co-operate to track down the real murderer the better, Herr Panewski.'

'No more time, Commandant. If you wish to discuss terms, you must approach the Bernbach & Co. warehouse, alone, on foot. Your car must be left at least a hundred metres away. And you must be there in exactly fifteen minutes. I shall be watching out for you and will make my presence known through a simple, unmistakable signal. If you arrive any later than that, I won't be there any more. I can't risk betrayal.'

The man's delivery was assured and confident. He knew his own worth. Not bad going for a criminal on the run for his life, Blessed thought. He was rapidly revising his opinion of Panewski as no more than a crude thug.

'Let's give this a little more thought,' he said, trying him just one more time. 'It's in your interests—'

'Fifteen minutes from now. Take it or leave it. I know you can get here in time. And I warn you again, Commandant: I shall know if you're not alone.'

The line went dead. There was no longer any time to argue. Hardly time to think it through. Only time to act.

Remember Lebanon. Remember Jamail . . . Yes, but . . .

The clock said just before five to one. Blessed ran down to the bathroom, sluiced his face and hands. Back in the bedroom he slipped on his gabardine windcheater, collected his SIB identity card. Then he unlocked the drawer in the corner chest and took out his police Webley automatic. He snapped an ammunition clip into the magazine.

Remember Jamail . . . But this time he had the situation under control, he was betting on a near-certainty . . .

Pocketing the gun and two spare clips, Blessed climbed the stairs to Gisela's attic, pushed open the door and called out her name.

'Yes?' She sat upright and before she covered herself with a sheet he saw that she was naked. 'What has happened? Are you drunk?'

'No. I have to go out, urgently. I've been called to an incident.'

Gisela shrugged sleepily. 'You often go out at night on police business. Why do you wake me up to tell me this?'

'Because one thing may lead to another. I probably won't be back tonight. Make sure Daphne gets off to school on time, and tell her what's happened.'

'Is this dangerous, what you are about to do?'

'I hope not. I don't think so.'

'All right.' She managed an uncertain smile. 'Good luck, and be careful. We would all like you to come back to us.'

Suddenly Blessed knew he wanted her. He longed to make love to her and then just sleep and sleep and sleep. Instead he nodded mechanically and said, 'I'll try.'

Remember Jamail . . . But this time it was all right, because he wasn't involving anyone else . . .

He backed out of the room, then turned and hurried off down the stairs.

Outside the front door, his way lit by the fat moon, he made for the garage. As he was unlocking its big double doors, the window of the flat above opened and Thwaite's head poked out.

'What are you doing, sir?' he said. 'Christ, you had me worried there. I thought some bugger was tryin' to nick the motor.'

'I'm going out.'

'Hang on a sec. I'll drive you.'

Remember Jamail . . . No Driver Lemberger to blame himself for. No Driver Thwaite . . .

'No time,' Blessed said quickly. 'In any case I promised to go alone. It's to do with Panewski. I think I've got him.'

'Bloody hell, sir.'

A moment later, Blessed was in the driver's seat, sliding the key into the ignition. It fired sweetly at the second turn. Less than a minute after turning his back on Gisela, he was out of the drive of the Villa Hellman and heading southeast towards the Schönwalder Allee.

Remember Jamail . . . But Berlin wasn't Lebanon . . .

The tree-lined suburban avenues were straight and comparatively well-repaired, there was no traffic, and so he pressed his right foot flat to the boards and gave the Horch full power, taking it well beyond the speed limit. He had just over seven minutes to make it to the warehouse by the Havel, close to the Eiswerder Bridge, and he wanted time to spare.

Remember Jamail . . . But this time it was just Jim Blessed, wasn't it? Jim Blessed, win or lose . . .

THIRTY

IT WAS SIX KILOMETRES to the meeting-place. Eiswerder was an island in the middle of the Havel, which at this point widened to half a kilometre or so across. The bridge mentioned in the phone call provided a link to Spandau, while another, smaller one ran to Haselhorst and Siemensstadt on the eastern shore. All along both river banks, and on Eiswerder itself, were factories, warehouses, utilities, docks, now either destroyed by bombs or largely stilled by the combined effects of the power shortages and the Soviet blockade.

Blessed passed the turning to the Eiswerder Bridge a couple of minutes before the deadline. Half a mile to the south he glimpsed the imposing shape of the sixteenth-century Spandau Citadel, guarding the place where the river and its tributary sister, the Spree, flowed together. Blessed followed the northerly curve of the Neuendorfer Strasse for a while and then forked right towards the river again. The Citadel had looked beautiful, but then tonight even the factories, gas-holders and warehouses were flattered. The big moon, without street lamps to neutralise its light, silvered the city, lent it the exact but subtly romanticised tints of a daguerrotype or a Hollywood backdrop.

He arrived on time, perhaps even a little early, in the broad cobbled street near the river. Parking the car the agreed distance from the meeting-place, he got out and surveyed his surroundings. The Bernbach warehouse was easily identifiable. The firm's name was painted on the wall in huge gothic letters, just as had been promised, but the place amounted to no more than a burnt-out shell, probably the most seriously-damaged building on the entire crowded waterfront. Nevertheless he began to walk towards it.

When he was about halfway, Blessed stopped and sniffed the humid summer air, inspected his surroundings. He was humming with adrenalin, calm and alert. Lucky he hadn't been hitting the whisky tonight, as both Harriet—and Gisela, come to think of it—had expected. *No weakness in that direction at least, Jimmy-boy.* If Panewski was here as he had promised, he would have seen the car drive up and stop. Blessed decided to light a cheroot, show he didn't intend to be rushed, establish a kind of moral equality with his quarry. A now-habitual glance at the sky. There were the usual aircraft lights overhead. The airlift went on twenty-four hours a day. Apart from the thin drone of aircraft preparing to land at Tempelhof or Gatow, or climbing to begin their flights back to the western zones, there was silence, or as close to silence as any city ever gets. It was so quite that he could hear river-water lapping on the far side of the buildings.

So Blessed waited, one hand in his windcheater pocket where the Webley nestled heavily.

He heard a long, shrill whistle. It came, not from the Bernbach warehouse, but from a building further back and to the right. At first Blessed thought it was a goods train. Then he remembered that since the blockade there were no goods trains in Berlin. He made no acknowledgment, did not even turn his head.

The whistle came again, definitely a summons and definitely from the second floor of the three-storey warehouse to the right of Bernbach & Co. It was an impressive Victorian building, even though it had lost most of its roof. The lower two storeys were boarded up but looked reasonably sound. This place had no name. Now that he looked closely, he could see that the main front doors showed signs of having been forced open.

Blessed's grip on the Webley tightened. He changed direction as he walked, stopped twenty yards from the open door. 'Panewski?' he called out.

Only that damned whistle for an answer. From the second storey on the left-hand side.

There was always a chance that Kelly was right, and that Panewski was a compulsive killer who had Blessed on his list. Not much of a chance, but enough to make him glad he had brought the pistol with him. He cautiously slid inside the doors, found it suddenly dark. He moved towards the wooden stairs with the Webley levelled and the safety-catch off. The first stair felt slightly rotten, so he slowed down, feeling each step with the toe of his shoe before he took it, and so reached the first landing. Along a landing straight ahead of him he saw the Havel, glistening forty, fifty feet below, framed by an open loading-bay. There were storage areas to the left, to the right a narrow corridor leading into what looked like an office. Behind him was a large, boarded-up window that faced out onto the street he had driven along a few minutes previously. Blessed carefully turned the corner, put his foot on the first of the steps leading up to the second storey, then paused.

'Panewski!' he repeated without much hope of an answer.

After a short wait, Blessed continued up towards the second storey, still feeling ahead with his exploratory toe. He had a sudden, irrational fear of tripping, or falling through a rotten step, and loosing off his pistol by accident, making a fool of himself, frightening off his quarry.

The second landing was a repeat of the first. Ahead another loading-bay, open to the night and the river. To the right a short corridor, an open door, an office. To the left the entrance to the storage room. That was where the whistle had come from.

Blessed felt self-conscious, framed as he was in the doorway, an easy target. 'Panewski!'

No answer. But also no turning back. Blessed took a deep breath, stepped forward, emerged into a high-ceilinged, musty-smelling room about sixty feet long by forty feet wide. It was completely bare. He guessed that it had probably been stripped by Berliners looking for firewood or for boards to keep the weather and their fellow men from their own homes. Ahead and to his right were tall windows. What panes were left had been painted over years ago, as a black-out precaution. Above the near end of the storage room was a platform reached by a rickety-looking staircase. Only a few unequal beams of moonlight penetrated here, but Blessed could see well enough to make out the burly figure sat bolt upright in a rickety wooden armchair in the middle of the room. Karl-Heinz Panewski was staring at Blessed with a lopsided grin, but he still refused to acknowledge his presence.

'Panewski!'

He advanced towards the chair, suddenly angry rather than frightened, angry at the theatre this involved, and the waste of time. He could be snug at home, he found himself thinking, instead of playing dupe to an arrogant psychopath with an overdeveloped sense of drama. Only when Blessed came a step or two closer did he realise that Panewski was not going to answer him, would never answer anyone again. There was a bright-red stain on the front of the man's white shirt just underneath the heart. A quick, relatively clean in-and-out with a pointed blade, by the look of it. If this was the same killer who had despatched Price, Heidemarie Sanders and Floh, then in Panewski's case he had been economical, even merciful, in his choice of deaths. That comforting illusion lasted until Blessed looked at Panewski's huge hands, which he saw were tied to the arms of the chair. All the fingernails had been ripped out, leaving bloody, raw tips where they had been. The same had been done to the nails of his bare feet. The lop-sided curl into which Panewski's lips had petrified, and which Blessed had almost mistaken for a smile, was merely the final, grimacing anticipation of death.

So who had damned well whistled when he had been waiting outside? And what was that noise behind Blessed now?

The sound was not a footfall or a shuffle, but a kind of pendulum creak and somewhere high above him an intake of breath. All this Blessed registered in the short time between his realisation that Panewski was dead, and the beginning of the sound that answered his inevitable question: What now?

Blessed had half-turned on his heel when something heavy swooped down at speed and crashed into him, knocking him headlong and sending the precious Webley flying out of his hand. Even as he toppled, he heard the gun bounce on the wooden floor, slide away beyond immediate retrieval. Then his head struck the ground, and he was rolling hard to one side, away from the danger.

'*KEP-TEN!*'

The strange, hoarse shout coincided with the thump of feet landing on the floor somewhere close by.

Blessed knew he had to get back on his feet, or be at the mercy of whoever had hit him. Mercy? No mercy. Think of Panewski's pain-distorted features, the savaged, bloody remnants of his hands and feet.

'*KEP-TEN BLESS-ED!*'

Blessed rose, found his hand made contact with a wall, which meant he must have fallen, pitched and rolled fifteen or twenty feet. He steadied himself and turned. There was a rope suspended from a hook in the ceiling, and it was still swinging gently back and forth across the huge room between Blessed and the bound corpse of Panewski. He realised that the weight that had hit from behind had been a man's. The assailant had been waiting on the platform up here above the door, the rope already in his hands, had watched Blessed enter the

306

room and move towards Panewski, had chosen his moment to swing down, legs outstretched.

He had to establish his bearings. A glance around told him he was standing on the right side of the warehouse hangar now, with the windows behind him, and to his own right the opening through which in better times cranes had swung pallets and crates of goods destined for storage here.

'*KEP-TEN BLESS-ED! YOU PAY ATTENT-ION YOU DUMB-DUMB HAT, OR I DON' WAIT, I KILL YOU NOW!*'

Blessed looked in the direction of that murderous adolescent voice. Something flashed brightly—brighter by far than the hesitant fillets of light that played through the high windows. It was, unmistakably, the metallic glint of a knife-blade, and as the blade jabbed forward in his direction he saw that it was fixed not to a conventional handle but to a set of brass knuckles, making it an extension of the wearer's fist. It was a gangster's weapon that had become popular in Germany since the end of the war; Blessed had viewed these savage tools as exhibits, been shown photographs of the damage they could inflict. The wielder of the blade took a step forward and revealed himself. He stood, feet planted apart, with an exquisite sense of theatre, in the centre of the floor.

'You pay, *ach scheiss*, you pay attention, Kep-ten! 'Cos I know this moment and this mo-ment is to me precious, yes *precious beyond belief*!' The boy spoke in a peculiar way, sing-song and alien, German but not German, and in some ways—this was the most chilling thing—deliberately hardly human.

Many things fell into place at the sight of this preening figure opposite him, with the stiletto glinting on his knuckles like a piece of jewellery. The boy-man—or better, the boy-murderer—stood about five feet ten in his army boots and flapping greatcoat, was sallow and wild-haired, and no more than eighteen years old. A boy. Hardly more than a child. And he fitted Herr Jauch's description of the the elder boy seen emerging from the cellar after the burglary at Heidemarie's and Anna's flat.

'Talk!' The blade arced out in a petulant hand-movement. 'Kepten, I want to hear you *talk*!'

Blessed nodded deliberately. Talk? 'Did you kill Panewski?' he said, because it was the first thing that came into his head.

'That Hat he cheat me/ That Hat he dies/ You don' stay living/ When you tell Boss lies . . .' A derisive laugh. The boy indicated over his shoulder in a gesture of contempt.

'Did Price lie to you? Did Floh? Did Price or Floh cheat you? Is that why you killed them?' Blessed asked. He knew he must keep talking, and as he spoke he shifted a couple of steps towards the opening of the loading-bay. The important thing was to gain space before this boy closed in on him, made it impossible for him to move without putting himself within range of the blade.

The boy shrugged, made a little grimace. 'A story,' he said tersely. 'A whole story, real story. My story . . .'

'And Heidemarie? What could she possibly have done—?'

'Kep-ten!' A flash of warning. The eyes, which were deep-set and smoulderingly bright, flickered rapid signals. 'Heidemarie? O Heide the lover? *Forget it*. Oh I *know*, everylittlething I know *too much*. She lied 'bout it after, ever-ever-after. Wrong, wrong, wrong . . .'

'What do you mean?'

The boy's vivid, bizarre scrambling of language would have made a fascinating study under any other circumstances but these. So would the headlong violence, the frantic evil of his psychology. Everything was connected. What factor buried in his past had made him that way? This was the question the fashionable analysts would ask. Or did such things just happen by bad grace, by the luck of the birth-lottery, as traditionalists would claim?

Now, two little steps to the right, towards that loading-bay, take it as easy as you can . . .

'The . . . dead . . . don't . . . mean . . .'

'Who *are* you?' Blessed interrupted him. *Three steps*. What he intended to do, most rational, normal human beings would consider insane. But then most rational normal human beings would never be trapped in an empty warehouse room with a murderer.

The boy stared at Blessed suspiciously. 'I am the boy who is his own hero, Mister Kepten,' he said eventually. 'I am the boy with no name.'

One step. 'Everybody has a name.' *Another step*. Just about there. Blessed knew he mustn't look. He mustn't even glance out of the corner of his eye, because that might give him away, enable the boy to anticipate his route and cut him off. The danger was, if he wasn't careful the boy would finish him off now without warning or fuss. Simple slaughter. Never fails. That was why he had to use this kid's insane need to communicate in order to gain time. He had to harness the killer's madness to his own survival.

Perhaps the boy understood what Blessed was trying to do.

'Enough-enough-enough!' he barked, and shook his head, as if waking himself from a troublesome dream. 'Now, Kepten Blessed of His Majesty's British Army in British-occupied Berlin,' he continued, twisting the words into a snarl, 'it's the end-time, no more talking, 'cos now I got to come for you, 'cos you know I got to stop you, 'cos you know after everything everything everything that happened, it's either you, Kep-ten, or—Gad-help-me—me.' He half-turned, motioned towards the doorway.

Blessed's heart missed. He saw two figures appear in the door and advance into the room until they were close behind the boy. Their presence explained how Panewski had been overpowered and held captive. Blessed also realised they had probably been behind him all the way from the street, and he hadn't noticed a thing. They had no weapons on display. For now, they seemed there just for protection. This was the boy-murderer's game, the boy-murderer's exclusive pleasure. The killer extended his knuckle-blade, began to inch forward. His eyes were keen, searching his prospective victim's face intently, almost lovingly.

Blessed was wondering how this boy had killed Price and Heide. Perhaps he had cut Price's throat first, exploiting the element of surprise, and then killed Heidemarie/Suzy at his leisure. As for Floh and Panewski, perhaps they had tried to keep him talking, believing that they might somehow out-play him with talk, pleas for mercy, improvised psychology, all the adult ploys. For his part, Blessed had already rejected these alternatives, had decided on an almost moronically simple approach: *I shall not let this person kill me*, he kept repeating to himself over and over as he prepared to make his move. *I might die in the next few seconds or minutes, but it will not be this boy who kills me.* That resolve was all that mattered. That was what everything had shrunk to.

Blessed took two quick steps to the right and then two seemingly wild but in fact carefully-calculated ones forward, pitching himself almost to within range of the waiting blade. As he had intended, the boy was so surprised by Blessed's apparent aggression that he gave ground, lashing out protectively with the knife, all but backed into Panewski's body in its armchair. His two helpers closed in swiftly to ensure that Blessed could come no further. To his surprise, he saw that they were not teenagers but conventional Ku-Damm criminal types, one very overweight and the other taller and wiry, both blandly, professionally brutal. They were completely different from the boy.

Of course, in their understanding, which was that Blessed had intended to overpower the boy, the crisis was over. After a temporary flurry of confusion there was a phalanx facing Blessed, solid and immovable. And if he ever considered hesitating on the second stage of his plan, he knew he couldn't now, because the rangy, almost scarecrow-like thug was reaching into his pocket and pulling out a gun.

'Kep-ten!' the boy whispered evilly. 'Kepten, I kill you now, now, now!'

But by now Blessed had turned his back on him and was running for his life, towards the open loading-bay door twenty feet away, the only part-unknown element in the equation and therefore the only hope. Not just that, but he was gathering speed, so that he hit the last plank of the floor like a long-jumper, going for all the bounce he could get, and launched himself out full-length into the empty darkness. In the distance, as he leaped, he suddenly glimpsed mysterious and beautiful lights far away across the water. Either he was already in the antechamber to heaven, or the suburb of Haselhorst must have its electricity on at this hour of the night.

Blessed began to fall. So odd. He felt an almost ecstatic fascination with those unexplained lights, and with the awesome, deliciously chill rush of air on his face.

THIRTY-ONE

BLESSED HAD TRIED to execute a perfect dive, arms straight together outstretched, head tucked in. Even so, the slap as he hit the river's surface was so hard that he told himself, this is how it is to die of falling—body smashed against the unyielding earth, face first, unrecognisable when the relatives come to identify the broken corpse. Then the whole of him was received by the oily waters of the Havel. First he was sucked into its surface warmth, then into the colder maw of the depths. Finally he touched the bottom. There lay good Berlin sand, a soft landing-place at last. He kicked off hard, began to rise again. A much more dangerous world awaited him above.

His head broke the surface. He trod water. All around was the stench of engine-sump, mixed with an acrid cocktail of human and industrial waste.

'*Kep-ten!*' He heard a shout when his ears cleared.

There were two figures silhouetted in the loading-bay entrance forty feet above him. One of them was the boy-murderer. The other, the scarecrowlike gangster with his gun. Blessed inexpertly kept himself afloat and considered his options. The man fired a shot down into the water. Fortunately he was way off target, showing that they hadn't yet pinpointed his position in the darkness.

The quayside beneath the warehouse was only ten feet away. As Blessed had trusted when planning his leap, there was just a narrow concrete catwalk where boats and barges had once tied up before unloading their cargoes. He weighed up his chances of reaching land and making a run for it. He decided he would never make it to the street, let alone the car. To put a respectable distance between himself

311

and death, he would have to keep moving in the river. Turning, he struck out in a laborious crawl, heading downstream, northbound and parallel with the shore.

He travelled seventy or eighty yards away from the quayside. His clothes were weighing him down, and getting heavier as they absorbed more water. On his left now was a large factory-building. Ahead lay another, and another. Landing would be difficult, and he had no idea who would be waiting for him. On the other hand, he could feel exhaustion beginning to eat at him. He had to land, and take his chances.

It was then that he saw the gleam of a domestic light, faint but unmistakable, not too far ahead. Without hesitation he began to swim for it, switching to a steady breaststroke. This was slightly easier and enabled him to look ahead towards the light, to home in on it. He heard a distant shot but kept on. Now his muscles were protesting. Now his body might be considering surrender . . .

The last few times he dipped his head into the water, Blessed thought he might not come up again. A bad way to die, but better than being filleted by the boy-murderer with the knuckle-blade. Then suddenly his hands scraped against brick. After some scrabbling and struggling progress along the quay, he gripped a metal ring. He hung there, head thrown back, gulping in the heavy, faintly rancid air. He was still waterbound, but he was almost a land animal again.

It was not easy to climb ashore. The dockside was too high to haul himself up. He rested and said his prayers, then started to travel bit by bit along the dock, half swimming, half relying on fleeting purchase provided by cracks and holes in the brickwork.

There came a point when, reaching forward to feel the brick, Blessed met no resistance. He plunged with a loud splash, was submerged for an instant. Then his finger-tips discovered a smooth, horizontal rectangle of stone, and a vertical one of the same size laid on top of it. He realised that what he had found were steps leading up out of the water.

Looking like a sick seal, he crawled slowly up the steps on his chest, using his hands like flippers. Only when he got to the topmost step did he half rise, defying the buzzing, rushing darkness that was beginning to fill his head. The last thing Blessed saw before the darkness conquered him were two shadowy figures advancing towards the steps, one of them carrying a long, heavy object tucked under his arm.

*

Blessed regained consciousness in time to feel the toes of his shoes bumping over the top step, dragging against cobbles. Then he was turned over on his back and eased down onto grass.

'Well, is he alive?' one German voice said.

Blessed opened his eyes and saw a man standing over him, pointing a shotgun at his chest. The man had a thick, curly moustache, upturned at the ends, of the kind favoured by Kaiser William II and RAF pilots. He was in his sixties. His companion was younger but extremely unfit. At one time he had obviously been unusually obese. Now the fat had gone, leaving his skin to hang off his body like a very badly cut suit. He had a grotesque, pendulous fold of skin under his chin, which wobbled, turkey-like, when he spoke.

'He just opened his eyes,' turkey cock panted. Dragging Blessed across the quayside had taken it out of him; he was breathing very heavily.

'He probably thinks he's died and gone to heaven, and we're angels,' the older one said, and guffawed heartily.

'Some heaven. Some angels.'

They were nightwatchmen, as it turned out, keeping an eye on a small warehouse full of sugar and candles. Maybe the stuff was black-market, maybe it wasn't. Blessed made no comment. In fact, he said very little at all until, with their help, he regained his feet and managed to walk the short distance to their quarters. These were in a cabin attached to the warehouse which doubled as an office. This was the single light he had seen from the water.

From somewhere the man with the Kaiser moustache produced a blanket, ordered Blessed to take off his jacket and shirt.

'No. I have to contact someone. Do you have a phone?'

'Were those shots we heard anything to do with you, eh?' the old man said, his eyes shrewd. 'That's why we come out armed. Not the first time there's been a shoot-out round here by the warehouses.'

Blessed nodded, made an impatient gesture.

'You're in a hurry, I see. Trouble with the law?'

He shrugged. Instinct told him to play things strong and silent until he had managed to contact the outside world.

'You don't say much, whoever you are. Anyway, you're safe here. They probably think you drowned. Which, to be honest, you bloody nearly did.'

'I need to get out of here. Phone for help.'

The old man smiled, pointed to a tiny doorless cubicle out the back. 'In there. Be quick. The owner of this place is my cousin.'

313

'Two phone calls. Short ones. I promise.'

The telephone was a battered old apparatus from the twenties. Nevertheless, he was able to get through to 248 Company by direct dialling. As calmly as he could, fighting against spasms of weariness, he told the Warrant Officer in charge at the Knesebeckstrasse his location and phone number, explained the circumstances. A car was to be sent immediately to pick him up. Kelly was to be woken and sent over here. They would need a forensic team as well. And extreme caution was to be exercised, because there might still be armed criminals in the vicinity.

Then Blessed rang Weiss's home number. The inspector answered the phone, sharp-witted and awake. Perhaps his family's electricity had also come on, and they were busy with domestic tasks.

'James! I didn't recognise your voice. You don't sound your usual self.'

'That's because I'm not. Listen: Panewski is dead. The killer is a young teenaged boy. He murdered all of them. Price, Suzy, Floh too . . .'

'My God. James—'

'It's *the* crazy boy we've heard so much about. I know, because he tried to kill me too just now. And he damned-near succeeded!'

'First things first. Are you somewhere safe?'

'I think so.'

'Good. Where exactly are you?'

'In a warehouse near the Nordhafen. The point is, what happened tonight confirms everything I suspected . . .'

'I will meet you there. I can bring some of my own people. If you haven't yet called your SIB colleagues, I will do it for you, of course.'

'No. It's all right,' Blessed said quickly. 'I've already rung the Knesebeckstrasse. They're sending a car for me.'

'Ah, yes. Whatever you say. As long as you are all right.'

'I'll live. We have a lot to discuss. You and me and Kelly. *Everything about this case has changed*. We have to look at everything afresh. You never really believed in the children, did you Manfred? Do you now?'

'It seems as if I have no choice. I will meet you at your office.'

When Blessed squelched back into the room, the Kaiser stared at him balefully.

'I overheard you, I could not help it. You are a policeman. Even worse, you are a Tommy policeman,' he said. 'And I let you use my cousin's telephone. He will never forgive me.'

There was nothing either he or turkey cock could do now, of course. The Military Police were coming here, they knew the exact address. It might have been a different matter if they had known Blessed was a policeman before he had picked up the telephone and told the world where he was.

'I saved you,' the Kaiser continued. 'I—we—rescued you from a watery grave. We could have left you to die. May God preserve us.'

'I'm very grateful. But what are you so worried about?'

Kaiser and turkey cock exchanged looks.

'I said, what are you worried about?' Blessed repeated. 'So far as I am aware, the business conducted here is perfectly legitimate. Why should your cousin be angry with you for helping the British authorities? You have done his standing with the government nothing but good.' He eyed the ancient shotgun, which was almost certainly unlicensed. 'Mind you,' he added. 'I'd get that out of sight, if I were you, before we let the MPs in the door.'

Understanding dawned on the Kaiser. The old man grinned, dug into his coat pocket, pulled out a crumpled packet of cheap German cigarettes.

'A smoke for the Herr Englishman, who speaks such good German,' he said, thrusting them at Blessed. 'And—' he snapped his bony fingers to rouse turkey cock to action '—get that blanket for him. Make that two. There is a whole pile somewhere. The Herr English Officer must not catch cold . . .'

'This is exactly as we found your vehicle, sir,' the CMP warrant officer said as they approached the Horch. The car was still where Blessed had parked it two hours before, but it was not quite as he had left it. 'We haven't touched anything, in case there's prints on the doorhandle or the radio knobs. The driver's door had been forced open, as you see, and the radio tuned in to the police frequency. There's little doubt they were listening in.'

Blessed nodded. He was wrapped in blankets like an Indian, sipping hot oxtail soup from a mug. 'Very professional of them.'

'It's lucky there was very little radio traffic, and especially nothing referring to your whereabouts after you rang us, or I suppose they might have sought you out and had another go.'

'Too risky, once you were on your way. You might have turned up in the middle of the proceedings, and then where would they have been?' Blessed said. 'I think it's more likely they had someone stationed here at the car from the moment I went out of sight, first to keep an eye on the street, second to eavesdrop on the police frequencies, just in case I had ordered up reinforcements before I got here.' *Which like a bloody idiot you hadn't*, was the message he saw written in the WO's involuntary grimace of accusation.

A car and a covered jeep turned into the street, stopped by the Horch. Kelly got out of the car, carrying a parcel which turned out to contain a complete change of clothes, including Blessed's 'German suit' from the office. The two men in the jeep were from forensics. They didn't look too pleased at losing yet another night's sleep.

Before he could change out of his wet clothes, Blessed had to tell the forensics boys his route into the warehouse so that they could use the same access. One stayed behind to check for possible prints in the Horch, while the other went ahead to make initial preparations at the scene of the crime. At last Blessed was free to strip off the rest of his wet clothes. While he got changed he briefed Kelly on the night's events. The sergeant listened impassively, made no comment until Blessed had finished.

'If, as you say, one of the blokes had a shooter, I don't know why they didn't just put a bullet in you and have done with it,' Kelly said then. 'Why make such a bloody meal of it? The kid's obviously a nutter.'

'He does like to chat a bit first, it's true. I think he likes to carve his victims up a bit too, before he puts them out of their misery.' Blessed, buttoning his fresh shirt, frowned thoughtfully. 'He takes his time, our boy-murderer. With me, he took just a little too long for his own good.'

Suddenly a surge of elation hit him. He had won the only kind of victory that really mattered. *No Jamail fiasco this time. Jim Blessed had handled this alone and come through alive. No deaths. No explanations or letters to bereaved families . . .*

Blessed put on his jacket, glanced at his watch. It had stopped shortly after he jumped into the Havel. The glass protecting the dial was cracked.

'What's the time, Kelly?'

'Five minutes to four, sir.'

'Is it really? Well, we'll only get in the forensic boys' way if we stay here, so you can drive me to the office in your car. Someone else can take me home later. Poor old Thwaite could do with an undisturbed night.'

*

By half-past four, they were climbing the stairs to BlessForce. Weiss was in one of the empty offices, dozing. On the desk in front of him was an empty sandwich plate, and a mug that had once contained tea. Kelly gently shook him awake.

Blessed sat down behind his desk, fished a packet of cheroots out of the drawer, lit one. 'Has there been any progress in identifying this so-called orphanage director?' he asked. 'This has suddenly become crucial. It could be the one thing that leads us to the heart of this case. I believe that if we find out where those kids came from, we'll be close to finding the boy killer. Perhaps they're sheltering him at an orphanage, a youth club, a school, for some reason. Perhaps they don't even know what he's done. But we have to find them, Manfred. Not tomorrow. Not next week. *Now!*'

Weiss looked very unhappy. 'We're doing our best, given the resources available—you know my difficulties with headquarters. I have three men assigned to this case full-time. Two of them spent yesterday at the Magistrat making enquiries about the orphanages. Again, this is in the Soviet Sector—' He threw up his hands. 'The third man has been frequenting Panewski's old drinking-haunts, seeing if he can find out something of his movements. Now, for obvious reasons, this man can be released for other duties.'

'I want your men to visit personally every juvenile institution in the central boroughs. We'll start with the orphanages. We have to find the director, or Buster. In a way it doesn't matter which.'

'I told you, I have only three men—'

'Listen carefully. This boy has killed four people,' Blessed growled. 'So far. He even made a carefully-planned attempt to murder me, and I'm an officer in the Military Police, in case you forgot. The nature of this investigation has changed quite drastically in the past few hours. I don't think anyone, British or Russian or German, can deny that this case deserves the highest priority. So for Christ's sake, Manfred, don't talk to me about problems with manpower. We're faced with a murderer in Berlin who's very young, and very frightening—I can tell you that from direct experience. We have to find him before he does any more harm. Do you understand that?'

Weiss had not been able to look him in the eye for the last part of Blessed's tirade. When the Englishman relaxed back into his chair and took a long pull on his neglected cheroot, Weiss continued to stare at his hands for some moments. Then he found the strength to look up.

317

'I owe you an apology, James,' he said heavily. 'You are right. Things have indeed changed greatly. I'll make a request for more men later today. Will your people back me up?'

'Of course, Manfred. I'll be seeing Colonel Harrison later this morning. If necessary, I'll have the question raised directly with the Russians at the most senior level.'

Kelly had been silent, making notes in a small exercise book. He looked up. 'What if these boys are from outside Berlin, sir? Say, Potsdam or Falkensee? Isn't that going to make them very hard for us to track down?'

'Yes. It would.' Blessed thought for a moment, then shook his head. 'But I'm sure they're Berliners. They know this city, especially the centre, like the back of their hands. Those kids are city rats. I'd stake my life on it.'

'But the sergeant has a point,' Weiss said. 'If the boy and his supposed helpers are based even just inside the Soviet sector (around the Friedrichstrasse, say) then things will be much more difficult for this investigation.' He smiled sourly. 'When it comes to politics, as we know, the Russians rule with a rod of iron. But in other matters they are often very lax. The black market is such an example. It undermines the economy of the western sectors, but it brings the communists many covert benefits. Also, it is a good way of acquiring western currencies unofficially . . .'

'I know. The black market's been my speciality for the past year. And I remember what happened to Wachtmann Pilzinger when we wanted to ask him some slightly more pointed questions . . . But would the Russians go to such lengths to protect a mentally unbalanced teenaged murderer? And if so, why?'

Weiss shrugged. 'Their reasons may follow a logic that we cannot understand. Remember, we still don't know what lay behind the original murders of Corporal Price and his girlfriend.'

Blessed could feel the uncomfortable truth of Weiss's words. 'I'm no closer to understanding motive,' he conceded. 'Why Price? Why the girlfriend? The killings of Floh and Panewski make some kind of sense. The boy and his friends tried to frame Panewski for the Price-Suzy murders, throwing in the killing of Floh for good measure—complete with a blade bearing his fingerprints. Who knows how they arranged that? When it looked like the frame-up was going to fail, they used Panewski as a bait to draw me in—and killed him as well, because he knew too much . . .'

'And you?' Weiss said. 'Why this interest in you?'

'I don't know. I honestly don't know. Perhaps I'm closer to catching that boy than I think. He likes to play cat and mouse. Yes he does.'

'Want me to draft a request to the Russians, sir?' Kelly suggested.

'Why not? For the moment, we'll keep looking in the western sectors. The boy and his friends—not all of whom are kids—certainly operate in our part of Berlin. They're pretty sure to show themselves here again.' Blessed stubbed out his cheroot, smiled. 'One never knows. He might have another crack at me. I'll have to have myself very carefully watched, won't I?'

'In my opinion this no joking matter, actually,' Kelly said with schoolmasterly severity. 'That boy doesn't sound as if he gives up easily. They've been following you. They obviously know your telephone number and where you live.' He leaned forward earnestly. 'You should arm yourself and have a permanent escort from now on, if you ask me.'

'You may be right,' Blessed had to admit. 'It might be a good idea to organise some protection. I'll take the spare Webley from the safe to replace the one I lost. Could we arrange for a bodyguard? We'll have to borrow one from 248 Company. I can't go pulling a man off this investigation just to play nursemaid to me.'

'And your family, sir.'

'And my family, I suppose,' Blessed agreed. 'Which reminds me. I'll go off home in a bit and change back into uniform. Sergeant, will you make an appointment for me to see the colonel at about nine? And if Captain Dracoulis from Tempelhof has any astounding information for us, you can tell him to ring me at home.'

Kelly nodded. 'Very well, sir.'

'I want that so-called "orphanage director" very badly,' Blessed said to Weiss. 'That's the main task for your boys today. Apart from that I need to see mug-shots of all juveniles between, say, fifteen and twenty years old, arrested for smuggling and black-market dealing, especially drugs, in the western sectors during the past year.'

'I will see. It's not my department, of course. If we're unlucky, you will probably end up having to look through hundreds, even thousands of photographs, James.'

'It won't take me long. I'll recognise that boy's face the moment I see it. There'll be no mistaking him.'

'I'll phone the records people personally.'

Weiss made a note of the request. Blessed noticed that his hand was shaking as he wrote. Though he tried to conceal it, Weiss was clearly exhausted, emotionally drained. Blessed hardened his heart.

319

Everything hung in the balance today. He knew he dared not let up.

'Come to think of it, the boy used a lot of American slang,' Blessed said. He turned back to Kelly. 'Get in touch with American CID—Captain Appleyard would be the man. Give him my regards but for Christ's sake don't tell him what happened to me last night or it'll be all over Berlin by lunchtime. See if they can supply us with mug-shots of juveniles within the specified age-range who've been picked up in the past twelve months or so on suspicion of illegal dealings with American servicemen.'

'Dealings to do with drugs especially, sir?'

'Drugs especially. It's a bit of a longshot, of course, because if the boy had been pulled in by the CID, he'd probably be behind bars now instead of running around Berlin killing people. Still, it's worth a try.'

Time to go home and change. Blessed got to his feet. 'I'll be back in about an hour and a half. Then work starts in earnest,' he said crisply. 'In the meantime, why don't you both catch up on your sleep? It may be our last chance for some time.'

THIRTY-TWO

IN HIS HOLLOW, SLEEP-STARVED STATE, Blessed should have fallen asleep the moment he collapsed into the back of the Military Police Riley they had found to take him back to the Villa Hellman. But his brain was seething, his body nervously alive with a kind of fragile euphoria. Perhaps it had something to do with escaping death so narrowly. Perhaps it was a result of all the new developments in the Price case, the new possibilities, the world that was being opened up under the scalpel of his determination.

I am the boy who is his own hero. I am the boy with no name.

Blessed suddenly found himself remembering the boy murderer's haunting words, and his own reply: 'Everybody has a name.'

'Pardon, sir?'

He looked up, saw the eyes of the tall lance-corporal in the driver's seat examining him in the rear-view mirror.

'You said something, sir, about a name.'

Blessed smiled to cover his embarrassment at being caught talking to himself. 'It's all right,' he said, 'I was just trying to remember a quotation.'

'I see, sir.'

After some hard work by Kelly, Lance-Corporal Cave had been co-opted to act as Blessed's chauffeur-cum-bodyguard. The lance-corporal was supposed to be one of the most outstanding pistol-shots in the entire Corps of Military Police, which Blessed hoped was true, but his driving was maddeningly slow and cautious. The trip home seemed to be taking an eternity. Blessed began to long for Thwaite's quick, uncompromising style. He wondered how long it would take to

321

get the Horch back from forensics, how quickly the door-lock could be repaired and the car made available again. In the meantime, he would need a replacement. Another thing for Kelly to arrange. He would ring the office the moment he got home. Kelly could do it when he woke up from his nap. If he was taking one. Kelly never let him down. Kelly was the kind of assistant everyone wanted. Kelly was a treasure.

Blessed had to guide Lance-Corporal Cave on the last bit of the journey through suburban Spandau, which at least kept him awake. The motion of the car had started to lull him into sleep, despite all the competing tensions in his body, the feverish thoughts chasing each other around his mind.

The Riley drew up outside the front door of the Villa Hellman just as the early-morning sun was starting to warm the ground. For those who had leisure, it would be a day perfect for picnicking, boating, sunbathing. The lance-corporal came round and opened the car door for him. Blessed clambered out, stretched, sniffed the air. There was a pungent-burnt smell about, like a bonfire of dubious things, but no smoke.

'First we'll put the kettle on, shall we, Lance-Corporal?' he said, to put Cave at his ease.

'Smashing, sir. A nice cup of tea would be just the thing.'

'Gisela will probably be up and about. She's learned to make it rather well,' Blessed said as he led the way towards the front door. 'I suppose it's considered an essential basic skill, a step towards penetrating the mysteries of "the British way of life" that the poor old Germans are always being lectured about on the radio. You know, along with cricket and "fair play". From tea-making to parliamentary democracy in ten easy lessons.'

'Well, personally I like my democracy with milk and two sugars, sir,' Cave said with a laugh.

But when Blessed came to put the key in the lock, the door gave, swung partly open, and the smell of burning, which he now recognised as cordite, became very strong indeed. He took out his new gun from his pocket, eased off the safety catch, motioned to Cave to do the same, and kicked the door fully open.

There, sprawled out on his back on the floor in the hall, his dark-red life-blood already soaked well into the expensive green-and-gold pile of the Kreisleiter's Flemish carpet, was the body of Blessed's driver. Thwaite had been shot in the chest at close range, judging from the size of the wound, and left where he had fallen.

322

Ignoring Cave's warning shout, Blessed ran up the stairs, taking them two at a time. Oh, suddenly he knew exactly what had happened. Oh, suddenly he understood the boy-murderer so terrifyingly well. How could he have let this happen? He should have realised that if the boy couldn't get Blessed himself, he would take instead what Blessed held most dear.

Daphne. Truly and not in jest, not in exaggeration. Truly, as the boy had said last night, *precious beyond belief*. This was so absolutely cruel.

Jamail! Jamail!, a voice screamed in Blessed's head. *Not better than Jamail this time, after all, but worse. The very worst . . .*

The boy-murderer had taken the captain's daughter. Daphne.

PART 3

PRECIOUS BEYOND BELIEF

Was hat man dir, du armes Kind, getan?

Johann Wolfgang von Goethe,
Wilhelm Meister: 'Mignonslied'

THIRTY-THREE

'YOU'RE A FELLOW-PROFESSIONAL, Captain Blessed, you know we have constantly to hope for the best, but unflinchingly to consider the worst. It comes with the job. So there's no point in my hiding the unpleasant possibilities, now, is there?'

'No. No point at all.'

Inside his head, Blessed clearly pictured Daphne dead. Dead like Panewski. Like Floh, Price, Suzy. He fought the image. His own voice sounded far off to him, as if he were halloo-ing from a distance on a stormy day.

'You're remarkably calm,' Major Dalgliesh was saying. 'Of course, I recognise the *effort* that must be costing you. But there are still one or two *pertinent* questions we need to discuss. Can you bear with me a little longer?'

'Whatever's necessary. Whatever.'

Dalgliesh was a burly Scotsman with red hair and a red moustache. Years in the Middle Eastern sun had turned his pale celtic skin lurid as cooked lobster. Those unexpected emphases and that aggressively formal vocabulary of 'officers'' English, shot through with traces of nasal Gorbals, betrayed a determined struggle up from Scottish working-class origins. They were talking in a spare interview room at the Knesebeckstrasse which had become the major's temporary headquarters. The walls had been freshly painted in a drab shade of yellow, but the place still managed to smell musty, forgotten, hopeless.

'OK, then,' the major began. 'There's still some unanswered questions about the German nanny.'

Blessed nodded mechanically. 'Gisela. Yes. What about her?'

'The, er, *fondness* between your daughter and the German nanny,' Dalgliesh rasped, ticking off something in his notebook. 'D'you think it was genuine?'

'Gisela is heartbroken. You've spoken to her yourself.'

Dalgliesh leaned forward onto his elbows, looked at Blessed through narrowed eyes. 'I've met a lot of good liars in my time, Captain. I'm not saying that's what this girl is, but, well . . . She's from a pretty *fancy* family, eh? Riding pretty high, eh, before the Third Reich got its come-uppance. D'you understand what I'm saying?'

'She came from a family of academics,' Blessed said with difficulty. The death-image kept flashing back whenever he tried to put his attention on the conversation. 'From what I can gather, they weren't Nazis. She doesn't talk about it much. She's certainly never made a thing of it. Her parents are dead. Possibly killed by the Russians or the Poles during the last winter of the war.'

'Ah. That's not without significance. What I'm really getting at, though, is the fact that the educated ones—the ones who've fallen the farthest, you might say—are often the worst. They resent us most, but because they're clever, they can hide it. Take my word for it! I've come across these cases in Cairo. One minute these natives with their high-sounding degrees will be chatting to a European about the latest literature and what-have-you; the next they'll be plotting to cut his throat and murder his family. It's called "striking a blow against the imperialists", I'm told!'

'This isn't Egypt. And the British here are certainly not imperialists.'

'Germany is an occupied country! And the Germans are a proud breed! Don't forget: this girl was one of the most privileged members of the master race. Her lot thought they were going to rule the world. Now her parents are dead—murdered by the victors, as you just said. She's an orphan, reduced to working as a mere household servant! Ask yourself: Would it be all that surprising if she secretly resented you and your family?'

Keep control, Blessed commanded himself. *Don't pick a fight with Dalgliesh, because he has the power to exclude you from the investigation altogether, and then they might never, ever find Daphne.* 'She's privileged compared with most Germans,' he explained patiently. 'Have you any idea how hard life is for the rest of the population?'

'The minds of the common folk may work along the lines of simple self-interest, Captain. When it comes to these educated wallahs, though, you never know . . .'

The theme of a German plot to murder British soldiers and their families was already one of the major's favourites. Until May this year, he had been with the military police in politically-restive Cairo. Ten days ago he had started his duties in Hamburg. And three hours ago, knowing nothing about the case, or Germany, or the Germans, Dalgliesh had landed in Berlin and taken Blessed's place in charge of the hunt for the boy-murderer—which since this morning had meant for Daphne Blessed. Just—like—that.

'Has she got any boyfriends?' he asked unexpectedly.

'No!' Blessed swallowed hard. 'No. She hasn't.'

Dalgliesh looked at him quizzically for a moment. 'Are you absolutely sure, Captain? She's a nice-looking girl. Doesn't she ever go out?'

'Hardly ever. Twice in the past year. Both times, to the opera. She's very fond of opera.'

'A culture-vulture, eh? Any surviving relatives?'

'One cousin. Somewhere in Bavaria. They write to each other occasionally, I think.'

'No other friends in Berlin?'

'No.'

'We're dealing with a recluse here. A nun,' Dalgliesh grumbled. 'What about the shopping? Didn't she get out of the house to do the shopping?'

'Quite often, I suppose.'

'Ah.' Dalgliesh tensed, like a cat ready to spring. A marmalade cat. 'Now, would she have been involved in the black market, by any chance? I'm told there's plenty of our German employees who are making their fortunes from the ration coupons with which we so blithely entrust them, eh?'

'I think you're making a mistake about Fräulein Bach, sir. I've never heard of a case of a German employee who has hurt or neglected a child.'

There was a lull. Dalgliesh was nodding, the movement tiny but the meaning absolutely clear.

'You have faith in the girl, I gather,' he said drily.

'Yes.'

'You believe her when she says they locked her in the wardrobe in her bedroom, and after that she neither saw nor heard anything of what went on?'

'She had absolutely no reason to help the kidnappers,' Blessed said. 'And if she had, why should she have stayed behind afterwards?'

Dalgliesh sucked in his cheeks. 'It's mysterious,' he agreed. 'But what I'd still like to know—the thing that makes me ask these questions—is, why did these people not kill her along with your driver? Human life is evidently not precious to them . . . D'you understand what I'm getting at, Captain?'

Blessed muttered a soft, held-in affirmative.

'I want you to understand that I will leave no stone unturned!' Dalgliesh concluded. 'Now, the girl will be effectively in your safe-keeping and may be required for questioning at any time. Do you vouch for her good character?'

'Without reservation.'

Dalgliesh noted that down. 'I hope you're correct on that score, I honestly do.' He checked the time. 'Eight o'clock. You must be dead on your feet. You're sure you're happy to go back to Spandau? You're aware that you'll be acting as bait, encouraging the criminals to return and finish the job?'

'Of course. It was my idea in the first place.'

'Right. Just making sure. For the record.' Dalgliesh sighed, closed his notebook. He laid his fountain pen beside it on the table. 'That's that, then.'

'Just promise me one thing,' Blessed said. 'Promise me you'll pay attention to the five empty orphanages that Weiss's men found today. They've all been registered with the city Magistrat and the military authorities, drawing ration cards, allowances, and so on, for at least two years. Especially, check the orphanage in the Bernauer Strasse. It seems to have been abandoned within the past twenty-four hours.'

This was the longest speech he had made in the past twelve hours. By the time he had finished, he felt as if he had spent a bucket of blood.

'All possibilities are being considered,' Dalgliesh said briskly. He glanced at his watch again. 'But our priority at the moment is this so-called orphanage director, and since he could be anywhere—'

Blessed looked at himself through Dalgliesh's eyes. Beneath the civilised façade he fancied he detected the most ancient form of contempt—the primitive, hunter-warrior's lack of respect for a man who fails in his first duty, which is to protect his own. Under the circumstances, the major would be polite to him, even kind, but why should he follow his advice?

Dalgliesh was already on his feet, holding out a meaty hand. The square fingernails were meticulously trimmed, but their colour was that of browned ivory. 'And now I must get on. We shall spare no effort to find her and to arrest those responsible, you can be sure of that.'

'You'll ring the moment there's any news.'

'Of course.'

'I'm available at any time . . .'

'You just get some rest, eh?' Dalgliesh said quickly and a little too emphatically. Then, as if realising he was being unfair, he softened slightly, even allowed his linguistic guard to slip. 'Captain, I'm awfu' sorry about your little girl. It's a shocking thing that's happened . . . You said her mother was on holiday in England. How's she taking it?'

'She's extremely upset. She's returning to Berlin by air tomorrow morning.'

'Well, I've no children of my own, but I can guess how you'll both be feeling. Mind you tell Mrs Blessed we're doing all we can, eh?'

As Blessed left the room, he began to feel a buzzing pain behind his eyes. He wondered how he was going to get through the night without losing his sanity, or taking to the streets with his service automatic.

Gisela was sitting on a hard wooden bench by the front desk, dressed in a thin cotton coat and a headscarf, to all appearances just another hapless German civilian drawn into the net of the occupiers' law. She sat with her head in her hands, still and pale and drawn, and so preoccupied that she didn't even see Blessed approach. She glanced up with a start when he spoke to her.

'We've been told to go home and stay there,' he said.

'You too?'

'Especially me.'

'How awful for you. You look so pale . . .'

Blessed didn't seem to have heard her. 'Lance-Corporal Cave, who was with me when we found you this morning, will also be staying at the Villa Hellman,' he continued in a toneless voice, as if he were explaining the accommodation arrangements for some boring residential course. 'And there'll be policemen keeping an eye on the outside of the house.'

'Yes. Yes, of course.'

'Despite the precautions, there's an element of danger. I mean . . . I *want* them to attack the house, that's the whole point. So if you . . .'

She shook her head. 'I want to be there. I want to know what is happening.'

'Wait here, then,' Blessed said, still showing no emotion. He approached the desk-sergeant. 'Is there anyone left in the repair workshops?'

'I think so, sir. There were several jobs needing to be finished tonight.'

'Make sure Lance-Corporal Cave is ready, will you?'

Blessed went out into the yard, found a couple of mechanics still at work. The lock on the Horch had been mended, though no one had authorised them to release the vehicle. But they knew about Thwaite, who had been a friend of theirs, and they knew about Daphne, and they recognised something about the look in the captain's eye. When he said he had to have the car, there wasn't a soul in the workshop who was prepared to argue with him.

Cave followed them quietly out to the car, with a duffle bag slung over his shoulder containing spare kit and some underwear, his eyes scanning the street, and his pistol in his right hand as if it were a part of himself.

'Are you sure you should be driving?' Gisela said as Blessed opened the front passenger door for her. 'You look terrible.'

'I need a car. I must stay mobile.' He nodded to Cave. 'Get in the back, OK? The door's not locked.'

Blessed manœuvred the Horch through to the Kantstrasse, headed due west into the sunset. On the corner by the Wilmersdorfer Strasse U-bahn station, a crowd had filled the street to listen to one of the American Sector's new mobile broadcasting vans. The RIAS vans provided a vital morale-boosting supply of news and entertainment for Berliners whose own radios had been silenced by the power cuts, and this one's big, roof-mounted speakers were broadcasting Beethoven's Pastoral Symphony. Many listeners had brought chairs onto the cobbles so that they could enjoy the programme in comfort. Children played at the adults' feet. Despite the casual, festive look of the gathering, the underlying tone was one of a shared spiritual experience—a miracle in cynical, materialistic Berlin.

The Horch was forced to slow down to walking pace. Blessed leaned on its horn until the crowds began to part and let him through.

His mind, as he inched his way forward, was a cinema-screen, subjecting him to an uncontrollable, unstoppable, ever-repeating theatre of Daphne's pain and death. He tried to exorcise his demonic visions by concentrating on the real world, the way ahead, the passersby. But each boy lounging with his friends in the shelter of a wall became a gang-member; each shadow in an alley a potential murderer; and each little blonde girl clutching her mother's skirt was Daphne.

Even when he recognised their innocence, momentarily acknowledged his own madness, Blessed still felt only a dull, helpless hatred for them all. He could no longer care about anything that happened here, good or bad. This was no longer his adopted place. His old love of Berlin had turned cold the moment he had returned to Spandau and found that Daphne had been taken from him . . .

He noticed that Gisela had turned her face towards the window. She was crying quietly. Blessed could find no words to comfort her—how could he, when he had none for himself?—and so, like an automaton, he kept driving on through the twilight. Still with her face averted, Gisela wept and wept, all the way back to the Villa Hellman.

Home.

THIRTY-FOUR

AS THIS LONGEST of nights wore on, Blessed's guilt engulfed him, ate at him like an illness. He stood alone at his study window high in the eaves of the house, looking down like a knight in his castle keep—or a suicide about to make his leap. From up here, the garden became a distant landscape, inhospitable and dangerous; its eerie, silver-tinted bushes resembled crouching animals in the moonlight, the lawn a pale square, a catching-sheet.

He turned back into the room with a sudden restlessness, as if movement could help him to escape from his impotence, his self-loathing. All the time he was feverishly willing the phone to ring. Every taut fibre of him screamed for news. Any news. *Lord, let me know the truth about Daff, however terrible . . .*

Lance-Corporal Cave was settled down in the conservatory on a camp bed, minding the access from the garden, while two teams of military policemen in jeeps were parked outside, to cover the front. *Fortress Hellman.* And Blessed was effectively held prisoner here, waiting for Major Dalgliesh to phone, or for a shot to be fired in the street outside. *For something to happen.*

In search of distraction, Blessed's attention wandered restlessly over to the shelf above his desk. It was then that he realised something was wrong, incomplete. He struggled to focus, organise his thoughts. Aunt Lotte's paperweight. *Yes.* His mother with Daff as a baby. *Yes.* His and Harriet's wedding picture. *Yes.* The Steinhuder Meer . . . *No.* The picture of his eel-fishing triumph last year—him holding the fish, Daff with her gap-toothed, trusting grin. *The boy-murderer had come in here and*

334

taken it. Just as he had stolen those photographs from Suzy's room in Moabit.

Blessed stumbled from the room, down the attic stairs and onto the main landing. First he checked his and Harriet's room. Nothing gone. He forced himself to keep going along to Daphne's room. The fear grew as he approached the door, deadening his mind and chilling his heart.

He flicked on the light. He had sat in here for twenty minutes earlier in the evening, after the forensic team had finished dusting for fingerprints, until he could stand it no longer and had retreated to the study. The unnerving thing, then and now, was the way the room looked so normal. Untidy, of course, but with no indications of violence. The abduction must have been over very swiftly. Perhaps that was why he hadn't looked to see if anything was missing. One by one, he began to itemise . . . There was the single red slipper left by the door. The unfinished jigsaw-puzzle of an English woodland glade still strewn on the floor. The copy of *Swallows and Amazons* that Daff had been reading, still open on the bedside table . . . Blessed's eyes moved on to the right of the book, and confirmed his most terrible fears.

For a long time he stood there as if turned to stone, hardly breathing. Then he left the room. Slowly he descended the stairs, walked through to the dining-room, opened the cupboard, and took out a full, virgin bottle of whisky.

'I could not sleep,' Gisela said. 'I heard you moving about down here. I must say, you are not quiet.'

'I don't *feel* quiet. I'd like to scream and shout.' Blessed shifted heavily on the sofa, fixed her with a defiant stare.

'How many whiskies have you had, Captain Blessed?'

'Only three. Well, this . . . this is my fourth. Have a drink yourself if you like. It passes the bloody time.'

She shook her head, pulled her bathrobe tighter around her. 'I suppose you must have something for comfort . . . but, please, what has happened? You weren't like this when we arrived home.'

'You've changed too. You're calm and collected. You were in a bad state then. Crying all the time.'

'The crying helped. I still feel very sad, but I am clearer about things. Now, please tell me what has happened.'

'I found out,' he said unsteadily. 'I found . . . they . . . took our most special photograph. The one on Daff's . . . bedside table . . .'

'The picture of you and her, just the two of you?'

'Yes. Like . . . stealing . . . my—*our*—soul . . . They took the one from my study too . . . but somehow the other photo . . .'

'I understand that this is shocking, that it feels like a violation,' Gisela said. 'But a photograph. Even *two* photographs. What is this significance that you are suddenly so depressed and hopeless?'

Blessed stared down at his half-full glass. He coughed out an ugly, despairing laugh.

'How could you know?' he said. 'The fact is, the murderer also took photographs from Suzy's place. They are obviously . . . fetishes. They play some kind of role in a private ritual before . . . before . . .' He fought to get the words out. *'Before he kills!'*

Then he rose to his feet. He hurled his glass of whisky across the room. The tumbler smashed against the wall, exploding whisky and glass fragments all over the Kreisleiter's expensive flocked wallpaper. Blessed's face, deathly white just a few moments before, flooded with colour. His eyes stared wildly. He was swaying stiffly on the spot, a statue come violently to life.

'Damn my stupidity! Damn my upbringing!' he bellowed. *'Damn my life!* Damn, damn who I am!'

Gisela stood her ground a few feet from Blessed, looking at him calmly and kindly, with just a touch of reproach.

'Why do you hate who you are?' she asked finally. 'Why this self-hate? If you know why, maybe you will be able to continue fighting the murderer. If not, the battle will be lost even before it begins.'

'Don't you understand?' Blessed growled vehemently. *'He kills! He has killed! It means that Daff . . . that Daff . . . oh, Christ . . .'*

'No. We must keep hoping. We must stay strong,' Gisela interrupted him. 'I hear Lance-Corporal Cave coming from the conservatory to see what is going on. I will tell him not to worry. Then I will make some good, black coffee.' She began to move towards the main hallway to intercept Cave. 'Afterwards, you must tell me the real reasons why you think you are stupid, and why you hate yourself so much. That, Captain Blessed, is an order.'

'. . . So you see,' Blessed said. 'So you see, if I hadn't been completely obsessed with the Price case, I would have realised the danger days, even weeks ago.' He drained his cup of black coffee. 'The signs were all there, starting with the scruffy boy who followed you and Daff home that afternoon, even before Harriet left for England. I ignored them. That's the terrible thing: When I spoke to my wife on the phone today and she blamed me, she was right—absolutely bloody well right!'

Gisela leaned over the kitchen table, poured him some more coffee. 'Keep drinking the coffee. And keep talking. I can see why you feel this way now, but the fact is that you always felt like this about yourself, I think.'

'Gisela, I can't—'

'You must not collapse. You must tell the truth. I will help you.'

Blessed hid his face in his hands for some time, breathing hard. Then he looked up. He was still pale and gaunt, but his red-rimmed eyes had begun to regain some of their directness, their penetration.

'I'd like to tell you a story,' he said in a low, harsh whisper.

'I'm listening. I have all night. Neither of us has anything else to do.'

'All right . . .'

His cheroots were still up in the study. He had found some cocktail cigarettes of Harriet's in a drawer here. He reached for one, then decided against it. Virginia tobacco didn't appeal to him, and neither did being reminded of his wife's cocktail-habits.

'Once there was a little boy,' Blessed began. 'His name was James. He lived in a nice, ordinary London suburb. His father, Alan, was a local doctor. His mother had a good, old-fashioned German name—Gertrude. Trude for short.'

'This is your family. You, your father, and your mother, who was German.'

He nodded. 'This little boy adored them equally. You know how small children are—their parents are godlike beings, as perfect, as permanent and unchanging as the moon and the stars. Are you with me?'

'I felt the same way about my own parents. I remember it very well.'

'Anyway, James was seven when he realised something was badly wrong. His parents were very unhappy. He used to hear them at night, arguing—or, more accurately, inflicting pain on each other. His mother was devastated by some mysterious problem, his father contrite over what he called his "weakness". He kept harping on about this "weakness".'

'He had a mistress, yes?'

'Nothing quite so ambitious. Although he was a doctor, he wasn't at all rich, because he practised in a poor area and didn't charge very much. In fact, he often didn't charge his patients at all.' Blessed

337

hesitated. 'No, he had been visiting a local prostitute. But I'm going too far ahead in the story, because naturally little James didn't know any of this, and wouldn't have understood even if he had. He just knew his parents were unhappy and so on . . .'

'You don't have to go on if it's too much.'

'I'm OK.' Blessed's face had returned to something resembling its normal colour. 'A few weeks later, James's world collapsed,' he continued eventually. 'His father was found dead. The coroner's jury returned a verdict of natural causes, but the family wasn't fooled. They knew Alan had killed himself by an "accidental" drug overdose. Things were successfully hushed up. Little James suffered greatly, not just because he had lost his father, but because for a long time his mother was mysteriously ill. Even after she got better she was depressed, and prone to strange behaviour. She sent James to a very strict Church school. Whenever relations between men and women were mentioned, it was as if we had touched something unclean, poisoned.'

'I think the whole thing made her a bit mad,' Gisela murmured.

'Oh, yes. When he was twelve she made him look at a book that contained photographs of all the hideous diseases you got from "doing it" with girls outside marriage. James never forgot that, even when he thought he had . . .'

'All this because of your father?'

'Yes. But I didn't know that until I was much older. That was when James, the future military policeman, solved his first case, the Case of the Disappearing Father.' He was staring up at the ceiling, not daring to look at her. 'My father picked up syphilis from the prostitute, but before he knew he had it, he slept with my mother and infected her too. That was why he killed himself. My mother had to take a long course of sulphur treatment. Penicillin didn't exist then. So, that was why she was fanatically determined I would never "stray".' Blessed forced a crooked smile. 'She succeeded. I'm the last of the Victorians, the man they can rely on never to accept bribes or the offer of a bit on the side . . . I'm Honest Jim, who would never, *never* betray his wife or his family. Not like weak, philandering Dr Alan Blessed . . .'

'It doesn't sound like your mother was much fun in bed,' Gisela commented matter-of-factly. 'Your father decided to pay for his pleasure. Poor man.'

'He certainly paid for it in the end. With interest.'

'So did you. And you're still paying.'

Blessed nodded. 'That's why I couldn't let go of the Price case, I think. The fact is, both Price and his girlfriend had syphilis. He'd given it to her, exactly as my father infected my mother.'

'And so when you found this out, the grownup James was forced to repeat his boyhood quest, yes?'

'Something like that. Anyway, I just couldn't give up.'

'The orphan, determined to find out what the adults had done . . .'

'Come on, really—'

'You were made an orphan. It's true. Or a half-orphan, which is almost as bad. I think such a child who loses his security and happiness like that, he has two choices: he turns into an outlaw or, like you, he becomes rigidly a part of society. But the strange thing is, in either case he is still terribly alone . . .'

There was a pause. Then Gisela sighed.

'This is also why you tolerate such outrageous behaviour from your wife,' she said. 'Because of this rigid indoctrination in virtue and marriage and so on. But it's not important. All that matters is, you must be strong for the fight ahead.'

'Fight? What if there's no point to it. What if . . .' Blessed bit the words off, one at a time. 'What—if—my—Daphne—is—dead . . .'

'Then, orphan or no orphan, you will find the person who did this,' Gisela said with quiet emphasis. 'And you will make sure that he is punished.'

'*Cap-tain!*'

The German accent. The urgent, whispered demand . . .

Blessed tore himself from the turbulent limbo between sleeping and waking. Suddenly he was wide-awake, crouched naked on his and Harriet's double-bed, searching the half-darkness with his eyes. And pointing the automatic he had hidden under his pillow at the slender figure outlined in the open bedroom door.

'*Stehenbleiben!*'

The warning faded on his lips as soon as he identified the intruder. In any case, it was hardly necessary. Gisela knew enough not to make any sudden movements until she was sure he had recognised her.

He laid his gun aside on the bedside table. 'Christ. You gave me a shock. What time is it?'

'It's about half an hour since we said goodnight.'

Gisela took a step forward towards the bed.

'What do you want?' he asked.

She shed her robe in an easy movement, let it drop to the floor. Now she was naked also.

'I think you know very well,' she said in her calm, quiet voice.

'I'm sorry,' Blessed told her finally. He rolled away from her onto his back. 'I'm sorry. I want to, but I can't.'

'It's all right. The situation is not easy.'

'It was a bad idea. How could I even think of it at a time like this?'

Gisela placed her hand on his belly, caressed him lightly, almost absently. 'It was I who thought of it. You needed to be comforted. What could be more natural? Why do you always find an excuse for feeling guilty?'

'Daphne—'

'Yes, of course. But do you want me?'

'Under any other circumstances—'

'You need this, at such a terrible time more than ever. As for me . . .'

'Yes. What about you?'

She looked at him gravely. Her eyes were gentle but unyielding. 'It's quite simple . . . I want you before you see Harriet tomorrow. I want you to bear my mark.'

She was blatant. Blessed had always known that lust and greed could overrule most moral codes, most inhibitions; this was something else, though—something more. With a small shock of wonder, almost awe, he realised how much he still had to learn about the ruthlessness of love.

'Lie back and relax,' she said. 'At least, as much as you are able to.'

And Gisela slowly, thoroughly, patiently coaxed him into life. Then, when she was sure of his hardness, she encircled him with her arms and drew him onto her once again. *Oh Jim liebchen*, she whispered over and over, soft but insistent, like a spring wind rising in the trees, *Oh Jim liebchen I need you and you need this love so badly* . . . In their lovemaking there was simple pleasure, skin-to-skin comfort, but as the climax came closer, and they moved each other towards release, something more primitive and vital took them over. Mutual, lonely desires were transformed into a shared rage for life and its wild affirmation—for their own sakes, as man and woman, but also, in a very strange way that no outsider could ever have comprehended, for Daphne too.

340

Afterwards they lay together, their limbs still intertwined, lips still pressed to lips. A long time passed before they moved apart again.

'I have loved you ever since I first set foot in your house,' Gisela murmured, breaking the silence. 'All that time, I have desired this. It is so sad that it happens under these circumstances . . . but seeing you tonight, in such agony, somehow gave me the courage . . .' She lifted his hand and kissed the fingers lightly. It was as if this were something she had been doing for so long that it was scarcely a conscious act. 'Now, whatever happens, I will have this memory of you. And you will manage to stay strong for tomorrow.'

'Harriet has already accused me of sleeping with you,' Blessed said. 'She has uncannily sharp instincts.'

'Yes. What do you plan to do?'

'I said I would pick her up from Gatow. She's Daphne's mother. I have duties . . .' He read the uncertainty that suddenly clouded Gisela's face. Love was ruthless, it was true, but not entirely shameless. 'I don't regret what we've done,' he reassured her. 'But you have to think about whether you want to be here when she comes home tomorrow.'

'Don't worry,' Gisela said evenly. 'I know it will not help the situation for Harriet to know what happened tonight. I shall be here, and if the necessity arises, I am quite prepared to lie to her.' She took a deep breath. 'What will you do once Harriet is safely established here?'

'That's the other problem. I can't just sit around at home, holding Harriet's hand, waiting for Dalgliesh . . .'

'Do you intend to ring him? Perhaps make sure he follows your advice?'

There was a silence. Blessed thought carefully before he answered.

'I'm not as strong as I'd like to be, but strong enough to do more than that,' he said. 'I may make some phone calls before I leave for Gatow, but they won't necessarily be to Dalgliesh. I shall certainly go somewhere after I've done my duty by Harriet, but it won't necessarily be to the Knesebeckstrasse.'

'Be careful.' She kissed his hand again. 'Please take care.'

'Of course. But I have to do this. I am bound to it.'

'Yes.'

'That's why I can't stay here with Harriet and you. And why I can't talk to you about love. Not yet. The fact is, I don't have a right to anything, not even to life itself, until I've done all I can for Daphne.'

'I understand,' Gisela said. 'And remember this, James Blessed: I will do whatever you want, if it helps you and Daphne. If you need something, all you have to do is ask. You will never have to ask twice. I promise that solemnly to you. No matter what happens between us here, or out in the world, you will never have to ask twice.'

THIRTY-FIVE

THE KINDER WERE WELL INSIDE East Berlin, had been for twenty-four hours. Riese had donated the underground part of an abandoned rubber factory that he controlled somehow, maybe by bribing the Commies. And so after their headlong abandonment of the Kinder Garden, after their anxious, scuttling exodus in safe little groups of twos and threes, after crossing the East-West border and sneaking through the graveyard quiet of the sleeping Russkie-sector, the Kinder had come here to an uneasy rest. Here they had set up camp.

It was a new era—more exciting—and the first big Kinder-meeting of this scary new regime was already under way.

Boss-Kind had chosen as their living-space an echoing industrial cavern, one of the former factory assembly-floors. It had been stripped of its machines by the Soviets, was now empty but for a few rusting brokens and immovables. And this was where he was holding forth tonight.

Most of the Kinder were confused. What about all this killing? And what about the inert bundle that Boss-Kind had brought here this morning in Fatski and Thinski's van, rumoured to be—of all things!—*Kepten Blessed's girlie*? All day and night now, that bundle had been hidden away in a storeroom, unseen by anyone but the Boss.

The slaughter-stories circulating among the tribe were hourly getting wilder. Two different reactions divided the Kinder-tribe. Some were thrilled by the uncertainty, placed in even greater awe of the Boss by his evidently growing capacity for violence. Fearful though they might be, these Kinder worshipped ruthless action. For them it was an addiction, like bootleg schnapps, or chocolate. On the other side,

343

there were doubts—particularly inside the older, cooler heads. They reckoned this violence was too close to home. Big risks were being run! But was Boss-Kind consulting his fellow Kinder? You beddabelieve not!

Everyone—whichever of these camps they belonged to—needed questions answered. Everyone wanted reassurance. The old life was over. Like it or not, they were on the move out into an unknown future. The violence and upheavals, especially leaving the old Kinder Garden in the Bernauer Strasse—most of them could remember no other home—had stirred up murmurings that had somehow to be stilled if the Boss was to stay in control.

From his perch close to the yard door, Benno watched, listened, and kept his own counsel. He knew the risks the questioners were running. He knew that Fatski and Thinski were still lurking in the factory somewhere. There was no doubt in his mind that the Boss was out of his wits. The question was, what to do about it? He would see how the older boys succeeded in their challenge.

'Boss-Kind, *what?*' Banana was saying. 'What are we doing among these Stalin-sucking Commies here?'

Seventeen, tall and slender, liverishly pale and stooped from years of ducking to avoid basement ceilings, Banana had always been close as a shirt to the Boss. Now he was questioning him angrily, in front of the whole tribe.

'Boss-Kind, we know this hideout here is in the Russkie-sector,' Banana continued. 'But justalittle while ago, you tol' us Kinder we would never—no *never*—go back to the Russkie-sector. You tol' us, soon the Kinder go to stay in the Hershey-Zone forever . . .' Banana paused meaningfully. 'But now where are we if not in the gadawlmighdy Russkie-sector? And now *what?*'

Boss-Kind was quiet, so attentive, almost humble. No sign of his blade.

'Ba-na-na,' he began in tones of pure velvet, like he was doing the stroking and Banana was some kind of a dog. 'Real question,' he acknowledged. 'I told you 'bout my change of plan. I told you 'bout the new Kinder Garden in the Hershey-Zone, dollar-plenty and Kinder-safe beyond all belief—'

'Eck, but *when?*' someone growled from the back of the room.

The Boss ignored the interruption. 'You say, *ach scheiss*, take us to the Hershey-Zone *now!* But *first* . . .' Boss-Kind opened his hands. He was now a merchant proudly showing his wares. '*First* . . .' he repeated, 'we got one last deal before we leave, the biggest and the best.

This deal with Riese will give us everylittlething we always wanted! A new Kinder Garden! Sweet dollars in our pockets! Hotdogs every day from the PX! All the promise of the Hershey-Zone!'

The Boss unwisely left a silence, while he paused for rhetorical effect. Banana decided to fill it for him:

'But meanwhile, we are *stuck* yes *stuck* here in the Russkie-sector. And also, *we are on the run*, Boss-Kind! Truly on the run from the Allies!'

Boss-Kind gave this solemn, silent thought. Then he said, in a gentle, hurt voice: 'Since when were we Kinder scared of the Russkies? Old Ivan is *not* so Terrible! Let me tell you—you and all the Kinder—that at this moment, this here Russkie-sector is a haven safer than *heaven*!'

Boss-Kind's voice had dropped to a slow, hypnotic murmur. He was working hard to weave his old magic, to bring the room back under his spell again . . .

Benno was neither entranced by the Boss, nor was he aggressively questioning, like Banana. A lot of the time he was dreaming about the Blesseds' house in Spandau—Daff-nee hop-skip-jumping through that front door with Nannypie, the Kepten and his lady fighting and fucking on that beautiful sofa, with him watching all the time through the window. Daff-nee, he knew, lay in the little shed on the other side of the factory yard. She surely wasn't hop-skip-jumping now. Maybe she never would again. Her fate was another of Boss-Kind's secrets—one that Benno intended to crack before the night was out.

Nevertheless, he forced himself to follow the discussion. It was impossible to sneak out in the middle of such a crucial Kinder-meeting. And he badly wanted to know what happened next in this power-struggle.

What worried Benno was, everything now happened only courtesy of Boss-Kind's friend Riese, the Hat with the famous, supposedly wonderful *deals*. From all the clues he could put together—from Boss-Kind's crazy behaviour with the knuckle-blades, to the sinister activities of Fatski and Thinski, to his glimpse of the wretched Bigman-Panewski that afternoon at Riese's headquarters—his suspicions of this alliance and of this entire move were sharpening by the hour. Benno the Watcher had no idea what to do or how. All he knew for the moment was, he must pay attention.

'Three days!' Boss-Kind announced in his seductive croon. 'Three more days only in the Russkie-sector. Then we begin our flight from Berlin to the Hershey-ruled, freedom-loving West of Germany.

Meanwhile, relax! I guarantee there is no more danger, now that I have fixed that Kep-ten Bless-ed . . .'

'You? *You fix Kepten?* Who are you *kidding?*' It was Banana's voice again. 'You *fix Kepten?* Blessed went for a nice swim in the Havel, good for his health!' Banana continued, piling on the sarcasm. 'So instead you raid his house and do a little soldier-killing, plus some kidnapping. Which means that instead of a dead Kepten, we got the Kepten's *girlie* here. And now we got to run from every Hi-Hat in all Berlin, in case we get recognised as this evil murder-kidnap-gang . . . So, Boss-Kind, you actually fix *what?*'

This was a real challenge. Every Kind held his breath, awaited the inevitable explosion. Just then, the Boss's smile was as cold as a butcher's in Lent. There wasn't a soul in the room who didn't expect his blade to flash out.

But Boss-Kind surprised them all. He leavened the deathly smile with tolerant understanding, injected it with warmth by willpower alone. By a titanic effort, he remained Mister Reasonable, Mister I-Got-the-Answers.

'We aw-w-w-l-l gotta stick together, just like the Kinder always do,' he purred. 'So long as we got the Kepten's girlie, we are holding all the aces in the pack.' He held up a first finger. 'Ace one! Kepten Blessed is *out* of the police. *Schluss*-finished! They send him home! I know this. I know everything.' Up popped a second finger. 'Ace two! If the Hi-Hats find us, we have this precious girlie to get us out of any trouble . . .'

'And if the Hi-Hats don' care about Blessed's girlie? What if they don' care a poor polack's wallet about her, whether she is alive or dead, they just want to catch the Kinder and put 'em in jail—even *hang* 'em?'

This demand came amazingly not from Banana but from Granit. *Granit, he was Palace Guard.* So loyal, Kinder joked that if the Boss told him to eat his own shit, Granit would only ask, 'With a fork, Boss-Kind, or with a spoon?'

'Impossible,' Boss-Kind said flatly. 'You beddabelieve, what you are saying there is out of the question, Granit . . .'

'That don' answer me,' Granit persisted grimly. Granit's strength was his stubbornness. He was slow to reach conclusions, but once his mind had fastened onto something, it didn't let go. 'What if those Hi-Hats come anyway? What to *do?*'

'Then we got that Kepten's girlie. And we got *this.*' Boss-Kind reached into his coat pocket and pulled out a service-issue Webley automatic. 'You see, Granit, we got the Kepten's gun! We took the

Kepten's gun from him as well as his poor girlie. Yeah, and we also got . . .'

How Fatski and Thinski had managed to appear at the bottom of the stairs at just that moment, Benno never knew—not even much later, when many sinister details became clear to him. Maybe they had been hiding close by, in the shadows on the unlit stairs. Maybe Boss-Kind producing Blessed's gun was some kind of signal. Anyway, Boss-Kind grinned, waved to them, as if their being here and disturbing the Kinder-meeting was the most normal, harmless event in the world.

Each of Riese's thugs smiled in his own way back at Boss-Kind: Fatski as tight as if he had a gut-pain, Thinski wide and inviting, like a hungry alligator on the cruise. Each showed his own gun. That made three weapons in the room on Boss-Kind's side, including the Boss's own. Hard odds for the rebels, if real revolt was what they had in mind.

Boss-Kind was preening himself like one of the famous, much-admired peacocks that used to screech the nights away in the Tiergarten years ago, before Point Null and the Russkie-terror, before the brilliant creatures had been eagerly scooped into cooking-pots by bird-lovers of a different kind.

'See?' he declared. 'We are *protected*! With our Kinder-unity strong, with these allies and their guns to help us escape from the blockade-trap that surrounds old Berlin, how can we Kinder fail?'

Banana and Granit both took the hint quickly. Granit sat down, folded his arms and went into himself in the way he did when his strength was no use to him any more. Banana smiled weakly, nodded.

Now that Boss-Kind had a truly captive audience, he would probably launch into an interminable political poem in praise of the alliance with Riese. Benno groaned inwardly, squirmed on the cold concrete that was slowly numbing his behind, and settled down to wait.

Later he would be able to satisfy his curiosity about Daff-nee. Later he would find a way.

In the chill of the hour before dawn, Benno stirred, scratched himself, looked around, letting his eyes accustom themselves to the darkness. Sleeping Kinder sprawled out on the floor, just where they had collapsed into sleep after the Kinder-meeting. His friend Gurkel lay nearby, emitting his usual high-pitched, chuckling little snores. He didn't know where the Wonder was. Probably with the Boss in some other part of the building.

347

He stood up slowly, careful not to knock against his boots, which he had parked just beside him last night, and began to pick his way, barefoot, between the slumbering forms. The soles of his feet made tiny *petch-petch* padding sounds as he progressed, but he knew no one would be woken.

And in any case, why shouldn't he be creeping out in the dead of the night? Was he supposed to pee on his Kinder-friends' heads, or what? This would be his response if anyone questioned his movements.

Benno found himself in a small, cobbled yard surrounded by factory buildings. It was open to the sky several storeys up, and he could see the very first pale streaks of daylight above him. To the right was the derelict men's washroom, the pretended object of his journey, while directly across the yard lay the real one: the door to a store where Boss-Kind had deposited the Daff-nee bundle yesterday, all trussed and immobilised.

First he did the washroom stuff, to satisfy the technical requirements of his cover-story. Then, returning to the yard, he paused as if taking the air. The place was quiet as a cemetery, and he hated it. After a few moments Benno steeled himself, padded over to the storeroom door. On the outside, to his surprise, it was secured only with a simple steel bolt now drawn back.

Battered wood. Cracked. But still stout enough. It was tempting to open the door quickly and steal inside, but caution won out. He searched for a good-sized crack in the door, put his eye to it and stared through into the room beyond.

A shock of instant recognition. Benno thanked his stars he hadn't burst in without preparation, because there, crouched on his haunches in the far corner, open-eyed—maybe in some kind of a trance—was Boss-Kind himself. The Wonder was curled up close to him, asleep like an exhausted puppy. Faint light was beginning to enter the room from an opening somewhere.

Swallowing hard in acknowledgment of his lucky escape, Benno moved round so that he could see what or who was on the other side of the room, on the receiving-end of Boss-Kind's weird stare. And he saw Daff-nee, lying there, half in shadow still, identifiable by a soiled night-dress and a hint of tangled fair hair. Her hands and feet were bound. Since she was half-turned away from him, he couldn't see if she was also gagged. But not a muscle in her body was moving. Something about this stillness was truly terrible.

As his eyes became able to pick out detail on the room on the other side of the door, a further chill ran up Benno's spine, electrified his hunched young shoulders. Boss-Kind had laid his knuckle-blade in front of him, pointing at the girlie-bundle, like a ritual device. And Boss-Kind held a square, shiny piece of paper clutched in his long-fingered hands. A page from a book or a magazine? A drawing? Maybe a photograph? Yes, a photograph! And in the grey, cold light that seeped in through the unseen window, Boss-Kind was smiling.

THIRTY-SIX

A LIGHT, MISTY DRIZZLE was drifting across the apron at Gatow. From where Blessed was waiting on the ground he could hear the drone of engines long before Harriet's plane became visible. Its eventual appearance was dramatic and sudden; the aircraft, a civilian airliner under charter to the RAF, emerged out of the low cloud only a few hundred feet above the runway, with its landing-gear already engaged, and slid awkwardly down through the remaining fall of air.

Once safely down and guided by ground-staff to its haven on the crowded tarmac, the aircraft disgorged its human cargo: a cheerful, though visibly queasy group of German children returning from holidays and stays in sanatoria; pensioners coming back to Berlin from family visits in the Western Zones; military and civilian government personnel. Harriet was among the last to emerge. She wore a smart grey suit, grey hat and gloves. As ever, her instincts had dictated the perfect outfit for the situation, sombre without being funereal. She descended the gangway slowly, staring at Blessed all the way down but avoiding actual eye-contact.

'You're in uniform,' was the first, predictably frosty thing she said to him. There was an exchange of pecks at the bottom of the gangway. 'I thought you'd been sent on leave.' Her make-up was thick, to hide the pallor and the worry-lines.

'The uniform makes it easier to get through the entry formalities quickly. Idiotic, I know, but a fact of life.'

'I'm sure you're right. Any progress while I've been airborne?'

Blessed shook his head. Enquiries are proceeding, and so on. The new man promises to do his best. He specifically asked me to tell you that.'

'Major Dalgliesh, wasn't it?'

'Yes. Officially, it's all in his hands now.'

'And are they capable hands?'

Blessed thought for a moment, then shrugged. 'He's thorough.'

Harriet looked at him in a furious, hurt way, as if he were wilfully robbing her of hope, but said nothing. Blessed picked up her suitcase. They joined the stream of passengers making for the administration building. There was the usual paperwork to be dealt with before they continued on to Spandau.

When they emerged from the other side of the building a few minutes later, the next plane was roaring in to land, and the Horch was waiting at the kerb. Lance-Corporal Cave was in the driver's seat.

'Lord . . . poor Thwaite,' Harriet said. 'Is . . . is that his successor?'

'Not exactly. More in the way of a bodyguard, actually. He's an excellent shot, has performed what they call close-protection duties for VIPs.' Blessed paused. 'I must have protection, they've decided.'

'Christ.'

Blessed put her suitcase in the boot. Cave had been told to stay in the car, to avoid behaving like a servant. 'It's something we need to discuss.'

'What do you mean? Discuss what?'

'The question of your safety. You, as a non-combatant, so to speak.'

He spoke with a harsh realism, even a certain brutality. In his new world of ruthless expediency, where everything was subordinated to the task of finding Daphne, Blessed wanted Harriet to feel all the dangers and problems of the situation. He needed her to be so angry and worried—and so frightened—that she would keep away from him until he had finished what he had to do.

He felt for the agony of this woman he had loved for so long, the mother of his child. But he neither said nor did anything to comfort her, because sympathy might get in the way of the only goal worth striving for. And because he knew that all the pity in Berlin wouldn't bring back Daphne.

The two jeeps were still on duty in the street opposite the Villa Hellman. Blessed explained why they were there. When the Horch

351

stopped outside the front door, Cave got out first, pistol at the ready, and covered them while they walked quickly into the house. Harriet shook her head in disbelief, but she wasted no time getting indoors.

Gisela was in the kitchen. 'Any news?' Blessed asked.

She shook her head. To Harriet she said: 'I'm so terribly sorry, Mrs Blessed. I'm sorry we could do nothing. They had guns, you know.'

'Yes. Yes I know that.'

Harriet seemed cold, withdrawn. Gisela's own manner was perfectly natural, just as she had promised Blessed it would be.

They went through into the living room, leaving Gisela to make some coffee. Harriet lit up her first cigarette, Blessed his umpteenth cheroot. She sat down in an armchair, while he stayed on his feet, paced the centre of the room.

'The place feels so empty,' she said with a shudder. 'And yet it's like a prison . . . How can you bear it?'

'Part of the reason for my staying here is to act as a sitting target. A bait. To see if they have another go at me.'

'You're extraordinarily calm for a man whose daughter has been abducted.'

Blessed shrugged, said nothing.

Harriet glanced towards the kitchen. 'Miss Germany's pretty OK too, by the looks of her. I notice the men who took Daff didn't harm a hair on *her* head.'

'No, they didn't.' Blessed checked his watch, moved towards the table where the phone sat. 'I think I'll ring Dalgliesh, see what's going on.'

He got through to the Knesebeckstrasse. Dalgliesh was out, and so was Weiss, but Kelly happened to be there.

'We're all looking for this orphanage director, sir,' he told Blessed. 'That's all I can say at the moment. Footslogging, records work, things like that. Just keep plugging away until you get somewhere.'

'Have you identified him yet?'

'No, sir. You can't really see his face in any of the photos, can you? Getting people to identify someone just from a description is not easy, as you know. Anyway, Inspector Weiss is organising that side of things.'

'Thank God he's still involved. What about the abandoned orphanages? Have they been thoroughly searched?'

'It's all in hand, sir.' Kelly was becoming more uncomfortable by the moment. 'Look, Major Dalgliesh told us, if you rang we was just to tell you we're working hard, getting out on the streets . . .'

'Mrs Blessed has arrived back in Berlin. She's here with me at the moment. Naturally, she'd like to talk to the major.'

'He's intending to ring her later. I'm sorry, but we're working hard. That's all I'm entitled to say, sir . . .'

Blessed put down the phone.

'He's out but he'll ring. Dalgliesh, that is,' he told Harriet.

'I know perfectly well it's all an illusion, anyway,' she said with an impatient gesture. 'An illusion of *doing* something.' Then she looked straight at Blessed for the first time since her return. 'You may think the fellow's rather unimaginative, but . . . well, to be honest I don't see how he could do any worse than you. Good grief, he might even do better.'

'I told you, I understand how you must feel,' Blessed said quietly. 'I've got no excuses to offer. But nothing changes the fact that I know a lot about this city, and a lot about this case . . .'

Harriet kept glancing towards the windows. She was disturbed by the embattled atmosphere of the place, the presence of Cave in the conservatory and the armed guards in the street outside. All that, and the memories . . . For a moment she came to the verge of tears, but a dab with a handkerchief and a good puff on her cigarette seemed to pull her back.

'I'm not sure you should wait here,' Blessed said. 'Those people who tried to kill me may try again. If they do, and you're with me, your life will also be endangered. Why should Daff lose both her parents?'

'Gillie said I could stay with her and Harry if I wanted to,' Harriet said tentatively. 'If I didn't want to be in the house.'

'When did you speak to her?'

'Yesterday. Before I left. I had to talk to someone . . .'

'I presume she knows everything. Does she also know to keep her mouth shut?'

'Of course she does. I told her how important it was that nothing got into the papers. Neither she nor Harry would do anything to endanger Daphne, surely you realise that?'

'I'm sorry. Anyway, perhaps you should take her up on her offer.'

'Perhaps,' Harriet said. Suddenly she was puzzled, even suspicious. 'And what about you? Where will you stay? And what will you do if I'm not home?'

'I'll base myself here, but . . . well, I owe it to Daphne, and to you, too, to do everything I can to find our daughter.'

'What do you mean? I thought you were under suspension.'

'I can still make myself useful. Freelance, you might say.'

Just then, Gisela entered with the coffee. She handed Harriet her cup, put Blessed's on the table near him, turned to leave.

'Will *she* stay here in the house too?' Harriet asked pointedly.

'Gisela!' Blessed said. 'Just a moment.'

'Yes, Captain Blessed?' Gisela stopped, turned on her heel to face them. 'Is there something else?'

'We both want to know, would you rather stay here or go somewhere else?'

'I will stay here at the Villa Hellman if that's all right with you and Mrs Blessed. Naturally, I'll do everything I can to help during this difficult time. If you would prefer to be alone here, of course, that is your right . . .'

'Thanks, Gisela. That's all.'

'Very nice,' Harriet said when they were alone again. 'Very prim. Impossible to fault, as ever.' She wearily passed a hand across her forehead. 'I'm sorry. I just can't bear the fact that she's all right, apparently none the worse for wear, while Daff's . . . Just as I can't bear you standing there with yet another bloody cheroot stuck in your face, telling me you'll help find Daff, when she wouldn't be gone if you'd been bothered to protect her properly in the first place!'

'I can't make you go to Gillie's. I just feel it would be the best thing. I'm obviously not being much comfort to you.'

'Well, that at least is true.'

'Look,' Blessed said, 'the fact, is I don't intend to sit around here and just wait for Dalgliesh to come up with something. Can you understand that?'

'James, haven't you learned *anything*? After the appalling fiasco—'

'We're all paying for my lack of foresight. Especially Daff. But the fact is, the investigation was progressing well until she was kidnapped.' He paused, searching for the right words. 'You see,' he continued, 'there are certain important aspects of the case that are unexplained, leads that need following up. I know Dalgliesh won't pursue them, because he doesn't have the knowledge or the connections. If I'm wrong, and he can find our daughter, that will be wonderful. But I can't sit idly by and wait for that to happen.'

'You're a *fanatic*!'

'Perhaps. But the safety I intend to risk from now on is my own.' He stubbed out his cheroot in the ashtray by the phone. 'We both know there's no future for you and me, Harriet, but for Daff's sake I'm asking you to consider staying with the Donaldsons. You'll be safe, and Gillie will be far more comforting than I could ever be—'

'I knew it. You're intending to leave me here alone, aren't you?'

'Talk to Gillie on the phone while I'm out. See how you feel then. Obviously, if it weren't for the danger involved, I'd suggest she came over here to keep you company. Until you make your mind up, Gisela will be here.'

'Damn Gisela! She's German! Make me believe Daphne's all right! Go on, you bastard! Tell me my little girl's alive!' Harriet was on her feet now, screaming at him, her eyes streaming tears, balled fists pummelling the air.

Of course he had to try to comfort her, and of course she cried in his arms, even though she hated him.

While Blessed held her, waited for her to calm down, he saw Gisela appear from the kitchen. She glanced in her serious, appraising way into the living room, then walked away again.

THIRTY-SEVEN

THE ORPHANAGE HID BEHIND a plain street door, without a sign, on the northern side of the Bernauer Strasse. It was on French territory, as Blessed had realised as soon as he saw the address. There were two bellpushes outside. One was unmarked, the other accompanied by a very old, dirty brass plaque that announced: '*Dr V Barnhelm, Direktor-Privatwohnung.*' The orphanage director had his own separate apartment.

Blessed mentally tossed a coin, decided to inspect the main orphanage first: that was where Weiss's boys—especially if they were looking for the orphanage director—would have tended to skimp their work.

Using his rank and a mix of bluff and bluster, Blessed had succeeded in getting a key from the city Magistrat's impossibly-overworked child-welfare department. Being a British officer still counted for a lot in Berlin. Not that this particular captain would have baulked at breaking and entering if they had refused his request.

He signalled to Cave to cover him, turned the key in the lock, gently eased open the door.

As usual, the lance-corporal was vigilant, obedient, impassively efficient. Blessed had stopped worrying about watching his own back. He was fast coming to the conclusion that the choice of this man as his bodyguard had been Kelly's last great service to him—in no way diminished by the fact that it had been unintentional—before the sergeant transferred his allegiance to Major Dalgliesh.

The inside of the building was dark and musty. Blessed and Cave entered a wide hallway. A staircase led off upstairs, while on the right was an open door which revealed a kitchen-cum-washroom. A glance inside told them that it was filthy.

Cave wrinkled his nose. 'Gawd,' he whispered. 'You wouldn't keep pigs in here, would you? This was an orphanage? A kids' home?'

'Apparently. The director was last seen some days ago, the kids the day before yesterday, or at least that's what the neighbours told Weiss's people.'

'I can't believe this'd be allowed. Not even with Berlin such a mess.'

'It probably couldn't have gone on for much longer. The city fathers are slowly getting on top of the housing problem. Let's check the other floors.'

In the two dormitories upstairs there were a handful of old iron bedsteads, without sheets or covers, and a few smelly, damp mattresses. At the end of each room hung a battered print of an idealised golden-haired Aryan Jesus preaching to improbably plump, beautiful children. There were no other decorations or ornaments, certainly no toys or evidence of play. Blessed ventured up to the attic and found it completely empty except for cobwebs and an ancient bucket put there to catch drips from a hole in the roof.

They arrived back on the ground floor and stood in the entrance hall.

'D'you mind if I say something, sir?' Cave asked shyly.

'Go ahead.'

'It's not just that this place is bloody filthy. The simple fact is, it doesn't look lived-in. Yet the German police reckon the kids left only the other day! Are you sure we've come to the right orphanage?'

'Absolutely. There were four or five other empty children's homes, but apparently they'd been abandoned some time ago. My guess is they were all part of one racket. Someone was running non-existent orphanages, somehow managing to claim all the rations and allowances for them, pocketing the lot.'

'A hell of a bloody risk.'

'There's always an element of risk in crime, but so long as the rewards are high enough there's always someone prepared to take it.'

Blessed started to move slowly down the hall past the kitchen, looking for further rooms. He tried the cellar door. It was locked. He cursed under his breath, shook the handle. The handle and door alike were flimsy, probably secondhand replacements installed quite recently.

'Of course, Weiss's men said they checked the basement,' he said, 'but I daresay they were in a hurry, eager to get on. Don't you think?'

He lifted his foot and kicked out at the door. It shook on its hinges. Two more kicks and he had it open, revealing a flight of concrete steps. When they got down into the basement, things became clearer. There was, for instance, another broken window. It was perfectly possible to get a good look at the room from outside in the backyard. Blessed decided Weiss's men had probably scrambled down into the yard and checked the cellar by this method.

There was, it seemed, so obviously nothing here.

The cellar was quite big, about thirty feet by twenty. Again the room was bare except for a hopelessly damaged horsehair sofa and a crudely-made table. Blessed had brought a pocket torch with him, and he shone it into all the corners. There was a wardrobe, shoved into the far right-hand corner, and to the side of that an inscription painted in green in laboured gothic script, the handwriting they had taught in the classrooms of the Third Reich. It brought back for Blessed another day, almost another world, when this investigation had been just a job, and when the late Karl-Heinz Panewski's reference to the name of a child-gang had filled him with curiosity rather than sick foreboding. It said in German: *HERE IS NO KINDER GARDEN*.

Blessed moved in closer, keeping the torch pointed at the wardrobe, and found his feet skating on unseen rubbish, including American Coca Cola and German beer bottles. He turned, quietly asked Cave to come closer, handed him the torch.

'Keep shining it on this corner.'

Cave took the torch and did as he was told. There were hand and finger marks on the walls around the wardrobe. Blessed pulled on its doors, which were of cheap pinewood. They were locked. This time he took a few steps, picked up a chunk of masonry lying nearby. On the fourth blow, the lock gave and the doors swung open.

'Torch!'

When the light was directed into the wardrobe, its beam revealed an inner door, solid and steel-lined. A flame-proof bomb-shelter door. Blessed's heart sank, until he saw that it was ajar. The Kinder had trusted the false wardrobe as sufficient protection. In the case of Weiss's men, they had been right.

There were three main chambers on the other side of the door, as far as Blessed could tell. He and Cave explored each in turn by the light of the torch. The first was a small anteroom, containing a decent table and two chairs. The second was a room the size of the cellar they had just left, with chairs and a table in the middle, mattresses arranged around the edge. A dormitory. Nothing here was very clean, but it had obviously been tidied from time to time on a systematic basis. The third room was a kitchen, with a gas cooker and fire, plus a long table. This seemed to be a communal eating place. There was not a soul about. Weiss's men had been right; the building was deserted, including even this secret catacomb. There was a little light from a grille on the street.

'We've found it,' Blessed whispered, standing with Cave in the kitchen.

'Found what, exactly, sir?'

'The Kinder Garden! A criminal named Panewski referred to it. No one believed me when I suggested it might actually exist.' Blessed shook his head in wonder. 'Upstairs, the kitchen and institutional rooms, no wonder they looked so filthy and neglected. *This* was where those boys really lived. This was the thieves' kitchen. The Kinder Garden.'

'Some *kids* built this bunker?'

'They didn't build it, though they've probably adapted it quite a bit during the past few years, since the end of the war. At one time a street entrance probably existed, and they must have sealed that off, to keep homeless refugees from coming in and taking it over.'

Blessed was already scanning the corners of the room for signs of a bricked-up street entrance. 'You realise we're right on the border between the Soviet and French sectors, don't you?' he said to Cave. 'The kids must have been able to come and go at will. The border patrols would have known them, probably never bothered to do spot-checks on their papers, like they would do with other civilians. A marvellous cover for smuggling currency, food, cigarettes . . . and drugs.'

'The French are especially slack too, sir. At least where the Germans are concerned. Their sector would be the perfect place for a fiddle like that. And even if they inspected the place, they'd never find this, would they?'

'Unlikely. Let's go back into the dormitory. I can't see anything in here.'

Returning to the largest room, they searched more thoroughly. Still they found nothing. When they got back to the first room, immediately inside the bomb-proof doors, Blessed was beginning to feel discouraged.

Cave was restlessly playing the torch around the walls of the room when Blessed saw something interesting just to the left of the main staircase. Only when the lance-corporal concentrated the torchlight did he realise that he was looking at a narrow door. It had been painted the same dull grey as the walls, making it all but invisible to a casual glance.

The door, also made of steel, opened onto a narrow corridor about twenty feet long. The far end of this, once a doorway, had been bricked in. That solved the puzzle of the former street entrance. Then Blessed saw a half-open door two-thirds of the way along on the right.

The space they entered could either have been described as a small room or as a large cubicle. It contained a bed, still with a crumpled, dirty sheet on the mattress, an armchair and a low table. There was no other furniture or decoration except for a huge, large-scale plan of Greater Berlin, which was pinned to the table-top like an army general staff map.

Blessed went over to the table, stood for some time there, staring at the city map.

'This must be where the gang-leader used to do his planning. Sending the other kids off to do smuggling-runs, to thieve, to keep watch on all of us at the Villa Hellman,' he said.

'Gives you the willies.'

'Yes.'

There were pieces of torn paper scattered over the plan's surface. Blessed made to brush them off the table, stayed his hand at the last moment. He picked up one piece of paper, noticed that it was photographic paper. He squinted at the others in the torchlight; they were definitely fragments of a photograph or photographs, upwards of twenty pieces. When he shone the torch on the ground, he realised there were even more down there, among the dirt and the cigarette-ends.

'Come over here, please,' he said to Cave, who was waiting in the entrance. 'I want you to hold the torch while I get down on my hands and knees and hunt for treasure.'

He collected all the fragments in his cap. Then he carried them upstairs into the orphanage kitchen, where there was at least a supply of natural light. They cleared the table-top. He tipped the pieces onto it and they set to work.

Whoever had torn the photographs to pieces had done a thorough job, but Blessed knew he couldn't afford to let that defeat him. Their task was considerably helped, it turned out, by the fact that one of the two photographs had been printed on matt paper, while the other was on glossy. Cave concentrated on collecting and fitting together the matt fragments, while Blessed did the same with the rest on his side of the table. They laboured in silence, occasionally sighing when something didn't fit.

Cave was the first to come close to finishing, close enough for him to be able to exclaim with a kind of appalled triumph: 'So! There you are! Not very nice, but clear enough.'

Blessed glanced over at the upside-down photograph. 'Half the top is still missing,' he said.

'But look, sir. You can tell what it is.' Blessed walked round to Cave's side of the table. 'You see,' the lance-corporal said. 'It's a baby. Or I should say, a toddler of about two years old. Some bugger's been drawing across his face with a pencil. Bloody kids.' Cave frowned. 'I'll continue, sir. If you think it's worth it.'

'Oh, I'm sure it is,' Blessed murmured, trying to keep calm but unable to suppress the mixture of anxiety and elation rising within him.

Ten minutes later, the two pieced-together photographs were as complete as they were going to be. Blessed and Cave stood back and surveyed them.

Cave's photograph was of a handsome baby, probably a boy by the length of the hair. The features had been defaced with two violent cross-strokes from a heavy pencil. Blessed's, on the other hand, showed a man and a woman in a nightclub. Someone had drawn a black 'x' on each of their faces too.

'Well, was it worth it, sir?' Cave asked. 'Any idea who these pictures might be of?'

Blessed didn't answer immediately. He lit a much-needed cheroot. Suddenly he was back with the sights, scents, horrors of that morning in June when he had first embarked so blindly on this pursuit. He exhaled slowly.

'I don't know for sure about the baby,' he said eventually, 'but I know about the man and woman in the photograph. They are Corporal Ronald Price and Heidemarie Sanders—also known as Suzy—the murderer's first victims. This photograph was stolen from Heidemarie's apartment in Moabit about a week ago. So, probably, was the other. I think it's of Heidemarie's child. The kid died many years ago, so I'm told.'

'Poor buggers, all of them,' said Cave. He looked around ruefully. 'A miserable bloody place this is, too.'

'Yes,' Blessed agreed. He was still transfixed by what he saw on that table. After a long silence, he turned away. 'We'll have to do our best to keep these intact during the drive back to Spandau,' he said. 'They're important, really important, I'm sure of it. I just wish I knew exactly why.'

THIRTY-EIGHT

As Blessed brought the Horch round the final bend in the drive, he saw that there were two cars outside the Villa Hellman. One was a stately Humber staff car, the other an Opel in the traditional dark green of the Berlin police.

'Visitors from 248 Company,' he muttered. 'Good news or bad?' Harriet had insisted on waiting here until he got back. He hoped she had come to no harm—and herself had harmed no one.

Lance-Corporal Cave leaned across to get a better look. 'That's Colonel Harrison's Humber, sir,' he said. 'See the APM's badge there on the grille?'

'Then we're honoured. I think.'

Blessed parked next to the Opel, got out quickly. The front door was on the latch, pushed open easily. There were unnerving parallels with how everything had been on that other homecoming, when he had found Thwaite dead and Daphne gone. Except that those were official cars parked in the drive, and when he entered the house there were English voices coming from the kitchen.

Kelly was in there with another man from BlessForce, drinking tea. The pair of them put down their cups and saluted. Before Blessed could ask the obvious question, Kelly said: 'Er, Major Dalgliesh is in the lounge, sir. I think you'd better go through and have a word with him.'

So their uninvited guest was the pushy Scotsman from Hamburg. He had even managed to pinch Harrison's car. Not bad going for someone who had been in town for less than twenty-four hours.

'What are you lot doing here, Sergeant Kelly?' Blessed demanded.

'There's, er, been a development in the case, sir. I think Major Dalgliesh had better explain. If you'd like to go through . . .'

Blessed strode into the living room and found Dalgliesh there with Weiss. Gisela was sitting stiffly in an armchair. There was no sign of Harriet.

When they saw Blessed, each of the men reacted in his own way. Dalgliesh, who had been crouched on the sofa, jumped up like a terrier on guard. A growl, even a leap at the newcomer's throat, wouldn't have been out of place. Weiss rose with slow dignity, made a helpless, embarrassed gesture. Gisela stayed where she was, met Blessed's eye in her calm, unreadable way.

'Good afternoon, gentlemen,' Blessed said. 'Might I ask what you're doing in my house?'

'Sergeant Kelly!' Dalgliesh bellowed through the open door. While they waited for the sergeant to come, he said, 'I tried to ring you, but you were out.' He cleared his throat. 'We have a warrant, of course, although we knew you wouldn't object under the circumstances.'

'*Knew I wouldn't object?*' Blessed exploded. 'I do bloody well object! Especially since no one's explained to me what you're bloody well doing here!'

Kelly had appeared in the doorway. Dalgliesh seemed satisfied with the balance of power in the room at last.

'Well, Captain,' he rasped, 'I have to inform you that the Fräulein here is under arrest, on suspicion of trading in illicit substances. Inspector Weiss has explained this to her in her own language, and has also informed her of her rights under military law, such as they are.'

'How long have you been here?' Blessed asked.

'Just under an hour. You've turned up just in time. We were about to take her down to the station.'

'And where's my . . . wife . . .?'

'She was very upset by this latest development. It was the last straw, eh? I must say, I'm surprised you left her here alone at a time like this.'

'There was something I had to do. Is she upstairs?'

Dalgliesh shook his head. 'A friend . . . a Mrs Donaldson . . . kindly came to fetch Mrs Blessed a short while ago. Your wife is now at her house.'

'I'll ring her as soon as we've got this business sorted out,' Blessed said. 'Gisela? What have you got to say?'

'Captain Blessed . . .' she began formally. 'I don't know what more I can tell you or the major . . . I think he is convinced I am guilty.'

364

'So, have you decided that Fraulein Bach is a criminal, Major?'
Blessed demanded, angry as well as sick at heart. 'You'd better have
a darned good reason for this, because you're taking time off *from
looking for my daughter*!'

Dalgliesh smiled grimly. 'You believe this is some kind of a red
herring? Let's see if you still think that after you've accompanied me
upstairs, eh?'

Gisela's room was just as neat as she usually kept it, except that the
bottom drawer of her clothes-chest had been taken out and placed on
the bed. Some underwear had been removed so that they could get at
what lay beneath.

'Take a nice long look at that, Captain,' Dalgliesh said with a wave
of the hand. 'But please don't touch, eh? This is vital evidence.'

The remaining contents of the drawer on the bed consisted of two
ten-pack cartons of Lucky Strike cigarettes—enough, if traded on
the black market, to feed an entire German family for a couple of
months—and a plump manilla envelope that had been slit open,
revealing a trickle of white powder.

'Is that what I think it is?' Blessed asked.

The major nodded triumphantly. 'The cigarettes speak for themselves, but the stuff in that envelope there is morphine—badly
adulterated, I'll grant you, but nonetheless worth a fortune if you
know where to hawk it.'

Blessed got slowly to his feet, his mind racing with possibilities, all
of them horrifying. 'What made you decide to search Gisela's room?'

'A tip-off. Anonymous.'

'German?'

'Yes. Some underworld type. He helped us bag the orphanage
director, too, for what it's worth.'

'Oh? What do you mean by that, Major?'

'By the time we got to the old bugger—in some hell-hole of a
cellar in Schöneberg—he was in a coma, suffering from a massive
drug-overdose. He's in a military hospital near here, still unconscious
and apparently likely to remain so. He's been turned into a vegetable,
Captain—we may safely assume, through injecting himself with the
same morphine that your Fräulein what's-her-name keeps so handy
around her boudoir.'

'Her name is Bach. Gisela Bach. And there's a strong possibility she's
been framed,' Blessed said coldly. 'These items were probably planted
here two nights ago when my daughter was kidnapped.'

'Can she prove it? Can you, since you feel so strongly about the matter?'

Blessed shook his head. There were many reasons he could never explain to Dalgliesh; reasons that would only make the situation worse. 'She would have had nothing to gain, and everything to lose—'

'I can't waste time on such speculation,' Dalgliesh interrupted. 'As you yourself said, our priority is the search for your daughter. This arrest has Colonel Harrison's personal approval, and the commandant's office is being constantly updated on our progress.' Suddenly he seemed to become sympathetic, confiding. 'My dear Captain,' he said. 'I didn't take this step lightly, I want you to know. When we got the tip-off, we checked on the whereabouts of the orphanage director first. That proved correct—he had his ration-card on him, plus a tidy sum in dollars—and so we knew for certain that the information had been supplied by an insider.'

'You had his ration-card? What was the address?'

'Oh, somewhere in Wilmersdorf,' Dalgliesh said. 'One of the empty orphanages. Been empty for six months apparently, so what's the use? Anyway, the point is that then—and only then—did we come and search Fräulein Bach's quarters, with results that are staring us both in the face. Good God, this could be our breakthrough, can you not see that?'

'It could also be a calculated attempt to mislead. Think about it: why should someone give you these tip-offs except to put you off the scent?'

'Well, the fellow who rang said he had a contact in the gang.'

Blessed's heart leaped. He forced himself to abort the hope before it could form, take on life, cause pain.

'Does he know where Daphne is? Does he know what's happened to her?'

Dalgliesh cleared his throat, obviously searching for the right words. 'Perhaps I shouldn't be telling you this,' he said. 'I don't want to raise your hopes unduly, but our informant assures us that your daughter is alive. He doesn't know where she is, but that much he claims to be certain of.'

'He would tell you that, wouldn't he? It's standard practice in kidnap cases. No live hostage, no bargaining counter.'

Dalgliesh refused to respond. 'I didn't tell Mrs Blessed about this,' he continued. 'I thought it best not to excite her further at that stage. As her husband, and as a professional, you're doubly qualified to decide if she should be informed. I leave the matter to your discretion.'

Blessed nodded. He needed to concentrate on this duel with Dalgliesh, because he knew it was about to enter a critical stage.

'Has this supposed informant actually given you any names?'

'No, but—'

'OK. Then did he tell you anything about the make-up of the gang? How many of them, what their motives might be, that kind of thing?'

'No, no. But that's hardly surprising. You know how these grasses operate. They're canny, and they're cowardly.'

'Look, what do you think he's up to? What does he want?'

'A reward, of course,' Dalgliesh declared, as if only a fool would need to ask. 'You'll be pleased to know that the city commandant has authorised us to offer the fellow a very substantial sum—on the strict q.t., naturally. If the nanny tells us what we need to know, it may enable us to wrap up the case. If she is an accomplice it would explain a lot. But our informant also said he was still endeavouring to find out your daughter's exact whereabouts.'

Even if I didn't know Gisela Bach, Blessed told himself, I'd still give good odds that this is all part of the frame-up. But I wouldn't hazard my daughter's life on it. If I were in Dalgliesh's shoes, I'd have to do what he's doing and follow it up.

'All right, Major,' he said, realising that further struggle was pointless. 'You've brought me up to date with your work. Now I think it's time I confessed to you why I went out earlier today, and exactly what I did.'

Standing there in Gisela's room, with everyone still waiting downstairs, Blessed told Dalgliesh about the orphanage in the Bernauer Strasse, about the underground catacomb where the Kinder had lived, and finally about the two torn-up photographs and what they showed.

It was obvious that Dalgliesh didn't know exactly what attitude to take to the evidence—or to the fact of Blessed's freelance detective work.

'Well, you can't expect a man, especially a policeman, to sit on his hands when his daughter's been kidnapped,' Dalgliesh admitted in a reasonable fashion that somehow also managed to convey the simmering anger beneath. 'However, there's an extremely vexing question of interference with evidence here . . .'

'I'm sure the photographs are important. They provide us with a key to the killer's state of mind.'

The Scotsman's face was slowly turning puce. 'They've also got yours and that lance-corporal chappie's fingerprints all over them now!' he barked. 'And so, presumably, has everything in that cellar you just told me about!'

'So far as the orphanage is concerned, I thought of it yesterday,' Blessed answered calmly. 'I told you. Yesterday. And nothing was done.'

Dalgliesh's eyes narrowed. He knew that what was at stake here was power, not whether Blessed's advice had been right or wrong. 'I've got every sympathy for you, Captain, I really have,' he said slowly. 'But I'm in charge of this case now, and I intend to stay that way. I want—I demand—your word that you won't meddle in this way any more! Give me your word.'

'How can I do that?'

'Because, Captain, otherwise I'm afraid I shall have you put under house arrest. You'd better realise that this case is not just a personal tragedy for you and your family. It has ramifications. Real *ramifications*. I have a job to do, and I warn you, if I find myself crossed I can be a bastard. A twenty-four carat, unfeeling bastard.'

The two men stared at each other for fifteen, twenty seconds. Dalgliesh had scaled the greasy pole of promotion by being prepared to carry out his orders at all costs. The humiliation of a middle-class officer who got in his way would count as a luxury. The major might not be a deductive genius, but he was tough all right, and he meant what he said, Blessed decided reluctantly.

'Very well, Major,' he said stiffly. Don't overdo the reluctance, but don't make it look like he's won an easy victory, he told himself. Just enough resentment to make things seem sincere.

'If I ever suspect you of breaking, or undermining, any aspect of this undertaking . . . well, I guess we both understand the inevitable consequences, eh?'

Blessed nodded. Like many proletarian toughies, Dalgliesh had a sneaking respect for 'gentlemen' such as himself. What is more, he probably harboured the romantic notion that when 'gentlemen' gave their word, they could be trusted to keep it. Blessed hoped so. He dearly hoped so.

'I'd still like to ask you what you intend to do with those photographs, though,' he said, to keep up the impression that he was reluctantly handing everything over to the major and finding it very hard to let go.

'I'm a questions-and-answers man, to be frank, Captain,' Dalgliesh said with a sigh, almost companionable again now that he had got his way. 'So far as those photographs are concerned, naturally I shall send them over to the lab, all the usual things. Every little helps. The building in the Bernauer Strasse will be carefully examined. But . . . well, you can't interrogate a picture the way you can a man . . . or a girl, eh?'

'I'm convinced they're important,' Blessed pressed him.

'Perhaps you're right,' Dalgliesh said. 'Just as you may be right about the Fräulein here's being "set up". But . . .' He smiled with sly satisfaction. 'On the other hand, what if the *photographs* were planted, as you put it? What if it is all an attempt to lead *you*, and thereby *us*, up the garden path. Have you thought of that one, eh, Captain? Have you?'

THIRTY-NINE

ENTERING THE ENCLOSED YARD, Benno heard raucous shrieks of laughter coming from the storeroom, and he hesitated.

Boss-Kind hadn't been seen around the factory-refuges for a couple of hours. So the watcher had decided this was the time to satisfy his curiosity about Daff-nee's fate. But was the Boss really out? Or maybe he was already back from his trip, returned for some different kind of amusement.

Benno almost retreated back to the main building. There was such a cutting-edge of cruelty in what he heard. But his curiosity once again got the better of his caution. He stepped over there as quietly as he could. He noticed that the door was unbolted again. He reached it, bent down to the same spy-crack he had used before. And he looked.

The girlie-bundle was still in the corner. She moved. Immobilised but alive. Looming over her were two figures. Not Boss-Kind. Absolutely not the Wonder.

Benno quickly fixed on the identity of one of the figures. It was Solo, a brawny fifteen-year-old who often hung around in the guardroom. Solo was known to be a drooling admirer of the Boss, and of his recent high-violence tendency. His big problem lay in the fact that he had polio as a baby and was pretty lame in his left leg as a result. This was why, Solo complained, he was never allowed to go out hunting with Boss-Kind and the other big Kinder. His friend went by the Kinder-name of Bug. As skinny and dark as Solo was big and fair, Bug also worked mostly on guardroom duties because he wasn't quick or strong. But they both had vicious reputations—no less because there was nothing heroic about their roles in the Kinder-tribe.

370

Solo was doing the actual girlie-baiting. His sidekick, Bug, a stick in his hand, was egging him on. The big boy was just two or three feet from where Daphne lay, standing with his feet splayed, swaying and throwing feral grunting sounds in his victim's direction. He half-turned as Benno watched, revealing that the front buttons of his pants were open, and his small but active extra limb of a prick was exposed, twitching with each jerky movement of his adolescent body. And all the while they were both laughing fit to bust—the same, ugly sound that had alerted Benno when he had first come within earshot.

Benno pulled open the door and moved forward. Exactly why, he wasn't sure, but in a couple of moments he was inside the storeroom, feeling unaccountably clear and light-headedly *right* in a way he had never quite felt before.

Solo spotted him, took his prick in one hand, waggled it enthusiastically at Benno by way of greeting.

'Showing that English girlie a special bit of Old Berlin, that's what, little Benno!' he boomed. His crony Bug guffawed obediently. 'Maybe she never saw a Kind's *Schwanz* before, eh?'

Bug subsided into helplessness because he thought this was so funny. Still gripping his prick, Solo started to caper clumsily like a drunken folk-dancer, facing first to Daphne, then back to Benno. Maybe they thought he wanted to join in the game. Certainly they were weakened by hilarity, and not expecting any prompt, definite action from a Kind so much younger than themselves.

Still without saying a word, Benno took two steps, grabbed the stick from Bug's hand and was lunging at Solo, disregarding the fact that the fifteen-year-old stood a good head taller than himself and was twice as broad.

Furiously but with intense, solemn concentration he started thwacking at the insolent pink snake that was bobbing outside Solo's trousers. Solo jigged away towards the other corner of the room, his escape slowed by his limp, but his stubby fingers hastily tucked his prick back under cover with surprising deftness. All the while, Solo was broadcasting a mixture of ripe curses and wild threats to keep Benno's stick at bay.

To tell the truth, Benno was surprised—and impressed—by his own violence. He dealt a smart whack at Bug, who was non-too-effectually grabbing at him from his other side. The blow struck the Kind four-square on the breastbone, causing him to let out an agonised croak and withdraw, clutching his chest and gulping like a drowning man.

371

Silence fell. All you could hear was Bug's choking struggle over by the door. And, for the first time, the sound of shallow, half-stifled breathing coming from Daphne Blessed. Benno glanced at her. Her eyes were wide open but somehow no longer seeing, like a blind beggar's. Her skin was corpse-waxen, her hair greasy, and she stank of all the familiar fear-smells.

Then Solo said in an aggrieved voice, treacly with feigned innocence: 'What is *wrong*, Benno? It's just the English girlie and us playing . . .'

Benno didn't know what to say. He had a problem. He couldn't criticise them directly for what they had been doing. That would be embarrassing, against the code, maybe even dangerous. In the Kinder-world, if you wanted to show mercy to an outsider, then you had to dream up a cold-blooded *practical* explanation why they shouldn't be treated bad.

'You think Boss-Kind will give you a medal for waving your *Schwanz* around,' he said finally. 'What we have here is *serious* Kinder-business. Maybe, if I tell him what you did to his precious insurance, Boss-Kind might just give you *ach scheiss* so quickly *award* you a taste of that free-flashing blade of his . . .'

Bug was still having trouble, still clutching at his chestbone, but he could get a few words out now. '*Du Arschloch*, Benno,' he panted. 'Only an asshole talks to equal Kinder like that in front of a girlie . . . Maybe we tell Boss-Kind *that*, too . . .'

Out of the corner of his eye, Benno saw that Solo was slowly starting to manœuvre his way forward, getting ready for a counter-attack revenge-lunge. Benno braced himself, took a firm hold on the stick.

'Maybe *what*, Bug? Maybe *what*, Solo and Benno?' The piercing accusation sucked the life out of the room, stopped them all in their tracks. '*Maybe you tell me what you are doing here?*'

Boss-Kind towered in the doorway, eyes blazing. As he spoke, he had his right arm thrust out towards the terrified Kinder. On the knuckles of his right hand gleamed his famous blade, bared and ready for action.

'*Explain.*' He took a slow, deliberate step forward. '*Yes. Explain this to me. NOW!*'

Of course, the Boss had been listening at the door for some time. He knew the situation. And he wasn't really interested in hearing any explanations—only in enforcing his will.

He told them all to stand exactly where they were, went over and crouched by the bundle. There was the same bizarre tenderness Benno

372

had seen during the night in the way he touched the girlie, stroked her face. Benno noticed that she had shut her eyes now, and that her mouth was a tight line of imploded fear. Boss-Kind didn't seem to mind. Eventually he got to his feet, leaving her where she lay, and faced the boys. He was no longer smiling.

Solo had got himself and Bug into big trouble. It counted as tribal folk-knowledge that the Boss never went with girls, or for that matter with boys. He was in fact liable to be frighteningly unpredictable if faced with the sex-frolics and general gawky *sexuelle Schweinerei* that other adolescents indulged in. It was one of the Boss's particular oddities.

'Kiss that girlie,' Boss-Kind said.

Solo was looking at the knuckle-blade. 'Kiss?'

'*On . . . her . . . face.* And say *sorry*.'

The Kind with the game leg lurched over, his face pink with humiliation and his eyes flickering with fear, and he got down. A last look at the Boss for confirmation.

Boss-Kind nodded.

Solo pushed his mouth onto her forehead. '*Sorry*.'

After he got back on his feet, the Boss beckoned him over.

'You did it wrong. You did it wrong.'

'Wrong? But Boss, I—'

'You said *sorry* to that *girlie*. But you were supposed to say it to *me*!'

'*SORRY! SORRY!*'

But the blade snickered out and the next moment Solo clutched his face and groaned. Blood seeped between his fingers from his cut cheek.

'You,' the Boss said quite calmly to Bug. 'Now you kiss and ap-ol-og-ise.'

Bug hastily ducked through the ritual. He didn't peck, he almost slobbered. Girlie twitched in helpless horror. And then he stood and squeaked at the Boss, salaaming like a slave, '*SORRY! SORRY!*'

'Come here.'

And Bug did. He stood quaking within the Boss's reach. And waited.

'You're too small to be cut, Bug,' said Boss-Kind eventually. 'You can go help old Solo, who doesn't know how to behave. Help him all you can. And tell everyone what happens when you tamper with my girlie . . . *MOVE!*'

He tested the edge of his knuckle blade with intense professional concern as he waited. 'You need to say sorry too, Benno?' he asked after Bug and Solo had gone.

'Maybe for being curious, Boss-Kind,' Benno said. His hands were shaking. 'You see, well, I heard those noises of Solo and Bug . . .'

'*I know.*'

'What?'

'I saw from upstairs, from a window. I just finished seeing Erich. I heard the noise, I saw you go in, and so down I came to see what was going on.'

Benno nodded. Nothing he could say or do would make this better or worse than Boss-Kind had already made up his mind for it to be. He knew that.

'Brave. You are brave, Benno,' Boss-Kind said.

Suddenly he smiled. He snapped his blade back into its knuckles, slipped them off and returned the closed weapon to his coat pocket. He looked down at the girlie-bundle thoughtfully.

'Trust,' the Boss muttered. 'This problem . . . you can' be the Watcher on the Kepten any more, because he saw you . . .' He looked up shrewdly at Benno. 'Can I trust you?' he demanded.

'Trust? Boss-Kind, yes! *Ach scheiss*, you know you can . . .'

'Yes!' The Boss nodded. 'Then,' he said in his efficient, I'm-the-leader voice, 'you will help me. I am too busy to mind girlie. I gotta go out. I gotta see Riese . . . I gotta plan . . . So *you*, my little watcher, will mind girlie . . .'

'Me? Mind Daff-nee? In this room?'

'Correct, Benno-*liebchen*. Just as girlie is, she will stay, until I am ready. She is our *guarantee*, our *insurance*. And you will be her *jailer*. This is now your *job*. See what a reward you get for your *curiosity*!'

This the Boss seemed to think was funny. He snorted with amusement, pointed to the stick that was still in Benno's hand.

'Yes, my little soldier, you will protect the body of my girlie. And if anyone else comes, and they won't pay you any attention, then you call for the Boss—and *I will cut 'em like I cut Solo!*'

Boss-Kind shut the door behind him, leaving Benno alone with just the light from the street, and girlie. He crouched down on his haunches, resting the stick on his knees. What now? he thought with mingled fear and fascination.

In the corner there was a tiny, gasping cry. He looked over. Girlie was choking on her gag. There were tears rolling down her cheeks.

FORTY

BLESSED SAT ON THE SOFA in his living room, the glass in his hand full of iced lemon-tea. Whisky, the great temptation, had stayed on the forbidden list since last night. He was looking through some notes when the doorbell rang.

The lance-corporal appeared from the kitchen to answer it, gun in hand. Blessed heard him call out, 'Who is it, please?' He didn't catch the reply, but eventually the door opened and there were voices in the hall. The visitor was Manfred Weiss.

The Inspector hovered on the threshold, uncertain, but still smiling his worldly, all-comprehending Berliner's smile.

'I hope I'm not intruding, James,' Weiss said, 'but I had no chance to talk to you when you arrived home this afternoon—and afterwards, of course, it was my duty to escort Fräulein Bach to the military police station.'

Lance-Corporal Cave was still standing close behind him.

'You can get back to your Glenn Miller,' Blessed said.

The lance-corporal nodded, wandered off back to the kitchen, where he was listening to dance-band music on the Forces' Radio.

'I'm surprised to see you, Manfred,' Blessed said. 'And pleased, it goes without saying.' He offered Weiss a cheroot, which the German accepted with a rueful grin. They both sat down. 'Well,' Blessed said quietly, 'are you here because you have news for me?'

Weiss shook his head. 'Not so far as your daughter is concerned, I'm sorry to say.' He paused. 'I have been sitting in on Fräulein Bach's interrogation, actually.'

'How is that going? And how is she holding up?'

Weiss made a so-so gesture. 'She continues to deny everything. I am impressed with her dignity and her consistency—or is it just her barefaced cunning? Everything depends on your point of view, doesn't it?'

Blessed felt almost ashamed of the intense relief that flooded over him. 'Is Dalgliesh going in hard or soft?' he asked.

'What do you think, James?'

'Well, I'd guess hard is the only way he knows.'

Weiss nodded.

'But he's still getting nowhere. Well, that doesn't surprise me. I'm pretty sure she was framed, Manfred.'

'Perhaps.' Weiss's expression gave away nothing of his personal opinion. 'Such things happen. Not very often, but . . .'

'So what else is Dalgliesh up to? Any change of mind about the Kinder Garden?'

'I have done my best to convince him, but the man can't be rushed. The forensic people are scheduled to visit the Bernauer Strasse tonight. Major Dalgliesh himself may inspect the place tomorrow—"to get the feel of it", so he says.'

'He's obviously just going through the motions. What's he done about the photographs I found?'

'The fragments have been sent to an RAF laboratory to be reassembled and rephotographed. I have no idea what he intends to do with them then.' Weiss made an unmistakable gesture of contempt. 'File them, maybe.'

'You don't think much of Dalgliesh, do you?' Blessed said bluntly, deciding it was time to move things along.

'Ah . . .' Weiss checked that the lance-corporal was out of earshot. 'I will tell you the truth. He is not a bad man, in his limited way not a bad policeman, but I feel he is out of his depth. He's under pressure, so he's looking for simple solutions, quick breakthroughs . . .'

'He's looking for a conspiracy. When you don't really know the *why*, you're tempted to invent it.' Blessed sighed. 'God knows, I've tried to get inside that boy's head . . . and I still haven't worked out his reason for killing Price and—maybe more to the point—Suzy in such a frenzied way. So, why should Dalgliesh be able to make sense of things?'

'He will not do that. Not in months,' Weiss agreed. 'It will take him a week to accept the conclusions we arrived at days ago.'

'I'd rather been hoping he might listen to you, at least a little.'

Weiss snorted disdainfully. 'A little? Oh yes!' He crooked his index finger and thumb together. 'This.' He squinted at the infinitesimal gap between them. 'This is how little he listens.'

'The prospects sound bloody hopeless.'

'They are not good, it is true.'

'No more word from this mysterious "informer"?'

'Not a peep.'

There was a silence.

'And how is Mrs Blessed?' Weiss asked. 'A truly terrible day for her . . .'

'After you had gone I rang the place where she's staying. The doctor had already given her a sedative.'

Weiss stared at his battered brogues, puffed thoughtfully away on his cheroot, as if he were waiting for a signal.

'Why did you bother to come all the way out here, Manfred?' Blessed asked softly. 'Just to tell me what a cock-up they're making of looking for Daphne? Or should we be discussing something more concrete?'

Weiss didn't answer immediately. He looked at the piece of paper on which Blessed had been writing notes.

'You are still having thoughts about the case, I see.'

'I can't help it. One has to do something . . .'

Weiss nodded slowly. 'I'm glad your morale is still strong.' Once again he glanced towards the kitchen, to ensure that Cave was still in thrall to the slow, smoochy arrangement of 'Stardust' on the radio. 'James, I came here to find out what your plans are,' he said. 'Because, if you have plans to continue this investigation alone, I am prepared to help you to the best of my ability. Do you understand what I am saying? Do you know what it means that I, an old-fashioned Prussian civil servant, make this offer to you?'

Blessed looked at Weiss carefully. 'Yes, I do,' he said. 'And I'm very grateful. The trouble is, I don't know what you or I *can* do now. I've reached a dead–end. I'd hoped I could persuade Dalgliesh to make the Kinder the focus of his investigation, but after what happened today with Gisela, he's not paying much attention to my opinions.'

'I know,' Weiss said. 'This is why I came here. First, to tell you the worst so far as Dalgliesh is concerned. Then, softly-softly, to find out if you still intend to continue with your own investigations . . .'

The phrase *your own investigations* hung in the air for a moment before Blessed broke the silence.

'I've promised Dalgliesh I won't interfere any more.'

'I know that. He told me. I had little doubt that you lied to him, to get him off your back. I would have done the same in your place.'

'You're saying you're prepared to help me if I work on my own, unofficially, against Dalgliesh's orders.'

'I am at your disposal, professionally and personally, in every way.'

'What about the boys in your team? Can we use them too?'

'Harder to arrange. I'll do what I can.'

Blessed looked at Weiss appraisingly. 'You're taking a big risk.'

'Perhaps. But I know you won't give up, James. You are probably the most obstinate man I have ever met, in a profession full of obstinate men. So . . . I tell myself, since you will go ahead anyway, I should come along for the ride. And if we were successful, hah! I might even find myself promoted to a permanent job with the British!'

It was typical of the man, Blessed thought, to lay a cynical gloss on an essentially sentimental gesture, just so that no one need feel embarrassed.

'Well, I must go, James. When I made my excuses, I told Dalgliesh I would be away just for an hour. Best that I keep him happy for the moment, I think.'

Weiss got to his feet. Blessed stood too, and after they had shaken hands in the formal German way Weiss insisted on finding his own way out.

Blessed stayed where he was for a while, listening to the cosy blare of Cave's dance music. Then he went back to his notes. Before Weiss had arrived, he had been writing down everything he could remember about the night before last, when the boy-murderer had tried to kill him and Daphne had been abducted.

Now he decided to read through the orders he had given to Weiss and Kelly that night. 1. *Weiss to provide mug-shots for me to go through*, he had written. Difficult to do that now, he thought. 2. *Weiss's men to check orphanages*. That had been done, and it had yielded the Kinder Garden and the photographs. Which Dalgliesh seemed set on ignoring. 3. *Kelly to ring American CID, Cptn Appleyard, to check on arrests of youths for drugs etc*. Now that was something Blessed could follow up on. His office exchanged a lot of information with Bernie Appleyard's. They had met from time to time in the course of their work. He liked him, though Appleyard was a little talkative for his taste. For present purposes, though, that garrulousness could be turned to positive advantage.

Ten minutes on the line to the CID headquarters in the American sector drew a blank. Captain Appleyard was out of the office, and they didn't know where he was. They didn't give out officers' home numbers under any circumstances, they said. Not even to someone who claimed to be with British SIB.

Blessed put down the phone, stared at the wall. He had never become chummy enough with Appleyard for them to exchange home numbers. He tried to think of someone who would know where to find Appleyard, and remembered that he had last met the CID officer socially at one of the Donaldsons' soirées, seven or eight months ago.

He was grateful that it was Harry Donaldson who answered the phone, and not his wife. Gillie had been extremely frosty when he had rung earlier.

'How bloody all this is, Jim,' Donaldson said awkwardly. 'I say, you haven't got any news, have you? If you were wanting Harriet, I'm afraid she's still asleep . . . the quack said we mustn't wake her for a while yet. I think she'll be staying here. For tonight, at least.'

'That's probably the best idea. Anyway, there's no news. I wish to God there were. No, what I need is help. To be more precise, I need a phone number.'

'Ah yes,' Donaldson said, sounding a little disconcerted. He always found directness unnerving and unEnglish. 'Well, fire away.'

'You had a man named Appleyard, an American CID officer, to dinner when Harriet and I were round, oh, some time before Christmas. Do you remember?'

'Yes, yes. A nice chap. Is this to do with finding Daphne?'

'Yes. I'm doing a little private information-gathering.'

'Absolutely, dear chap. Wait a minute. I'll nip upstairs and fetch my little black book.'

Some time later, Donaldson came back to the phone, gave Blessed Appleyard's phone number and address. 'And if that doesn't work, I'll tell you he usually hangs around the Tabasco of an evening. He has a taste for big blondes who don't wear clothes, and at the Tabasco they're the house speciality.'

'Thanks a lot, Harry.' Blessed was about to ring off. Then he asked, because the information could be crucial, 'Does anyone else know about what happened to Daphne? Have the rest of the press been briefed?'

'No. So far as I'm aware, I'm the only journalist who knows, and I'm not going to blow the whistle, so don't worry.'

'Well, thank God it's not going to be all over the papers.'

'No chance of that,' Donaldson said. 'The powers-that-be know that I know, and they've already been on the phone to me, making blood-curdling threats about what'll happen if there's a leak and they trace it to me.' He paused. 'Jim,' he continued eventually, 'I daresay you're in a hurry, but if you want my personal opinion, I think they're afraid. They're afraid that if the story were to break in Fleet Street—you know, "little English girl abducted in wicked Berlin"—it might cause a big wave of ill-feeling against Germans, thus undermining the ordinary British taxpayers' support for the airlift, which last is obviously vital, because it's costing them a bloody fortune. Do you see what I'm getting at?'

'Yes. I see only too well what you mean.'

Blessed tried to sound calm, accepting, but his mind was seething. He recalled Dalgliesh's threatening Glasgow snarl: 'This case has *ramifications* . . .' It all began to fall into place, fuelling his determination to go on alone.

So the British authorities wanted to sweep this incident under the carpet, Blessed thought. Of course. Donaldson, who hid a shrewd mind under that deceptively casual manner of his, was probably right: If Daphne's kidnap were to be made public, it could cause a strong wave of anti-German, anti-Berlin feeling. And if that happened, any suggestion that Britain should make major sacrifices to save Berlin would not be enthusiastically received. Unless it could be pinned on the Soviets, of course. Perhaps that would be Dalgliesh's new theory, that the orphanage director and Gisela were Communist agents, out to undermine the trust between the British people and the people of Berlin.

Blessed heard Donaldson let out a heavy sigh over the line. The journalist had misinterpreted his silence.

'Christ, I'm sorry, Jim. I've upset you, haven't I? I shouldn't be talking politics at a time like this. What a bloody awful mess. Our hearts go out to you and Harriet both. So I'll just shut up and say that if there's anything else I can do . . . If you need a sympathetic ear, or just a good stiff drink and some company, all you have to do is give me a ring.'

'It's all right, Harry. You haven't upset me. But I think I'd rather keep busy,' Blessed said. 'We'll find Daphne one way or another, at least if I have anything to do with it. Just tell Harriet I'll ring the moment there's any news. Goodbye, Harry.'

He immediately dialled Bernie Appleyard's number. He let it ring for about a minute, then put down the phone and swore quietly.

Outside, in the deceptively ordered expatriate enclave surrounding the Villa Hellman, the shadows were merging into the dark wash of twilight. The second day was coming to an end. The second day since his world had been destroyed. Despair threatened to overwhelm him. Hope was like fuel, and it was running low. Blessed closed his eyes for a moment. He saw Daphne dead. Then he forced himself to see her as he remembered her, and a fragile picture formed of her face—pale and desolate and terrified, but alive . . . He cradled his head in his hands, felt his heart tear to the edge of breaking.

Lighting a cheroot, Blessed steeled himself to his task. First he would ring the Tabasco and ask for Appleyard. If he wasn't there, he would try the Rio Rita. In fact, before this night was out Blessed was quite prepared to ring every nightclub and bar in Berlin, if that was what it took.

FORTY-ONE

BENNO BEGAN PREPARING to untie his prisoner's gag in order to feed her some cold lung-soup. He was just doing his job well. That was how he saw it. After all, what use would Daffnee be to the Boss if she went and *died* now, while she was still valuable *insurance*?

Everything about the ungagging and the feeding was high-security. Benno was taking the process very seriously. Even though Daffnee was helpless—wrists tied together with strong twine, ankles bound with rope—he daren't take the slightest risk with the exclusive property of the Boss.

When Benno moved over to her side and squatted down, holding the bowl and a spoon, she winced, struggled weakly.

Scheissdreck, he said to himself. *Does she think I am gonna hit her with this soup? Don' she know we Kinder respect food too much for that?*

'Now, Girlie-Daffnee,' Benno whispered. 'You bedda behave! OK?' He made a grotesque face and drew an imaginary knife across his throat, then continued haltingly, summoning up his sketchy knowledge of proper English: 'No . . . skrimm! You no . . . skrimm! *Nicht schreien. Verstanden?*'

She looked at him blankly. Terror was there, dominating everything for her, but she knew what was going on. Benno could talk to her.

'No skrimm?' he repeated. 'You promise you no skrimm? If yes, nod. OK?'

Still only empty terror. Putting the soup back to one side, he folded his arms and waited. 'Nod. Yes. To say, you no skrimm.'

A moistening of tears at the corner of her eyes again. Slowly, imperceptibly, a painful small movement of her head. A nod.

'Promise no skrimm! Goot gurrl! *Brav bist du doch, Daff-nee* . . .'
Benno struggled with the tight knot of the gag, unpicked it and worked
the gag loose, freeing her mouth and therefore her breathing.

At the moment he released the gag, there was a hiss like a tyre going
flat. Daphne hiccoughed. Her face went pink and she looked as if she
was going to throw up. He waited, staring at her, just in case she
screamed after all. But she didn't. That was a good start. It meant
girlie kept her promises.

Soon she was breathing steadily, though in short gasps. Benno was
disconcerted to see that she averted her face, as if she couldn't bear the
sight of him.

Now that he was close to her, he wanted to reach out and pinch her
peach-smooth cheek. The temptation was strong. Anyway, she was his
prisoner. So he went ahead and did it. She started, looked back at him.
Tears poured down her cheeks, and a sound came out of her mouth,
half sobbing, half speaking.

'Hurt. Oh. That *hurt* . . .'

Benno had no idea what she had said. But he saw that where he had
pinched her there was now an angry little oval of sore flesh. A wave of
confusion came over him. He grabbed the bowl, thrust it under her
nose.

'No cry! Itt ziss. Soop.'

He dipped the spoon into the cold, porridge-like substance, scooped
up a portion, manœuvred it between her feebly-resisting lips.

'Itt!' he urged, like an owner addressing a stubbornly disobedient
dog. At last she gave in, allowed him to feed her.

The grimace that followed was a perfectly understandable expression
of disgust at the way the soup tasted. It was encouraging that girlie had
kept her sense of taste and smell. Benno looked at it this way: He had
been eating the stuff for years, and he still loathed it, so why shouldn't
she?

'*Noch* . . . more . . .' Another mouthful. 'Itt!'

Her hunger overcame disgust, as it did with everyone in the end.
And after she had eaten her fourth mouthful, and he had also given
her a drink of water, she managed to utter some more words—this
time ones he understood, because they were so close to the German.

She croaked softly, in her swollen, hoarse voice. Benno leaned
closer.

'Thank . . . you . . .' Daphne Blessed mumbled. The expression on
her anxious, pale face was confused and puzzled. 'Thank . . . you . . .'

★

Benno stood outside in the yard in the near-darkness, leaning against the storeroom door in his proprietorial jailer's way. He was feeling depressed, uneasy. What was the Boss's ultimate plan? None of these questions had been answered at the Kinder-meeting. Just a show of brute force. That had been the Boss's argument! That had been his answer when the Kinder questioned his actions!

Throwing away the miniscule remnant of his handrolled cigarette, Benno looked balefully up at the moon, filled with resentment of this hateful factory-refuge here and this prison of a life. To listen to the Boss you would believe that the Kinder were freer than anyone in Berlin, in Germany, in the *world*! Eck, this claim of Boss-Kind's would be a real good joke, except it was not so gadawlmighdy funny . . .

Benno spotted the Wonder scuttling out of the door, heading through the yard towards an unknown destination. Benno hailed his old friend enthusiastically. The Wonder looked scared, but also strangely euphoric. He was moving his matchstick limbs as if every Kripo cop in Berlin was on his heels.

'Hey, Wonder!' Benno called. 'The Olympic Games is *next* month!' He laughed in welcome. 'Take it easy, or you will disappear to nothing.'

The Wonder stopped. 'Benno, you speak no less than the very gadawlmighdy Kinder-truth,' he panted.

At first Wonder looked as if he might disappear again at any moment, but Benno offered him a cigarette and he gave in easily to the temptation of a smoke and a sympathetic ear. The Wonder felt like complaining, that was the truth of it. And that was what he stood there and did.

'Eck, Benno, all you gotta do is mind girlie!' he whinnied. 'Easy job! She just lies there, tied up!'

'Easy job? Try it sometime! But what you doing here this fine night, eh?'

'Benno, Boss-Kind takes me everywhere, says, "Wonder, you run this message to this place", "Wonder, take this to that place", and "Wonder is coming with me to Riese's hideout". No rest! Just 'cos Boss-Kind don' need any rest . . .'

'You don' have time to get bored like me, Wonder, eh?'

'Nah. You are so lucky, Benno, sitting around minding that dumb girlie 'cos you got seen by the Kepten her father. Boss-Kind he was explaining to Riese about girlie Daff-nee, see, and I know the Boss is punishing you just a little.'

'When was Boss-Kind talking to Riese?'

384

Benno had gone onto full alert. He wanted badly to know the whole story about how things were going between Boss-Kind and Riese, the Hat they had got themselves as an ally. The Wonder knew that story from the inside, and now was Benno's chance to wheedle and coax it out of him.

But the Wonder didn't answer him straightaway. He acted shy. Then he said with a knowing chuckle: 'I see you got plenty cigarettes, Benno. You know, I don' have none 'cos I been working with Boss-Kind and I got no time to trade or steal any . . .'

Benno couldn't believe what was happening. The Wonder wanted a *bribe*. The ridiculous thing was, all he really had to do was to *ask*, and if Benno had cigarettes, he would share. But now, Benno was reminded once more, the Kinder Garden was nearly over. Now they were moving into a time when Kind would demand bribe from Kind. No more sharing, Benno told himself with a desolate certainty, only buying and selling and bribing, just like Hats.

But he didn't show any hint of his despair. He just said coolly, 'You never asked for that kind of swap-deal before, Wonder. You need cigarettes, I got 'em. You wanna tell me 'bout Boss-Kind and Riese, you tell me.'

And Benno handed over four precious doses of nicotine, each in its homemade white jacket.

The Wonder lit one, put the others in his shirt with a satisfied grin, smug as a politician at payout time. Benno hated that grin more than he could say. And the Wonder was still blabbering, telling him things like, 'Well, these days you gotta look after yourself' and 'That's how the world is . . .'

Benno waited patiently, smiling and smiling, even though inside he felt like *killing*. And finally the Wonder got to the point.

'Well, you know, I just heard Boss-Kind and Riese are meeting tonight here,' he said. 'To talk 'bout the big deal coming up, to arrange everything so we can move to the new Kinder Garden in the Hershey-Zone and live high on Ami-dollars.' He puffed on his cigarette. 'You know, I am doing the big consignment tomorrow—to Frankfurt with real good stuff, then back the day after tomorrow. For this big, special job they chose me, Benno, only me . . .'

'Con-grat-u-lations, Wonder,' Benno said. 'I just hope you don' get caught, that's all.'

Wonder laughed. 'Never. You know, Reise and Boss-Kind fix everything so no one suspect me. What's the matter, Benno, you scared yourself or what?'

'I believe in this famous day of us all getting on planes to the Hershey-Zone when it happens, not before, Wonder.'

'Benno, it's all fixed!' Wonder said, looking pained. 'You know, they already arranged those planes that will carry us out off to Frankfurt, Mannheim, Wiesbaden . . . only two, three Kinder on each plane, so we don' make the Amis suspicious . . . Riese has big plans for Boss-Kind, youbeddabelieve it!'

This was interesting, Benno thought, but it was not yet the information he wanted and needed. He would have to probe harder, and quickly. The smoke was almost finished. 'And us? What about Riese's plans for the Kinder?'

The Wonder was staring at Benno. 'Benno, you know Boss-Kind *is* the Kinder,' he bleated. 'Without the Boss, no Kind is safe.' Suddenly he looked worried again, realising he had already stood talking for too long. 'So the Boss meets Riese tonight, to make sure everything will go right for the new Kinder Garden. This Boss-Kind tells me, his friend and fetcher!'

'Oh yeah? And where is this famous meeting happening, Wonder? I don' have an invitation. Maybe Boss-Kind forgot me!'

'The meeting is in the old manager's office up top above the factory. Around midnight, yessir. Just Riese and Boss-Kind. We don' need to be there, Benno. Boss-Kind will tell Riese what oh yes what is necessary to bring all us Kinder safely to the Hershey-Zone, just like he promised.' The Wonder leaned forward confidentially, dropped his voice. 'Fact is, Riese thinks he is *using* Boss-Kind. But the Boss is *using Riese*. You will see, Benno! Boss-Kind is the most *schlau*-smart operator around. You should trust him—we all must trust him to the very end, you beddabelieve!'

And so, having finally told Benno what he needed to know, as well as a few things he would rather not have heard, off the Wonder scampered, a nervous, speedy little creature of the night.

'You . . . goot gurrl. Wait! No es-kepp!' Benno muttered. '*Nur keine Fluchtversuche bitte Fräulein!*'

Did she understand? He had taken girlie's gag off again, but she wasn't saying anything. He had even loosened the twine around her wrists and ankles, eased the ropes that confined her, to help the blood to circulate. But whatever he told her—in pidgin-English or Kinder-German—she just stared at him. He wished he could explain to her what his plan really was. He wished he was really sure of it himself, for that matter . . .

'I . . . go.' He made a scuttling motion with his fingers on the floor. '*Im-por-tant!* I come back.' Fingers returning in haste. 'You no es-kepp, OK? Promise?'

Benno did his fierce cut-your-throat motion again, in an attempt to intimidate her, but his heart wasn't in it. He was too busy thinking of midnight, of Boss-Kind's and Riese's all-important meeting, and of the Wonder's naïve but highly informative burblings out there in the yard.

'No es-kepp! Promise?' This question had become a bit of a game. Daff-nee still said nothing.

Benno found her lack of understanding maddening. Particularly since she was now breathing more normally, and her eyes were definitely clearer. He abandoned trying to make her give her word. How could she possibly escape, anyway? What difference would it make if he left her bonds loose? Was she going to hop-skip through that bolted door, up through the Kinder-infested factory-building, and then across Berlin back to the British sector?

Nevertheless, girlie's silence disturbed him. Because it occurred to him that, in fact, she understood precisely what he had asked her to do for him. From now on, he realised, Kepten Blessed's daughter wouldn't make any promises she didn't mean to keep.

FORTY-TWO

IN BETWEEN TELEPHONING every nightclub, bar, brothel and officers' club in the entire city, every half hour Blessed had been trying Appleyard's home number again. Just in case. At eleven-ten, suddenly someone answered. It was a German woman, but she spoke in American-flavoured English. There was music playing in the background.

'Hello,' Blessed said wearily. 'I want to talk to Bernie Appleyard. Have I got the right number?'

'You sure have, English,' the woman said. 'He's just gotten into bed.' A giggle. 'He's not quite decent . . .'

'I don't mind how indecent he is. Please tell him it's Jim Blessed from British SIB.'

'OK.' He heard her wander away from the phone, calling out, '*Schatzi!* There's an Englishman on the phone for you, his name is Bless-ed . . .'

Eventually Appleyard picked up the phone, breathing a little heavily.

'That girl'll be the death of me, I swear it,' he began. 'But Jim, what a way to die! Anyway, howya been?'

So Appleyard didn't know about Daphne. Fine. No point in telling him. Policemen were used to being roused in the middle of the night. Just keep it friendly but to the point, business as usual between allies. Routine.

'All right, Bernie,' Blessed said, summoning the strength to appear unhurried. 'I don't need to ask how you're getting on; I just heard her. Tall? Blonde?'

'You got it exactly. Her name's Elfrieda.' Appleyard paused, then got down to business. 'So, to what do we owe the honour of this call, Jim?'

'Apologies for ringing so late, but it's important.' Blessed heard the woman laughing in the background. He pressed on. 'Bernie, my sergeant, Kelly, got in touch with you today, or he should have.'

'Wait a minute. Yes. There was a Kelly, but he didn't mention you. Something to do with a certain Major Dalgliesh. He was making an enquiry about a delinquent juvenile, asked me to look through my records. He said there was no hurry, but I followed it up anyway.'

'And?'

'Well, I came up with a kid who fitted the bill. My fellows picked him up last winter, along with a bunch of other Germans, in a bar where cocaine and morphine were being sold to GIs. The raid was a joint operation with the local Kripo, and it turned out to be a real fuck-up. You know: one of those *Razzias* that goes so wrong, you wonder if someone tipped the bastards off. In the end we had to let 'em all go, including that boy . . .'

'Long hair? Crazy-looking? A very strange way of talking?'

'Precisely. And, you know, this is why I recall him so well, the kid kept on saying over and over, he didn't have a name. *No name*, he kept repeating. Even when we found a ration card with a name on it. But we were letting him go anyway, so we just stuck whatever-it-was on the paperwork.'

'Have you rung Kelly back yet?'

'I intend to get my own sergeant to do that in the morning, actually. Glad to be of help, as they say. Presuming I've got the right kid.'

'I'd say you have.'

'OK. So, er, who's this Major Dalgliesh? We like to know who we're going to be dealing with in future on your side.'

'Dalgliesh's been brought in to run various criminal investigations while we concentrate on the airlift stuff,' Blessed lied smoothly. 'But of course, there's a lot of overlap.'

'Uh-huh. Maybe I'll meet him soon. Well, ah, if that's all—'

'Just a minute, Bernie. Listen, I know it's ridiculous, but I want to know the personal details of that boy, the one who said he had no name.'

'Jesus. Can't it wait till the morning?'

'I need to have the information now, actually, Bernie. You know how it can be when you're working on a case.'

389

Appleyard muttered a soft expletive under his breath. 'OK, OK,' he said then. 'You're lucky. We have someone on duty in records right around the clock . . .'

'I knew you wouldn't let me down.'

'Actually, you're in luck twice over, because it also happens that I'm a nice guy. Give me your number so I can call you back.'

Blessed spelled out the digits. 'Thanks a lot. I'd do the same for you Bernie, honestly.'

Appleyard rang back fifteen minutes later. 'No more requests, please. Elfrieda is waiting. You wouldn't believe what she—'

'Don't tell me. Just the boy-criminal's details. Then I'll let you go.'

'Promise? OK, the details with regard to your boy are as follows, OK? Name: Möller, Johann-Peter. Address: Wilmersdorf, Hildegard-strasse.'

'Are you sure? Of the address, I mean?'

'Listen, I just took fifteen minutes out of my evening to get that information for you. It practically cost me the devotion of the woman I love. Of course I'm fucking sure.'

'Apologies. Off you go then, Bernie. I'm very grateful.'

'It's nothing . . . well, let's say, nothing much,' Appleyard said. 'I'll see you around town, Jim. Give my regards to, er . . . Henriette and that cute kid of yours, OK?'

'Same to Elfrieda.'

'To know her is to love her.'

Blessed looked at the address Appleyard had supplied for 'Möller'. It was in Wilmersdorf, whereas he had expected it to match with that of the building in the Bernauer Strasse. But then, according to the information he had gleaned from Dalgliesh, the orphanage director had also been registered in Wilmersdorf, at an abandoned children's home. All right. It was fair to assume that the addresses of the boy-murderer and the director would turn out to be the same. Probably each 'orphan' had several ration-cards, each bearing a different address, as part of the welfare racket. Wilmersdorf lay in the British Sector, the Bernauer Strasse in the French . . . so the orphanages were spread among the different occupation bureacracies, reducing the risk of anyone cross-checking their welfare claims.

Restless, dissatisfied, Blessed got up and walked around the room. Cave's radio was no longer playing dance-music. The lance-corporal was clattering about in the kitchen, whistling to himself. Oddly, he seemed much more at ease since Gisela had gone. Blessed realised that his bodyguard had a possessive, motherly streak. In all likelihood, Cave would soon be through to ask him if he'd like a cup of tea, and perhaps an egg on toast.

Lighting up a cheroot, he wondered where the boy-murderer was tonight, and what feelings were in that wild head, and what in the name of God he and his Kinder were planning to do next. Gisela had said that an orphan became either an outlaw or a cop. Perhaps that really did give Blessed a unique perspective, made him the only investigator who could begin to get inside the boy-murderer's mind. After all, the boy-murderer was the one and only key to everything, wasn't he?

Wasn't he? Or could there possibly be another way to the heart of this case, another way to find Daphne?

Blessed sat down again, started to go back over his notes one more time. Cheroot between his teeth, he worried at the complex puzzle of evidence, experience and hunch, knowing that somehow he must force his mind into new channels, find insights that would give him the breakthrough he needed.

Then something happened. Suddenly it was staring at him. Blindingly clear. Apparently impossible and yet also totally, frighteningly obvious. A single connection was made, causing a hundred others to snap into place.

Within minutes, after one more phone call, Blessed's whole world had been transformed. Now—if he was right—everything was just a question of time.

He needed twenty-four hours. No more. Perhaps a little less. And he needed to become, while this lasted, the most ruthless operator in Berlin.

FORTY-THREE

ONCE OUT OF THE STOREROOM, Benno proceeded silently and secretly, slinking through the shadows like a dog that's been driven from the pack, heading for the fire escape that led up to the old factory-manager's office. He was in a state of fear. This was not only because of Boss-Kind's blade and Riese's gun, and what they would do if they discovered him listening and watching outside their meeting-place. The fact was also, Benno feared the future, any future.

He reached the bottom of the third and final flight, caught sight of a faint light in the manager's office. This confirmed the Wonder's story. His stomach did somersaults. His heart beat faster. He prayed there were no guards posted, able to spot even an agile and small intruder such as himself.

In the Russian sector, of course, they had electricity. There was no blockade, therefore no power cuts, and for propaganda reasons the Commies wanted everyone to know it. From here, as he steeled himself for the final stretch, Benno had a panoramic view of East Berlin. He could see the lights of the big apartment blocks and official buildings of Soviet-ruled Berlin, patterned in wondrous thousand-petalled flowerbeds of brightness, each point evidence of a window, a lamp, a human life. Benno's fear was alloyed with exhilaration, a sense of power that he was alone above the city.

But when Benno managed to tear his eyes off the haunting vista below and look up, his heart sank. Instead of more fire escape above, there were only bare stumps of twisted metal. Maybe the fire escape had been vaporised by a stray Soviet shell back in forty-five, or maybe during that battle for Berlin the German defenders of the factory had amputated the steps so that the Russkies couldn't climb up and shoot down on them from above. No matter. For Benno's mission it had the same shitty result. With a tightening in his gut, he considered the prospect of failure.

Somehow I got to get up there, Benno told himself. *Somehow. Anyhow.*

A second later, his eyes lit on a pipe, an old, nasty-rusty cast-iron waste pipe, rickety and cracked, that went right up the side of the wall, maybe three feet to the right of the fire escape.

Pray those bolts are still fixed to that wall just a little, Benno thought feverishly. *Pray the pipe is as sound and steady as it looks. Pray.*

He did not hesitate. This had always been his secret. A long time ago, Benno had learned that those who were too careful, who worried all the time about failure and its consequences, paradoxically were in the most danger, because in a crisis their hearts were timid and their survival instincts failed them. This insight had little to do with what more privileged beings talked of as 'courage'; to Benno it was simply hard-won war-wisdom, a way of action suited to survival in this treacherous environment that had once been a civilised city.

Perched on the highest surviving step of the fire escape, Benno pulled his feet out of his giant boots and flexed his toes like a monkey. The boots he placed tidily in the shadows, to await his return. He reached out a wiry arm, gripped the pipe and shook it gently before deciding it would have to do. Then out went one strong, bare foot, curled round the pipe. And he pulled himself over, was all at once hanging in nothingness, and the pipe was holding his weight. There wasn't much space between the pipe and the wall, maybe three inches, but he quickly resigned himself to getting grazed knuckles and knees. Benno started squirming upwards.

As he inched towards that light, that window, he heard the murmur of voices. Soon he could make out individual words, tell Riese's voice from Boss-Kind's. At last, wrapped around that pipe for his dear life, he cautiously popped his head up above the sill. He saw Boss-Kind and Riese amid the shabby splendour of this long-gone Generaldirektor's office.

It looked as if the Russkies had used the sofa for bayonet-practice, but those two were sitting there comfortably enough. Benno could easily follow their talk. For all the pain it had cost, and for all the almost unbearable effort of holding himself up there, he was elated at his own achievement. But as he tuned into the conversation, his triumph dissolved into shame, and his eager curiosity turned into cold anger.

393

Because there was Boss-Kind, sitting at a table, with a whisky-glass in his hand and a cheap cigar clenched between his teeth. And *ach scheiss*, he was talking just like a Hat.

'Slow down,' Riese was saying. 'If I had one piece of advice for you, kid, it would be, slow down.'

Boss-Kind gulped down some more whisky. He could feel a flush warming his cheeks, and his head was starting to spin, but it really didn't matter. There was nothing to do tonight except talk to Riese, finalise their plans. And he needed this drink, something fierce to celebrate and also to mourn the end of the Kinder Garden. 'I don' wanna live my life slow,' he said. 'I want fast happenings, yes . . . you beddabelieve it, yes.'

Riese put his own glass down on the table. He got to his feet and started pacing. He turned round and saw that Boss-Kind was still staring straight ahead.

'No more scotch for you, kid,' he said. 'You have to learn to take your drink where you're going, just like you have to learn how to talk and act like a normal human being, if you want to be accepted. You'll be living among normal people, not these weird orphans.'

Boss-Kind nodded slowly. Then he tossed his head. 'It's OK, OK,' he said. 'I know all these things. I want to get this leaving over, that's all . . .'

He was trying hard not to speak like a Kind, instead to imitate Riese and the others. Riese appreciated it. He clapped Boss-Kind on the shoulder.

'I understand that. Everything takes time. Growing up takes time. But we all have to do it, kid.'

Riese was only five feet five, but built like a wrestler. Now that he had status to protect, he wore an expensive suit and topcoat, whatever the weather, but tonight, alone with Boss-Kind, he had taken off his jacket and rolled up his sleeves to show his powerful forearms and biceps. His real name was Otto Haselhuhn, but everyone in Frankfurt and in Berlin jokingly called him 'Riese' or 'giant', at least behind his back. Since returning from an American POW camp in 1946 he had become a Reichsmark billionaire, and with sufficient holdings in diamonds, gold and American dollars to keep afloat even when the recent currency reform had wiped out his paper fortune. He dealt in drugs; in scarce medications such as penicillin; in prostitution, and in precious metals—all the staple items guaranteed to earn a man a crust in the uncertain postwar world. His time as a prisoner of the US

Army, followed by extensive illicit dealings with American personnel, had given him an impressive vocabulary of American slang, a way of talking and dressing that he liked to think of as transatlantic, and a taste for the benefits of freedom—at least of the financial kind.

With the aid of Boss-Kind and the Kinder, Riese was currently moving all his operations and his valuables out of besieged, ever-vulnerable Berlin and into the American Zone, where there was no threat of Russian invasion, and a man was free to travel, move himself and his money around where he wished. The Allies were planning to set up a new West German state whose financial capital would be Frankfurt, not Berlin. Riese knew that to exploit opportunities you had to be in the right place at the right time.

'The first thing we have to do once we get to Frankfurt,' he was saying, 'is to get you a new ration book and identity card. Is Möller your real name?'

'No name,' Boss-Kind muttered peevishly. 'You know that.'

'Come on . . . Did the orphanage give you the name, that's why you hate it?'

Boss-Kind shook his head.

'All right. Who cares? You can choose your own name when you arrive, start afresh. My printer can make you anything you like. Just don't call yourself Adolf Hitler, OK? We don't want to attract unwelcome attention.'

Boss-Kind smiled dutifully at Riese's little joke, then steered away from the subject of names. 'I forgot to tell you, Dackel and Engelchen got back from Tempelhof at around six. They took the package for the pilot Engelchen's been cultivating. It was the diamonds, stuffed inside a homemade wooden doll.' He smirked with satisfaction. 'For his little cousin Greta in hospital in Frankfurt. He even showed the dumb pilot a *photo*!'

'Who was picking it up at Rhein-Main?' Riese asked coolly. He rarely found any aspect of business amusing.

'Carlotta. She's the best, Herr Haselhuhn. I saw her in action when I went to Frankfurt a couple of weeks ago to get away from the heat. Carlotta always intercepts the pilot, no chance he can renege or forget. And you know she's so convincing, I mean, she could charm any Hershey-American until he would do anything, anything. They all want to sleep with her, but she says she must hurry. They press her, she blushes, says here is her phone number. It is a fake, of course.'

'Fine. I'm only interested in results. And I don't think we'd better use her to meet tomorrow's arrival. It's our last run, and the biggest consignment of all. I'll call Frankfurt later, get them to substitute. No matter how good Carlotta is, if one of those pilots she's already fooled recognises her around the place, we're in trouble.'

'She wears different wigs and clothes every time. It would be—'

'My instincts are always right, that's how I got so successful so fast,' Riese snapped. 'And my instinct is, we've pushed our luck far enough. That package the Wonder is taking with him to Frankfurt tomorrow morning contains twenty thousand dollars' worth of pure cocaine. You think I want some sharp-eyed Ami seeing Carlotta and saying, "Hey, aren't you the girl who was that *other* kid's aunt, last month? What's going on here? Is that *really* a wooden sailing boat that kid's got there? Let's take a closer look . . ." '

'*Ach scheiss*, you know—'

'No argument!' said Riese. Boss-Kind went silent. 'I didn't hire you for your opinions about couriers. I took you on because you can control those orphans, and because of the way you handle that knife.' Riese poured himself some more whisky. 'Though I might add, you're a bit too ready to cut people up, boy. You're going to have to learn to control yourself.' His frown deepened into a scowl. 'Instead of steadily exporting small amounts of stuff with legitimate parties of kids going west, we have to chance it all on a few do-or-die runs. You know why? Because you blew the whole orphanage front by deciding to kill that British corporal and his girl. Jesus, I *still* don't understand that. Then one thing leads to another . . . If I hadn't agreed to get you out of trouble, you'd be finished by now. Know what? You'd be sitting in that English captain's lock-up waiting for the hangman to come calling.'

Boss-Kind swallowed hard, but didn't argue. 'One thing, Herr Haselhuhn. I have one thing to ask,' he said.

'What is it?' Riese was irritable now.

'I want to take the Wonder with me to the West. I don't want him to . . . go with the others. He is very useful to me, you know. He can get into places, find things out . . .'

Riese's voice was soft and low, but somehow all the more intimidating for that. 'I can't let you do that, kid,' he said.

'He is useful. That's the reason, oh yes that's the reason.'

'He's no good to us. Worse, he's a liability.' Riese took the top of Boss-Kind's head in one big hand and turned the boy's face so that he was looking up into his eyes. 'We can't afford to be sentimental. We can't leave any witnesses around. None.'

Suddenly there was a flash of the old, princely Boss-Kind. 'He's different,' he hissed, shaking himself free of Riese's grip. 'The Wonder is mine. He is my—my—'

'Little brother? Is that what you were going to say? Let me tell you, there's no such thing as family in this business, kid. You I can use. Him I can't. That's the truth of it.'

Riese stepped back. The warning bulge of a compact pistol was visible in his pocket. 'You can choose life with the grownups in the real world, boy, or you can go to hell with the orphans,' he said. 'In forty-eight hours, after we hear from Frankfurt that the last consignment has been delivered and paid for, we blitz everything here, orphans and all, and catch the first plane west, with you cleaned up, hair cut, nice bib and tucker and manners to match. That's the deal.' Riese looked hard at Boss-Kind, a chill, professional's appraisal that was without either malice or pity. 'OK?'

Riese waited impatiently. Boss-Kind was staring at the floor, his brow knitted with the intensity of his mental conflict. Then he looked up. 'OK,' he said in a resigned voice. 'The Wonder must go with the others.'

'Good. They used to say, you can't make an omelette without breaking eggs,' Riese said. 'Put it another way, for everyone who goes up in this life, someone else has to go down.' He shrugged his broad shoulders, bared his teeth in a grimace of a smile. 'So the night after next, this place gets torched—along with the English girl, the orphans, and—so far as the cops are concerned—you too. Then there's no one left to point the finger, and you're free to start again, to join the grownups in a new city with a new name. You'll work for me. And you'll be a *good boy* . . .'

'I have called a meeting. More explanations. These Kinder love explanations, a new one every night and they are happy!'

'Lie, cajole, threaten, fart the entire works of Beethoven. I don't care what you do so long as there's no problems. They have to think they're coming with us to the American Zone. All you have to do is to keep those orphans happy for another forty-eight hours. That's essential, kid, and that part's all up to you, because from the moment my boys and me leave this building tonight, we're going to be too busy elsewhere to get you out of trouble . . .'

Boss-Kind was nodding slowly, rhythmically. Riese obviously thought it was the drowsiness brought on by the alcohol, but from his watching place Benno knew better. Boss-Kind was already rehearsing the big poem he would deliver soon, the one that would keep all the Kinder happy, innocent of the horrifying fate Riese and their leader had in mind for them.

Oh Kinder-truth hurts, Benno thought grimly as he shinned back down the pipe. Oh Kinder-death looms . . .

The outlook, not just for the Kepten's girlie but also for the rest of them, was far worse than he had conceived even in his wildest imaginings. But anger had now replaced fear as his predominant emotion: what he had learned tonight absolved him from any lingering tribal loyalties. He was thinking instead about his survival.

So if what Riese said is true, I am safe for forty-eight hours at least, he told himself. There is time to make a plan. But still the old question, the old conundrum: What to do? Where to go, when all my life I have known only the Kinder Garden? How am I to live?

He thought then about the importance of Daphne Blessed. It was good that he had started to be kind to her, maybe even to gain her confidence a little. The Kepten's girlie, you see, was still an insurance policy for someone, for the person who knew how to keep her safely. And to present her to the right people, in the right place, at the right time. For the pay-off.

Benno safely returned himself to the fire escape, retrieved his boots. Silently, cautiously, he set off back down the stairs.

FORTY-FOUR

BERLIN WAS BEING BATTERED by one of those brief, violent summer showers that descend without warning out of an apparently cloudless sky. His trenchcoat thrown around his shoulders for protection, Blessed had run the length of the Knesebeckstrasse and had almost reached the headquarters of 248 Company when he came face to face with the human being he least wanted to see.

Harriet Blessed stood a few feet away in the shelter of the building's entrance. Beside her a military police driver was struggling to unfurl an umbrella before escorting her to one of the official cars parked further along the street.

Once his wife had seen Blessed, there was nothing for it but to brazen things out. He splashed up to her and greeted her as gracefully as he could, which was not very. The lack of enthusiasm seemed mutual.

'Oh, God. It's you,' Harriet acknowledged him.

There was an uncomfortable pause. Blessed turned to the driver, who had got the umbrella open and was now waiting uncertainly. 'Look, just nip back inside and wait for a bit, will you?' he said. 'We'd like to talk privately.'

Harriet made as if to object, then let the driver make his escape after all. She had been about to put on her gloves. Slipping them back into her handbag, she nodded to show she was prepared for a temporary truce.

Blessed's manner softened once they were alone. 'How are you managing, Harriet?' he asked.

'I'm fine, Jim, just fine!' she said with a bitter laugh. 'I've got pills to make me sleep, more pills to keep me calm, and pounds of make-up to help me look more like a normal human being . . .'

'This is a terrible time. I'm sorry I had go out yesterday, especially because of what happened with Gisela. But I got some results . . .'

'Dalgliesh mentioned your detective work,' Harriet said. 'He doesn't approve.'

'No,' Blessed agreed, because there was no sense in denying it. 'Any news, by the way? Makes a change for me to be asking you that question.'

'No news of Daff, no. But at least Dalgliesh seems like a sensible man. Step by step, no fantasies.'

And getting nowhere, Blessed thought, but he knew he could never say it to Harriet. It would be unkind to undermine her current set of illusions.

'The major is an old pro,' he said in the end. 'But I can still give him the benefit of my local knowledge.'

'He has other people who know Berlin just as well as you do, James.'

'Perhaps.'

Harriet turned her face away, stared at the cream-painted wall of the lobby. 'I've made my mind up. After this is over, I never want to see you again,' she said. 'But first I want to ask you a couple of questions. About Daff. I was going to ring you, but since you're here . . .'

'Ask away.'

'First, why did they kidnap her?' Harriet said. 'Just out of spite?'

'Partially. But since they'd failed to kill me, they did it because they knew it would effectively put me out of action, cause me to be taken off the case.'

'Oh, so you fancy they were that frightened? You think you were that close, do you?' Harriet was making herself do this. Her voice was brittle.

'I was getting very close, yes.'

'All right. Then I want to know if you think, with all your experience of the macabre, I want to know if you think those people have murdered Daff.' Harriet spoke very quickly. She caught her breath, then finished: 'That's really what I was building up to, and I'm asking you as a policeman who also happens to be the father of my daughter.'

'The short answer is no. Even though there've been no demands for a ransom, no conditions laid down for her release, there's still hope they haven't murdered her.'

'Thanks. And what would the long answer be?'

'The long answer would be the same, except that I would add that I think Daff is of use to them in some way we don't understand. I think they are up to something, planning some coup that will save their hides. Once they have what they want, things will change. I hope they will then release her.'

'But there's no guarantee that they will. In fact, there's no guarantee she's alive.'

'I told you I have hope. But the people who took Daphne from us are not everyday criminals. They're evil, and worse than that, they're clever. I never imagined just how clever. Whatever happens, I'll have to live with that mistake for the rest of my life.'

'And trusting that little tart Gisela too. *What about that mistake, James Blessed?*'

Always ready with shock tactics, whatever the occasion, that was Harriet. His wife almost shook him out of his emotional numbness with the force of her anger. So had Gisela confessed to Dalgliesh that she and Blessed had been lovers? Or was Harriet still guessing?

'Has she been charged?' he asked, trying to keep the conversation crisp, matter-of-fact.

'Not yet, but Dalgliesh isn't going to let go of her, you can be sure of that. That's why he asked me to come in and see him. He wanted to know what I knew about her background, whether I could remember any suspicious behaviour . . .'

A military police sergeant whom Blessed knew slightly came in out of the rain, shook himself like a dog. Then he noticed the captain and his wife, hastily saluted and mumbled a 'good morning' before hurrying on into the building.

'And what did you tell him?' Blessed persisted. It was important he know how Gisela was doing, and how much Dalgliesh had found out.

'The truth, of course. I said I hadn't noticed anything suspicious in her behaviour, at least towards Daphne.' Harriet paused significantly, as if waiting for Blessed to react. He didn't, and so she pressed on: 'But, of course, it's obvious now that everything she did was carefully calculated.'

'I don't think it's obvious. Possible, yes . . .'

'I'm sure she was always after you, for instance,' Harriet said harshly. 'And I told Major Dalgliesh so. I still don't know whether she got you . . .' From the way she was looking at him, this statement amounted to a question.

'We've already discussed that,' Blessed answered without hesitation, knowing he dared not falter or stumble. 'The other night when you phoned from London, I said I wasn't sleeping with her. It was the truth.'

And now he knew he was using a trick to avoid an outright lie. He was avoiding that lie only because Harriet's antennae were extremely sensitive, and he might not get away with something more direct.

Harriet looked at him doubtfully. 'Well. The evidence that she was working with the kidnappers is overwhelming now, isn't it? Even you have to admit it.'

'If I were Dalgliesh, I'd be asking that girl some very hard questions. But I wouldn't be relying exclusively on getting a confession out of her.'

Blessed remembered that the evidence against Panewski had also seemed decisive. If only he could work out why they needed to frame Gisela, he would come a lot closer to the boy-murderer's motives for other things. He was so nearly there. A few more threads of evidence, then a turn of the mind, a new way of seeing . . .

'Oh, really? And what *would* you be relying on, then?' Harriet snapped.

Blessed shrugged wordlessly.

'James?' Harriet was staring at him with a kind of furious pity. 'Haven't you got anything else to say?'

'I'm sorry. I understand how you feel. We'll all do our best to find Daff in our own ways.'

'Oh God, I think I want to go now. Will you call my driver?'

Blessed leaned through the doorway, beckoned to the driver, who was sitting on the bench near the reception desk.

'All right,' Harriet said when he turned back to her. 'I know I shouldn't be making things more difficult. I have to make myself be practical, absolutely practical. So . . . I'll be at Gillie's for the rest of the day. Will you be at the Villa Hellman if anything comes up?'

The driver had reappeared. He resumed his wrestling-match with the umbrella, then realised that it was no longer raining. The storm had stopped just as suddenly as it had begun.

Blessed nodded. 'Unless I'm called away, yes.' It seemed the safest thing to say under the circumstances.

Harriet fished out her gloves. Without another word, she turned and walked through the door out into the Turkish-bath humidity of the Knesebeckstrasse. Her movements were abrupt, her shoulders hunched. She had the marionette-look of a woman who was keeping going by sheer, desperate willpower.

Blessed continued into the building and announced himself to the warrant officer on duty there. He said he urgently needed to see Major Dalgliesh.

Unsurprisingly, he was kept waiting for almost half an hour before being shown into Dalgliesh's office. The major was even frostier than he had been at the Villa Hellman. In fact, his manner had become downright hostile.

'I have a meeting with Colonel Harrison at twelve, which is in twenty-three minutes,' he said. 'Is there anything you particularly want to discuss?'

'Naturally, I'm anxious to know how things are progressing, sir.'

'Right. We're covering all airports, major border crossings, checking orphanages, disused schools and residential institutions, factories . . .' Dalgliesh intoned, as if he were quoting from a press release. 'It's a big job, and the most difficult part of it is avoiding publicity. Anyway, I spoke to the Americans and the French this morning. They're doing their best with the limited resources at their disposal. If you ask me, the kidnap gang have gone to ground in the Russian sector. It's part of a pattern, isn't it, eh?'

'They could well be in the Russian sector, sir, but I don't think it's part of a pattern, no.'

Dalgliesh was staring at Blessed with cold hatred. 'Captain,' he said, 'I am endeavouring to be polite and considerate to you, since you are, after all, a man whose daughter has been kidnapped.' He puffed himself up into the fighting-cock pose he liked to assume for confrontations. Whether by accident or design, he was positioned in front of the portrait of King George VI that hung on the wall, as if ready to defend it from outrage. 'However, I have to confess that I find this degree of restraint extremely difficult, since I consider your treatment of your wife appalling, your professional conduct at best eccentric—*and your liaison with that German girl despicable!*'

Blessed went rigid. He could feel the first prickling beads of a cold sweat forming on his forehead. 'Is that what my wife said, sir?' he asked with great deliberation. 'That I had a liaison with Fräulein Bach?'

'She voiced her strong suspicions, and I took it on from there. That's why I kept you waiting! I wanted to confront the girl with this matter immediately.' Dalgliesh strutted a couple of paces, then back-stepped. 'You know, I'd had my own private thoughts on the matter! I mean, ordinary, decent folk would be brought together by such a tragedy as this, eh? But not in your case, Captain Blessed! Anyway, by careful questioning within the last few minutes, I have been able to confirm that Mrs Blessed's fears were completely justified. While your lady wife was away, and *even after the abduction of your daughter*, you were . . .' Dalgliesh made a disgusted gesture '. . . with the nanny.' He drew himself up to his full height and looked up at Blessed. 'Well?' he barked. 'What have got to say for yourself before I pick up that phone and tell Colonel Harrison about the entire sordid business, eh?'

The important thing was to avoid being arrested and put out of action, Blessed told himself. Nothing else mattered. Of all the insults, lies, misunderstandings, none mattered. The only thing that mattered was to keep going, with or without the co-operation of the righteous Major Dalgliesh, until he found Daphne. Everything was justified to that end.

'My wife is completely mistaken,' Blessed said, taking refuge in a pompous police-report style. 'I'm aware that she has long harboured suspicions regarding the girl—such outbursts had become common recently, contributing to the deterioration of the marriage. Harriet is a highly-strung woman and now, understandably, quite distraught. I wish I could be of more comfort to her, but . . .' He shook his head slowly. 'Let's say this is no great surprise . . . As for the nanny, I really cannot imagine why Fräulein Bach should make a such a claim. Unless she hopes that by threatening to "expose" a scandalous affair with a British officer she can save herself from prosecution.'

Dalgliesh, who had seemed so sure of himself, was not exactly convinced but he was visibly deflated. This conversation had not gone the way he had imagined it would. Instead of a contrite, pliable Blessed, he had a man denying all impropriety. It was the last thing he had expected, and it opened up a chink of uncertainty.

'Well, eh—' Dalgliesh began.

'Sir, if you're right about the girl, don't you see that this might have been the intention all along?' Blessed interrupted him, as if he had just experienced a revelation and couldn't bear not to share it. 'The girl saw her chance to embarrass the British army! She thought, if Mrs Blessed, in her confused state, decides to give an airing to an old fantasy, why should I deny it? What have I got to lose? Why not make a little extra mischief on the way?'

'I suppose that's just about possible, Blessed. But I'm still not happy,' Dalgliesh said testily. 'I feel I should discuss this matter with Colonel Harrison. You may as well know that I had intended to ask him to suspend you formally from duty, pending an inquiry.'

'All right,' Blessed said. *Had intended* rather than *still intend*. It was a small retreat, but an encouraging one. 'But first, sir, I think it only

404

fair that I be given the opportunity to confront Fräulein Bach and see if we can sort the matter out. We can't let these red herrings get in our way, can we?'

Blessed had to protect himself against an official suspension from duty. In effect, he was already suspended, but informally so, and that made all the difference. He must make sure he kept the car, the access to information, the status that went with his rank and position.

Dalgliesh's mouth opened and closed several times. And then because, as Blessed in his new found cynicism had been calculating, the major was at heart a cautious man, he called for Gisela to be brought into the office.

Blessed did not stand or acknowledge Gisela when she came into the room. He only looked at her when Dalgliesh coughed, pointed. Then he nodded in her direction, waited for Dalgliesh to ask her to sit down. She looked even paler and more frightened than at the time of her arrest. He hated himself for caring. It was a weakness, when all that mattered was to keep going, to find Daphne.

'Captain Blessed wants to have a word with you, Fräulein,' Dalgliesh said. 'Just answer his questions truthfully. If you know what that means.'

Gisela looked in a bad way, but her eyes, when he met them, were intelligent and gently penetrating as ever.

'I have a problem. Do you know what it is?' Blessed asked gruffly.

She said nothing. Her calm was extraordinary, almost eerie.

Blessed coughed. 'Very well . . .' he continued, doing his best to appear awkward, embarrassed. 'Then I'll be specific. The thing is, Major Dalgliesh says you told him this extraordinary story . . . you, er, claimed that we had been having, er, relations . . .'

No answer.

'Come on, Gisela! Why have you decided to make so much trouble for me, at a time like this? Why did you lie to the major?'

Still she stared at him, said nothing. As the silence deepened, Blessed feared that she intended to stick to her story. If she didn't, she was beginning to overdo the defiance. Then, quite suddenly, he realised what she was waiting for. He remembered her promise during the one and only night they had slept together.

'I *never* thought I'd have to ask twice,' Blessed said.

Their eyes met again for just an instant. Then Gisela rounded on Dalgliesh. 'You told me he had already confessed to this thing, after his wife made the accusations,' she said. 'Why did you do that when we all knew it was not true?'

Dalgliesh reddened, pursed his lips. 'Never you mind. Just answer the captain's question, will you, my girl?'

'Very well.' Gisela shrugged. 'He had not slept with me, of course, but at that moment I thought, why not for once tell the major what he wants to believe? Then perhaps he and the others will leave me in peace for an hour or two. I was so exhausted, I would do anything to get some sleep. But . . .' She bit her lip in shame. It was so convincing that for a moment Blessed feared that this was genuine, that Gisela had not understood his coded reference to her promise '. . . But seeing Captain Blessed here now, and knowing what he is going through, I cannot continue with this deception.'

'This won't do you any bloody good, my girl!' Dalgliesh blustered, leaning forward and jabbing his index finger threateningly in her face. 'I haven't finished with you, not by a long chalk!'

Blessed sighed. 'I always thought she was a decent girl, as I've said. I still don't think she had any contacts with the kidnappers, but I don't know about the rest.' He faced Gisela. 'All right,' he said, 'now you've told the truth about this slander, come clean about the drugs. Were you just minding them for someone? A boyfriend, a relative? There may have been extenuating circumstances that could get you a lighter sentence, providing you give evidence against your confederates. What do you say, Gisela?'

For a moment he thought he had gone too far, but she responded perfectly.

'Please. Take me back to my cell, Major. I know nothing about those drugs. I cannot make trouble for Captain Blessed, but I have nothing else to say on the other matter. Please, now I must rest.'

Dalgliesh looked at Blessed, who shook his head to indicate a hopeless case.

When Gisela had been escorted from the room, Blessed said, 'Well, what more can I do? Of course, I accept that you must act as you see fit, Major.'

Dalgliesh sucked in his cheeks. 'This matter will have to be cleared up, but maybe at this point . . .' He looked at Blessed. 'She's a tough nut, isn't she?' he said. 'These bloody Germans are so barefaced. No morals, eh?'

Despite this apparent suspension of hostilities, Blessed was by no means sure that Dalgliesh had believed Gisela's denial. The fact was, rather, that the major no longer had the clearcut evidence he'd been preparing to take to Harrison, and he wasn't either stupid or headstrong enough to risk making an idiot of himself. It was obvious that Dalgliesh still believed Blessed to be a bad man and a bad officer. Now, though, he couldn't be sure of proving it, and since he knew the APM liked and respected Blessed, he had decided to back-pedal. For the moment.

'Yes, sir. I always thought Fräulein Bach was better than most of them, but there you are. One lives and learns,' Blessed said sympathetically. 'By the way, sir, have you had any messages from the Americans this morning regarding a boy named "Möller", possibly identical with the boy we're looking for in connection with this case?'

Dalgliesh was looking at his watch. 'Yes. Yes,' he said. 'As a matter of fact, we have.'

'The address on this "Möller's" ration card is one of the empty buildings which, according to Weiss's men, had been registered as an orphanage.'

'Quite,' Dalgliesh said impatiently. 'It was one of the matters I was about to take up with the colonel. How did you, er, know about this?'

'I made the original enquiry before you took over the case. I know the American officer who supplied the information. We meet from time to time. I just wanted to make sure that loose end had been tied, that's all, sir.'

'That's very kind of you,' Dalgliesh thanked him unconvincingly. 'Now, why don't you stop worrying about all these details. I'd suggest you see if you can be of any help to that good lady wife of yours. She needs you, Captain. She may not think she does, but . . .' He nodded like a judge passing sentence. 'And now, if you'll excuse me, I have to be at that meeting with Colonel Harrison. He and I have a lot to discuss. Still.'

As he escorted Blessed out of the room, carrying the thick file he intended to present to the colonel, Major Dalgliesh's entire posture said, *I didn't get you this time, but I haven't given up yet, Blessed. Just you wait.*

As for Blessed, the Scotsman's personal opinion of him was irrelevant. He had managed to see Gisela, to encourage her and to confirm something that was vital to his peace of mind. He had staved off the threat of suspension. And he had got Dalgliesh to confirm that the address on the boy-murderer's ration card was that of an empty orphanage. He still had some calls to make. Soon, however, all the moves would have been made. This was the beginning of the end-game.

Once Blessed was safely out of the building, he paused to light a cheroot and to feel the healing touch of the sun on his face.

Nothing must be hurried, he told himself. This time I must know everything. This time I must be totally prepared. And this time I must do everything right. Or my daughter will certainly be lost.

A brisk five-minute walk took Blessed back to the far end of the Knesebeckstrasse. He had parked the Horch on some waste ground at a discreet distance from 248 Company's headquarters, just in case Dalgliesh or anyone else had decided to question why, with no job to do, he still needed his own car. Lance-Corporal Cave was waiting in the passenger seat.

Blessed eased himself in behind the wheel, apologised for taking so long to return from his meeting. 'You must be bored stiff with all this sitting around,' he said. 'Are you still with me, Lance-Corporal?'

'Yes, sir,' said Cave. 'Absolutely.'

'Good. Now, the main thing I want you to do is to get out of that bloody uniform and stop following me about. You see, I won't be needing you as a bodyguard tonight.'

'Sir—'

'No arguments. Trust me.' Blessed turned the key in the ignition. 'I told you life would soon get a great deal more interesting, and I'm a man of my word. First, we've a couple of social calls to make. Then I have to be home and ready by the telephone. I'll explain everything during the drive.'

Blessed put the car into gear and pulled smoothly away from the kerb. Soon he was crossing the Savigny-platz, heading northwards in the direction of Moabit.

FORTY-FIVE

DAPHNE WINCED, bit back a scream, but he kept working, maintained the pressure despite the pain it was causing.

'Pliss. Goot gurrl,' Benno said. 'Chance. Ziss iss your chance . . . *Ach, darin liegt deine einzige Chance, verstehst du das?*'

She had a tiny bit of German, about as much as he had English. He didn't think she got three-quarters of what he said, but she understood the basic situation perfectly. Afraid this girlie most certainly was. Stupid she absolutely was not.

After being tied up tight for two days, Daphne was in no state to go anywhere. But he was determined to get her walking. This was why he had spent a lot of time massaging her legs, trying to bring back the feeling, loosen up the muscles. This brought pain for her. But if she couldn't move, his plan was no good. And if his plan was no good, she would surely die.

'Ziss . . . hurt. So sorry,' Benno muttered.

Daphne pointed to the rope still round her ankles. 'Take . . . this . . . off?' she hissed. At least the lubricating effect of food and water had made her voice easier to understand.

He shook his head. The trouble was, he had to keep her legs and arms more or less bound, in case Boss-Kind or one of his minions came in. The Boss was said to be out for most of the day—wouldn't be back until the big meeting tonight—but you couldn't be too careful. So he had loosened the rope as much as he dared: sufficiently slack for her to move her legs a bit, but still not enough to let her walk about. That would come during the last hour or two, the time before the Kinder-meeting, when all the tribe would be busy, with no chance of his being disturbed here.

He saw a shadow of distrust cross her face. Of course, she suspected he might be playing a game with her. He understood her fear. How could Daphne know his real reasons for helping her? How could she, the pampered British Kepten's girlie, understand why her jailer had decided to hazard his own fate upon her own?

'You . . . trust . . . Benno,' he urged. 'Benno . . . know how . . . make you . . . safe . . .'

Daphne looked bewildered for a moment. Then she made a little pointing motion with her hands. 'Benno,' she said simply. Maybe she even managed a fleeting smile; in this light it was hard to tell. This was the first time she had spoken his name.

But before the conversation could go any further, he heard footsteps outside in the yard, a short whistle, a glancing rap of knuckles on the door. Someone trying to get his attention, see if there was anybody home.

Hastily Benno tightened the slip-knots on her ankles and wrists until they almost broke the skin. He replaced the gag, making it as loose as he could. Then he went over to the door. He cautiously eased it open, ready to do his risky duty as her jailer-protector if he had to, but praying all the while that this wouldn't be necessary.

Gurkel sidled in. He stared down at Daphne with a kind of fearful curiosity. 'So girlie can't say nothing? She just lies there and stares at the wall? So boring! How do you stand it?'

Benno shrugged. 'I got the job. The Boss tol' me, so how can I fight it? Maybe others go crazy sitting here allthetime with girlie, but you know I don't let her get to *me*,' he said with a conspiratorial leer.

His friend grinned crookedly. 'Help-less . . .' he murmured. 'Help-less . . . Wow, I seen how ol' Solo got himself cut bad for playing on that help-less-ness when he shouldn't . . .'

'Eck, but you're right. We bedda go,' Benno said hastily. 'You know, if the Boss finds out I let you ogle his girlie-toy, we'll get cut too.'

Without further ado, he shoved Gurkel back out the door. Then he closed the bolt behind them to secure the prisoner. He fished out two ready-made cigarettes. This plan was costing him plenty of nicotine, you beddabelieve! They stood a way off in the little courtyard. It was midafternoon, and the sun was just disappearing westward over the top of the high factory building above them.

'Well, you know,' Gurkel began cheerfully when they had lit up. 'Well, you know that in a few days we shall all be safely in that sacred Hershey-Zone. *Jitterbug strictly forbidden*,' he said with a giggle.

Gurkel pronounced the English words with little accuracy but enormous relish. This was a sign he had seen in a dance-club frequented by GIs. He had memorised it because he loved the ridiculous sound, that *tschit-ah-boog*, and the even more absurd notion of its being not allowed. The American Zone, Gurkel hoped, would be full of such surreal signs.

'Sure, soon,' Benno agreed. 'Me I like to eat hamburgers, that's what I like.' After several near-misses, he managed to blow a perfect smoke-ring. 'Hey, I been so busy, now I gotta ask you, Gurkel, how many more smuggle-trips to Rhein-Main before we all of us head for the Hershey-Zone forever?'

'You don' know the plan?' Gurkel grinned. 'Benno the watcher, he don' know what's going on?'

'Been busy guarding girlie, you know that,' Benno defended himself. 'Course, I don' care. I just wait and go when we all go. But naturally I am just a bit curious. Better I know what's going on, or what?'

'Better. Yes.'

'So?'

'So . . . the Wonder is already on his way from Tempelhof to Frankfurt-on-cottonpicking-Main, and this is the very last smuggle-flight.'

'The very last?' Benno echoed, as if this was hot news to him, as if he had never risked all to eavesdrop on Boss-Kind's and Riese's very confidential conversation up there in the old manager's office last night.

'You beddabelieve! Word is, Riese fixed that. Riese got contacts and the Wonder's cover-story all worked out. How do you like *that*, Benno?'

Benno didn't answer, only laughed politely. 'What then?'

'Tonight is the big Kinder-meeting, you know that. Boss-Kind will tell us everything 'bout how we all fly to the West. Everyone will be here for the meeting—'cept Wonder, of course. He will still be in Frankfurt.'

'And what time is this Kinder-meeting? You know that?'

'Seven, eight. Boss-Kind promised good eats. He will explain everything-everything. This is the big deal, Benno,' Gurkel said excitedly. 'This is why we Kinder got ourselves allied with Riese!' The look on his face became knowing, almost sly. 'I know you didn' like that alliance, even though you didn' tell no one how you feel. Now you see you are so wrong! Now is the pay-off for the alliance!'

'Alliance?' Benno exploded, unable to stop himself. 'You call this thing an *alliance*? Gurkel, don' be dumb. We are *working* for Riese, that *Hat*. We are like *slaves*—and so is Boss-Kind, *especially* Boss-Kind . . .'

Before he had even finished speaking, Benno knew he had made a terrible mistake. Gurkel was staring at him, angry and tight-lipped.

'Benno,' he said, quietly but far from softly. 'Benno, you make it hard for me and the Wonder. We go by what you say, you beddabelieve we would all end up in Reform School for ever and ever eternal, 'stead of living high and happy in the Gee-Eye paradise of the Hershey-Zone.' He took a long last drag on his cigarette, tossed it away. 'Now I gotta go. You stay here with that girlie. And when we get to the Hershey-Zone, maybe you feel different. *Ach scheiss* maybe you come to your senses again, be like old times. Maybe.'

'For sure, Gurkel—'

'And you bedda be at that Kinder-meeting and you bedda listen *care-full-y* to everylittlething the Boss says!'

FORTY-SIX

In the seven hours and twenty minutes since leaving Dalgliesh's office, Blessed had not stopped scheming, planning, meticulously working things through. Now, with the day conquered and survived but the uncertainties of this night still ahead of him, he sat alone in the Horch in a strange street in an unfamiliar area of Berlin. He smoked. He watched the sun setting over the weathered, charcoal-grey crags of the tenements. And he waited for the first of the evening's encounters to begin.

This part of Steglitz was a decent, thrifty neighbourhood, made up mostly of sturdy four and five-storey apartment blocks built in the 1870s and 1880s to accommodate the new lower middle-class of minor officials, tradesmen and industrial clerks whose numbers had mushroomed in Berlin after it had become the capital of united Germany. These buildings were a crucial step up from the insanitary, dark rookeries of Berlin's proletarian east, but they were still a world away from the elegant villas of the western suburbs. And inflation, war and defeat, had eaten through the underpinnings of petit-bourgeois respectability, even here. The once-impressive facades of the surviving buildings had a battered, neglected air.

Blessed had rung Manfred Weiss at his home twenty minutes earlier to request an urgent meeting. Short notice, and necessarily so, but he was sure that the Kripo inspector wouldn't renege on his offer of help, not on the most important night of Blessed's life.

Weiss came out of the doorway of an apartment building just down the street. He wore his usual threadbare suit and trilby, and he carried a light raincoat over his arm. It was a warm evening, but there was still

413

a chance of rain. After looking briefly about him, Weiss made his way over.

'Good evening, James,' he greeted Blessed through the open car window. 'No bodyguard, I see. Is this wise?'

'I got rid of him for the evening. I couldn't take it any more. The boy can use a pistol, but he has no idea of anything else.'

'Yes. Please excuse me for not inviting you in to meet my family, but my youngest is still very sick. With so many children and so little space . . .'

'It's OK, Manfred. I'm not in the mood for socialising.' The last thing he wanted was to meet Frau W and all the little Weisses. Not tonight of all nights. 'Why don't you get in the car?' he added. 'We need to talk.'

Weiss walked round the vehicle, opened the door and slid into the front passenger-seat. He indicated his neatly-folded raincoat. 'You said you wanted to take a walk, so I brought this with me.'

'You may need it later. Smoke?'

They went through the accustomed ritual. Weiss relaxed back in his seat, glanced sideways at Blessed. 'You said there has been an unexpected development,' he said. 'It must be important.'

Blessed nodded. He took a deep breath and said, 'Manfred, an hour and a half ago I had a telephone call from a boy—or rather a young man. He wouldn't give his name. All he would say was that he was one of the Kinder, of the boy-murderer's gang. He said he wanted to talk, to help save Daphne.'

'My God,' Weiss murmured in hoarse amazement. 'This is . . . well . . . extraordinary!' He squirmed round in his seat to face Blessed. 'What practical proposals did he make?'

'None as yet. He wants to meet. Tonight. Just after dark. And I want you to back me up. In case it's a set-up—like the supposed phone call from Panewski that almost got me killed three nights ago.'

Weiss shook his head. 'James, this is outrageous! You should have warned me when you first rang! I am unprepared. I have no weapon on me . . .' Then he chuckled drily. 'I can see exactly why Major Dalgliesh finds you so impossible. Unlike me, he doesn't know you also have some good points!'

'But you'll come.'

'Of course. I told you to ring me if you needed me.' Weiss sighed. 'Well, you phoned, and here I am. I can pick up my gun from the office on the way.'

'We haven't got time. We're going in the other direction. Towards Spandau.' Blessed reached into his glove compartment, took out a Webley automatic and handed it to Weiss. 'They gave me this after I lost the other one at the warehouse. You're used to a blowback automatic, so you'd better have it.' He patted his left side. 'I'm wearing a shoulder-holster. Nothing for it but to take my old Enfield ·38 service revolver out of mothballs.'

Weiss weighed up the unfamiliar weapon, nodded. 'So where are we meeting this boy?'

'I suggested we meet at the cemetery near Daphne's school. Do you remember, I told you I chased a boy there one morning?'

'Of course. A macabre choice, nevertheless.'

'There are plenty of places to hide there, Manfred,' Blessed said. 'I want us to get there in plenty of time, so that you can take up position and cover me. Just in case it's a trap. All right?'

'Fine.'

Blessed checked the time, tossed away his cheroot. 'We'd better go if we're going to get there early.'

The drive took them north, away from the respectable poverty of the area where Weiss lived.

'Why do you think this boy has contacted you, James?' Weiss asked as they drove. 'Presuming this is not another trick, of course.'

'A mixture of conscience and self-interest, I suppose. The usual reasons. Perhaps he's dissatisfied with the situation in the gang, or frightened of what's going to happen next.'

'And you have no idea who he is?'

'He didn't say much. But he was convincing enough.'

'Perhaps this is genuine. They would realise that you would be unlikely to fall for the same thing twice.'

'You may be right,' Blessed said. 'Though they might reckon I'd do anything, however risky, to find out what's happened to my daughter.'

'Ah, yes.' Weiss looked away, tight-lipped. 'It never occurred to you to involve Dalgliesh?' he asked a little later.

'Dalgliesh would never follow my advice. He'd insist on doing things his way—and Daphne could pay for that decision with her life. Better it's just you and me, Manfred. Well-armed and well-prepared.'

'You are very determined. From somewhere you have found strength, James. I am proud to help you.'

'Let's start getting proud when we've pulled this off,' Blessed said.

Weiss nodded gravely, lapsed back into thoughtful silence.

Blessed drove with great care, even though there was little traffic about and it was a fine evening. He wanted to keep everything calm and undramatic. What mattered tonight was coolness, professionalism and timing.

Above all, timing.

The scissors were blunt from a hundred haircuts, and certainly Benno was no expert at wielding them, but he persisted, hacking remorselessly at what was left of Daphne's once-beautiful golden hair.

'I don' know this hair-cutting thing,' he apologised as he sawed through another matted curl. 'You know, another Kind, he does it for all of us . . .'

Benno's policy now was to speak a kind of modified Kinder-German. This seemed to work. Daphne seemed comforted by being talked to, however incomprehensibly, and he thought she had, at last, begun to trust him.

That afternoon Benno had crept off and explored the entrances and exits from the factory. At first the hunt had been unsuccessful, but just when he had been reduced to making plans for risking the main gate for their escape, dreaming up implausible ways of distracting the lookouts' attention, he had noticed a door. Through that door had been a dark corridor, at the end of which a narrow steel service ladder went straight up a disused air-vent. Thirty feet up the ladder a removable grille at ground level opened onto a lane that ran between this factory and the one next door. It would take time to leave by this route, but it was far safer than trying the main gate.

'Boss-Kind, he will be back soon. That's why you gotta keep some girlie-hair, Daff-nee. So if he looks in here, he don' see nothing different. This also is why you stay in girlie-clothes until we can start for Spandau.' Benno trimmed off a final inch, appraised his work. 'But I think the Boss will go straight into the Kinder-meeting. They are getting *restless* in there . . .'

'Spandau?' Daphne spluttered, like a numbed swimmer spotting a lifeboat. 'We go to Spandau?'

'Breet-isher sec-tor,' Benno agreed, switching to his own brand of pidgin-English. 'We go Breet-isher sector. You follow me.'

OK, he thought. The haircut was convincing enough. In the dark you could take her for either a girl or a boy. For sure, no longer a spoiled Kepten's daughter. Now, a street-kid. One of the Kinder.

416

Benno gestured at the spare pair of shorts, the filthy sweater and the tattered canvas shoes that he had ready for her to slip on just before they left. The shoes would be a poor fit, but there was no helping that.

'Soon you put on Kinder-clothes.'

Daphne nodded blearily. Then: 'We will be all right?'

'You beddabelieve! Everything—yes *everylittlething*—will be all right!'

Maybe it was stupid, but talking helped increase his confidence. Even though girlie understood so little, sound was better than silence.

'Now . . .' Benno unpicked the twine round her ankles, completely removed it for the first time. 'Stand . . .' he said, gesturing for her to rise.

Daphne struggled. Even when he held her still-bound hands and helped her, she tottered like a calf taking its first steps. But finally she was on her feet, moving stiffly around the room. He let her walk around for a while, gaining in strength and confidence.

Then Benno put a finger to his lips, signifying silence. He went to the door, listened carefully. There was a roaring sound coming from the main hall.

'Down!' he rasped, pointing to the corner.

Daphne obeyed instantly, understanding that she must keep up the pretence of being a helpless prisoner, in case anyone came into the room. Benno quickly gathered up the twine and tied her up again.

'Something is happening in there,' he whispered, testing the knots. 'I better go see what it is. When I come back, we will put on your Kinder-clothes and leave, Daff-nee. You beddabelieve this, and say some prayers—English, German, every other language you can think of.'

They arrived round the corner from the school just after sunset. Blessed wound down the car window, pointed to an alleyway across the street.

'OK, Manfred,' he said, 'I want you to go down that alleyway. After two hundred yards, you'll see a gap in the fence to your left. There you'll be able to get into the cemetery. Just squeeze through. Understood?'

'Absolutely.'

'Once inside, work your way round into a position where you can cover the gravedigger's hut in the middle. In a few minutes, I'll walk over to that hut. I'll be relying on you to be nearby, covering me with the Webley.'

417

Weiss nodded. 'Of course. Where do you think he will be coming from?'

'If he's got any sense, he'll approach from the far side of the cemetery. I should imagine this way in is too public for his purposes.'

'Ah yes. Well, I'll go now. Good luck, James.'

Weiss was nervous, but he was also cool and economical with words and feelings, just as Blessed had expected. The German left the car and disappeared into the gathering darkness without a backward glance.

A gentle breeze had picked up, cooling the air just enough to take the sultry edge from the night. There were the usual aircraft lights in the sky. Blessed closed his eyes for a moment and breathed deeply and calmly, then opened them again and stared around. Weiss was nowhere to be seen. Blessed began to count slowly to fifty, tapping his finger gently on the steering-wheel of the Horch to beat the time.

Fifty. Blessed patted his shoulder-holster, opened the driver's door and stepped out into the street. There was no one around, not even a suburban dog-walker. He began to walk along the road, saw the school buildings coming up. He crossed where he had watched Daphne scamper off to school that rainy morning, had turned and seen 'Buster', the boy with the ridiculous shorts. Blessed entered the waste ground, crossed the bomb-site, and paused. A little more than five minutes had passed since Weiss had got out of the car and disappeared into the alleyway leading down to the cemetery. That should be more than enough for the German to get into a good position. Everything had been timed perfectly, and now there was just one last piece of timing to get right, one last trick to pull off.

Blessed forced himself to walk unhurriedly, almost casually across the cemetery to its heart, picking his way between the neglected and damaged graves. There were no longer any paths discernible. When he arrived at the keeper's hut, he took up position by the plain little building and lit a cheroot. He eased his right hand into his raincoat, resting on the cold comfort of the Enfield. He wondered who, apart from Weiss, had been watching him when the match he had struck illuminated his face.

No haste this time, Jimmy boy, Blessed told himself. A few nights ago you were too hasty. You let the enemy take the initiative, and once you'd lost it you never regained it, from the moment you parked the car outside the warehouse by the Havel to your arrival at the Villa Hellman to find Thwaite dead and Daphne gone . . . But now, Jimmy, you've learned some hard lessons, and this time it's going to be different. If you've guessed right you'll soon know the truth about where Daff is and what the kidnappers have done with her . . .

Blessed checked his watch, concerned that too long a time had elapsed. Then he scanned the horizon and his body tensed. His heart faltered in its rhythm.

A figure stood watching from the western boundary of the cemetery, seventy or eighty yards away, silhouetted by the last, feeble glimmer of daylight behind it. It did not move for some moments, and Blessed studied it carefully, praying that somewhere nearby Weiss was doing the same, taking everything in. The figure was tall and rangy, dressed in a long coat, and as Blessed stared it began to walk towards him, moving slowly but with loose-limbed purpose.

Blessed knew this was time to throw away the rest of the cheroot and then edge a little closer to the hut, so as not to present too easy a target. He thought of making some gesture, a sign to ensure that Weiss was alerted to the stranger's presence, but he decided against it. The man covering his back would be watching, keen and impassive as a hawk. That was Weiss's nature.

When the figure was about thirty paces away, the coat became unmistakably recognisable.

When the figure had come another few yards closer, the stranger tossed his shock of unkempt hair, then ran his fingers through it and swept it away from his pale face.

At that moment, Blessed stepped forward and spoke in a voice that must have been audible to Weiss and probably also to the advancing stranger.

'Oh Christ,' he said. 'Christ, I just don't believe it—'

There was a moment's silence, while the figure kept coming and Blessed stood in the open, staring as if spellbound with fear.

Then came a dull click from behind him, quickly followed by another.

Even before the second click, Blessed had spun on his heel, his hand reaching automatically for the heavy service Enfield.

'Light!' he shouted. 'Light!'

From the direction of the approaching stranger came a bright torchbeam, illuminating the whole corner by the hut where Blessed was standing. The beam revealed Manfred Weiss, blinking in the glare. He was still pointing the borrowed Webley straight at Blessed's chest and trying yet again to fire a shot.

419

Blessed had his Enfield levelled at Weiss. The beam began to waver, as the figure holding it broke into an ungainly trot.

'Don't bother, Weiss,' Blessed said calmly. 'I disabled the gun this afternoon, so it's no good to you.'

By the time Weiss had let the useless gun drop, the shock-haired, dark-coated figure had arrived. Slightly out of breath, Lance-Corporal Cave stepped straight past Blessed, and approached Weiss. In one easy, practised movement he grabbed his wrists, clapped them together, and snapped the handcuffs shut. He dragged Weiss some way closer to Blessed. Then, like a cooped-up thoroughbred hunter, he shook his unkempt mane.

'Christ, sir. Can I take off this bloody wig now? I'm sure it's harbouring fleas and Lord knows what other creepy-crawlies.'

'You certainly can, Lance-Corporal. I hope this evening is proving interesting enough for you.'

Momentarily Blessed had felt overwhelmed with the pain of Weiss's betrayal confirmed, his friendship destroyed. Now, as he began to move to the next phase, his hurt became absorbed into the power of his righteous fury, and the freedom that came from knowing the truth.

Through Weiss I can find Daphne, he told himself. And if Weiss is guilty, then Gisela is innocent.

Blessed was examining Weiss. The German's face had hardened into an impassive mask, expressing neither fear, nor anger, nor regret—not even embarrassment. He still had not uttered a word. He had retreated to a place deep inside himself in preparation for what he knew must come next.

'Well . . . our exciting evening's not over yet,' Blessed continued. 'Weiss here is going to talk to us. He has a lot of explaining to do, and in a very short time. I want to know why and how he's been betraying me. More than anything, I want to know where my daughter is, and whether she's dead or alive.' He gestured with the Enfield. 'And if he won't tell me that, I shall kill him.'

Boss-Kind seemed in euphoric mood. Only half an hour into the Kinder-meeting and by every appearance he was riding high. He had hope as his weapon. And the remnants of the Kinder's trust. Perhaps most of all, he had Captain Blessed's old gun, the Webley automatic he had appropriated at the warehouse by the Havel, and which he displayed like an emblem of office.

Boss-Kind had been whetting their appetites, sketching in the arrangements for the coming exodus: how they would fly westwards in their twos and threes, threes and fours, as 'sick children' or 'youth groups' or 'Bible students', to Rhein-Main, starting the day after tomorrow.

'And the Wonder *has* gone to the Hershey-Zone,' Boss-Kind declaimed. 'But he is coming *back* tomorrow, and then for one more night we shall all be together here in the Russkie-sector. For one more night only!'

One more night, before they split up, supposedly to reassemble in the Hershey-Zone of all their dreams, that mythical land of milk and honey, where flourished the dollar-tree, and rose the candy mountain. Thus was Boss-Kind treacherously disarming the Kinder, just as Riese had demanded of him the previous night in the Generaldirektor's office while Benno had watched and listened.

And yet, and yet. Even among the loyal Kinder, there were one or two who were sensitive enough to identify the fragility of Boss-Kind's high spirits. So much effort to keep sadness from showing, from exploding out from the place deep inside where it had festered for so long. There were loyal Kinder who had that sadness within them too, and perhaps that was why, without realising what they were noticing, without even feeling anything except a vague unease, they noticed it in the Boss tonight.

'To live in the Hershey-Zone, you know we gotta have an ally like Riese,' Boss-Kind continued. 'Who books our seats on planes? Who opens bank accounts in our name? Who knows 'bout dollars, pounds and new Deutschmarks?'

'Why, you are describing any old Hat, Boss-Kind!' called out someone. It might have been Granit, emboldened by the fact that even if Boss-Kind did have a gun, he no longer had the support of Riese's boys.

But Boss-Kind didn't react badly. He laughed as if Granit or whoever had made a witty, throwaway crack. 'You know, you gotta learn to use Hats,' he said. 'Yes! Oh yes, get them under control, get them in as good allies who do what we tell 'em. That is the *use* of Hats, after all.'

Then a younger voice piped up from the back. 'But . . . what if those Hats—like Riese—are not allies of us Kinder at all? What if *really we are working for them like slaves?*'

Boss-Kind stopped chuckling. 'Who-is-that?' he asked in a low, angry voice, his eyes seeming to search every face in the room. 'Who-is-that?'

421

Gurkel had to confess it was him. He was smiling his Gurkel-smile, but he was pants-shitting scared. Because suddenly Boss-Kind was pointing the Kepten's gun straight at him, and the joke-time was over.

'It's a real question,' Gurkel pleaded desperately. 'It's a real question. I hear another Kind ask this question 'bout slaves.'

'*Who?*' Boss-Kind hissed. 'What other Kind asks this question? Who dares say that me and the Kinder are *slaves* of *anyone?* You . . . tell . . . me . . . who . . .'

Gurkel hated himself for what he was about to do. He hated himself for his weakness and his treachery, but still he blurted out: 'Benno. Yes, you know Benno ask that question 'bout slaves! That is the gadawlmighdy Kinder-truth!'

There was a long silence while Boss-Kind pondered. Finally the silence ended. Boss-Kind lifted his arms like a prophet, roared: '*WHERE IS BENNO?*'

And everyone looked around the room and asked along with the Boss, where *was* Benno?

'I think he went out 'bout ten, fifteen minutes ago. When we only just started the Kinder-meeting,' someone said. 'I think he got to do something connected with girlie Daph–nee.'

But Boss-Kind was not really paying attention. He had already made his mind up about something. He was peering along the barrel of his purloined automatic, taking a bead on a terrified Gurkel. And now he began to chant softly:

> seek
> a sneak
> seek
> a sneak . . .
> hate a
> traitor
> hate a
> traitor . . .
> good-bye
> spy
> good-bye
> spy . . .

Then, to Gurkel's relief, Boss-Kind lowered the gun. He turned slowly, pointed with his finger to a group of older Kinder, ones who usually supported him. He had in mind the classic diversionary tactic of every dictator, big or small, who had seized on a scapegoat when the questions got awkward. Boss-Kind turned to those Kinder, and he yelled at the top of his strong young lungs:

'*Find me Benno! You find me that Benno! This besserwisser sassy shit been going on too long, we got to FINISH it now! You find me Benno the traitor and the spy and you bring him to me HERE!*'

FORTY-SEVEN

'WE ARE IN DEADLOCK,' Weiss said. His voice was quiet, steady. Those pale, vigilant eyes of his never once left the gun that Blessed held in his right hand. 'If you kill me, you will be throwing away your only chance of resolving this situation. But, James, if we can come to an arrangement—'

'*Don't call me James!* Just tell me what I need to know. And quickly.'

A ghost of a cold smile. 'I must still ask, what is in it for me?'

'Nothing much,' Blessed said. 'Only survival.'

'Really, such drama—'

'You're straining my patience, Weiss. Now, for the last time: What have they done with my daughter? And where is she?'

'I think to shoot me would not really be your style, as they say.'

'Who said anything about shooting?'

Blessed nodded to the lance-corporal. Words seemed unnecessary. They had prepared a procedure for exactly this eventuality.

Smiling faintly, Cave produced a cotton bandage from his pocket. He grasped the handcuffs and dragged Weiss close to himself, then moved around behind him. Working from the back, rough and quick, he yanked the bandage between Weiss's teeth for a gag. He pulled the ends painfully tight before knotting them hard at the nape of the neck.

Weiss's eyes bulged in surprise. The colour drained from his face. The first inklings of real, physical terror. He fought for breath.

'Come on, Weiss,' Blessed said.

With the lance-corporal pushing from behind and Blessed dragging Weiss forward by the handcuffs, they covered a hundred yards from the hut at an uncomfortably fast pace. Weiss stumbled over headstones, bruised a shin on the corner of a mausoleum, but still they hauled him inexorably forward.

The journey ended by a far boundary wall, a long way from the nearest houses. Behind them lay the silent graveyard, ahead on the other side of the wall the first trees of the heavily-wooded Berliner Forst. Weiss looked around wildly. There seemed to be no reason to have come to this place.

Until the lance-corporal shone his torch and Blessed began to speak to Weiss in a voice that was all the more disturbing for being so reasonable.

'Look carefully,' he said. 'See this?'

Weiss was looking. Weiss could see it.

'This was especially dug for me earlier this afternoon,' Blessed continued. 'By the municipal gravedigger. It didn't take him too long—as you can see, it's narrow. This is deliberate, to make it difficult for the person down there to move about. And it's not quite the usual six feet deep, because we thought that wasn't necessary. In any case, it would take too long to fill in. Take a very good look at it, Weiss.'

The lance-corporal helpfully shone the torch in the appropriate directions. The freshly-dug grave was about four feet deep and a few inches narrower than the usual. A man who fell down there—and certainly a man with his hands fettered—would find it impossible to rise again.

'All right?' Blessed said almost conversationally. He nodded and Cave switched off the torch. 'The gravedigger did this in exchange for two kilos of good coffee,' he continued. 'As you can see, he also left us his shovel. Plus plenty of nice fresh earth piled up there, so we can refill the grave in a matter of a few minutes.' He smiled. 'The gravedigger didn't want to know what we wanted this hole for, and he didn't care, so long as he got his coffee.'

Weiss had turned away from the grave. He was staring at Blessed, calculating what the next move was, planning what to say when they removed the gag—as they surely must. Then the lance-corporal moved in.

Cave made to push him backwards. Understanding this, Weiss sidestepped desperately. Cave grabbed him, held him, gave him another powerful shove. Weiss lost his balance, struggled to keep some purchase on the loose, giving soil. One final, almost tender push sent him toppling helplessly into the cold womb of the open grave.

*

'Weiss?'

The dark outline of Blessed's face appeared over the edge of the trench. For some time he stared impassively down, waiting and observing.

Weiss had fallen flat on his back, but he was trying frantically to squirm and push his way into some kind of an upright position. It was a waste of time. He couldn't use his hands to lift himself, or to get a purchase on the sandy earth sides of the grave. Every time he wriggled, or pushed out with his legs in an effort to rise, more earth would tumble down onto his body and his face. Every movement only made things worse. Finally he forced himself to lie still, to concentrate on the simple struggle for air.

'Good. You've realised you can't get out,' mocked the distant voice on the surface. Then the torch shone down. Weiss was dazzled. He couldn't see Blessed, but the Englishman could see him. A shovel sliced into the pile of earth above. A large clod hit Weiss's chest, followed by a shower of gritty soil. Again. And again.

No matter how Weiss thrashed around, the dirt kept coming, slowly filling the grave, until he could feel movement becoming more difficult, almost impossible.

This was what it felt like to be buried alive. This was the ultimate nightmare . . .

Then, suddenly, the earth stopped descending. Despite the sandy soil that had almost stopped his ears, Weiss heard Blessed's voice again. The Englishman was speaking slowly and clearly, as if to an idiot.

'Weiss?' he said. 'Another two or three good shovels full of earth, and I will have buried you.' Blessed paused. 'Nod if you can hear me, Weiss.'

Weiss nodded frantically.

'Fine. I can see your face well enough to make it out when you nod. The rest of you is half-buried, you see. So here's my last question. Will you tell me what I want to know, completely and unconditionally? Nod again if the answer is yes.'

Weiss thought wildly, this man has changed. This man has become a monster. He began to nod and nod and nod . . .

It took them a lot longer to get Weiss out of the grave than it had to pitch him in. Eventually they hauled him up onto the grassy earth, to the scent of flowers, the summer air and the stars. Weiss wept with relief. They laid him down and Cave loosened the bandage, pulled

426

it down so that he could speak. Weiss spat dirt, snorted repeatedly through his nostrils to clear them.

Blessed leaned over him. 'We're leaving that gag close at hand, just to show we mean business,' he said in that clinical, easy way he had adopted since he had confirmed Weiss's betrayal. 'So if you're just playing games, we can pop it back on and shove you back in the hole. I'll give you about thirty seconds to catch your breath. Then we start talking.'

For some moments Weiss lay as if asleep. His breathing, rapid at first, became steadier. At last he opened his eyes.

'You have proved your point,' he said thickly.

Blessed shifted position so that he was looking down into Weiss's eyes. 'Now,' he said, 'let's get the most important question over with. Is Daphne alive?'

Weiss's answer would be the turning-point, and all three men knew it.

'Yes,' the German said quickly. 'Or at least she was this morning.'

Blessed sensed a lightening in his chest, a partial return of feeling. But there was still so far to go . . .

'If you're lying, I'll do things that make this grave seem merciful by comparison, Weiss. I swear it.'

'I'm telling the absolute truth.'

'OK. Is she still in Berlin?'

'Yes. But the place where they are keeping her is in the Soviet sector.'

Blessed closed his eyes in a silent agony of disappointment. 'You're sure?' he murmured.

'I promised you I would tell the truth.'

'So be it,' Blessed said finally. 'Now, I need to know a lot of things in a very short time, so that I can decide what to do next. I want the story from the start. All the hows and the whys of it.'

Weiss looked at Blessed. There was a sense of defeat in those watchful eyes, of a light fading. 'But first . . . please . . . I need to know . . . *How did you find out about me?*'

'One small piece of luck, and a sudden putting together of a whole lot of tiny, disturbing details. I spoke to a man called Bernie Appleyard of US Army CID, and as we talked he described a *Razzia* in which the boy-murderer had almost been caught by the Americans. It was a joint operation with the Kripo, and Bernie half-jokingly said the thing was such a spectacular failure, it was as if the villains had been tipped off.'

Blessed could see a sour look of understanding on Weiss's thin face.

427

'I didn't put two and two together immediately. It came to me some time later, quite suddenly . . . and then I rang Bernie and asked him if he could remember the name of the German police officer in charge of the Kripo's team for that particular raid . . .'

Weiss sighed. 'I always feared that such a coincidence would find me out.' He shrugged his bruised shoulders.

'Yes. Now, we don't have much time. Let's have some explanations.'

'Very well,' Weiss said. 'I had nothing to do with the kidnapping of Daphne. Naturally, I informed them that you had survived both the attempt to kill you and your dip in the Havel. It was Boss-Kind—you call him the boy-murderer—who carried out the kidnap, on his own initiative. Pure improvisation, brilliant in a way—except that it pushed you to extreme measures . . .'

Blessed cut him short. 'Why did you betray us?'

'My police salary was never high. Since the war it has become worthless, because the old Reichsmark has become worthless. A good enough reason in itself, perhaps, but things are rarely that simple. There was another reason at the beginning.' Weiss licked his dry lips. 'As you know, I have responsibility for seven children, including my brother's. Two of them are in poor health, needing medication that it is impossible for us Germans to obtain legally.' His voice had become weak and cracked, like that of an old man. 'I was offered those medicines, including penicillin, if I would inform Riese of any projected moves by the Kripo or the Allied police against his business interests . . . I was a clever choice, since I enjoyed the trust of Allied officers like you and Appleyard.'

'We were dazzled by your anti-Nazi record. We thought you must be incorruptible.'

'Ah yes . . . and perhaps I once was . . . Strange, but in the Nazi time it seemed easier to do the right thing. Maybe by the end of the war I had become tired of virtue. Maybe, being only human, I expected greater rewards from the end of the Hitler-regime. Certainly I felt passed over.'

Blessed showed neither blame nor sympathy, only the cold need to know. 'Those were your motives at the beginning,' he drew Weiss on.

'Yes. But after that I was "hooked". Riese had taken my virginity and for me there was no going back. Soon came not just medicines but cigarettes, and wonderful foods that no one else could find no matter how they tried, and whisky and precious kilos of black-market butter. Rewards at last—though not from virtue!'

'You never looked like a well-fed man.'

'It took discipline and self-denial, the old Prussian virtues, to resist this life of luxury that might have given me away,' Weiss said wryly. 'So I exchanged most of the food and luxury goods for American dollars. This hard currency I saved for a new life after I had left the police.'

'When was that going to be?'

'This month. I intended to resign as a protest against communist infiltration, so becoming a political martyr into the bargain. But then unfortunately . . .'

'Yes?'

'Then, of course, that little shit Boss-Kind killed the British corporal and his girl. I was forced to stay, to keep an eye on the investigation and do my best, obviously, to hinder it.'

'Were you told to arrive at the scene of the crime and attach yourself to me?'

Weiss nodded. 'That's why the child, one of the Kinder, was ordered to "find" the bodies. So that we could control the timing, the sequence of events of that morning. It worked beautifully.'

'Except for the wretched Wachtmann Pilzinger. He had to be taken out of circulation later so that I couldn't question him too closely about the child who found the bodies. Did you denounce him to the Russians?'

Weiss nodded. 'Anonymously, of course. They'll give him a few months "re-education", then release him. Personally, I would have let you interrogate him again. It would have done you little good. The denunciation was Boss-Kind's idea, so you would think everything was a Soviet plot.'

'The thought did occur to me. It appealed even more strongly to my superiors. I suppose it was Boss-Kind's idea to plant the black-market contraband in Gisela's room as well.'

'He did it on his own initiative. So he would have a further weapon against you if need be.'

'Very thoughtful.'

'Boss-Kind is crazy and dangerous. No one would claim he is stupid.'

'Tell me more about him and your relationship to him.'

'He never called me by my name, only referred to me as his "eyes" or his "ears". He would say, "And what did *my eyes see* today?" or "What did *my ears hear*?" I can tell you, I wasn't pleased at having to take my orders from him. He is too erratic. He is not a rational criminal like Riese . . .'

'So, do you think the Price–Suzy murder was just crazy, irrational?' Blessed asked.

'That was never properly explained. Maybe Boss-Kind and the couple had an argument. Maybe Boss-Kind was drunk, or under the influence of drugs. I never knew. I didn't *want* to know.' The inspector's eyes flickered with a brief spark of defiance. 'Why? Does it matter? Do *you* have a pet theory?'

Blessed ignored his question. 'OK, I think I know enough about Boss-Kind,' he said. 'But who is this "Riese"?'

'His real name is Haselhuhn. Otto Haselhuhn. He's a big black-market dealer. Clever and very ruthless. Any problems with clients or associates, he doesn't believe in negotiation. He just sends in his boys and they remove the problem.'

'Why did he put up with this Boss-Kind killing so many people and causing so many problems? Boss-Kind and his gang were smalltime thieves and drug-pedlars. Why should Riese protect them?'

'He needed them. And he needed Boss-Kind. You see, Riese is pulling out of Berlin, transferring all his operations to the American Zone. He's been using Boss-Kind's gang—the Kinder—to smuggle currency, diamonds, consignments of drugs, his working capital—over there.'

'And how have they done that?'

'By posing as kids visiting sick relatives, kids recovering from illnesses and needing the fresh air of the Taunus, that sort of thing. Riese fixed them up with the papers. I wasn't the only civil servant on his payroll.'

'Dalgliesh thought the orphanage director was the evil genius.'

'Dr Barnhelm? He's a pathetic wreck, a morphine addict,' Weiss said with a curiously puritanical distaste. 'Boss-Kind could control him by regulating his supply of the drug. The Doktor presented an acceptable face to the authorities, but Boss-Kind actually ruled the orphanage, through a skilful mixture of charismatic leadership and simple, naked terror.'

'The orphanage was a perfect thieves' kitchen, a smugglers' haven, right on the border with the Russian sector.'

'Exactly,' Weiss said. 'That's how Riese first became involved with them. He used the kids as couriers. Then he started to use Boss-Kind as an enforcer. You've seen that knuckleduster-blade of his?' Blessed nodded. 'He cut up a couple of enemies of Riese so badly, so *enthusiastically*, that even hardened criminals were intimidated. When Boss-Kind murdered Price and his girl—he did business with

Price, and with Floh and Panewski, it was quite separate from his arrangement with Riese—the transfer of Riese's assets to the American Zone had already started. So Riese needed Boss-Kind and his Kinder. He had no choice but to keep supporting Boss-Kind, despite the inconvenience of a murder investigation. In any case, everyone thought you and your superiors could be neutralised . . .'

'I was made a fool of. And it wasn't because Boss-Kind was all that damned clever. It was because you were betraying me every step of the way.'

There was a short silence. Blessed was the one to break it.

'So,' he said quietly. 'Where exactly is my daughter?'

'In an underground factory in Lichtenberg, in the Soviet sector.'

'Have you been there?'

'Yes.'

'Describe the place.'

'It used to make tyres and other rubber fittings for army trucks. It was one of the bomb-proof underground plants that the Nazis built towards the end of the war, when the air-raids got really bad. The Soviets tore all the machinery and fittings out in '45, shipped it all back to Mother Russia.'

'Who else shall we find there—apart from Daphne?'

'Boss-Kind and his Kinder. The whole tribe decamped there three days ago.'

'No one else?'

'The place has sometimes been used by Riese for hiding contraband, and for meeting contacts like me. He must have bribed some communist officials, maybe even Russians. I don't know. But I know Riese and his boys are not there any more. They are in West Berlin, making plans to fly out to the West. One of the Kinder has just carried out a final, very important smuggling trip and will be returning to Berlin tomorrow. Then,' Weiss concluded heavily, 'the factory can be abandoned— and then I think Daphne's usefulness as a hostage will be at an end. Along with the usefulness of the Kinder.'

'Delicately put, Weiss. You mean, they intend to kill her.'

On balance, it seemed likely to Blessed that he could trust what the German told him. If they succeeded in rescuing Daphne and turning Weiss in, then the 'full cooperation' the German had given would help his case in court. If they failed, on the other hand, Blessed and Cave would probably end up dead—in which case, what did it matter what Weiss confessed to him now, when the urgent priority was to save his own skin?

431

'How many are there in Boss-Kind's gang?' Blessed pressed on.

'Twenty-five or so. I usually met only him and his immediate lieutenants. The others were always scattered around, or out on gang business.'

'Are the Kinder armed?'

'Only Boss-Kind has a firearm,' Weiss said. 'He has that small automatic of yours. The others have knives, knuckledusters. Street weapons only.'

Blessed nodded, turned to the lance-corporal. 'How does that sound?'

'I've been up against worse. And we'll have the element of surprise.'

'You're going to have to forget that these are children we're up against,' Blessed said sharply. 'Can you do that?'

Cave looked at him, patted the holster he had concealed under the greatcoat. Blessed had never really noticed before how cold the lance-corporal's eyes were. He turned away.

'Take us there, Weiss,' he said. 'Take us to Lichtenberg.'

FORTY-EIGHT

IT WAS ONLY A COUPLE of minutes after Benno and Daphne had squeezed out of the grate from the air-vent and started to run—in her case, a rapid hobble—towards the Frankfurter Allee, that a whistle and a whoop went up. All at once Benno knew that they really had to fly yes fly for the British occupied sector of Berlin. *Because the Kinder were in hot pursuit!*

Despite their communications-difficulties, the oddly-matched pair of escapers had managed to agree on a plan. They would head at the best pace possible for the Tommy-sector, and there throw themselves at the first British soldier they met. (As Benno kept insisting, by mime and sign and German and English, they couldn't put themselves at the mercy of the Russkies, because you *never* knew how they would react, *never*.) The best idea was to slide in at the Brandenburg Gate. There at the hardly-guarded sector-border they would be able to cross smartly and unobtrusively, and report immediately to the welcoming British MP post on the Tommy side.

This had seemed like a great plan! A plan that could be carried out with ease, even allowing for girlie's weakened state, while the Kinder were still over at the big Boss-Kind-explains-all meeting!

So what could possibly have gone wrong?

'Hurr-ee, yes quick-*schnell*, Daff-nee!' Benno puffed.

The first necessity was to reach the relative safety of the Frankfurter Allee, which was usually well-lit and well-peopled. Daphne, awkward in her borrowed shoes, was now keeping up a brave pace, though her poor condition placed limits on how fast they could travel. Benno held

433

her hand, determined not to betray his terror, uttering constant words of encouragement.

'Es-kepp! We make best es-kepp, OK? *Ach scheiss* you hurr-ee . . .'

If only courage were the answer to everything! If only every optimistic word put an extra metre between them and the pursuers! Because the older Kinder at the head of the posse would be gaining fast. They had those long legs that could run faster, faster for sure than poor Daphne's.

They reached the boulevard of the Frankfurter Allee. And there was no one about! At this time on this night, there was no one about! The Kinder would be able to scoop them up and bear them off without a witness to pity or save them!

Hope was draining from Benno's heart. A quick glance over his shoulder let him know that the Kinder—headed by Boss-Kind and Banana—was only thirty, forty yards away. The look on the Boss's face was cruel, and his long legs were eating up the distance between himself and the fugitives as if he was devil-driven.

Benno refused to give up. He dragged Daphne out into the boulevard, searching it for something, anything, that could be used to their advantage . . .

'A Russkie-truck!' he yowled, unable to contain himself. 'A gadawl-mighdy Russkie-truck!'

This canvas-topped Russkie-truck was backing out of a building that looked like a garrison club, or a store—anyway, it had a big red star outside, plus the hammer-and-sickle, the whole gadawlmighdy Russkie-Commie *tool-box* portrayed on the usual banner. Benno pointed, saw that Daphne had got the message, and they changed direction. He didn't dare look behind, only forward. He just kept the truck in view, concentrated on closing the gap.

The vehicle had finished backing out. It was turning . . . and . . . yes, the truck was planning to head towards them, west along the Frankfurter Allee, which soon became the Stalin-Allee, newly named after old Joe, the Killer in the Kremlin. At the moment it was still moving pretty slowly. Perfect! Benno gripped Daphne's hand even more tightly, and increased his speed.

One final glance behind them. The big Kinder were bearing down on them. If this trick failed, he and Daphne were lost. Those Kinder were baying like wolves. Or was that just his own ears playing tricks? Daphne seemed to stumble, almost let go of him. Then, gaining some last strength from somewhere, she righted herself, renewed her grip on Benno's hand.

A second later, he was up. And she was up there beside him, hanging on as the Russkie-truck picked up speed. In no time they were sailing at a sedate but impossible-to-match forty kilometres per hour away from the now vainly yelling posse.

Benno couldn't resist laughing and waving as the distance between the truck and the hunters increased. Till they were swallowed by the darkness. Till they were three-quarters of the way to the Alexanderplatz. And till he saw that the canvas at the back had parted and they were being leered at by a big Russkie—a real terrible Ivan with a face like it had been put together out of old spare parts, and in a pretty slapdash way, too.

But by then, the truck had begun to slow down, preparing to turn right, just before the Alexanderplatz. So Benno yelled to Daphne and together they sprang down to the cobbled street. They stumbled and rolled, scraping more skin off their hands and knees, but then they struggled to their feet. He half-dragged her across the Stalin-Allee. In no time they had lost themselves among the crowds that drifted aimlessly, day and night, around the huge square that for more than a century had been the meeting-place, the greeting-place, the beating heart of this great city.

Crossing the Alexanderplatz presented no problems. Here in the darkness, they were just two more scruffy, weary kids among scores of others. Daphne was suffering badly from exhaustion. They slowed right down. Benno even recovered his sense of humour. He shivered theatrically, stuck his tongue out when they passed the old Berlin police headquarters. He could have told Daphne that when a criminal from these parts talked about 'being taken down the Alex', it meant he was under arrest. *Maybe this would be possible later*, he began to fantasise. *When he learned more English, at the Kepten's house in Spandau. When he, Benno, would be fêted as the hero of the hour, Daphne Blessed's special, personal saviour* . . .

With the crowds behind them, they tottered on into the Kaiser Wilhelm Strasse. And when they reached the end of that and were on the west side of the Schlossplatz, they had arrived at the top of the famous Unter den Linden, old Berlin's east-west axis. There, down the far end of that lucky Linden-Avenue, rising to their two pairs of eyes like a massive thanksgiving-hymn in carved stone, was the Brandenburg Gate. It marked the end of Russkie-ruled Berlin, the beginning of the Tommy-sector.

They were a few hundred metres from safety. Unter den Linden in this year, 1948, was a strange and eerie thoroughfare, as empty as the

Alex was crowded. Once lined with government buildings, Wilhelmine wedding-cakes celebrating Prussian power, and elegant embassies, its trees and vistas had been praised by every poet who ever glimpsed its colonnades. It was now a sad, shattered place, with the wedding-cakes wrecked and the embassies in ruins, the trees uprooted and used for firewood.

Benno and Daphne were not saddened by these gloomy memorials. In fact, as they made their way from the Schlossplatz towards the Brandenburg Gate—he leading the way, she doing her best to keep up with him despite her tiredness—their mood had a hint of holiday, of celebration. But then, as they were passing the old Interior Ministry on their right, Benno's exuberance suddenly faded and the look on his face belonged to that of an animal that has just glimpsed an almost forgotten old master who used to beat it and starve it. One sight, and cruel memories come flooding back.

'What . . . Benno?' said Daphne, noticing the change.

He didn't point, so as not to attract attention, but Daphne was able to follow his eyes. Ahead of them, like catchers in a sheep-pen, there were Kinder fanning out on the empty boulevard.

They would all have knives, blades, everything, Benno told himself. They must have realised that we were heading here 'cos we took the Stalin-Allee instead of crossing at the Potsdamer Platz. That was Boss-Kind's thinking.

He looked to the right, to the north side of Unter den Linden. If they headed through those ruins they would reach the Wilhelmstrasse. From there they could cross the sector-border by the Reichstag. No other choice.

'Benno?' Daphne was waiting for him to decide what to do, trembling now, as if already afflicted by the chill touch of death.

No choice. Benno's mind too was racing with hideous thoughts. *Or only one other choice. Ditch this slow-moving girlie. Leave her to the Kinder. Save your own skin. Head back into the Russkie-sector. Lose yourself in the crowds and live to fight another day. Somehow. Somewhere. Alone . . .*

He hesitated only for an instant. He grabbed Daphne's hand and leaped over the wire into the ruins. Then Benno began to run as never in his life before, dragging her with him.

Soon they were forced to slow down. After a hundred yards or so they found themselves hopping over rubble in the darkness, one behind the other, trying to follow the lanes that had been cleared between clusters of white crosses. For this, as Benno knew, was not only a bomb-site but a graveyard. Hundreds of people had been killed here in the bombing, but the bodies had not yet been recovered—possibly never would be. The families and friends of the victims had had these simple memorials placed here. Benno cursed them roundly, without remorse.

But on they scampered, cutting across a corner of the extensive grounds attached to the old Interior Ministry. Benno started to bring them round to the left, the westward side, until they could see a great hole that had been punched through the perimeter buildings by some Soviet gunner during the Berlin battle. This was their means of access to the Wilhelmstrasse beyond. The Kinder were still way behind. Benno didn't relax, but he did find himself thinking, well, maybe after all, we'll make it. Maybe there'll be a British army jeep prowling the border the very moment we arrive. Maybe . . .

Suddenly there was a whistle, piercing and loud. Another, answering the first. And another, another, until the air in all directions was raucous with the sounds.

The two fugitives stopped dead. Ahead, blocking their way through to the Wilhelmstrasse and the Reichstag, to the safety of the British sector, stood two, maybe three, large, determined figures. Benno and Daphne swivelled, their eyes searching back along the route they had taken from Unter den Linden. But Kinder-shapes loomed in that direction too, cutting off their retreat.

The whistling ceased. Except for their own tortured breathing, there was silence in the ruins.

'My fault,' Benno panted. 'I shoulda recognised the trap when they started to drive us in this direction.'

Her only reply was to take his hand and hold onto it firmly. Benno squeezed her hand in return. If this had to be, then let them face it as well as they could. Differences of language, upbringing, evaporated in that defiant hand-holding. They waited in silence, together.

At the Wilhelmstrasse end of the trap there was a small commotion. The guards stationed there parted ranks. An unmistakable figure stalked through, followed at a distance by his henchmen.

Boss-Kind halted four, five feet from them. On his right hand, his knuckle-blade gleamed ominously in the moonlight.

'Eck. Benno-*liebchen*,' he hissed. He shifted his gaze to Daphne. 'Eck. And the Kepten's girlie . . .'

Slowly, without taking his eyes off them, the Boss reached into the pocket of his coat. He took out a stiff piece of paper, held it up towards them. It was a photograph. He snapped his fingers. A minion jumped forward, lit a match to illuminate the picture. During the brief life of the flare, it revealed a photo of Daphne together with Captain Blessed, her father.

Daphne let out a little whimper. Boss-Kind smiled. He tore the photograph into two. He put the pieces together and tore them into four. Then eight. He tossed the fragments away into the darkness. His face had taken on an expression of near-ecstatic power.

'*Adieu*, girlie,' he breathed. 'Poor girlie. Nevermore see Kepten your father. Nevermore see Mummypie.'

His blade clicked open. He took a step forward, looked at each of his captives, unable to make a final decision. Then Boss-Kind shook his mane of hair, and started to tap his foot, as if he could hear music that they could not. It was Benno whom he harpooned at last with his killer-stare while he intoned, softly and chillingly as a surgeon bearing bad news:

> Seek
> a sneak . . .
> Hate a
> traitor . . .
> Goodbye
> spy . . .

FORTY-NINE

THE HORCH CROSSED THE SECTOR boundary at the Friedrich-strasse, north of Unter den Linden. There was no trouble, for which Blessed gave thanks. As army-of-occupation personnel travelling in a military vehicle, Blessed and Cave were entitled to go anywhere they liked in Berlin, including the communist-controlled East. The same useful privilege allowed the Soviets to roam the western sectors at will, so neither side was interested in introducing restrictions just now, despite the crisis. But sometimes there could be problems. Blessed had feared that if they were flagged down by a Russian patrol for a document-inspection, there could be a serious delay if the Soviets decided to have some fun deciding whether Inspector Weiss was on legitimate business on their territory.

Blessed followed the raised S-bahn tracks around the north edge of the Alexanderplatz. Weiss, who was sharing the back seat with Lance-Corporal Cave, spoke only to give him essential street-directions. There were hardly any private cars on the street in East Berlin, but plenty of Soviet military vehicles. From time to time a pedestrian or a cyclist would be caught in the headlights. More than once, such civilians dived into side-streets and doorways when they saw the sleek, official-looking Horch approaching.

After they had been travelling southeastwards on the Frankfurter Allee for several minutes, Weiss leaned forward slightly in his seat and said quietly, 'Turn left at the next opportunity. The factory is about five hundred metres along on the left. Be very careful how you approach. There will be guards at the main gate. They will be alerted if a car draws up right outside.'

'Is there another way into the factory?' Blessed asked, slowing down to make the turn.

'Not as far as I know.'

'You're being surprisingly helpful, Weiss.'

'It's not surprising at all. Just primitive self-preservation. I want us to get in and out of there in one piece. If we were ambushed in the dark on our way in, they'd probably cut me up just as thoroughly as you and Cave.'

Blessed still didn't trust Weiss's helpfulness, but he did trust his instinct for self-preservation. He parked the Horch a hundred yards away, on a piece of waste ground shielded from the factory gates by a more or less intact brick wall.

'Do these Kinder know you by sight?' Blessed asked before they got out of the car.

'Some. I don't think they necessarily know who I am, but the guards, here or at the Bernauer Strasse, have been instructed to admit me . . .'

'All right. Out we get. You can lead the way. If someone challenges us at the gate, just smile a handy greeting and ask for you and your friends to be admitted into the august presence of Boss-Kind.' Blessed patted his shoulder-holster. 'And we'll be right behind you, in case you don't do the right thing. Understand?'

Weiss nodded. They got out of the car. Blessed first. Weiss next. Then Cave. They rounded the wall, walked along the pot-holed lane that led to the factory. There was a hint of rain in the air now, and here in the Russian sector, Blessed suddenly realised, no airlift planes overhead.

The 'gates' were grandly named. They may have been more substantial at some earlier time, perhaps of steel or wrought iron, but if so the Russians had stolen them, or Germans had taken them for scrap, because now they were rusty chickenwire on a wooden frame, without even a padlock. In fact, they were open, as if someone had left carelessly and quickly.

'That's the watchman's hut,' Weiss whispered, pointing to a concrete hut about ten yards inside the gates.

Blessed signalled to the lance-corporal to take a look in the hut while he drew his Enfield and watched the German. Cave crept over, glanced in through the window, came away shaking his head. Blessed turned on Weiss.

'How do we get in here?' he demanded. 'If you've been lying . . .'

440

'This is right. I know it,' Weiss whispered. 'I don't understand. It was definite that they would be here for at least two more nights.'

He led them to the entrance. Double doors opened into a hall with a concrete floor. Steps ascended to the upper floors, but Blessed and Cave followed Weiss along to the end of the hall and through another pair of double doors which gave immediately onto a flight of stairs leading down to the bomb-proofed part of the building.

As they prepared to descend, Blessed made two observations. First, a faint light was shining somewhere beneath the factory. Second, someone—someone quite small—was standing at the foot of the steps. As he looked, this little figure ducked back into the underground complex.

They advanced cautiously. At the bottom of the stairs was an open door, somewhere beyond which originated the source of light. When they reached the door, Cave covered Weiss while Blessed moved forward to investigate whatever lay on the other side.

The light was coming from a single naked bulb in the middle of a huge underground room. It was about sixty feet by twenty and contained a table, some chairs. Blessed noticed that there were a few old blankets scattered around. Some chipped cups. A bowl or two. Signs that the place had been hastily abandoned, possessions left just where they lay. *Why?*

'This is the factory hall. This is where they would be,' Weiss whispered. 'I *swear* I told you the truth. Where have the Kinder gone?'

'Wait here by the door, both of you,' Blessed ordered quietly. 'I'm going in there.'

He advanced warily into the room. The small figure that had slipped away as they arrived at the top of the stairs was in here somewhere. But where were the others? And above all, for God's sake, *where was Daphne?*

Blessed's gaze swept the room, found nothing. Then he halted. His eye had been caught by something on the floor a few feet away. Something very familiar.

He half-turned, glanced back at the doorway to ensure that Cave was still there, covering Weiss. A moment later, walking quickly over, he knelt down, retrieved the filthy, rolled-up ball that had been his daughter's nightdress—all she had been wearing the night she was kidnapped. Slowly he raised the garment, touched it against his cheek, closed his eyes . . .

When Blessed opened his eyes again and began to make for the door, Weiss knew what was coming. He made a quick move in the direction of the exit. Cave blocked his path, forced him at gunpoint towards the nearby corner.

'I didn't know anything about this, Captain,' Weiss pleaded hoarsely, backing off as Blessed strode inexorably nearer. 'Believe me, if anyone had told me they were planning to . . . .'

When he could retreat no further, Weiss put his hands up over his eyes and waited.

When he was only three or four feet away, Blessed stopped. He let Daphne's nightdress flutter gently to the floor, like a mourner dropping flowers on a loved one's grave. He slipped the Enfield back into its holster. Then he hit Weiss with brutal deliberation, right in the middle of the face.

The blow sent Weiss crashing against the wall. The back of his head hit the concrete with a loud, dull cracking sound. Weiss sank to his knees, his fettered hands clutching his face. Blessed reached down, pulled him to his feet, wrenched his hands away from what they were covering. Blood was pouring from Weiss's nostrils. His left eye was already closed. Blessed let him fall. Without giving him another glance, he turned back to Cave.

'We'd better look for that kid,' he said. 'Perhaps he has nothing to do with all this, but we'd better look for him anyway. Handcuff Weiss to that heating pipe. In the meantime, I'll get started with the search.' He sighed. 'The little bugger's got to be here somewhere.'

Then a voice from behind spun him round. As he turned, he was already wrenching the Enfield from its shoulder-holster.

'You are, yes you are the *Kepten!*' Gurkel repeated. He had popped up from a rusty old iron water tank in the farthest, gloomiest corner of the room, where he had taken refuge. 'You are Kepten Bless-ed, *girlie's father!*'

Blessed released the safety-catch on his pistol, pointed it at the boy. This was not a child to him, only a potential murderer—perhaps even an actual one.

'Get out of there slowly and very carefully,' he said in German, and began to walk towards the boy. 'Take it easy. Absolutely no sudden movements.'

Gurkel, tipsy on an exhilarating cocktail of fear and excitement, eased himself over the rim of the old tank and slid down to the ground. There he stood with his hands above his head, wearing his best, most winning grin.

442

Weiss had been manacled to the defunct heating-pipe. He was slumped on his knees now, with his back to the room, moaning thickly.

'Good. Now come here and search this one, please,' Blessed called out to Cave.

The lance-corporal hurried forward. His search of Gurkel's pockets turned up a a half-smoked cigarette, a few worthless old-currency coins.

'He's all right, sir. Clean.'

Blessed moved closer, put away the Enfield, looked hard at the boy. 'What's your name?' he asked.

The boy laughed nervously. 'Gurkel,' he said.

' "Gurkel"—that's gherkin in English, probably a nickname. What's the name on your ration-card?'

'Ach . . . that would be Hans-Georg Mielke,' the boy said, as if reciting a formula learned by rote. 'But *ach scheiss* you know Boss-Kind, he would never allow that, he cut you for using that name 'cept once a year maybe when the orphan-inspector come, you beddabelieve it. Boss-Kind, he is so *strict* 'bout this, you know that all Kinder got no no no no *no* name!' The last part was delivered in a machine-gun imitation of the boy-murderer's voice.

'OK. That's enough,' Blessed said. He braced himself and asked: 'Do you know what they did to my daughter? Tell me the truth. Don't be afraid . . .'

Gurkel smiled crookedly. Which concept—truth or the absence of fear—he found the more risible, it was impossible to tell. His look turned sly.

'See, Kepten, I tell you what. See . . . they didn' do nothing at all to her! *Nothing!* That is the gadawlmighdy total and absolute Kinder-truth!'

'She's alive?'

Gurkel nodded enthusiastically. 'You beddabelieve!'

'Then where the hell is she? Where are the rest of your gang?'

'Daff-nee escaped with Benno,' Gurkel said. 'All the Kinder gone to look for them 'cept me. I came back here and I hid. 'Cos Benno he is my friend, and I don' want to catch him, oh no.'

'But that's her nightdress,' Blessed murmured, still disbelieving. 'There.'

Gurkel nodded solemnly. 'Sure. Benno organised Kinder clothes for her to wear. They found that nightie-thing in girlie's prison, brought it for the Boss to see.' He brightened. 'I hope the Kinder didn' find girlie and Benno after all. Maybe they get caught themselves by Russkies.'

443

Blessed realised he was looking at someone who had just sensed it was time to change sides. As for Daphne, she had escaped just at the wrong time, just when help was on its way. He stood there for a moment, wondering what really lay behind this child's ingratiating smile; what everyday diet of danger and intimidation, how much casual death and horror. If Daphne had been recaptured, he realised, these children would show her no pity. Why should they? In their savage world such comforts were unknown.

'When did this happen?' he asked eventually. 'When did they escape?'

Gurkel's freckled brow wrinkled with the effort of calculation. 'Well, I don' know exactly. I think one maybe yes almost one and a half hours ago they find Benno and girlie gone. This was right in the middle of the Kinder-meeting and Boss-Kind got mad, oh *killing* mad . . .'

'All right,' Blessed said. 'So, who is Benno?'

'Benno? Oh Kepten, Benno is the best watcher! And he helped girlie Daff-nee escape! And you beddabelive *he* is *my* best best best Kinder-friend, and *I* am *his*.'

'How did he help Daphne escape?'

'Oh yes he ran off with her, let her out of the storeroom where she was kept.' Gurkel jerked a thumb in the direction of the courtyard and the storeroom on the far side. 'See, they crack through air-vent and get out into the street, then they escape! Unlucky, oh very unlucky that so soon after this, Boss-Kind suddenly decides to check on Benno and girlie Daff-nee . . .'

Gurkel shrugged as if to say, these things happen.

'I have no reason to think this kid's not telling the truth,' Blessed said to Cave.

It means Daphne could be anywhere, he thought. She could even be in West Berlin by now. Christ, she could have tried to ring the Villa Hellman, and there would be nobody there . . .

So the question was, should he stay here or return to the British sector? If this were happening on British-controlled territory, now would be the time to confront Major Dalgliesh with this incontravertible evidence. Impossible here. Here there was only one course of action open to him.

'Catch,' Blessed said, tossing the car-keys to Cave. 'The Horch is yours. I'll help you put Weiss and this boy into the car. You will then drive back into the British sector. Report to the first military police post you find, hand over Weiss and the boy, and demand to phone the

Knesebeckstrasse. Once you're through, insist on speaking to Major Dalgliesh personally. Explain what's happened. Tell him that a certain Otto Haselhuhn and colleagues are to be arrested if they attempt to fly out of Berlin. And tell him also that I'm here. If I'm not back in the British sector by first light, he's to inform the Soviet authorities and . . . well, do as he sees fit.'

Blessed wrote down three things on a page from his notebook: The address of the factory, the name 'Otto Haselhuhn', so that Cave would not get it wrong, and lastly the simple statement, 'Inspector Manfred Weiss is to be taken into custody for aiding and abetting in illicit trading and as an accessory to murder. This boy is a witness and is to be taken into protective custody.' He signed the paper in the small space still available, 'J. Blessed (Capt SIB)' and had the lance-corporal button it into the breast-pocket of his shirt.

'What about you, sir?' Cave asked. 'I'm not happy leaving you here.'

'You have to go. You have to turn Weiss in, see this witness is delivered, ensure Haselhuhn is arrested before he can leave Berlin. You're my insurance that the truth will be known and that some, at least, of the guilty punished,' Blessed said. 'I have to stay. I don't know whether Daff and her friend have got back safely to our sector. I daren't move from here until I know for certain that they have.'

'They have phone boxes over here, don't they? We could find one and ring the Knesebeckstrasse,' Cave said stubbornly.

Blessed shook his head. 'The telephone lines from the Soviet sector to ours are routed via Hanover,' he said. 'It can take hours to get through, Lance-Corporal. My place is here. I'm prepared.'

Between them they managed to drag Weiss to the car and put him into the back seat. They positioned him with his face buried in the corner, as if asleep, so no Soviet soldier or communist policeman glancing in the window would see the mess he was in. The boy went into the passenger seat, with the promise of swift retribution if he caused any trouble.

Blessed watched the Horch until it disappeared from sight. Provided there were no problems, Cave should be back in the British sector in ten or twelve minutes. He walked back to the deserted factory, slowly descended the steps into the basement. Now he was without protection, but he was also free of encumbrance. And if he was too late to save Daphne, there would be no adults to witness what he did next.

Carefully placing Daphne's night-clothes back in the middle of the room where he had found them, Blessed took a last look around the underground hall, memorising the entrances, the main furniture. Then he pushed open the door that led out into the courtyard.

When he got outside, the storeroom door was open. He walked over, stared into the dark cell where Daphne had been imprisoned. The smell of squalor, the lingering presence of terror here, brought Blessed to the brink of nausea. But he made himself stay there for some time. To harden his heart.

Finally Blessed crossed the yard again, leaned himself against the wall by the entrance to the main hall. The door he left open just a chink, so that he could see into the big room without being seen. It was in this position that he settled down to await the return of the boy-murderer and his gang. The Boss and his Kinder.

FIFTY

When blessed was wrenched back into consciousness he felt a momentary panic. Then the fear gave way to shame. He had fallen asleep on his feet, leaning against the wall. Forty-eight hours virtually without rest had finally taken their toll. He cursed himself for giving in to his body, *now* of all times. Then he heard noises from the far end of the building – distant voices, echoing footsteps descending the stairs – and he knew the time for guilt was past. Swinging himself into position by the door, he dipped one hand inside his coat to retrieve the Enfield. Adrenalin flooded through his system. Only seconds remained to the moment when he would know if his only child had lived or died.

Blessed waited, keeping watch through the chink between the door and the wall.

The first arrivals were four boys in their mid-teens. They burst noisily into the room, looked around, quickly satisfied themselves that everything was as it should be. One of them went back upstairs. The remaining three lit cigarettes thin as toothpicks. They slouched by the door in the self-consciously 'tough' way common to adolescent males everywhere.

Don't weaken. Forget their age. Dismiss pity from your mind, Blessed commanded himself.

A great, ringing din of steps announced the rest of the gang's approach, the sound augmented by a swell of voices, a chilling, triumphant growl. Blessed was reminded of how soldiers might sing when returning victorious from some brief and bloody battle.

And suddenly there was the boy-murderer at their head, waving the pistol he had stolen at the warehouse. He was flanked by two older

447

kids with knives in their waistbands. Blessed could not know it, but these were Granit and Banana, restored to the leader's favour in this crisis. Once in the room, the boy-murderer took a few steps forward. He lifted Daphne's nightdress with the toe of one boot, tossed it high and then stomped on it where it landed.

Pick him off now! Have your revenge for Daphne. Now!

The temptation grew to take aim, to kick open the door, to kill. Blessed's finger ached on the trigger, as if it possessed a will of its own. So easy to squeeze off that first shot, have it over. Easier than yet more waiting, more uncertainty . . . Then the rest of the gang surged forward to surround their leader, forcing Blessed's decision, saving him from himself.

Because then he glimpsed Daphne, being carried between two older boys, and everything else faded into insignificance.

Until now the mob had been pressed together like a scrum, as if its members were concealing something. But as they swarmed into the room the tight bunch opened and there was his daughter. They must have borne her through the streets like that, to foil adults' prying eyes.

Blessed still couldn't determine whether his daughter was alive or dead. But as he watched . . . she moved, and one of the two kids who had been carrying her was guiding her towards a corner. *She was alive.*

Stay cold! Now Blessed knew he had to stick to his plan, keep dealing only in the possible, the practical, refuse to allow this intense feeling of relief to distort his judgment. *Daphne wasn't safe yet.* To fail her now, after all these agonising days and hours, would be unforgivable, impossible. *For God's sake, stay cold.*

She looked very different from the neat little schoolgirl of three days ago. Her hair had been cropped, she had been forced into filthy boy's rags, and she was clearly petrified with fear. Nevertheless, she had suffered no obvious harm. Not so her helper. There were cuts on the boy's face and neck, evidence of casual torture. With a shock he realised that this was the kid he had chased at the Spandau cemetery that rainy morning, whose photograph he had spotted in the *Tagesspiegel*, the one he had dubbed 'Buster'. Was this Gurkel's Benno?

More than once during the moments that followed, Blessed took a bead on the boy-murderer, considered the chances of a surprise-shot. But even presuming he managed to kill him cleanly, the danger to Daphne would not be over. Those kids looked hard. They were probably ferocious cop-haters. He held his fire for the moment. If Daphne came under immediate threat, he would rely on shooting fast and straight, and on reaching her in time. Meanwhile, the cold, wise course was to watch and wait.

The atmosphere out there was becoming formal, almost ritualistic. The boy-murderer was busy conferring with the older kids. Then, quite suddenly, he turned and bellowed like a crier:

'THE TRIAL BEGINS. THE TRIAL OF BENNO!'

Benno was dragged into the middle of the room, while Daphne crouched in her corner staring listlessly at the events as if past all care or feeling. The Kinder were forming a circle around Benno and Boss-Kind. They sat down. Benno didn't move. Like Daphne, he seemed for the moment uninvolved. Boss-Kind, by contrast, prowled the inside of the circle, both ringmaster and shaman. Among the long shadows cast by the solitary naked light, this was a sinister campfire meeting, the wide basement a buried clearing in the concrete forest of Berlin.

'*The trial is opening!*' He raised his fist in an angry, decisive gesture. Then he forced Benno to the floor.

A subdued ripple greeted Boss-Kind's words. His audience, perhaps suffering from anti-climax after the excitement of the hunt, seemed at this point dutiful rather than enthusiastic.

Not to say there was no hate against Benno. Every Kind in the room considered that he had betrayed them by running off with the girlie. Every Kind knew that he and Daphne had been about to report to the British Military Police at the Brandenburg Gate when they had been run to ground. Every Kind was convinced that the two escapers would have turned the entire tribe in.

But Boss-Kind was astute enough to realise that there was also an undercurrent of distrust directed against himself. That was why he hadn't stuck Benno like a pig there in the ruins behind the Wilhelmstrasse. That would not have been the Kinder-way. Therefore, although for Boss-Kind a rabble-rousing show-trial of Benno involved undeniable problems and dangers, from a political point of view it was nothing more or less than a gadawlmighdy *necessity*.

'So?' began the Boss in a low, growling voice. His eyes travelled round the circle. 'Benno who was once the Watcher has betrayed us with girlie by escaping. Yes or no, Kinder? Am I right or wrong?'

There was a murmuring. But again it was Granit who, in his slow, unstoppable way, expressed the Kinder's innermost thoughts.

'Boss-Kind,' he said, 'that's a real question, oh yes. But I see trials and I hear 'bout them, and I tell you we got to ask *him*, I mean *Benno*, if he is pleading *guilty* or *not guilty*.'

'This is such *shit*, Granit!' Boss-Kind sneered. 'This Kind here, the only thing he should be pleading for is *mercy*. But . . .'

'Plea! There must be a plea!' Granit insisted.

The Boss had been looking around, and from the faces he knew that the mood was against him. He was going a little fast, the Kinder wanted the trial to last a little longer. For them this was a solemn occasion.

'Well, maybe,' he said in a more measured way. 'Well, yes.' He rounded swiftly on his intended victim. 'Benno, then what do you plead?' he demanded. 'And remember "mercy" is not allowed, oh no . . .'

Benno didn't answer his question immediately. But it seemed to have brought him back to life. The next moment he said in a voice as loud as he could manage, because Boss-Kind had cut his cheek back there at the Wilhelmstrasse and in the hour or so since, it had swollen and become painful: 'If I am justalittlebit guilty,' he said then, loud and clear, 'If this is so, *you*, Boss-Kind, *you* are so guilty you can't stand up straight and look anyone in the eye!'

'Enough! That is ab-so-lute-ly *enough*! You plead . . .'

'Truth is we Kinder don' know half the things this boy who calls himself the Boss done. None of us know! And I don' mean just the crazy killing, I mean the *treach-er-y* . . .'

Boss-Kind lunged forward with Blessed's gun in his hand. He lashed out at Benno, but because the younger one moved so fast, he only managed to strike him a glancing blow on one bony shoulder. This made Benno wince and clutch himself, though, and stopped his mouth for a little while.

'He *is* yes he *is* guilty! You hear that Kind admit it?' Boss-Kind accused, pointing a long finger.

He had raised the gun high and was preparing to smash Benno across the face with the cold metal of its barrel, to shut him up, but Granit intervened, reached out a restraining hand.

'Sure, he is guilty of running away. We know this,' the Boss's bulky henchman said heavily. 'Otherwise, what is Benno doing in the Wilhelmstrasse with the girlie instead of guarding her in the storeroom? The point is not this—this is simple and plain—but that he is entitled to say a few words for old times' sake before you slit his gizzard. As you are *dying* to do, Boss-Kind!'

Benno knew that now was his last and only opportunity. Now he had attention, a morsel of sympathy even, from Granit and the other Kinder. Now he must act, before Boss-Kind managed to silence him for good.

'There will be no flight to the Hershey-Zone for any Kinder!' Benno proclaimed suddenly. 'No Kind is going nowhere!' he plunged on. 'The plan of Riese and Boss-Kind—*yes Boss-Kind*—is that all the Kinder will *die*. Listen to me, oh my fellow-Kinder: *The traitor is Boss-Kind. I heard him plot with Riese, and this is why I escaped with Girlie Daff-nee . . .!*'

The swell of shock in the silence that followed was beyond measure. Granit's eyes were like weapon-slits of thought. Then his expression changed to one of fury. He no longer trusted Boss-Kind's leadership, it was true, but for him to believe Benno's charge that Boss-Kind intended to betray the very thing he above all other Kinder had created by thought and word and sometimes bloody deed—that for Granit was being asked to do too much. Just like Boss-Kind, Benno had gone too far, too fast.

Granit was still restraining Boss-Kind with one powerful hand. But with the other he was waving disgustedly in Benno's direction. 'Your words are shit in your own pants, in which you must sit forever, Benno,' he said. 'Don' try throwing it at *us* . . .'

Benno still managed to look defiant, but he knew he was finished. No Kind in that room wanted to know the truth. No Kind could conceive of such a huge, such an evil thing as the Boss betraying the Kinder Garden.

Benno could see that Boss-Kind was deferring to Granit. After all, he had only to keep the Kinder happy for one more night after this one, so what did it matter?

Boss-Kind said mildly, with a statesmanlike wave of the hand: 'Granit, you know these are wise words.'

Granit was pleased, as every Kind could see, at the power he was accumulating with such apparent ease. This was when he looked at Daphne, who was sitting there by the wall, still frozen with fear but lately with her eyes maybe more watchful, and Granit said, 'Girlie don' belong here, Boss-Kind. This trial, this is Kinder-business. Private, you beddabelieve. We can deal with girlie later.'

Again Boss-Kind was easy. He gestured, made a little shrug of maybe indifference, could-be agreement, with the gun.

'Boss-Kind, we should put her back in the storeroom.'

'I agree. This is our Kinder-decision?' Boss-Kind said quietly, raising the gun as if it were a baton of office or a sceptre.

He was answered with murmurs of agreement, nods of approval.

Granit handed her over to the same two kids who had brought her back after the escape attempt. Each took an arm and, just as they had then, half-marched, half-carried her towards the courtyard-door.

Blessed was waiting. He had stepped back, his mind working to cover the new situation, as he flattened himself against the wall beside the door. He knew the entrance was too narrow for the two boys to come through either side of Daphne; they would have to enter in single file and regroup in the courtyard.

Then in she came, struggling now and letting out furious little cries. A wiry boy of almost adult height was holding her in front of him. All the while he was laughing nervously, repeating, 'Go, girlie, go!' The Kind and his captive stumbled on across the yard, oblivious to Blessed, who made no move.

He waited for the second boy to come through. This one was shorter, stockier, with a cigarette stuck between his lips. The kid moved at a swift lope, anxious to catch up with his comrade and Daphne. He wore what had once been a white shirt, which made him easier to see in the semi-darkness.

Blessed thought about the boys' ages, the sheer horror of what he had to do . . . Then, by a huge effort of will, he erased every doubt from his mind.

After the second boy came through, Blessed stepped forward behind him and struck him sharply with the barrel of the Enfield in the nape of the neck. As the boy staggered and began to collapse, he caught him under the arms, kept him from falling, then shoved him forward, much as the other kid had been pushing Daphne but a lot faster and harder, using his body as a weapon. The other had now delivered his prisoner to her dungeon and was turning with a smirk on his face to greet his friend. Blessed all but hurled his stunned comrade at the boy, propelling both of them through the storeroom door. The boy he had hit with the gun fell hard just inside the threshold, cracking his head against the floor. By then Blessed had followed through. He had the second kid gripped by the shirt and was pointing the barrel of the Enfield straight at his right temple. It had all happened without a word being said. The loudest sound had been made by the first kid's head as it hit the ground. His cigarette still glowed on the concrete where it had landed, in the middle of the courtyard.

Daphne seemed stunned, uncomprehending, weirdly unmoved at the sudden eruption of violence in her prison. Then she recognised

452

that the figure in the doorway was her father. She made a keening sound, like a lost puppy found.

Blessed raised a finger to his lips. 'Don't speak, sweetheart,' he whispered. His daughter walked forward and felt his arm, as if testing the reality of this apparition. In return he touched her cheek.

All this time, the second boy had taken only one look at his unconscious comrade; since then he had been staring at the Enfield as if mesmerised. Blessed motioned to Daphne to start moving back towards the door, took a step back himself, keeping the gun trained on the boy.

'If you raise the alarm, I'll shoot you,' Blessed told him very quietly.

The boy nodded.

'And if you shout after I close the door, I will come back in here and shoot you. Understood?'

The boy nodded more vigorously.

'Out, Daff,' Blessed said simply, aware that she was still in shock and he mustn't overtax her.

He took one last look at the boy standing inside the room, and the boy unconscious on the floor. He backed over the threshold, closed the door and secured the bolt.

They gave themselves, father and daughter, only a couple of seconds for an embrace in the empty courtyard.

'I'm going to get us out without anyone getting hurt,' Blessed explained quickly. 'Stay close behind me whatever happens. Understand? *Stay close behind*. In a moment we're going through that door.'

Daphne was making strange mumbling sounds. Realising she was trying to speak, he ducked down, listened carefully.

'Benno . . .' he heard her murmur. 'Dad . . . save . . . Benno . . .'

Boss-Kind was in highest oratorical form, hammering nails into Benno's coffin.

'And what shall we do about this crime?' he was intoning. 'I mean this crime against me and you and the Kinder Garden—against *everything* that this Kind should have loved till death . . . *So what shall we do about it?*'

At that moment the door to the courtyard swung open wide, and from the half-shadow at that end of the room a voice rang out, firm and deep.

'No! What shall we do about *you*, Johann-Peter Möller! No one move! I have a gun, and unlike Boss-Kind I know how to use it!'

The Webley swung round wildly as Boss-Kind tried to get a fix on the intruder. His eyes were afire, with what emotion it was impossible to tell.

'*Kep-ten!*' he bellowed. But he did not move or shoot. Not yet.

'Quick! Drop that gun! It's only you I want!'

The gun in the boy's hand wavered. Boss-Kind's eyes were still on fire. His face was taut, betraying enormous strain.

'Drop that gun!' Blessed repeated. 'Listen: I'm arresting you in connection with four murders, but with one murder especially . . .'

'*No! Kep-ten, no!*'

'. . . Because, in fact, it led to all the others.' Blessed drew a deep breath. 'Johann-Peter Möller, born Berlin-Friedrichshain on February 5, 1931, last month you killed Heidemarie Sanders—'

'Kep-ten . . .' Now Boss-Kind's words were drawn out in a moan of agony. '*Forget it.* No name . . .'

'But there are so many names, Johann-Peter,' Blessed continued. 'They confused me for a long time. Heidemarie Sanders was only one of them. That was her married name, though, wasn't it? Her other name—the one she got from her father and mother—was Heidemarie *Möller.* So let's get it off our conscience . . .' His voice dropped to a whisper. 'Let's tell everyone here, shall we? *Let's tell all your Kinder friends that on the night of June 25/26 you savagely murdered your own mother . . .*'

There came the sound of a great gasp of breath from the Kinder. Into the teeming silence that followed, Blessed's voice again, gentle now in the door's darkness, but still relentless:

'Now . . . just . . . drop . . . that . . . gun . . .'

'No. No, Kepten,' Boss-Kind repeated.

'You will. You must,' Blessed said. He was sure that Daphne was behind him, shielded by his body. He was sure that he could talk them all through this. And he was nearly certain that, if he didn't, for an untrained shot like Boss-Kind to kill him at this distance would take a hundred-to-one chance. Nevertheless, he stepped a little to the left to ensure that he was really in shadow. He felt behind to ensure Daphne had followed him. She had. 'You are the last,' he continued. 'I have Weiss. I will soon have Haselhuhn, the man the Kinder call Riese. I know how you aimed to betray the Kinder with him. *Everything Benno said was true . . .*'

A growl arose from among the Kinder. This was evidence of a sea change, of instincts racing to instant new conclusions, of a hundred things falling into place in a score of minds.

454

'Nobody move!' Blessed said. 'I want to ask Boss-Kind something else. I want to find out how he knew about Heidemarie.' He fixed on the boy-murderer again. 'I found the pictures at the Kinder Garden, you see,' he said. 'That's what first made me suspect who she was to you. I confirmed it yesterday with Anna Löbke, then with the city registry. But how did *you* know, Johann-Peter? Did you recognise the pictures? Did you somehow remember her from all that time ago? Or did she recognise *you*?'

Boss-Kind was swaying, looking to the left and right to see what the other Kinder were thinking. When he saw that he still just held them, and that for the moment he could still talk, he said, beginning almost inaudibly and then building up to a stronger voice, though clearly the voice of a child, 'She tol' me . . . this Heide tol' me she had this boy, this boy would be the same age as me, but he *died*. You know she said that?' He gestured with the gun for Blessed to keep away. 'Now one day I see my . . . this thing called a birth cer-tif-i-cate. Doktor Barnhelm keeps it with all the others in his filing cabinet; only me, the Boss, can make him let me look at this thing, which no other Kinder have seen. I see the name of my *mother* . . . mother, no father, you know no father . . . and this was Heidemarie Möller. I tell you this. And you know when one day she . . . I was doing Kinder-business with the corporal, he went out for a while, and she sees this ration card of mine, somehow, and she says with a laugh, like I made a good joke, my name it was also Möller, this was my name before I married that dumb Hat Sanders and . . .'

'When was this?'

'A week, maybe a little more, before . . .'

'Before you killed her?'

'*Forget it.*'

'She said *you* were dead,' Blessed said with careful emphasis. 'How about that? She told everyone *you* were dead.'

Blessed knew he had him now. Boss-Kind looked at him and there were real tears in his eyes, he was a child at last.

'And you know what? Those orphan-keeping, creeping *Arschlöcher*, they tol' me *she* was dead, this is what they tol' me, so she don' exist. And so . . .'

'Did you tell her what you knew?'

'Not yet. But, you know, me and the corporal and her would meet sometimes in that place near the Tiergarten yes Potsdamer Strasse to do business, good business, no problems.' Boss-Kind was close to choking on his words. 'We met that night . . . and well, they tol' me they were leaving Berlin soon as they could, and bye-bye Boss-Kind, corporal taking Heide away forever. And so then I had oh *had* to tell her 'bout, 'bout . . .'

'About who she was, yes. And what was the reaction you got?'

Boss-Kind sighed long and deep. 'Well, you know she *laughed*. And corporal said, you are a crazy German boy. And she laughed again, so loud and also *scared*, and said, "My baby *died*, the corporal is right, you are a *crazy boy* . . ." And next thing, I cut the corporal in his neck, finish him *quick. Then her, but her I keep cutting again and again and again, oh again . . .*'

Boss-Kind's secret was out at last. Forget the drugs, the money, the seductive trails of criminal machinations. Everyone had thought that Price the smuggler got himself into fatal trouble, and what a pity the woman had to die too. Floh, Panewski, Weiss—probably the shadowy Riese as well—had looked at the deaths that way. And Blessed too. Despite the puzzling lack of a clear, criminal motive in the killings, until his conversation with Anna Löbke just yesterday, after his last trip to the Knesebeckstrasse, he had been fooled as well.

Only when Anna had told him her dead friend's maiden name, had Blessed finally been sure that Heidemarie-Suzy was the key. With that understanding, everything fell into place, and he had gained the power he was now wielding. Price, Floh, Panewski, all had been granted deadly bit-parts in a drama that was Boss-Kind's and Heidemarie-Suzy's. They had had to die because of her. Because, by chance, Taffy Price the drug-smuggler had introduced her to one of his clients, a teenage freak who was actually her son, her long-abandoned son, Johann-Peter *alias* Boss-Kind, a flesh-and-blood time-bomb, primed and waiting to explode.

'Steady,' Blessed said to everyone in the room. 'Keep steady.'

Of course, for the moment, all the watching Kinder were transfixed. This would end very soon, probably quite suddenly, Blessed knew. And so because he knew enough for now and because it was essential to keep the initiative, he ordered calmly but firmly:

'I'm going to count to four, Johann-Peter. At the count of four I want you to lock the safety-catch, then throw that gun into the middle of the room, slowly and without lifting it. Just scud it like a stone. All right. One . . .'

'*It was oh it was the only answer,*' Boss-Kind muttered.

'Two . . .'

'*And every Kind has a name, you are right. The Hats are right. Riese was right . . .*'

456

'Three . . .'

Boss-Kind had reached a kind of critical level of instability, Blessed knew. To defuse this human explosive, you worked your way into the circuits, disarmed the triggers and cut the wires, until you came to the heart, the detonator, and this was the most dangerous moment of all. Blessed felt behind him for Daphne, found she was there, whispered to her to be ready to hit the ground.

'. . . *And the name is worth nothing . . . even when you tell her . . . so you want everything to be dead, everything and everybody . . .*'

'Four . . . Drop it slowly.'

'*Dead—is—best—for—every—body . . .*'

But the gun, instead of falling was rising fast—a snake about to strike.

Blessed had already grabbed his daughter and pushed her to the ground. All in that moment, he wondered if Boss-Kind could really shoot, and he thought, yes, and he cursed himself for trying yet again to be too damned clever . . .

He hit the ground and rolled towards Daphne, finding and encircling her just before there was a shot. Then Blessed was pushing Daphne back further into the darkness, away from any more bullets, rolling back into the room and levelling the Enfield again towards where the boy-murderer and the circle of Kinder had been.

Finally, as Blessed's eyes found focus, he saw Boss-Kind's lanky figure sprawled—better, slapped like a piece of dough—against the wall. The Webley was still clutched in one out-flung hand, thrown back by the recoil. Blood was spreading down behind the figure's head, dark and new. Johann-Peter Möller, *alias* Boss-Kind, had not needed to take aim, only to thrust the barrel of the Webley into his own wide-open mouth and pull the trigger. Suddenly, in one last self-directed spasm of violence, his fierce, frantic emptiness was gone from the room and from the city, leaving only an equally hollow silence.

'Don't look,' Blessed told Daphne. Cautiously he stood up.

Her voice came from behind him, slightly muffled but stronger than before. 'Can't help it . . . see . . . Got to find Benno . . .'

'Don't—'

But Daphne was also on her feet, staring at Boss-Kind's body. Then she threw herself at her father and buried her face in his jacket. He held her to him, felt the damp warmth of her tears begin to soak through his shirt. He drew her even closer, stroked what was left of her hair. For the next few moments he lost all awareness of his surroundings.

When he looked up again, there was Benno, peering at them shyly from a few feet away.

'OK,' Benno said. 'OK, you beddabelieve.'

Granit appeared out of the gloom. Blessed watched as he walked slowly over to Boss-Kind's body, stared down at it impassively. He turned back and looked at the Englishman with a hint of challenge in his gaze.

'Don't touch that gun!' Blessed snapped.

Granit slowly extended a foot and kicked the Webley out of Boss-Kind's lifeless grasp, with enough force to ensure that it landed some distance from himself. Then he knelt down and quickly went through the dead boy's pockets. He found something in the breast pocket of the shirt, examined it, nodded to himself. Then he walked over to Blessed.

'Here,' Granit said, and offered the object to him.

Blessed took possession of a battered identity card which bore the name Heidemarie Sanders and her address in Moabit. This was the final piece in the puzzle. This was the identity card she had been carrying the night she was killed, and which Blessed had never found. Boss-Kind, the boy with no name, had carried this last proof of where he came from, and he had carried it next to his heart.

'I have no quarrel with you. You can do what you like,' Blessed told Granit. 'But I think you owe Benno something.'

Granit shrugged, then cuffed Benno briefly on the shoulder. It was the nearest that he, the new Boss, with his prestige to think of, was going to get to apologising. A moment later he turned to the other Kinder and clapped his hands. 'This story is *over!*' he roared. 'We go *now*. Yes we go quick-*schnell*! Banana, you go fetch those two from that storeroom!'

Benno grinned wryly, inched closer to his protectors.

When he had finished issuing his first orders, Granit relaxed a little. 'Good job, Kepten,' he said.

'No,' Blessed said. 'I lost Boss-Kind. I didn't mean to do that.'

Granit shook his head. 'He lost . . . that Boss-Kind, he lost himself, a long oh yes a long time ago.' There was no gloating, but equally no pity in the way he shot a quick glance at the body bent against the wall. 'Important thing is, now we are all free,' he said.

Blessed saw Kinder moving towards the storeroom to release their comrades. 'I hit one of your friends very hard,' he said. 'He should see a doctor. I can find you a good British one.'

'We have doctors, Kepten. They can be bought.'

'I mean to say, if you decide to go straight, just come to the British sector. I'll vouch for you, make sure you and your people are looked after.'

'Kepten, if we need you sometime, we'll shout.'

'I may not always be in Berlin.'

'Then we won't shout. We won't waste our breath.'

'You're growing up. Germany and the world are changing. The Kinder Garden can't last forever.'

Granit thought about that. 'The world is wide, and if we are lucky, life is long. But do you think any of those Hats up there know better than we do?' he said. 'If you think that, *ach scheiss* if you think that, then you are more stupid than you look. The only decision is, do we run the Garden well and safe, or do we run it like Boss-Kind ran it?' He nodded solemnly. 'Now before we go, we got to tidy up, bury that Boss-Kind somewhere, 'cos even though he was crazy and he was bad, without him there would be no Kinder Garden.'

And Granit began to round up his troops.

Blessed and Daphne, with Benno beside them, walked towards the steps that led up into the fresh air. Boss-Kind's ability to hurt, or be hurt, had died with him. His rage was over. There was nothing more anyone could do to assuage it, or understand it, or avenge it.

When they reached the factory lane outside, the sky was already dull silver. Soon dawn would be breaking once again over Berlin. There would be plenty of early-rising workers accompanying them on the grey streets leading west, and through the border-crossings. Blessed was grateful for that, and for the precious anonymity it conferred; because only when the three of them reached the British sector at last would they be completely safe. Nevertheless, his instincts told him that his brush with hell was over for now, perhaps for the rest of his life if he was fortunate and careful. Let the same be true for the children, every one.

He put the Enfield back in its shoulder-holster, smoothed his jacket over the bulge.

'Now, let's pretend you two are going to school, and I'm going to work. All right?' Blessed took first his daughter and then Benno by the hand. 'Just try to look normal, like a family.'

Benno, understanding at least the key words, snorted with amusement. '*Normal?* Like a *family?* What is *that?*'

Even Daphne managed a croaking little laugh, her first since being reunited with her father.

Blessed squeezed her hand. He thought about Harriet, about Gisela, and about his marriage. One thing was for certain, he reflected: whatever future now lay in store for himself and those he loved, it was hardly going to be conventional or easy.

He smiled wryly. 'Maybe I'd better rephrase that, so we can all be happy with it. Agreed? *Einverstanden*, Benno?'

'Agreed. You beddabelieve.'

'OK,' Blessed said. 'Then how about . . . normal like a Hat and two Kinder stepping out for a stroll.'